KILLERS

KILLERS

Laurence Gough

M&S

Canadian Cataloguing in Publication Data
Gough, Laurence
   Killers

ISBN 0-7710-3439-3

I. Title.

PS8563.08393K5   1994   C813′.54   C93-095203-0
PR9199.3.G68K5   1994

First published in Great Britain 1993 by Victor Gollancz Ltd.
A Cassel imprint
Villiers House, 41/47 Strand, London WC2N 5JE

Photoset in Great Britain by Rowland Phototypesetting Ltd.,
Bury St Edmunds, Suffolk
Printed and bound in Great Britain by
St Edmundsbury Press Ltd., Bury St Edmunds, Suffolk

McClelland & Stewart Inc.
The Canadian Publishers
481 University Avenue
Toronto, Ontario M5G 2E9

Author's Note

There is a Vancouver Public Aquarium, and it does indeed have a board of directors as well as a large salaried staff, many enthusiastic volunteers and the two captive orcas; Finna and Bjossa. But with the exception of the above-named whales and a marmalade cat named Barney, the inhabitants of *Killers* are mere figments of my imagination and are not intended to portray real insects or animals or persons. Any resemblance to real insects or animals or persons, living or dead, is entirely coincidental.

1

Homicide detective Jack Willows tested the blade of the carving knife against the ball of his thumb.

Fellow detective Claire Parker watched him over the rim of a wine glass that had been recently topped up with a more-than-decent Australian burgundy, but was now somehow almost empty again. Parker's skin was pale, her shoulder-length hair jetblack, her chocolate eyes lively and bright. When she had first walked into Inspector Homer Bradley's office, back in '85, she'd been twenty-eight years old, stood five-foot seven and weighed one hundred and seven pounds. Time hadn't passed her by, but she still considered herself a reasonably young woman. She had managed, mostly due to the stress of the job, to keep her weight down. Perhaps it was the wine, but at the moment she was feeling pretty good about herself.

She and Willows ate together fairly frequently, but he rarely invited her to his house. So this was a bit of an occasion, and she had dressed accordingly. She was wearing a beige suede skirt and a low-cut black silk blouse. She looked very good, and she knew it. Her self-awareness and confidence showed in the way she held herself – loosely, but very much in control.

As Parker raised her glass, Willows noticed that the wine was just slightly darker than her lipstick. He sliced into the roast the way he did almost everything else – with manic, calculated energy. The cut meat, as it fell away from the joint, smelled hot and rich.

Parker drank a little more wine. There were birch logs in the fireplace, candles burning on the table. Moonlight shone through the mullioned french doors that led to the sundeck, and the backyard lawn was frosty and gleaming. The weatherman had predicted snow and it looked as if he might be right. The westerly that would bring cloud to blanket the city was already snatching the last dead leaves from the tossing branches of the apple, plum and cherry trees that Willows and his children had planted so many years ago.

Parker watched but said nothing as Willows served her exactly the right amount of paper-thin slices of rare roast beef, oven-glazed roast potatoes, fresh-cut green beans imported from California. She watched his wrists and hands as he worked; the graceful play of tendon and shadow, bulge of vein and flex of muscle, the ridge of scar tissue and permanently swollen knuckles of his left hand – the memento of a punched-out windshield.

Willows filled his own plate, and sat down. He raised his glass in a toast. "Happy birthday, Claire."

Parker smiled. Willows was two days early, but it was the thought that counted. Hard to believe, but she was thirty-six years old, had been crime-busting with Jack for eight years. A long time.

Longer than most marriages lasted, for example.

Willows chewed and swallowed. "I'm not going to ask you what you're thinking about, but I will tell you this – you look awfully damn serious. Something wrong with the food?"

Parker helped herself to a little horseradish. "No, everything's fine. I was just thinking about how old I'm getting. Imagining the hands of a giant clock spinning round at dizzying speed. Pages blowing off a calendar." She smiled. "Stuff like that."

A violent gust of wind shook the house. Curtains flared nervously. The candles guttered, and then held steady.

Willows said, "Morbid."

"Very."

He smiled. "Eat some red meat. It'll perk you up. Stop you from getting maudlin."

Parker ate some roast beef, a forkful of potato, a string bean.

"Everything okay?"

"Delicious."

Willows gave her a doubtful look. He emptied his glass and poured himself a generous refill. A birch log snapped in the fireplace, chasing a flurry of sparks up the chimney. Another gust of wind rattled the french doors. Willows sneaked a carnal, slightly feverish look at Parker. Maybe it was the weather, but he felt a desperate need to do a little hibernating.

Parker said, "Now it's my turn."

Willows gave her an enquiring look.

She said, "What are *you* thinking about, Jack?"

8

"Dessert," said Willows quietly, in a tone of voice they'd arrest you for, in some parts of town.

Parker felt her temperature shoot up; a dusky rose suffused her skin. She drank a little more wine, took refuge behind the glass. She was pushing forty and had the complexion of a chameleon: she was blushing like a child.

In the kitchen and entrance hall and upstairs in the den, telephones rang stridently.

Parker said, "When are you going to buy some decent phones – something made in the twentieth century, that *warbles*?"

"Never."

"Those things sound as if they need their diapers changed."

All three telephones rang five times, and then the answering machine picked up.

Willows said, "You ready for a little more roast?"

"I'm just fine, thanks. Aren't you going to find out who that was?"

"I know who it was." Willows smiled. "It wasn't you." He poured the last of the bottle into Parker's glass, and suggested she move into the living room and enjoy the fire while he cleared the dishes. He went into the kitchen, and she heard the clatter of the dishwasher. In the living room, Parker kicked off her shoes and curled up on the sofa. The birch logs were burning hot and steady. Parker felt the heat on her face. She shut her eyes.

What the hell was Jack up to?

The phones rang again and once again Willows let the answering machine handle the call. Parker opened her eyes as, looking slightly harried, Willows rushed over to the table, scooped up a pack of matches and disappeared back into the kitchen.

Parker called out, wondering aloud if he needed any help. She was rebuffed. A few moments later, Willows reappeared with a large, gaudily decorated and brightly lit cake. He knelt in front of Parker, placed the cake carefully down on the scarred pine trunk that doubled as a coffee table. He stepped back, and sang,

> Happy birthday to you
> Happy birthday to you
> Happy birthday, dear Claire
> Happy birthday to you

Willows had baked the cake himself, and covered it lavishly with chocolate icing decorated with hundreds of tiny multi-colored candies and many artfully designed pink flowers haloed in green leaves.

Parker said, "I appreciate the effort, but I refuse to count those candles."

Willows nodded, smiling. "Hurry up and blow them out, before the smoke alarm figures out what we're up to."

Parker took a deep breath and extinguished every candle on the cake.

"Does this mean I don't have any boyfriends?"

"One only. No extras."

"Unless you happen to think," said Parker, "that a single boyfriend is still one too many."

Willows handed her a knife. "Why don't you cut me a slice while I see if the coffee's ready."

He'd obviously gone to a lot of trouble, so Parker cut a larger slice of cake than she'd ordinarily have permitted herself. Willows was only gone a moment. He came back to the living room balancing two mugs brimful of his special blend of freshly ground Colombian and dark French beans, another bottle of wine and two clean glasses. He put the mugs down on the coffee table and then went over to the fire and tossed another length of birch on the coals.

Parker, watching him, admired his lean, angular frame and the way he used it, with precision and grace. With Jack, there was never a wasted movement, but all the movements were there. A rush of heat washed over her, spilled through her body.

Willows went over to the stereo. He slipped a Sonny Criss album into the CD player, pushed a few buttons and adjusted the volume. The bass and piano spoke briefly to each other and then Sonny's alto kicked in on "Until the Real Thing Comes Along", the notes tentative at first, then climbing into strength and slipping all over the scales, tight and silvery, fluid.

Willows sipped at his coffee, demolished the cake.

Parker said, "Appreciate your cooking, do you?"

"I've had worse." Willows opened the second bottle of wine. He sat back while Parker filled his glass and then her own. During the past six months she had spent enough time in Willows' house to feel comfortable and at home, relaxed. She tucked the suede skirt beneath her to make room as Willows moved a little closer to her. He had pinched the candles on the dining room table, and now the only light in the room came from the birch logs,

10

which burned evenly, bathing the room in a soft, warm yellow light.

Parker let the music swirl through her. The wail of the saxophone seemed to come at her from everywhere at once. It seemed to her that Criss played as if he was making love, and there was nothing he'd rather do.

Willows said, "Can I get you anything?"

"I'm fine, Jack, everything's perfect."

A log snapped, and a bright orange spark hit the firescreen and rebounded into the hearth. Parker's wine jumped in her glass. Willows put an arm around her. His fingers traced the line of her neck. Parker turned towards him and he took her glass from her and put it down on the pine chest.

Parker said, "Am I going to get my present now, Jack?"

The damn phones started ringing again. Almost as if someone was watching them. Now there was a thought worth repressing. Willows concentrated on Parker. The suede skirt was soft and warm, the black silk slippery as water. Parker's lips were the color of wine. Her mouth tasted of wine. She made a small, needy sound and drew him closer.

The damn phones finally stopped ringing.

An hour or so later, the moonlight pouring through the bedroom window was extinguished by a rolling front of pillowy cumulus that had moved in on the city from the west, across thousands of miles of open water and then the low-slung hills of Vancouver Island.

Willows felt the change in light, tactile as a subtle change of air pressure. He raised himself up on an elbow. The moon vanished and then reappeared with a ragged bite taken out of it. The spindly branches of the vine maple that had planted itself below his window less than five years ago and shot up thirty feet in the interval scratched restlessly against the glass.

The light dimmed again. The perfect white circle of the moon was speckled with grey.

Willows saw that it was still snowing. Fat white flakes that must have been carried miles from their source and were now spinning down out of a star-spangled sky. He turned to wake Parker and saw that he was alone in bed, experienced a split second of grief and acute loneliness and in that same tiny moment heard the muted thunder of the shower.

A swiftly moving wall of pillowy cloud smothered the moon.

11

Darkness fell into the room. Feathery white flakes of snow spiralled out of the night and crashed mutely into the window, slid down the panes of glass and thickened the mantle on the ledge.

Willows slipped out of bed and padded over to the window and looked out. The ground was covered in a smooth, glittery blanket of white. At the end of the block a cone of snow fell in the glare of a streetlight, as if it was being poured from a giant funnel.

He thought about joining Parker in the shower, but decided against it. Claire was in many ways a solitary creature. If she'd wanted company, she'd have let him know. He thought about easing back into the cozy warmth of the bed, and decided against that, too.

He'd go downstairs, check to make sure the doors were bolted and listen to the answering machine.

He slipped into a multi-colored terrycloth robe and left the room, walked silently along the carpeted hall and down the stairs. A riser creaked under his weight but he knew the shower would cover the sound.

He checked the doors to make sure he'd locked them and then went into the living room. A handful of coals glowed dull orange.

He went back upstairs. Parker was still in the shower.

In the den, the answering machine's red eye winked in sequences of five – there'd been two calls he hadn't heard.

He pressed the rewind button and listened to the mildly venomous hissing of the tape as it ran from spool to spool.

Sheila, confident that he'd recognize her voice, didn't trouble to identify herself. She said without preamble that she had something important she wanted to tell him. This vaguely ominous declaration of intent was followed by a lengthy pause. Willows thought she'd hung up. Then he heard the rasping of a match and knew she'd started smoking again.

Sheila exhaled noisily, just in case he'd missed the point. She promised to call back, and hung up without saying goodbye.

The messages that followed were simply more of the same, but Sheila sounded a little less sure of herself with each call.

The fifth and last time she left a message, she told Willows it was three o'clock in the morning, Toronto time. She assumed he was on a case, wished him well and then mentioned almost in passing that she and Annie and Sean were coming home.

Air Canada flight 857, departing Toronto at 6:50 p.m.

The flight from Toronto to Vancouver was scheduled to take five hours, but because of the three-hour time difference between the two cities, she and the children expected to arrive at the house about ten p.m.

A match rasped as Sheila lit another cigarette. Willows was staring blindly down at the answering machine when she cheerfully reminded him she still had a key to the front door, and hung up.

2

The tank held just over ten thousand gallons of fresh sea-water that had been pumped in from the harbor and then subjected to the most complex filtration system money could buy. The entire exhibit had been rebuilt only a year or two earlier, and was the largest in the building. The tank was rectangular, about twenty feet long by fifteen wide and ten deep. At one end, the sandy bottom was studded with a jumbled mound of large rocks which, along with a wealth of marine vegetation, provided sufficient cover for the pool's smaller and shyer occupants.

A skate with a six-foot wingspan drifted down the length of the tank. The huge fish seemed motionless, yet surely it was moving, its deceptive speed betrayed by a slate-grey shadow almost the exact color of its body, that rippled gracefully over the sand as the huge fish drifted along.

A school of bright yellow fish saw the skate coming and darted wildly about at high speed in a display of stunningly perfect but totally mindless synchronization that defied all logic – if you bothered to think about it.

Dr Gerard Roth glanced at his watch. Twenty past nine. The aquarium had been closed to the public since six, and the rest of the staff were long gone. Roth sat at the lip of the pool with his thin, hairy legs dangling in the water. He was in a small, comfortably warm room that had been constructed on the roof of the original building when the pool was enlarged. Access to the room was available only through a locked door. A floor-to-ceiling window at one end of the room provided light during the daylight hours, but it was impossible to see into the room either from the ground or inside the aquarium.

Roth glanced at his genitals. Checking his status, so to speak. He spread his legs slightly and reached down and adjusted himself. He glanced behind him, saw that he was still alone, tilted

14

left and energetically scratched his buttock. Even though it was late November, he still had a pretty decent tan.

Roth was all scientist, top to bottom. And proud of it too, if anybody cared to ask. But somehow he couldn't bring himself to swallow all that stuff about ragged gaping lethal holes in the ozone. Maybe the doomsters and gloomsters knew what they were shouting about. Or maybe they didn't. As far as Gerard Roth was concerned the jury was still out. Too much conflicting evidence. What he did know for sure was that old Mr Sun kicked ass with his arthritis and from early June right through the end of August he had hardly any acne problems at all.

Dr Roth clawed at his left cheek, his brow furrowed in concentration, then left off to swap hard looks with a black-tailed shark that had swum lazily to the surface and was now gnawing tentatively at his big toe with a view to swallowing it whole. The shark was only a couple of feet long, too immature to realize it was strictly a bottom feeder. It was vexing, the way mere confinement seemed occasionally to alter the behavior of certain species. It was unpredictable, and it pissed him right off. Dr Roth energetically wriggled his foot. The shark held tight.

What was the stupid creature thinking, if anything? Roth admired ambition. He loathed quitters. But at the same time, he strongly believed that every living creature, no matter how brainless or genetically depraved, should somehow instinctively know its limits.

He watched the shark as it squirmed and wriggled around his foot. It was smaller than he'd thought. It was only about eighteen inches long and kind of anorexic. Even so, it'd probably have tipped the scales at eight pounds easy. Fortunately Dr Roth swam two miles a day and had the legs of a dray horse. He effortlessly lifted the shark clear of the water, raised it so high that it dangled right in front of his face, only a few inches away, all splayed fins and white belly and tiny little puckered anus.

Dr Roth cocked his fist and hit the shark in the eye with a thundering overhand right.

The fish held on to his toe as if it was the last toe in the world.

Blood trickled down Roth's leg and into the water, each drop exploding like a little bomb. The shark had cut him. He was *bleeding*. Temper rising, Dr Roth wound up and slugged the shark again, putting his upper body into it, achieving excellent leverage and doing serious damage, he was sure of it.

15

The shark made a kind of desperate gurgling sound and defecated all over his genitals.

But refused to let go.

Roth lost his temper. He resorted to the kind of language he didn't normally approve of, and when he'd finally run out of wind, grabbed the shark in both hands and gave it a tremendous yank. His toe appeared to have been rubbed down with a sheet of number eight sandpaper. Now he was really pissed. He gripped the fish in both hands, so tightly that he squeezed all the air out of its bladder. It made a noise like a mortally wounded bagpipe. Standing, he swung the shark at the painted cinderblock wall three times, turning his wrists over the way his baseball coach had taught him so many years ago. As the unfortunate denizen of the deep repeatedly impacted against the unyielding cement, its dull yellow eye unflinchingly held his gaze.

God, it was staring at him the way mother used to, when he'd filled the toilet and then forgot to flush.

Roth caught his breath and then resumed slamming the wise-ass fish into the wall, smearing the painted surface with a slimy residue of blood and fish scales and tiny bits of inedible flesh. Eventually the force of the blows knocked the shark's offending eye right out of its head.

Gasping for breath, Roth tossed the corpse behind a potted palm.

His hands were *dripping* with blood and slime. It was a gimme that fish didn't sweat. But his hands were sure as hell covered with some kind of sticky, horribly repugnant, semi-liquid gunk. Dr Roth knelt at the lip of the tank and washed his hands as best he could and then ministered to his genitals.

Fish poo dried amazingly fast.

He tried to winkle the last of the stuff out of the intricate folds of his foreskin, accidentally gave himself a nasty pinch and uttered a shrill yelp of pain.

Bath time.

Dr Roth – Gerard to his superiors – slipped on his swim fins, which were roughly the equivalent of size forty-eight shoes, had more than two hundred and fifty square inches of surface area and allowed him to propel himself at near warp-speed through a liquid environment. He grabbed his mask and cannonballed into the pool in a frothy white maelstrom, causing a shock wave duly noted and filed away for extremely short-term future reference by every living organism within the confines of those two-inch-thick, reinforced clear acrylic walls.

Not only was Gerard Roth the largest fish in that relatively small pond – he was also the meanest. He allowed himself to drift to the surface, kicked himself into an upright position and rinsed his mask, freed a few strands of grey hair from the rubber strap.

When he had the mask adjusted to his satisfaction, he took a deep breath, lowered his head beneath the surface and grabbed his dick and shook it energetically.

Tiny fragments and tendrils of shark poo clouded the water, drifted away on the currents.

Dr Roth, penis in hand, suddenly had a creepy-crawly feeling that he was being watched.

Maybe Susan had finally showed up.

He raised his head, pawed at the water with the big blue fins as he turned slowly around, hitting every point on the compass, all three hundred and sixty degrees. But spotting no one.

Probably it was the surviving black-tailed sharks watching him, wondering what had happened to good old cousin Ralph. When the dying shark had evacuated its bowels perhaps it had released some kind of chemical – something that served to alert its buddies.

Or maybe it was the human blood that had fallen into the water, that had them watching him.

What in Heaven's name would Susan think of him if she knew he'd dipped his dick in fish doo-doo? He gave himself another shake, adjusted his grip and worked his foreskin back and forth like a tiny mute accordion. The current had carried him up against the viewing area. A covey of snails worked methodically but without visible effect at a field of bright green algae.

Not for the first time, but perhaps for the last, Dr Roth pondered the fact that there wasn't any cushy unemployment insurance or social assistance in marine-land. He believed the oceans were the last parts of the world where the work ethic still prevailed. No room down there for floaters. Either you worked your ass off, or you died. *Fin.*

Dr Roth pressed his evenly tanned butt against the acrylic, wiping out several square feet of algae and throwing the snails into a panic, making them scatter as best they could.

Next he mooned the school of rainbow trout swimming eternally against the current in the artificial stream on the far side of the dimly lit aquarium corridor.

17

Sometimes during working hours, especially when a bunch of schoolkids on a field trip were running around feeling each other up or making disconcertingly accurate fish-faces by the simple expedient of sucking in their cheeks, Dr Roth liked to insert himself into their midst and then imagine himself paddling starkers in the big tank. Imagine what he'd look like from the perspective of a grade sixer's close-set eyes.

Was this a little . . . perverse? He liked to think so.

A lady friend, following orders, had once taken a Polaroid of him cavorting naked in the tank, but the flash had reflected off the glass so it looked as if she'd taken a slightly out-of-focus shot of an empty mirror.

Kind of a Zen thing, she'd said. Now what the hell was that supposed to mean?

Shortly after that incident Dr Roth had given her the old heave-ho. Who could blame him?

Despite the warm temperature of the water, Dr Roth began to feel a slight chill. He decided to swim a few laps to warm up and kill time. There was a pint-sized moray eel he always kept an eye out for, that hung out under the rocks at the far end of the pool. He had named the eel Mr Vinegar, because of the sourpuss look on its ugly face. Other than the eel, which was still too small to do him any serious damage, nothing in the tank was worth worrying about.

You had to remember to keep moving, though, if you didn't want some damn thing to *settle* on you, and start *grazing*.

Dr Roth picked up the pace as he swam over the pile of rocks Mr Vinegar called home. He swam the length of the pool and back three times, and then broke his rhythm to take a quick look at his faithful stainless steel TAG Heuer.

It was quarter to ten. Susan, bless her young heart and lots of other parts as well, was due any time now. He was always early for his dates. He couldn't help it. A woman he'd known had made a joke about him always coming early. That was it for her. Another of his lady friends that he'd had a brief – but not brief enough – affair with had told him he was insecure.

Ha! He was as secure as Fort Knox.

Why, he'd even written her a letter and told her so, although of course she probably hadn't bothered to read it.

Dr Roth rolled over on his side, the better to admire the reflected image of his marvellous physique as he flippered along parallel to the glass. Part of the thrill of these watery evening sessions was the risk that one of the many porcine security guards who roamed the premises might suddenly appear in front of him.

Whenever Roth managed to arrange one of his little adventures – what it amused him to think of as a game of water pogo – he told the guards that he was doing some vital research and that the entire wing of the building was strictly off-limits; trespassers would be fired for just cause, terminated without notice.

The threat of losing their six dollar an hour jobs seemed without exception to strike unadulterated terror in the hearts and souls of the aquarium's grey-uniformed monoliths.

Or maybe, come to think of it, it was the thought of lost uniform privileges that frightened the brutes. Fair enough, no? Because otherwise what was the point of shaving one's empty head and spending all day pumping heavy, heavy iron and gobbling anabolic steroids if you had no spiffy uniform to wriggle into, come the midnight shift? Where were the babes, if you lost the Sam Browne and badge?

Gone, thought Gerard dispassionately. He was a scientist. He knew how things worked. Archimedes used a lever. Okay, fine. Back then, it was the only tool that was available to him. But this was the modern era. Archimedes was dead and buried. So was Charlie Chaplin. Nowadays psychology was all the rage. You wanted to get a handle on what cranked your date, psychology was the only way to go.

Dr Roth jackknifed, pumped hard and powered his way down to the sandy bottom of the pool. A dead fish that looked like an anchovy with measles lay half-buried in the golden sand. He tried a handstand. The old magic was still there. If the watch could be believed, it was thirteen minutes to ten.

A platoon of drab khaki-colored fish marched past. Left fin, right fin, left fin, right fin. Wasn't it amazing, how deceptive they were. The tricky little devils actually looked as if they had a purpose, knew exactly where they were going, and why. Their compact bodies had a unnatural rigidity, as if they were doing their very best to swim to attention. Their tiny, sleek faces seemed incredibly intent and their pinched, beady little eyes stared straight ahead, unwavering and to his way of thinking faintly psychotic.

He waited until the school had swum past and then tailed along behind. The fish seemed bound together by invisible wires. They

19

moved as one, with the stifling predictability of a clockwork mechanism or a bank clerk. Their purpose in life was apparently to display a total lack of interest in anything. Losing interest himself, Dr Roth swam down to the bottom of the tank, snatched a ghost crab off the sandy floor, ripped off its shell and disembowelled it with a twist of his thumb, then swam an interception course and tossed the greasy bundle of guts into the path of the fish.

The platoon homed in on the remains of the crab like a dozen cruise missiles. In a few brief, violent seconds they had torn it to shreds and consumed every last bit of it.

Dr Roth began to hunt for another crab.

When he grew tired of this boring game he checked his watch again and saw that he had killed approximately two minutes. Time sure crawled by, when you were looking forward to a session of hot sex.

Though he would never have admitted it – not even to himself – Gerard Roth was an extremely vain fellow. He was fifty-seven years old, but had what he liked to think of as a goatish constitution. Inevitably, his head swelled with pride whenever the rest of him managed to puff up with lust.

Sometimes that made straight thinking a difficult business. Too much trouble to bother with, in fact.

Staring admiringly down at himself, Dr Roth swam slowly around in a tight circle. As a consequence of the magnifying effect of the water, the doctor's head was so enormously swollen that he could hardly think at all.

So when the flat calm of the pool's surface was disturbed, and a rolling wave splashed over his back and shoulders, Roth didn't – wasn't capable of – giving it a moment's thought. So he was caught completely by surprise when, a few moments later, a slim arm encircled his neck, a weight settled upon him from behind and a hand slid down his belly and gave him an encouraging squeeze.

Dr Roth tried to rotate in the water to look behind him. His new playmate turned with him.

My, but she was agile.

In the swirling water, a drift of long blonde hair obscured his vision.

Susan.

Who else could it be? When he'd invited her to the pool for a starkers late night swim, he'd certainly made his carnal intentions clear. In fact the language he'd chosen to use would have made the devil blush, because his experience had taught him that talking filthy really turned women on. Either that or they threw up all over his shoes. Either way, no time was wasted.

The hand on him seemed to know exactly what to do next. He tried to turn around again, but the woman behind him had a leech-like grip, and all he managed was to bump face masks. He reached up behind him and managed briefly to cup a breast.

The thing was, even though he was enjoying himself, he had planned something a bit more intimate than a handshake.

He reached down, tried to free himself from Susan's grip.

She clung to him tenaciously as a barnacle.

Roth checked the TAG. Ten o'clock.

Normally it took him a minimum of three hours to fully recharge his sexual batteries, but he happened to have suffered through an exceptionally long and arduous day. A woman in Maui who owed him one and was eager to cancel her debt had called him first thing in the morning with the news that she'd lined up a hell of a deal on a couple of tiger sharks. He'd pitched the sharks to Tony Sweeting and got into a very ugly shouting match, both of them getting so angry they actually said things to each other that they really meant.

Tony was *such* an asshole. He'd sit there at his desk in his purple-colored velvet three-piece suit and yellow tie, smoking a goddamn *pipe* for chrissakes, and mumble on forever and a day about budgets and priorities and all that *crap*.

Gerard kept telling him, sharks were the new wave, all the rage.

The damn killer whales were killing the aquarium. They brought in schoolkids by the thousands, and plenty of tourists from the prairies, too. But the public was slowly learning the truth about exactly how limited life in an aquarium really was. And the cost of feeding the ravenous bastards was completely out of hand.

The phrase *completely out of hand* brought Dr Roth crashing back to the moment. He was getting pretty darn agitated. Susan's hand had the grip of a leech and the soul of a metronome. His breathing was more than a little ragged and he was so out of control that he was wriggling and squirming like a rabid puppy.

The disembodied hand picked up the pace.

21

The veins in Dr Roth's neck popped out as if small moles were burrowing just beneath the surface of his skin.

Susan – surely it was Susan – grabbed his right buttock with her free hand, pulled herself down and, never missing a beat, spun him around. He saw that she was naked except for her mask and fins, air tanks and a weight belt.

Pump, squeeze, pump, squeeze.

It was odd, but somehow she seemed a little bulkier than she should've been. Could it be the foreshortening effect of the water? He ran his fingers through her silky hair. She pulled him closer.

Pump, squeeze, pump, squeeze.

She removed her breathing apparatus.

Roth watched wide-eyed as his genitals disappeared in a huge cloud of silvery bubbles. His body shuddered from stem to stern, apocalyptically, like a huge ship that has foundered on a mythic reef. He threw back his head and howled, emptied his lungs in a long, orgasmic cry.

His lover replaced her mouthpiece and violently spun him around. She released him for a moment and then reached up between his legs from behind.

Dr Roth's lungs emptied and his orgasmic cry faded to a whisper. Timing it perfectly, his lover yanked him under, pulled him down.

If the lever's long enough, it can be used to end a man's world.

The woman kicked out. Dr Roth felt himself being pulled backwards through the water, down and down. By now his penis no longer afforded much of a handhold, so naturally she'd shifted her grip to his balls.

Roth clutched desperately at her but her body was coated with some kind of grease or gel, and his hands kept slipping away. Jeez, it was like trying to get a choke hold on a sea cucumber.

The seconds that had so recently oozed past were now racing along at full gallop.

Because he was a professional scientist, a small part of Dr Gerard Roth's feverish mind remained icy calm and continued to monitor his progress, even as he died.

He noted that his lungs felt as if they'd been filled to the brim with high-octane gasoline and set alight. He clinically observed that he had a terrible headache and absolutely no interest whatsoever in sex. He could not help notice that he was losing strength with terrifying rapidity, or that he had the eyesight of an earthworm and the reflexes of a garden gnome, and that his bladder was killing him.

Gerard finally wised up. He stopped struggling and concentrated on the only thing that mattered to him any more – positively identifying his tormentor.

By God it was . . .

The name slowly formed in his mind, vowels and consonants jouncing about as they struggled to arrange themselves in a meaningful order. It was something like a three-dimensional game of musical chairs. The last of the letters were about to fall into place when Dr Roth's thought processes were interrupted by nothing less than a high and lowlight package from his entire life, each scene zipping past like a brightly illuminated window in a passing train.

With a tormented squeal of brakes, the train came to an abrupt stop.

Dr Roth had an out-of-body experience.

His perspective was that of an angel, or perhaps a hovering sparrow. He watched himself float limply two or three feet beneath the surface of the salty water.

He was pleased to see that he had achieved neutral buoyancy.

The names of all the men and women he had known and abused or otherwise taken advantage of scrolled through the water in chronological order. The letters that made up the names were flat and extremely thin, in a variety of florescent colors, and translucent. As the letters drifted slowly through the water they were gobbled up by curious, voracious fish.

Then, in small, fuzzy, hellish-red letters outlined in black appeared the words

The End.

3

Parker didn't slam her fist into the pillow, or shout or even raise her voice, but her body was stiff with anger, there was a frosty glint in her eye and steel in her voice. She was furious – madder than hell – and not too tied up inside to say why.

Willows had poured himself a small Cutty on the rocks and brought it upstairs along with a glass of wine for Parker. But neither of them was drinking. It was too solemn an occasion, somehow.

Parker had turned on the bedside lamp. She'd dried herself quickly after her shower and there were still a few beads of water on her legs. She was wearing one of Willows' blue uniform shirts and sat cross-legged on the big queen-size bed with her back against the headboard. The shirt was so large that the cloth VPD flashers hung halfway to her elbows. Although he didn't dare say a word, Willows found Parker's slightly rumpled look just this side of totally irresistible. Apparently unaware of this, Parker said, "I just don't understand how you can let her get away with it."

Willows couldn't think of anything to say. He felt as if he were being interrogated.

Parker said, "Explain it to me, Jack. Is that too much to ask?"

Willows stared out the window. The wind shifted and the snow danced. The mantle of white on the windowsill was visibly rising. Why was it that the only time the weatherman hit it right was when he had bad news?

"Jack?"

Willows broke down and sipped at his Scotch. He said, "The way I see it, I don't have any choice in the matter."

"Come on, Jack. You can do better than that."

Willows hated it when Parker was sarcastic. She was so good at it. Her voice positively dripped with scorn.

He said, "What am I supposed to do? She left a message on my *machine*. It isn't as if we talked it over and came to a decision together. You know as well as I do that I didn't have a chance to say a single word to her. If she wants to buy a ticket and fly across the country, I can't stop her."

"No, but you could call her back and tell her there's no room at the farm."

Willows said, "You make it sound so easy." Now *he* was being sarcastic. Or was he just whining?

"I thought . . ." Parker pulled the shirt a little lower over her knees. "I thought we were trying to develop the kind of relationship that depended on making important decisions together."

"We do, we do." Willows rested a companionable hand on her thigh.

Parker pushed his hand away. "I'm not talking about sex, Jack."

"Neither am I."

"Well, what are you talking about? Commitment? Tell me something – where's the commitment when you let your wife waltz back into your bedroom just like that!"

Parker snapped her fingers under his nose.

She punched him in the shoulder, hard.

"Wake up, Jack!"

Willows said, "What about Sean and Annie?"

"They're welcome any time. They can stay as long as they like. You aren't married to your goddamn kids – that's the whole goddamn point!"

Willows drank some more Scotch. Why hadn't he poured himself a double? Because he needed a clear head, even if he didn't want one. He said, "I don't think either Annie or Sean is old enough or mature enough to understand the distinction."

"Well, you're wrong."

"Am I?"

"Call her back. Tell her she'll have to stay in a hotel."

Willows turned towards the bedside alarm clock. It was closing in on two – five in the morning, in Toronto.

He picked up the phone, dialled long distance and the Toronto area code, four-one-six, and then Sheila's number. He hadn't needed to look the number up in his book, and was acutely aware of the exasperation – or was it rage – pouring off Parker in waves.

There was a double click. Ringing. And then a doleful computer-generated voice told him the number was out of service.

He hung up.

Parker said, "What?"

25

Willows told her. He dialled his wife's number again, with the same result.

Parker swore with all the skill and authority of an experienced officer of the law. She gulped half her wine and swore again, but more specifically.

Willows downed most of his Scotch.

Parker said, "You see what she's doing, don't you?"

"Using the children," ventured Willows.

"That's right, Jack. She's got one tucked under each arm and she's using them to batter down the front door. And you're letting her get away with it."

Willows got his book out of the bedside table and looked up a number, started dialling.

Parker said, "What are you doing?"

"Calling her parents."

The phone rang twice and then Sheila's father picked up. His voice was clear and firm. Despite the hour, he sounded as if he had been interrupted in the middle of a good book. Willows knew better; Ross habitually rose at six in the morning and always got eight hours' sleep.

Willows identified himself. He assured Ross that nothing was wrong, and then told his father-in-law that he wanted to speak to Sheila.

"She isn't here, she's staying with a friend."

Willows said, "I phoned her, but the line's been disconnected."

"Yeah, well. She's moved. Didn't she call you?"

"A couple of hours ago. She left a message on my machine."

"Useful things, answering machines. Might even get one myself." Ross cleared his throat. "What happened, you got something new going?"

"That's one way of putting it."

There was a pause. Willows could almost see his father-in-law scratching his chin. After a moment Ross said, "She's been through some tough times, Jack. The past couple of years haven't been easy."

Willows said, "You can't turn back the clock, Ross."

"What about Sean and Annie?"

"They're welcome any time."

Ross said, "The way Sheila sees it, she and the kids come as a package. All for one, and all that crap. Don't quote me, by the way."

26

No fear of that. Willows heard a female voice in the background and Ross's words of reassurance. Then he said, "You want to talk to Elizabeth?"

"Say hello for me."

Ross chuckled into the phone. "Will do, Jack." He lowered his voice. "I've got to follow the party line, son. But you take care of yourself, understand?"

Willows said, "Sorry I woke you, Ross."

Ross disconnected.

Willows hung up. He sat there for a moment with the telephone in his lap, and then put it back on the bedside table.

He finished his Scotch.

Parker said, "Jack?" Her voice was soft and light as falling snow.

He looked at her.

She held out her arms, opening herself to him.

Willows snapped awake as violently as if he'd had a pistol barrel shoved into his face.

His heart pounded in his chest. In his sleep, he'd kicked off the sheets. He felt feverish, and his body was slick with a thin sheen of sweat. He lay quietly, listening so hard it hurt, until he was sure that he and Parker were alone in the house.

He turned his head towards the bedside clock. It was quarter past four. It came to him then, the reason he'd awakened, why he feared there might be an intruder in his home.

It was quarter past seven in Toronto. Sheila and the kids would already be up, eating breakfast or perhaps doing a little last-minute packing.

Parker was lying on her side, facing away from him. The swell of her hip was outlined in the snowy window.

He whispered her name, very quietly, then leaned into her, close enough to hear the slow, steady cadence of her breathing.

Suddenly he felt very lonely, and vulnerable as he hadn't felt since Sean was born.

The truth was, when he'd heard Sheila's voice he'd felt a twist of desire, a longing for the life they'd shared; complacent, perhaps, but full of trust. It was Sheila who'd made the decision to separate. Somewhere deep inside himself, he wasn't too sure he'd ever really let go. Parker had suspected as much, no doubt.

Willows lay there, wide awake, wondering what in hell to do, for a very long time. Finally he gave up on the idea of going back to sleep, eased out of bed and slipped on his red, green and yellow terrycloth robe and went downstairs.

In the backyard, the snow balanced precariously on the dark limbs of the fruit trees was over an an inch thick.

Willows poured a finger of Cutty into a lowball glass. He turned towards the refrigerator but decided not to risk ice because the clatter might wake Claire.

In the morning, the roads would be sheer hell. He'd be driving an unmarked police vehicle and it would be fitted with snow tires. But since the city rarely experienced more than two or three days of snow each winter, most drivers didn't bother with the expense of special tires. Even fewer drivers knew how to handle a car in the snow. Almost no one had sense enough to leave his car in the garage and take a taxi or the bus.

Willows drank some Scotch, held the glass up to the dim light coming in through the kitchen window. He started towards the living room, hesitated, and then snatched the bottle off the sink.

He'd put on the headphones, listen to a little more Sonny Criss, or maybe some Charlie Parker. Perhaps the music would help him find a way out of his predicament.

He sat down heavily on the sofa, unscrewed the cap from the bottle with a quick twist of his thumb. He'd have to watch himself, take care not to drink too much.

Yeah, sure.

4

There was a place downtown, about a hundred-fifty seater with a ten by sixteen foot screen, that showed art movies and National Film Board stuff, some pretty decent foreign films that hadn't been able to attract a distributor. Chris Spacy and his girlfriend, Robyn Davis, had gone to see an Italian animated film called *Gladiators*. Robyn thought the film was hilarious but Chris had trouble reading the subtitles and kept pretending to fall asleep, snoring like a chainsaw with his mouth wide open and his head lolling on her shoulder, heavy as a block of cement. After awhile the neighbouring intelligentsia became sufficiently irked to start hurling small coins as well as large insults.

So they'd walked out and it was snowing, who'd have guessed?

Chris drove a little four-wheel drive Subaru Justy that Robyn had been making the payments on pretty much from the day she'd bought the thing, three hundred dollars a month, rain or shine.

It was still early, and Chris suggested they take a spin around Stanley Park. Put the Subaru through its paces.

Robyn said Yeah, okay. Terminally bored. As if she was doing him the world's biggest favor. Chris knew right away where she was going because she'd taken him there so many times before. River country. *Cry me a river* country, to be exact.

He said, "Just once around the park. Where's the harm? Tell you what, you can be in charge of the tape deck, play whatever music you want."

"Pavarotti."

"Gimme a break."

Laughing, Robyn slipped the tape into the player and twisted the volume control.

Chris turned the key in the ignition, revved the engine hard. The wipers made a miniature snowstorm as they cleared the windshield. He manoeuvred the boxy little car back and forth in the parking spot and then put it in first gear, jumped on the gas and

29

popped the clutch. The sudden acceleration made Robyn drop her seatbelt. The buckle cracked her on the knuckles. She swore. Chris grinned maniacally at her as the Subaru charged down Georgia Street, letting the tachometer needle slide deep into the red zone before he bothered to shift gears.

Chris's philosophy of life in general and cars in particular was elegant in its simplicity: *Break it before it wears out.*

At that time of night traffic in the city was usually pretty light. Tonight, it was even thinner. The snow had kept a lot of people at home and the commuters from West and North Vancouver who drove daily into the downtown core to work in the towers had long since made the return voyage to their color televisions, gas fireplaces and family pets.

So, except for the odd taxi and occasional bus, Chris had the road to himself.

Driving at exactly twice the maximum speed limit, he was able to hit green lights right down Georgia all the way to the last one at Robson. From that point on he was inside the park and there were no more traffic lights, nothing but miles and miles of wide open road.

Chris had a minor control problem as he took the right-sweeping turn past Lost Lagoon. There was a bus route all the way down Georgia and the snow had been pounded to slush, but it was clear from the untrammelled state of the road that very little traffic had entered the park. He was toying with the idea that he might be going just a bit too fast when he hit the virgin snow. The Subaru, stricken, went into a graceless sideways drift. Chris cursed manfully. He lifted his foot off the gas pedal so energetically that his kneecap cracked against the underside of the steering column. He turned into the skid, but, due to inexperience, overcorrected.

Pavarotti – or maybe it was Robyn – screamed in terror as the Subaru pirouetted flirtatiously across two lanes reserved for oncoming traffic, jumped the curb and slid sideways down a snowy slope. A gaggle of drowsy Canada geese fled in disarray. The Subaru hit the pea-gravel walkway that encircled Lost Lagoon.

Chris noticed that the steering wheel no longer seemed to be connected to the rest of the car. For all the difference it made, he might as well be safe at home instead of sitting behind the wheel. He fumbled through the many pockets of his black leather jacket, found a joint and lit up.

The Subaru's front bumper nudged the trunk of a weeping willow.

Robyn said, "That was fun. Gimme a hit."

Chris passed her the joint. He tried reverse gear. Much to his surprise, it worked just fine. He backed up until he was in the middle of the pea-gravel path and eased into first, lightly touched the gas. A few minutes later they were back on the road again, good as new.

Robyn was a member of Greenpeace, the Sierra Club, Tree Huggers Unlimited, and half a dozen outfits Chris could never remember the name of. If there was a mailing list, she was on it. About a ton of plant material recycled and converted into desperate pleas for cash was vomited through the mail slot every single month. Robyn was a passionate joiner. She was crazy about meetings, loved to mingle. Her latest fad was an animal rights group that called itself Animal Action. Fifty bucks and you were in. She'd paid sixty for the family rate, although they weren't even engaged and probably never would be.

Chris had gone to one meeting and that was it for him. Guys who wore faded denim coveralls and wandered around with their hands in their baggy-ass back pockets with their eyes full of unfocused rage were definitely not his type.

Ditto for the legions of bright-faced girls who wore all-natural fabrics and shiny black Doc Martens and wouldn't touch red meat if their miserable lives depended on it.

Robyn thought they were okay, though. A little rough around the edges, but *sincere*. In Robyn's book, sincerity was a rare commodity, worth pursuing.

A few weeks ago, Robyn had paid ten bucks to join an outfit whose oddball name Chris couldn't recall, but whose sole purpose in life was to outlaw the capture and display of killer whales. Orcas, they called them. Huge black and white mothers the size of a 7-series BMW.

And Chris thought they were as nifty looking as a BMW, too. Sleek and shiny, with that ruthless get out my way or I'll gun you down look that Chris admired so much. On the road it was the BMW's famous kidney-shaped grille that filled your rearview mirror. With the whales it would be a three-foot wide mouth full of six-inch teeth that you'd see coming up behind you.

Same deal, essentially.

Driving along at a sedate twenty miles an hour, the Subaru

trailing a roostertail of snow as Pavarotti wailed away at them from both front and rear speakers, they cruised past the mock-Tudor bulk of the Coal Harbor Yacht Club, which Chris believed functioned primarily as a hangout for alcoholic rugby players. He'd lit another joint, and the Subaru's cramped little cabin was full of smoke. Robyn had burned her share of weed and was feeling pretty relaxed, enjoying the passing view. When Pavarotti finally ran out of wind she took her turn, started singing "On the Road Again" in a voice that sounded like a mouse on helium. Chris imagined a puffed-out mouse floating along at an altitude of ten feet or so as it sang a medley of Roger Whittaker hits. He couldn't stop himself from giggling.

Robyn said, "What's so funny?"

Chris shrugged.

"Tell me."

"Forget it."

"You want a good time tonight, sailor, you better speak up loud and fast."

Chris said, "Is that supposed to be a threat?"

"You better believe it."

What Chris believed was that he was starting to get the hang of it now. He steered the Subaru into the middle of the empty road, slammed on the brakes and spun the wheel.

The little car did a perfect donut.

Robyn shrieked with delight.

Chris said, "You better think of some other way to pry it out of me."

She stuck her tongue out at him, and he flicked at it with his finger, but missed.

She said, "Why is that, loverboy?"

"Because any time I want it, all I have to do is snap my fingers. And we both know it."

"Oh, is that right?"

Chris nodded emphatically. He said, "Because you need it more than I do. Your sexual appetite is out of control. And we both know that, too."

Robyn reached up and twisted the rearview mirror so she could look at herself. She brushed her hair back from her cheek. The joint dangled from a corner of her mouth. Still looking into the mirror, she said, "Are you accusing me of insatiability?"

Chris grinned at her. "Yeah. I guess I am."

32

"You're suggesting I'm some kind of nymphomaniac?"

"Hey, babe. It ain't just me!"

Robyn reached up and twisted the mirror back to its approximate original position. She smiled at Chris and said, "How's that – can you see okay?"

Chris glanced up at the mirror. Robyn tried to punch him in the groin but he brought his leg up and caught the blow on the thigh. Even so, it hurt like hell. He said, "Careful, toots. Hit me there, you're likely to break your hand."

Smiling, Robyn said, "You're such a jerk." She rested her hand gently on his thigh. "Take me to see the whales, okay?"

Chris fiddled with the mirror, getting it right. He said, "What happens when you pump a gerbil full of helium?"

"I don't know, what?"

"Figure it out. *Think* about it."

Robyn nibbled at her lower lip as she mulled it over. Chris ejected the Italian tenor and slipped a ZZ Top tape into the machine.

Robyn said, "It turns into a dirigible." She smiled sweetly. "Now take me to the aquarium."

"No can do, sweetheart."

"Baby, don't make me lose my temper."

Chris fiddled with the mirror, getting it right. Behind them, the road was white except for two parallel black stripes left by their tires.

He tapped the brakes and skidded to a gentle stop in the middle of the road. To their right a couple of hundred sail and power boats were moored in individual boathouses. As well, several big sail boats, all of them covered in snow, were moored out in the open.

One of the boats was occupied. A row of round yellow lights glowed along the line of a graceful hull. At the stern, an American flag drooped wearily.

The snow had drained all the color out of the world. It was as if they were looking at an old movie. Behind the boathouses, the city's skyline had been transformed into an abstract in black and white. It was very quiet. Chris rolled down his window. Somewhere in the distance a duck quacked grumpily.

Chris rolled the window back up. They drove through a metered parking lot and turned left. The wheels spun as they ascended a gentle slope. A scrim of rainforest loomed on their left. To their

33

right the low, flat concrete roof of the bear pit was almost invisible. Chris parked behind the stone-faced building that housed the zoo's collection of exotic birds and, at the far end, a handful of poisonous snakes stuffed into glass cubicles the size of a shoebox.

They climbed out of the car. Chris activated the burglar alarm. "Lock your door?"

Robyn shrugged prettily. She gave him a taunting, over-the-shoulder look. "Beats me, Chris. Maybe you better check it for me."

Chris scooped enough snow off the car's roof to make a nice fat snowball. Robyn stood there, smiling at him, snow falling into her hair. She'd get up in the morning and nibble at a piece of dry toast and go happily off to work – eight hours of zombie tedium she didn't seem to mind at all. And then she'd come back to the apartment at the end of the day and change into another personality as easily as she changed clothes.

Chris admired her for that – her ability to adapt to the terrain. She was a disciplined, feisty chick. Cute, too. Fine bones, a dairymaid's complexion, big green eyes and mysterious smile, a wild mane of flaming red hair beautiful as a postcard sunset. A wonderful laugh, endless energy. Deep in his gut, Chris knew that one of these days Robyn would see him for what he was – just another drifter with a nice smile – and take back the keys to the Subaru and kick his ass out of her life.

But that was later. This was now.

Chris finished packing the snowball and rolled it across the roof of the car towards her. Trusting her, providing her with the ammunition to do him in.

Robyn snatched up the snowball and cocked her arm. Chris held his ground. Laughing, she turned, adopted a bowler's stance, took three quick strides and rolled it down the road.

Chris watched the snowball gain bulk and gradually slow down, finally roll to a stop.

Kind of like life itself.

He lit a fresh joint, took Robyn's wool-mittened hand in his, and led her down a narrow asphalt path past the public washrooms and then the massive Bill Reid sculpture of a killer whale. The orca was made of bronze and the artist had depicted it at the apex of its leap above a small, frozen pool.

Chris dug into his pants pocket. He flipped a shiny new penny at the pool. It struck the ice with a clear ringing sound.

34

Robyn squeezed his hand. "Did you remember to make a wish?"

Chris squeezed back. "How could I forget?"

"What did you wish for?"

"I can't tell you."

"Why not?"

"Because then it wouldn't come true, would it?"

Robyn said, "I doubt it will anyway, Chris."

"What's that supposed to mean?"

"Remember last summer, when you threw some money into the fountain behind the art gallery, on Georgia Street. I asked you what you wished for and you told me it was always the same thing. And then whispered your filthy, disgusting needs into my shell-like ear?"

Chris said, "I've changed, honey. You *know* it's true."

"I do, huh."

Chris wiggled his eyebrows. He said, "Okay, I admit it – Somewhere deep inside I haven't stopped hoping you'll buy me a dishwasher."

They strolled around the outside of the building housing the monkeys, down a snow-drifted asphalt path that skirted a small pond. High above them in a fir tree, an unseen great blue heron croaked nervously, and then was still. They continued to follow the path until it dead-ended at a sheer eight-foot-high wall made of rough slabs of streaky orange rock.

Chris said, "It's cold as hell – you sure you want to do this?"

"I think it's kind of romantic."

Chris said, "Yeah?" Hopefully.

"Romantic, Chris. Not carnal."

"So what's the difference, exactly?"

At the base of the stone wall there was a narrow strip of black soil planted with a few small deciduous shrubs. The ground was lumpy and hard. Chris offered Robyn his hand but she ignored him. One of the things about her that vexed Chris and yet so attracted him was her refusal to be dominated in any way. Robyn was a strong-willed woman. Sex or a donut; if she wasn't in the mood, forget it. Somehow she instinctively knew what was good for her, and what wasn't. Chris envied her ability to define her needs and abide by them. In all facets of her life, strength of purpose seemed to flow out of her.

They made their way along the rock wall and then Chris knelt and braced himself against the cold stone, made a sling of his interlocked hands. Robyn stepped into the sling. He gave her a quick kiss on the mouth and she fleetingly kissed him back.

They'd paid unauthorized late-night visits to the whales several times before, and had gradually worked out a routine. Robyn held tightly to his jacket collar while Chris stood upright, then she reached up and got a grip on top of the wall, stepped on his shoulders and hauled herself up the rest of the way.

The stratagem had been a success on their previous trips, but now, in the middle of a snowstorm, it was much more difficult. Chris's hands ached with the cold. It was a lot more difficult to keep his balance. Snow tumbled out of the sky and into his eyes and down the back of his neck. Robyn's expensive leather boots were slick with mud and slush. He grunted as he boosted her a little higher. Her bootheel scraped his collarbone as she pushed away from him, scrambled up on the wall.

Chris waited until she was clear and then pulled himself up after her.

Robyn hugged and kissed him as he reached the top of the wall. She said, "God, Chris, you climb like a spider!"

Stooped low, they hurried towards the whale pool and out of sight of the path. The joint had gone out. Chris paused to fire a match, sucked smoke deep into his lungs and passed the joint to Robyn.

The whale pool was shaped roughly in an oval. The viewing area with its open seating was on the far side. Chris and Robyn squatted near a wall of mock-sandstone planted with a fringe of ferns and other small plants. The wall dropped almost straight down into the pool. A thin grey fog hung above the black water. Snow falling on to the quiet surface made a faint hissing sound.

Robyn passed the joint back to him. She put her arms around his neck and kissed him. Staring deeply into his eyes, she kissed him again and again.

Chris inhaled deeply, held the smoke.

"Love me?"

Chris said, "You betcha."

"How much?"

"More than, uh . . ."

Robyn tweaked his nose. "More than what? Words can say?"

36

Chris said, "Sounds good to me."

There was a heavy *whuffing* noise as one of the two killer whales in the pool breached and vented a rising column of mist.

Robyn turned towards the sound and, Chris could plainly see, forgot him in the moment of turning.

Robyn said, "Bjossa."

The whale's body was blacker than the black water. There was a flash of white saddle as the huge creature slipped beneath the surface, sounding at such an acute angle that its broad, flat, glistening tail rose high into the speckled air.

A second, smaller whale suddenly thrust its head out of the water at the far end of the pool. Chris caught a quick glimpse of a mouthful of blunt, rounded teeth and a darkly glittering eye, and then the whale crashed heavily down, sending a foaming wall of water into the snow-shrouded bleacher seats.

A moment later the surface of the pool had calmed and the enclosure once again was silent and lifeless.

Then Bjossa surfaced and the base of the whale's dorsal fin sliced through the water as she raced around the pool, completed a circuit and then slowed, abruptly smacked her tail flukes against the water, the impact loud as a pistol shot.

Robyn said, "Did you see that!" Whispering, as if she was in church.

Chris leaned into her and kissed her softly on the neck, just below the line of her jaw. He tried to cop a feel, but she was wearing so many layers of clothing he might as well have fondled a mattress.

The smaller of the whales, Finna, rose slowly out of the water directly in front of them, no more than twenty feet away. The whale continued to rise to about the level of its pectoral fins. Its interest seemed to have been captured by the snow, which was falling fast and thick.

Very slowly, almost reluctantly, Finna began to sink beneath the surface.

Neither Robyn nor Chris noticed the glass doors by the narwhal pool swing open, or saw the metal dolly with the naked corpse splayed across it, as it was pushed through the snow towards the pool.

At the far end of the pool Bjossa suddenly surged straight up out of the water like a slightly overweight black and white ICBM. The whale crashed back into the water and a rolling, foamy wave

37

slopped over the lip of the pool and turned a ten-foot span of snow to slush.

Chris said, "Holy Christ!"

Robyn's breast swelled beneath his groping hand. She was about to scream.

He clamped his hand over her mouth.

Dr Roth's corpse, naked except for the bright blue flippers and his face mask and TAG Heuer watch, rolled off the dolly, hit the slush and went *splat*.

Robyn's big green eyes were bugged out. She was hyperventilating like crazy. Chris held her tightly. He told himself that he and Chris were sharing the same hallucination and that the root of their common terror had to be an impurity in the marijuana – fertilizers or insecticides, some other essentially harmless chemical.

Or they might be the victims of some maniac farmer who'd dusted his crop with strychnine.

Dr Gerard Roth's acned butt was kicked hard and trembled like a lump of milk-white jello. The rest of him didn't move an inch.

The dolly rammed into him, hard. Chris flinched as the sharp sound of cold steel on dead meat carried to him across the body of water. He squinted into the glare of the lights from the aquarium. The snow was tumbling out of the night sky with such enthusiasm that it was difficult to see exactly what was going on over there.

Chris winced as he was once again assaulted by the distinctive thud of steel-on-flesh. Dr Roth's corpse slid across the slush towards the pool. The dolly smacked him on the hip. A ridge of slush was building in front of him as his progress towards the pool continued. His eyes were wide open and so was his mouth. The dolly hit him again.

The surface of the pool bulged smoothly. A darkly glittering eye assessed the situation and then vanished in a welter of foam.

The dolly's hard rubber wheels thundered across the snowy tiles and there was that nasty beef-bashing thud again, sharp as the crack of a whip.

Dr Roth's corpse slipped headfirst into the pool with scarcely a ripple, vanished beneath the surface so abruptly he might have been pulled under by some unseen subterranean presence.

Chris said, "Oh my God." He slowly realized that Robyn

seemed to have stopped breathing. He unclasped his hand from her mouth. She continued to stare at the pool as if hypnotized.

Chris said, "Robyn, honey. Are you okay?"

Bjossa breached with the naked dude held sideways in his huge jaws. He shook his head. Dr Roth was flung high into the air. Timing it perfectly, the whale smacked him with its broad tail, knocked him all the way to the far end of the pool.

A moment later Finna surfaced beside the corpse. The whale nudged Roth's torso with its blunt snout and then opened wide, fixed the doctor's weary head in its jaws delicately as a skilled jeweller wields a pair of miniature tweezers on an almost invisible screw. Roth was yanked under, slapped around. He might have been the rope in a not-so-friendly game of tug-of-war.

Robyn turned away and emptied her stomach over an azalea bush.

Dr Roth shot high into the air again, as if he had been fired from a large-caliber cannon. As he reached the apex of his arc he hung motionless among the flakes of snow for a fraction of a second, and Chris saw that the whales' boytoy had lost most of a leg.

No, wait a minute, he was wrong. Dr Roth hadn't lost his leg after all. Because there it was, bright blue swim fin still firmly attached, bobbing in the swell over by the feeding ramp.

5

The snow had slowed to a trickle and then stopped completely at a little past eight in the morning. But the air was wintry crisp and clear, the sky dark with low-lying cloud. The short-term forecast was for more snow, and plenty of it, and Willows believed the weatherman might hit two in a row, for once.

The streets were a mess; downed trees and power lines littered the side streets, and several main arteries were cluttered with dead buses, a tangle of dented automobiles and apoplectic drivers. At nearly every corner, milling knots of foul-mouthed, mad-as-a-hornet commuters fought over the few taxis that were available. The snarl of congestion added almost half an hour to Willows' trip. It was ten to nine when he finally parked his unmarked car in the underground garage across the alley from the Public Safety Building at 312 Main.

He locked the car, turned in the keys and hurried across the alley. As he took the elevator up to the third floor, he enjoyed the sensation of being snug and warm – inside.

As Willows made his way towards his desk, Eddy Orwell sliced the flat of his hand rapidly back and forth across his shiny blond brushcut, as if smoothing it down prior to sticking a tee in his skull and reaching for his putter. Willows gave him an odd look. Orwell noticed. He said, "I look like I've been up all night butting heads with a train, don't I?"

Willows said, "You could use a shave, Eddy. And a long hot, soapy shower as well as a change of clothes and a new barber. Toss in a good night's sleep and a three-egg breakfast, you'll feel like a new man."

Orwell said, "I'm consoled by the knowledge that no matter how terrible I look, Farley must be twice as bad."

Orwell's partner, Farley Spears, was slumped in his chair at his desk, his mouth wide open and the back of his left hand trailing on the pale grey carpet.

Orwell said, "You could stuff a smoke alarm up his ass and light him on fire, I bet he'd sleep right through it."

"Had a busy night, did you?"

Orwell yawned hugely. "Hear about the Russian?"

"What Russian's that?"

"Vladimir. Calls himself Vlad the Impaler. The guy and a couple of his brothers slipped into the country a few years ago. They operated a chopshop for a while, then moved into the wholesale drug business." Orwell scratched his jaw. He peered myopically at his thumb and then dug something out from under the nail. "Me'n Farley have been up all night, taking turns interrogating the guy. The way he tells it, he was simply scratching out a living the best way he knew how, intended to go legit once he'd satisfied his basic needs. All he wanted was a mansion in Shaughnessy, ski cabin in Whistler, a condo in Maui and – he admits he may have overreached himself here – a private jet and maybe some English lessons from Berlitz."

"How's he doing so far?"

"I know he's got the mansion and the cars, because I helped tear 'em apart. The rest of it he refuses to talk about. Modest, I guess."

Willows said, "You can't blame him for wanting to get ahead. In this imperfect capitalist world of ours, a guy's got to have a little ambition. Where'd Vlad go wrong?"

"His girlfriend liked to skinpop once in a while. Not that she was an addict, understand. Just that she liked the rush, during those really special times."

Willows leaned against his desk, folded his arms across his chest and listened patiently as Orwell told his tale of greed and woe and terminal incompetence.

It turned out Vlad didn't know all that much about the art of profit maximization – a simple process that depended largely on how much he cut, or diluted, his product. Consequently sweetheart had overdosed. While Vlad and a few friends were out in the backyard pool playing bare-ass water polo and drinking champagne from the bottle, sweetheart had nodded off in the middle of her fettucini, slipped under the table and asphyxiated and died.

The thing was, the two brothers volunteered that lately Vlad and the girl hadn't been getting along too well. In fact, a couple of hours before her death she'd tried to run him through with a fondue fork. So was her death an accident, or was it murder?

Orwell had seven hours of Q & A on tape, but nobody was any wiser than when they'd begun.

Dan Oikawà, who happened to be passing by, jerked his thumb at Spears. "He okay?"

"Righteous exhaustion," said Orwell. "You could nail a smoke alarm to his head and light him on fire, he'd sleep right through it."

Oikawa said, "I got ten bucks says you're wrong."

"Yeah?"

"And I'll even supply the materials. But you do the carpentry work."

"You're on," said Orwell. Winking at Willows, he said, "Where's Parker?"

"She's around."

"Yeah?"

"Yeah," said Willows.

Orwell said, "The thing is, Vladimir shows all the classic signs of genuine remorse. I think he really loved the broad."

"If you say so, Eddy."

"I do say so." Orwell stared down at the largest of the photographs of himself, his wife and child that cluttered his desk. "See, I've been in love, so I know how to recognize the symptoms."

Parker entered the squadroom. Orwell smiled broadly. "Morning, Claire."

Parker nodded tersely as she made her way to her grey-painted metal desk. She shrugged out of her coat, sat down and rifled energetically through her message slips.

Orwell said, "You're looking good this morning."

"What's that supposed to mean?"

"Well rested," said Orwell. "Rarin' to go."

Parker looked up from her messages, met and held Willows' eye, then turned to Spears.

"What's his problem?"

"Heart attack," said Orwell. "We got a pool going on when his wife'll phone to find out why he's late for dinner." He smiled. "Care to pick a month?"

Parker straightened some papers on her desk. She said, "You look awful, Jack. Have a problem getting to sleep last night?"

"As a matter of fact, I slept like a baby."

"Just make sure we don't catch you sleeping with a baby," said Orwell.

42

Willows said, "You're a sick puppy, Eddy."

"Arf!" said Orwell. He raised his eyebrows and opened his mouth and let his fat pink tongue hang out. Breathing heavily, panting, he stared bright-eyed at Parker as if waiting for her to take him for a walk.

"Down boy," said Oikawa, continuing on his way.

"Arf!" said Eddy.

Inspector Homer Bradley stood at his office door, his arms folded across his chest. He caught Orwell's eye. "What's Farley's situation?"

"He's been up all night, Inspector."

Bradley said, "Wake him up and send him home." He disappeared into his office.

Orwell rapped his knuckles against Spears' temple as if he was knocking on a door. Spears' eyes popped open. He sat bolt upright. In a perfectly clear voice he said, "I guess we can scratch the smoke alarm as a fund-raiser."

Orwell nodded. "Maybe so. But I bet if we put our heads together we can think of some other reason to light you on fire."

Spears said, "I'd like that, Eddy."

Orwell shot Spears a sly look. He winked, gave Parker a sideways glance and said, "Know who I'd really love to set on fire?"

Willows said, "No, Eddy. Who?"

"Vladimir," said Orwell, a little too promptly. He snatched up his giant-size bottle of Windex and grabbed one of the dozen gun-metal framed photographs of his wife and child that littered his desk. He triggered a fine spray of blue liquid, industriously wiped the glass clean with his handkerchief. "Want to know something, Farley?"

"Probably not," said Spears.

Orwell put the picture down and picked up another. Judith smiled lovingly up at him from the head of their dining room table. Orwell fired away. A jet of Windex hit her right between the eyes. He said, "Sometimes I wish this stuff was Mace, or even that new pepper spray we got. But Mace would be better."

"C'mon, Eddy. That's a terrible thing to say."

"Maybe so, but it's true. I admit being married has certain advantages. But there are times lately when I feel like a trapped animal."

"I'm sure I speak for all of us," said Willows, "when I say that comes as no surprise."

"Yeah?" Orwell looked pleased. He tugged at an earlobe. "Thanks, Jack."

Inspector Bradley reappeared in his doorway. He pointed at Willows and Parker, motioned them towards his office.

Parker pushed her chair away from her desk. She stood up.

Orwell said, "Hey now, don't go away mad."

Bradley waited until the two detectives were in his office and then shut the door.

Willows said, "What's up, Inspector?"

"I just got a call from a guy named Tony Sweeting. Ring a bell?"

Parker shook her head, no.

Willows waited.

Bradley said, "Mr Sweeting's the director of the Vancouver Public Aquarium. He phoned to tell us that a member of his staff has just discovered a body floating in the killer whale pool."

Parker said, "What kind of body?"

"The body of a naked male Caucasian. Possibly a staff member, although no positive identification has yet been made due to the fact that the guy's floating face down and nobody wants to touch him."

"If the body's floating face down, how can this guy Sweeting be so sure it's a male?"

"Hairy legs. Bald head." Bradley grinned. "Come to think of it, it's a lucky thing I'm standing here talking to you. Because otherwise it could be me."

Bradley opened a desk drawer and pulled out a box of wooden kitchen matches, lit one with his thumbnail. The match flared hot and bright. Bradley huffed and puffed. The flame was extinguished. The air stank of sulphur. Bradley waved the smoking match at Willows and Parker. "It's your case, kids. From what I understand, there's more than enough of the guy for the two of you." He wiggled his eyebrows. "Have fun!"

Willows checked a brown Ford out of the car pool. The car had blackwall tires, mini-hubcaps, four doors and a whip antennae. They called them unmarked cars, but he wasn't sure why. He drove against the flow of traffic down the one-way alley that ran behind the Public Safety Building, turned left on Cordova, made a right on Main and another left on Powell.

Parker sat quietly in the passenger seat, staring straight out the windshield.

44

Willows said, "Homer was in a pretty strange mood, wasn't he?"

Parker nodded, not looking at him.

Willows said, "Look, Claire . . ."

"What?"

Despite the heavy downtown traffic there was still plenty of snow on the roads and in places the surface was slick with ice. Willows eased his foot off the gas as brake lights flashed in front of him.

Parker said, "Have you made up your mind what you're going to do?"

Willows said, "It isn't that easy . . ."

"No? Well, that's too bad. But if that's how it is, I don't want to talk about it. Because it's your problem, not mine."

Willows nodded.

There was only one road to the aquarium, and so, once they hit the park, Willows inadvertently followed the route Chris and Robyn had taken over twelve hours earlier.

Despite the early hour and inclement weather, there were a dozen or more cars in the parking lot and several groups and individuals wandering around the zoo area, bundled up against the cold and somehow looking pathetic and lost.

The aquarium's director, Anthony Sweeting, had suggested to Bradley that the investigating officers use the staff entrance at the north end of the aquarium – door number five. Willows and Parker walked in and found themselves in a spacious reception area. Willows identified himself and said Tony Sweeting was expecting them.

"*Anthony* Sweeting," said the secretary, correcting him.

Willows nodded. "Sorry."

The secretary's long chestnut hair was swept up in a french twist. She was wearing too much lipstick on too much mouth, and the lenses on her oversized glasses made her eyes look small and close-set, myopic. She tossed a yellow wooden pencil in a ceramic mug, smiled at Parker. "He's out by the whale pool, I'll show you how to get there." She was wearing a thick patchwork quilt of a sweater with a maple-leaf design, and tight black Levis. Willows tactfully admired the way the Levis label sewed to the back pocket of her jeans fluttered like a little red flag when she walked. She caught him peeking and gave him a look that reduced him to nine parts pathetic and one part immature.

They walked down a long, windowless, carpeted hallway and then through a door marked "emergency exit" and down another hallway that connected unexpectedly to a wall of glass. The whale pool looked as if it were full of oil, slow-moving and glossy black. A heavyset man in a dark blue suit was crouched at the water's edge with his back to them. The secretary unlocked a glass door and pushed it open. The cold hit Willows, nipped his ears and pinched at the corners of his eyes.

The door sighed shut. Parker heard the click of the automatic lock. The whale pool was about fifty yards away. There were open concrete bleachers on the near side and an iron railing all the way around the pool. A diving board projected over the water on the far side. Parker supposed that's where the trainers stood when it was feeding time. She'd seen them on television, leaning far out over the water and pouring big metal buckets full of small silvery fish into the whales' gaping maws. And she remembered wondering what it was like, making the big adjustment from hunting and killing and eating everything from salmon to sea lions to minke whales to opening wide on cue for a bucketful of dead herring.

Willows had lived on the coast within sight and smell of the Pacific ocean almost his entire life, but had spent hardly any time at all in or on the sea. He knew several people who owned sail boats. Most of them went for a sail on the Labor Day weekend at the end of the summer, and that was about it. In the meantime they were forever grouching that a boat was nothing but a bottom-less hole in the water into which they were forever pouring their money. Yet they seemed without exception to take pleasure in the grim reality of it all.

Willows slipped and nearly fell on a patch of ice. His arms windmilled as he fought to regain his balance. His mind had been wandering. The point he'd been about to make to himself was that he knew very little about killer whales. Were orcas known to attack humans? Had a whale killed the victim? Willows fervently hoped so. Death by misadventure sounded exactly right. His plate was already overflowing, thanks to Sheila. The last thing he needed was a high-profile, time-consuming murder investigation.

Anthony Sweeting heard the crunch of ice behind him and turned, already raising a hand to shoo away the uninvited.

Sweeting was what people were calling vertically challenged, but what Willows simply thought of as *short*. He seemed determined to compensate for his lack of height by occupying a maximum amount of horizontal space. He was wearing an expensive dark blue suit, an orange silk shirt under a puce cardigan, a fish-shaped tie complete with a plastic eye that moved when he did, solid gold starfish cufflinks and the only patent-leather brogues Willows had ever seen.

Willows showed him his badge case. The director stared up at it, squinting. Despite the cold, his pale skin was pebbled with sweat. Willows could smell the mousse.

After a moment Sweeting said, "Cops?"

Willows nodded, introduced himself and Parker.

"It's about time you got here. This is Dr Gerard Roth. He was one of our employees."

Parker said, "Who found his body?"

"Me. I did." Sweeting hesitated. He gnawed at his pendulous lower lip for a moment, obviously mulling it over, and then added, "What I mean is, I found most of it. Everything but the leg. Bob found the leg."

Parker said, "Bob?"

"Robert Kelly. Head of security." Sweeting's knees creaked as he stood up. "Bob found the leg down there, in the holding tank."

At the far end of the pool a narrow channel led to a second, much smaller pool.

Parker said, "That's where you put a whale if you want to segregate it from the others?"

"Whales or dolphins."

"Do the whales usually have access to the holding tank?"

"Yes, of course. Unless it's in use, they can come and go as they please."

Within the confines of the pool, thought Parker.

Willows said, "How big is the pool, Mr Sweeting?"

"I'm not sure, exactly. About a hundred-twenty feet long by eighty wide. Somewhere in there. It was designed as an extremely irregular shape, so it looks natural. There's about nine hundred thousand gallons of water in there – more than the average person drinks in a lifetime."

Willows nodded politely. He and Annie and Sean had spent a week on the West Coast of Vancouver Island a few years previously. They'd taken a "whale watch" cruise from the overly picturesque and pricey village of Tofino. High seas combined with thick fog had kept them close to shore. They hadn't seen any

47

whales. But Willows remembered a bit of what the guide, who'd been a genuine enthusiast, had told them. Bulls grew to thirty-two feet in length and weighed as much as seven tons. They often journeyed ninety miles or more in a 24-hour period, and were capable of sustained speeds as high as fifteen miles per hour.

Orcas emitted complex sonar-like clicks in bursts of up to several hundred beats per second, both as a navigational aid and to locate prey. To communicate, they produced more than five dozen distinct sounds. Their sonar was effective up to six miles. Their natural lifespan was as long as sixty years.

In the aquarium, that sixty-year lifespan was reduced to a maximum of twenty years.

No wonder.

Parker said, "Let's take a look at the body."

The aquarium had been closed to the public, but parts of the complex were visible from the surrounding park. Bob Kelly had thoughtfully shielded the corpse from the public's prying eyes with a large blue tarpaulin.

Willows knelt and lifted a corner of the tarp. Dr Roth's left leg had been yanked off at the knee. Bob Kelly had placed the leg beside the body in the correct position, as if Roth's corpse was an exceedingly simple puzzle that had been successfully reassembled.

Willows said, "When you found the body, was there much blood in the water?"

Sweeting shrugged. "None that I could see. Was he recently killed, is that what you mean? There's no way of knowing. The entire contents of the pool are filtered every ninety minutes. It's an exceedingly expensive and very thorough procedure. I can show you the filtration system, if you like."

Parker said, "Do you have any idea what Dr Roth was doing in the pool?"

"No, not at all."

"Just out for a swim, was he?"

"It's possible. It isn't something we approve of, but there's no point in denying that from time to time staff succumb to the temptation of an unauthorized dip in one of the tanks."

"Wouldn't that be dangerous?"

"Yes, I should think so. Finna and Bjossa aren't accustomed to having people in the water with them. If someone was to enter the pool I'd expect them to become quite agitated."

48

"Angry?" said Parker.

"Not necessarily. Playful, perhaps."

Willows lifted the tarp a little higher. There were deep conical bite marks – what appeared to be bite marks – on Roth's torso and thighs. He said, "Are you suggesting Finna and Bjossa playfully ripped off Dr Roth's leg?"

A starfish cufflink glittered as Anthony Sweeting ran stubby fingers through his heavily moussed hair. He said, "The truth is, vigorous physical interaction is quite common among whales. If you take a look at the belugas you'll notice toothmarks on every single one of them. It's partly a domination thing; they're constantly rearranging the pecking order. And it's sexual as well, of course. But I think I see what you mean. 'Playfully ripped his leg off' sounds a bit callous, doesn't it?"

Parker said, "Let's not make any assumptions. We don't know how or when Dr Roth died. He may have been killed before he went into the pool."

"I don't understand. What do you mean?"

Parker shrugged. "It's conceivable he slipped on the ice beside the pool, fell and fractured his skull. He may have died instantaneously, or lost consciousness for no more than a few seconds. Either way, he slides into the pool and the whales start playing volleyball."

"You think that's what happened?" said Sweeting anxiously.

Parker said, "That's just the point. We have no idea how he died. Our purpose here is to try to find out."

Sweeting said, "You're homicide detectives. Does that mean you suspect foul play?"

"No," said Parker. "It doesn't mean that at all. We're here to investigate the circumstances of Roth's death, make a preliminary decision as to how he died. If it begins to look as if he expired as a consequence of someone else's actions . . ." Parker smiled. "Let's take it one step at a time, okay?"

"Fine," said Sweeting. "Whatever you say."

Willows let the tarp drop. He moved closer to the lip of the pool and trailed his fingers in the water. It was very cold. He became aware of a huge dark mass rising towards him. Before he could react, the larger of the orcas, Bjossa, surfaced near him and vented a blast of spray from its blowhole. Willows turned away, but too late to avoid a shower.

Sweeting said, "They tend to do that quite often. I don't know if anyone's done any research into whale humour, but it seems a likely candidate for a thesis, wouldn't you agree?"

Willows saw himself pulled effortlessly beneath the surface, emptying his lungs in a mute scream. He wiped his face dry with his coat sleeve. The whale rested quietly on the surface. Willows looked into its dark and solemn eye. A worm of fear wriggled through his heart. The whale sounded as best it could, given that the pool wasn't much deeper than its overall length.

Parker said, "He was checking you out, Jack." Then her attention was caught by something and she looked past him and Willows turned and saw Mel Dutton bustling towards him, moving pretty fast considering he had fifty-odd pounds of equipment strapped to him.

Anthony Sweeting, noting the Nikon in Dutton's hand, swept his fingers through his hair and glanced around as if looking for a stray mirror.

Willows introduced Mel to Sweeting, who offered his hand and had it perfunctorily shaken. Dutton said, "You're the director?"

"Yes, that's correct."

Dutton yanked aside the tarp. He brought up the Nikon. His face twisted as the camera's power winder whirred. He said, "So who's the cheapskate?"

"Cheapskate?" said Sweeting, frowning.

Dutton winked at Parker. He said, "What I mean is, it seems the guy was willing to give a leg, but not an arm." His smile faltered. "No, wait a minute. I got it the wrong way around, didn't I?"

Sweeting stared at him for several seconds before turning to Willows. His face blank, he said, "If you need me, I'll be in my office."

Willows thanked him.

Dutton waited until Sweeting was out of earshot and then said, "Notice the *tie*?"

Parker nodded.

Dutton smiled. "Me too. And from the look on his face, I'd say I got even."

6

Susan was amazed at herself. All that crazy self-actualization stuff was true, wasn't it?

You never knew what you could do until you decided to go ahead and do it.

Susan sat in front of her computer terminal, her back to the open door of her cubicle. She typed eighty words a minute and her fingers danced lightly across the keyboard as she fattened up the databank with Jerry Northcote's latest on Northern Cod. It was pretty dull stuff, but Susan didn't mind because it wasn't the kind of work that required much concentration.

Right now, for example, anyone looking in on her would assume that she was managing to function as if it was business as usual. As if Gerard were still alive.

As if Gerard hadn't been murdered.

She wondered when the police would find out what had really happened to him. She considered what little she knew of police procedure. Films she'd seen, and television drama . . . A word formed in her mind.

Autopsy.

There were quite a few autopsies performed at the aquarium, down on the second level, in small windowless rooms. They called them something else, though.

Necropsies.

Susan knew that both words meant the same thing – cutting things open and looking inside. "Murdering to dissect" as Gerard had put it. He was so smart, always thinking of clever, original ways of describing things.

Susan thought about Jerry Northcote or somebody just like him, inquisitive and humorless, striding briskly into a cold dark room, snapping on a light, staring down at Gerard and then choosing a scalpel and cutting into him.

Ripping him open, gutting him. Humming a popular song as

51

he poked around in there where no one had any right to be. Time passing. Then breaking for lunch and coming back an hour later, burping and humming.

Slicing tiny pieces off her lover, peering at him with monumental stupidity through the powerful lens of a microscope. Susan had been a psych major. She knew how it worked. When you got close enough to something and magnified it until it was no longer recognizable, you completely lost track of what it actually was, or had been. You *disassociated*.

And that's what had happened to her. She had no idea how she'd disassociated, or when. But that's how it went with self-defense mechanisms. When your mind couldn't stand the view, it pulled the drapes.

Susan leaned back in her chair. She stared at the terminal and saw that she had just finished typing *pull the drapes*. She giggled. That was what made Northern Cod truly unique. They had this thing about *privacy*.

Susan wiped the last few lines of the file. She sat there, staring fixedly at the flat grey surface of the screen as if in expectation that the answer to all her problems would magically appear at any moment.

She couldn't bring herself to believe that he was dead. That he'd actually died.

Susan picked up a pencil, pushed the point into the palm of her hand until the pain brought tears to her eyes. She told herself to be honest, to tell the truth.

Gerard hadn't exactly *died*, had he? The situation was a *little* more complicated than that, wasn't it?

He'd been killed.

Murdered.

There it was, out in the open. The "M" word. She tapped the keyboard and the word appeared in the center of the screen, in bold capital letters.

MURDERED

She tapped a few more keys.

MURDER MURDER MURDER MURDER MURDER MURDER MURDER MURDER MURDER MURDER MURDER MURDER

52

The word raced across the screen, filled line after line. In the space of a few seconds the entire screen was filled. Susan burst into tears. She pushed away from her desk and blindly slammed shut the door.

A hundred-twenty salaried employees work at the aquarium, as well as almost one thousand volunteers. Susan imagined she could hear the babble of all their voices through the door, as if they had all somehow managed to jam themselves into the corridor outside her cubicle. The individual words were indecipherable but the accusatory tone was crystal clear.

Someone knocked on her door. Her office was so tiny she hardly ever shut the door because she felt a bit claustrophobic with it closed, despite the window in front of her desk. She plucked a tissue from her purse and blew her nose. A disembodied voice wondered if she was alright.

She took a deep, shuddery breath and called out that she was just fine, but quite busy at the moment, thanks all the same.

Silence.

She had been told that homicide detectives would be investigating the circumstances of Gerard's death. She wondered how long it would take them to find out about her. Not very long, surely. The aquarium held few secrets. Everybody knew everything there was to know about everybody. Or so it seemed.

She wanted a cigarette very badly, but the whole complex was a no-smoking zone and her tiny window was hermetically sealed. She didn't dare step out of the office for fear of bumping into someone. She believed that the word guilt was written all over her face just as clearly as the word murder dominated the screen of her terminal.

She thought about being found out. Caught. She thought about what they would do to her. She tried to imagine what it felt like to be handcuffed, taken to a small room and questioned by detectives.

How long would she be able to keep silent if she was interrogated?

It was a ridiculous question. She was already crying her heart out.

Susan was an only child. If she was arrested, her mother was bound to suffer terribly. She imagined her neighbors reading about her in the papers, gathering to gossip about her and agreeing she was mortally flawed, somehow.

She wished she had been stronger when Gerard first approached her. But she was no match for him. He was too sophisticated. So experienced, and so slick. From their first moments together he had somehow known her so well, known her better than she knew herself. He'd instinctively realized exactly how far he could push her, to what degree she was capable of letting herself go.

Susan allowed herself to slip six months back in time.

It had begun with a nod of acknowledgement and a casual word said to her as they passed in a hallway or happened to sit at the same table or near one another in the staff canteen. Then one day Gerard had smiled at her, holding the smile just a little too long, as if there were something hidden behind his teeth. Soon he was delicately soliciting her opinion on immigration or the economy or violence in schools; whatever happened to be topical that day . . .

She'd bought a new raincoat – a plain blue poplin that happened to be on sale – nothing special. Gerard noticed the coat the first time she wore it, and made a point of casually complimenting her on her taste.

They began to meet for lunch. He took an interest in her work, hinted that she was overqualified and due for a promotion. He began to drop by her office at the same time every morning, just to say hello, hovering in the doorway and smiling, admiring her perfume or the way she'd done her hair.

Often Gerard was unable to think of anything at all to say to her. It was at these times that she was most flattered, for it seemed obvious that he simply craved her company.

She began to anticipate his daily visits, to look forward with great pleasure to his complimentary words.

Before long he was no longer content with lounging in the doorway. Soon he was walking into her office as if he worked there himself. By the end of a week he was resting a hip against her desk as he spoke to her.

Looking down at her.

She liked the mature, openly calculated way he dressed – his tweed jackets and Oxford cloth shirts in white or grey or blue, his determinedly colorful ties. She became addicted to his smile, the way he moved his hands when he spoke, the direct and yet non-threatening way he looked into her eyes when she was speaking to him, the strong, masculine odor of his aftershave and the way he moved, his clumsiness, bulk.

54

When he visited her in her office he often leaned over her shoulder to look more closely at something on her desk. Usually he took advantage of the moment to needlessly touch her, lightly press his hand against the small of her back or brush her neck with the tips of his fingers or perhaps rest his hand briefly on her shoulder. If she looked up at him he invariably smiled down at her with great warmth, but in that same moment he would withdraw from her, as if there were something he must hide from her, no matter what the cost.

In mid-August he dropped by unannounced as she was clearing her desk at the end of a Friday. He dolefully told her he'd intended to take his mother to the opera the following evening, but that she'd had to cancel at the last moment, due to a severe cold. He had two very good tickets and it seemed a shame to let them go to waste. Would she like them? Did she have a friend who cared for the opera? Susan hesitated. He suddenly had a *wonderful* idea – why didn't they go together!

Susan stared fixedly out her tiny office window as she coolly suggested it might be more appropriate for Dr Roth to take his wife to the opera, if he truly lacked companionship.

Lacked companionship. What a stuffy little fool she'd been . . .

Dr Roth – Gerard – was astounded. Yes, of course he was married, but surely Susan knew that he and Iris were no longer living together, that they'd separated more than a year ago.

Heavens, what sort of person did she think he was?

Taken by surprise, caught off balance, Susan said she needed time to make a decision. Gerard showed her the tickets. She couldn't help noticing how expensive they were. And he was right – it was a terrible waste not to use them. It suddenly occurred to her that the destruction of his marriage might explain why he was so relentlessly cheerful.

He had been badly hurt but he was doing his best to recover. He was being brave.

Susan agreed to go out with him but insisted they meet at the theater rather than have him pick her up at her apartment. And despite his objections, she would go only if she paid her own way.

That first time they'd dated, the way he treated her, so courteously, she might as well have been his mother.

They'd had a glass of white wine at each of the two

55

intermissions. Afterwards Gerard had suggested a nightcap. Against her better judgement Susan agreed to just one drink. Gerard knew a quiet little bar in a downtown hotel. He ordered two glasses of wine. Susan was in a festive mood, and they chatted gaily about the opera. Gerard explained the subtleties of the tragedy. He sang, very quietly but with intense passion, a few lines of an aria. He drank as he talked; very quickly, and despite her best intentions Susan found herself keeping pace. She excused herself to use the washroom and when she came back to the table her empty glass had been replaced with a full one.

Gerard was effusively apologetic. He'd indicated to the waiter that he wanted the cheque, but his signal was misinterpreted. Would she forgive him? They would leave immediately, if that's what she wanted.

It was midnight when Gerard finally paid the tab, and the single glass of wine had turned to four. Susan was a little drunk, but she was enjoying herself too much to be upset about it.

Gerard had a black Saab station wagon with soft leather seats and a compact disc player. He inserted a disc that contained highlights of the opera, and sang loudly and with good-natured gusto as he drove slowly through the late-night traffic.

At the door to Susan's apartment he had smiled and held her small hand in both of his, and told her with much energy that he'd had an absolutely wonderful time, and couldn't wait until his mother succumbed to another cold.

Then he'd kissed her on the cheek, very lightly, and turned and walked away.

Susan had heard vague rumors that Dr Roth was a womanizer. Now she was convinced that these rumors were unfounded. He was a naturally friendly, outgoing person, and that was all there was to it.

Two weeks passed and then he invited her at short notice to a Beethoven concert, and to his favorite bar afterwards for the ritual glass of wine. This time, as she said goodbye, he kissed her softly and fleetingly on the mouth.

From that point on their relationship developed so quickly that Susan could hardly keep up.

Gerard took her to the theater, films, concerts. He introduced her to Early Music, gave her armfuls of flowers, many small, inexpensive but tasteful gifts. He took her sailing on his Cal 20. He showed her how to cook pasta the way his mother cooked it.

He bought her books, introduced her to his favorite authors. No matter what they talked about – and it seemed to Susan that they talked about virtually everything – he never failed to respect her opinion. Soon he actively sought her advice when he had to make a difficult career or personal decision.

Gradually, Susan came to feel needed. Gerard was so much older, and yet so obviously depended on her in so many ways. Their relationship was perfect except for one crucial aspect. Susan had no idea whether it was Gerard's age or simply that a strictly platonic relationship was all he desired, but he was completely uninterested in making love.

Or so she thought.

In late September Gerard invited her to accompany him to Seattle to view a touring exhibition of modern art. Without giving it much thought, Susan said she'd love to go.

It was about thirty miles to the border and another hundred and twenty-odd miles to Seattle. The trip would take about three hours altogether, unless there was an unusually long delay at customs.

Gerard was at Susan's apartment at eight o'clock, Saturday morning. He was dressed a bit more formally than she'd expected: in grey slacks and a dark blue sports jacket, one of his more sombre ties. The Saab had been recently washed and waxed. As Susan got into the car, Gerard made a casual remark about how much he admired a woman who travelled light. When she asked him what he meant he grinned mischievously, revved the engine and pointed out that she hadn't fastened her seatbelt.

When Susan pursued the subject he turned up the disc player and burst into song.

The weather was so mild that once they were out of the city Gerard opened the Saab's sunroof. The breeze rippled Susan's hair, slid under her skirt and caressed her thighs. She felt a mounting sense of excitement – the trip to Seattle would be an adventure. Even though it was so close, America was a foreign country. They might not realize it, but Americans were very different from Canadians.

Gerard broached the subject of lunch. He seemed to know all of the best restaurants in Seattle. Susan asked him if he spent a lot of time in the city, and he smiled and told her he hadn't been across the border in years.

The highway speed limit was fifty-five miles per hour, but

Gerard kept the Saab moving along at a steady eighty. He'd never before driven above the legal limit in Susan's company. When she tactfully voiced concern he told her not to worry, that the Saab had the best radar detector money could buy.

Well, that was hardly the point. But Susan wasn't sure how to make that clear.

They drove nonstop except for a brief pause at an Exxon station to fill the Saab's tank, and arrived in downtown Seattle at quarter to twelve. Gerard drove swiftly and with a great deal of confidence – he seemed as familiar with the Emerald City as he was with the streets of Vancouver. Eventually he pulled up in front of a large, expensive-looking hotel. He helped Susan out of the car and said something she couldn't quite catch to a gaudily overdressed valet, then handed the man the keys to his car. Susan wasn't sure quite what to think. As Gerard guided her towards the hotel door he assured her the restaurant served the best seafood in the entire Northwest.

Despite the vast scale of the hotel, the dining room was small and intimate. Their reserved table was situated in a little nook close to the fireplace, next to a bay window that afforded a sweeping view of the harbor. The tablecloth was snowy white and the glassware and cutlery sparkled in the flame of a tall pink candle. A waitress brought menus and advised them as to the daily specials. She wondered if they'd like a drink to start, and Gerard cheerily admitted he would absolutely *love* a drink. They were on a holiday, why not enjoy themselves? He ordered a vodka tonic and asked Susan what she'd like. When she hesitated, he told the waitress to make it a pair.

The menu was in French. Gerard spoke the language fluently. He sat a little closer to her, the better to explain the various dishes. The sommelier appeared and, after a quick exchange in French followed by a moment's thoughtful reflection, Gerard ordered a bottle of wine.

The vodka tonics arrived, and the waitress took their order. Gerard insisted on a toast. They touched glasses and drank to a long and happy day. Gerard told Susan how much he'd been looking forward to the trip, that he'd been thinking of nothing else all week long.

They were well into their vodka tonics by the time the salads arrived. The sommelier bustled about with the wine, and a long-legged silver ice bucket. Susan surprised herself by wondering aloud if the bucket was really silver, and the sommelier smiled and showed her the sterling marks. Dr Roth examined the label on the bottle and nodded his solemn approval. The cork was pulled and Gerard examined that, too, rolled it about between his thumb and index finger and then brought it to his nose and sniffed with authority. As a splash of wine was poured into his glass he gave Susan a quick wink that made her smile. Then he offered the glass to Susan, explaining that her palate was less jaded than his, and more dependable.

Gerard watched her closely as she tried the wine, nodded her approval. The sommelier lifted the bottle but Gerard put his hand over the mouth of Susan's glass and said quite firmly that they'd have another gin and tonic and let the wine breathe a little, until the meal was served.

As it turned out, this took quite some time. It was mid-afternoon by the time they'd finished eating. Gerard ordered digestifs. He lit a cigar. This was something new. As she sipped her drink, Susan felt a little off-balance, vaguely alarmed. She was fairly confident that she wasn't exactly drunk. But not at all confident that she was going-to-church sober. She did know that she was enjoying herself immensely.

She asked Gerard if she could try his cigar. He gave her an odd look. Have a puff, she explained. She saw she'd unsettled him, and was ridiculously pleased with herself. He handed her the cigar and she put it in her mouth and blew a cloud of smoke at the ceiling, then gave the cigar back to him.

She noticed that he paid for the meal simply by signing the bill. That didn't make sense, although she wasn't sure exactly why.

Gerard tossed the hotel pen on the table – a casual, subtly controlling gesture. He asked Susan if she was ready to move along, then helped her with her chair and took her by the hand and guided her to the hotel lobby. She wondered aloud how long it would take to get to the exhibition. Laughing, he squeezed her hand and told her not to worry about it.

Everything in its own time, he said.

Gerard had led her to a bank of elevators, pushed a button. He made small talk about art. The doors slid open and in they went. Susan felt a giddiness in her stomach as they shot upwards.

She asked Gerard where they were going. He smiled and looked deeply into her eyes as he told her it was a surprise – she was going to have to try to be patient and that was that.

He leaned towards her, kissed her on the tip of the nose.

The elevator doors slid open. Gerard guided her down a discreetly lit hallway. He had a rectangular plastic card in his hand, silvery and punched through with rows of small round holes.

They stopped in front of a door remarkably like all the other doors. Gerard inserted the card into a slot beneath the doorknob, cursed softly and withdrew it and turned it over and stuck it in again. A tiny light blinked red and then green. Gerard pushed the door open. Susan blinked, peered into the dimly lit room. Gerard's hand pressed softly but insistently against the small of her back. His breath on her neck was warm and moist.

She stepped hesitantly into the room. The air smelled of fresh-cut flowers. Heavy gold drapes had been pulled across the window; the only light came from a wall lamp. A vase stuffed with long-stemmed red roses stood on a small table by the bed, next to a bottle of champagne in a clear plastic ice bucket.

Susan said, "Isn't this a surprise?"

Gerard hung a "do not disturb" sign on the door and firmly shut it. The deadbolt shot home.

Susan thought, It's about time. She tore a button on her blouse, cursed and laughed and plucked frantically at the remaining buttons, noticed at last that the great seducer was standing there with his mouth hanging open, in shock.

She moved towards him, dropped to her knees and reached for his belt. Gerard stared fixedly at the ice bucket. He seemed to have run out of small talk. But it was obvious things were going to work out just fine, as long as he remembered to keep breathing.

Someone knocked tentatively on the door. Before she had time to react, it swung open. Ginnie Schulman popped her head in and said, "Have you heard about Dr Roth?"

Speechless, Susan stared at her.

Ginnie said, "Have you been crying?" She came all the way into the office. "You poor baby!" She crouched awkwardly and gave Susan a clumsy hug that reminded her of Gerard and the way he had so often held her back in the good old days – with a great deal of passion and an endearing lack of natural grace.

Susan was blinded to everything but her grief and rage. She

hurled a box of tissues at the wall, cursed and screamed and burst into tears.

Ginnie Schulman, fresh out of compassion, eased back out of Susan's cubicle and quietly shut the door.

7

Mel Dutton ran a few frames through his Nikon, switched from a wide-angle to a 135mm lens and turned to snap several shots of the killer whales.

They'd been lying low ever since he'd arrived, then suddenly gotten frisky. Maybe they'd spotted the Nikon and smelled a photo op.

Dutton said, "Hey, Claire?"

Parker said, "No pictures, Mel."

"Wait a minute, don't be so negative. Check out the crime scene, look what we've got. Mist rising off the pool, a totally naked corpse, all this wonderful snow. A couple of photogenic homicide cops . . ."

"Count me out," said Willows.

"I shoot high contrast black and white film, two or three rolls max, we're looking, I guarantee it, at the next cover of *McLean's* magazine."

Parker said, "You take my picture, Mel, I'll stuff your camera down your throat." She smiled sweetly. "I *guarantee* it."

Dutton winked at Willows – or maybe he suffered from a nervous twitch. "No repressed coppers on the homicide squad, huh?"

Parker gave him a cool look. Six weeks earlier she'd arrived at the scene of a Kingsway shoot-out in time to watch Dutton, armed only with a remarkably insincere grin and a stale-dated pack of Camel filter cigarettes, con a coked-up teenage gangleader into posing, white-hunter style, next to the three totally dead teenage gangsters he'd just clipped with his Uzi.

At least a dozen cops had made damn sure the Uzi was out of ammunition, and then Dutton had handed it back to the kid, lit his Camel for him and stuck it in his mouth, used crude sign language and the simple but effective expedient of physically manipulating him into position; made him kneel with the Uzi clutched in his blood-spattered hands close behind the bullet-riddled corpses of his victims.

In the colorful snaps that resulted, the killer looked like a turn-of-the-century big-game hunter who'd gotten turned around in the high grass and accidentally popped a few bearers, instead of a lion or two.

Dutton took the sheaf of photographs to the crown prosecutor assigned to the case. The guy stuffed the pictures in his battered briefcase but didn't use them in court, possibly because the gang-leader pled guilty on three counts of first degree. When Dutton's request that his work be returned forthwith was ignored, he sent the prosecutor a double-registered letter containing a government pamphlet on copyright law for the layman and swore on his mother's grave never voluntarily to submit evidence to the crown ever again.

But ever since the Kingsway shoot-out, Dutton had been working hard to promote what he liked to call his *Crooks and Cops with Corpses* series. In his zeal he was so aggressively persistent that plenty of normally easygoing cops had turned against him.

When Dutton propositioned Parker, she immediately went on the defensive, assumed he was going to pressure her to – for example – strip to her bra and panties and shoulder holster, jump on a killer whale and do a few quick laps around the pool.

Dutton caught the look in Parker's eyes. He had no idea what she was thinking, but could see it wasn't good. He raised his hands in a gesture of submission, and went back to photographing the crime scene environs.

Willows had been examining the many abrasions and scrapes on Gerard Roth's body. There were a number of deep wounds that appeared to be bite marks. He shared a little of the horror Roth must have endured and then, with an effort, clamped down on his imagination.

Light glinted on a disc of silver. Willows turned and saw the medical examiner, Bailey "Popeye" Rowland making his way slowly and deliberately down the pebbled concrete steps towards the pool. It was Popeye's monocle that had caught the light. Above the monocle he wore a black trilby pulled down so low on his oversized head that it bent his ears double. His salt-and-pepper eyebrows were so thick they had to be clipped back like hedges, and his wiry beard overflowed his face like ivy run wild.

Popeye's fondness for anything alcoholic was the stuff of legends. He was a boozehound fit to roam the Baskervilles. Where his flesh was visible, it was dominated by burst capillaries and resembled a roadmap of hell. He claimed his glass eye had been hand-forged by Spanish artisans from a molten drop of the very best German crystal. The iris was blue as the Mediterranean and the pupil was a small stylized red heart that looked like a valentine candy. Popeye had used the eye many times to horrify unpleasant children or play marbles with his nieces and nephews.

Occasionally, when he was extremely nervous, he would remove the eye from its socket and roll it about in the palm of his hand while making metallic clicking sounds with his tongue. At bedtime he thoroughly washed the eye in contact lens solution and then stored it for the night in an old matchbox. His good eye, the one that worked, was a fuzzy black ball that looked as if it had been recently rolled in coal dust.

Strangers often confused the two eyes, good and bad, and concentrated on the wrong one. When this happened he was always considerably cheered. Over his protruding belly he wore a bulky overcoat, dull grey flecked with black, that was a full two sizes too large. He'd paid heavily to have the sleeves shortened and extra padding stuffed into the shoulders. When he wore the coat he looked almost exactly as wide as he was tall, and when he planted his feet and stood erect, he looked solid as a lump of granite: as if he'd been there forever.

Beneath the overcoat Popeye wore an expensive teal-blue cashmere sweater, and beneath the sweater a custom-tailored sleeveless vest of Kevlar body armour. Beneath the Kevlar, which he found a little stiff and scratchy, he wore a hot-pink silk shirt.

Some cops wore Kevlar but most didn't. As far as Willows knew, Popeye was the only ME who sported a bulletproof vest. He'd been wearing the miracle fabric ever since a stone-dead bank robber had sat up in the middle of being audited, spat out Popeye's thermometer and stuck the foot-long muzzle of a stainless steel Colt Python .357 Magnum up against his heart and pulled the trigger. The Python's hammer dropped on a spent cap and the perp was promptly and enthusiastically shot considerably deader by a frustrated traffic cop. Even so, it had been a *premium* negative experience. Popeye was guilty of a certain amount of self-inflicted kidney and lung damage, but aside from that, he liked to think of himself as the kind of guy who could learn from his mistakes.

So he bought the Kevlar vest and a pair of boxer shorts as well, and wore them faithfully.

Willows watched Popeye make his way down the wide concrete steps to the pool. Popeye's baggy black pants dragged at the heels of his ill-fitting, scuffed brown shoes. To confuse the issue of his sobriety or lack of it, the ME had developed a style of walking that owed a lot to Charlie Chaplin.

Popeye made it to the bottom of the steps. He put down his black bag in order to shake hands with Parker and Willows. His breath smelled strongly of tunafish. He peered down at Gerard Roth for a long moment. A mischievous grin took hold of his moustache and twisted it hard.

"Don't tell me what happened – lemme guess. The whales went after him and in his frantic attempt to get away he swam so hard his leg fell off."

"Not exactly," said Willows.

"We figure centrifugal force was the culprit," explained Parker.

Popeye lifted an eyebrow. The monocle fell into the open palm of his hand. He blew on the glass and rubbed it against his overcoat, screwed it back in place. He peered hard at Parker. "Mind if I smoke, darlin'?"

Parker smiled sweetly down at him. "Do whatever you like, Doc. Go ahead and burst into flames, if it makes you happy."

Popeye lit a cigarette. He'd started smoking the day the dead bank robber had pulled the trigger on him, and now he was hooked. But what the hell, at least he enjoyed it. Drinking was best, of course. But smoking came in a close second. Wasn't vice a euphemism for pleasure? He unzipped his black bag, found his digital thermometer and wedged the instrument under Dr Roth's armpit.

The largest of the whales, Bjossa, surfaced right at the edge of the pool. The huge mammal cleared its blowhole, spraying them with a fine, cool mist.

Popeye said, "He's pissed off. He wants his toy back."

The thermometer made a shrill beeping sound, a whine of complaint, perhaps. As if there was something about Roth's armpit that it didn't like, and it wanted out of there pronto.

Popeye carefully removed the instrument. He held it up in

65

front of his face. Cigarette smoke drifted into his functioning eye but he didn't seem to notice. He studied the thermometer for a very long time and then snorted loudly and said, "You want it in celsius or fahrenheit?"

"Celsius," said Parker in the same moment that Willows asked for the readout in fahrenheit.

"He's twenty degrees celsius," said Popeye. "About seventy-two fahrenheit. Either way you add it up he's deader than an ice cube."

"No chance of suspended animation?" asked Willows.

"He's dead, Jack." Popeye took another pull on his cigarette. "Look on the bright side – at least you don't have to try to resuscitate him." He flipped the cigarette butt in the pool, knelt and fished around in his bag until he found a small rectangle of cardboard with a reinforced hole punched in one end and a short length of twine attached.

"Got a pen?"

"Not until you give the last one back," Parker said firmly.

Willows offered his ballpoint. Popeye printed the date on the card in large block letters. "Got a case number?"

"Ninety-three dash three-niner."

"What's his name? And don't tell me Mark Spitz."

"Gerard Roth."

"Spell that for me, Jack."

Popeye wrote it all down, initialled the tag and used the twine to fasten it securely to the big toe on Roth's only foot. He zipped his bag. "For the record, in my professional opinion Mr Roth has earned a free one-way ticket to the morgue." As if playing a miniature piano, he lightly ran his fingers across the pale wrinkled toes of Roth's left foot. "These little piggies *all* going to market. Want me to call the ghoul patrol?"

"Got to wait for Ident, Popeye." The ME nodded dolefully, and turned away. Willows clutched his arm. "There is one small thing you can do for me, though."

"Name it, Jack."

"Gimme back my pen."

Willows went for coffee. When he returned the crime scene was being methodically searched by a team of crime scene technicians in baggy white one-piece coveralls, clear plastic shower caps and disposable slippers. Willows was reminded of the outfit he'd worn in the delivery room, when Annie and Sean were born.

66

One of the techs, a thin, dark man named Troy Hull, who for unknown reasons insisted on wearing a shower cap even though he'd been balder than a snake since his twentieth birthday, asked Willows if he had any explanation for the tracks in the snow and frozen slush.

Willows said, "Yeah, it looks to me as if he was pushed down to the pool on a dolly."

Hull's clawed fingers made parallel red streaks on his skull as he scratched himself through the shower cap. "That's exactly what I was thinking."

Willows said, "On the other hand, there could be any number of reasons somebody might wheel a dolly down to the pool. So let's not make any assumptions, okay?"

Hull said, "I already thought of that, too." His latex-gloved hands made tiny squeaking sounds as he briskly rubbed them together. "Cold, huh?"

Willows said, "Yeah? I hadn't noticed."

Hull's eyes lit up and then he realized he was being kidded. He turned and spat, then said, "You finished?"

Willows said, "Claire?"

Parker nodded.

A few minutes later they watched in silence as Dr Gerard Roth and his detached leg were zipped into a dark green plastic body-bag, lifted on to a gurney and wheeled away.

Willows said, "Now what? Sweeting?"

"He can wait. Let's see what goes on around here at night." A whale breached, and idly circled the pool in a counter-clockwise direction. Parker kicked a chunk of loose ice into the pool. She said, "I hope he isn't our only witness. How do you cross-examine seven tons of blubber?"

"Or find the right size handcuffs," said Willows, "if he decides to cop a plea?" He checked his watch. "You happen to notice if Troy took a water sample from the pool?"

Parker said, "While you were gone for coffee. I never did get my change back, by the way."

Willows said, "Double or nothing – will the water in Roth's lungs match the water from the whale pool – assuming he drowned?"

"You think he was already dead when he went for his swim?"

"Ask me after the autopsy."

*

67

The head of security, Robert Kelly, was an intense six-footer, the kind of man who had a hard time staying still. Kelly's black hair was combed straight back from his steeply sloped forehead. His eyes were large and dark. His wrists and the backs of his hands were shaded with coarse black hair. He ushered Willows and Parker into his cramped office and, his crowns flashing gold, volunteered that Gerard Roth's death was an untimely tragedy.

Willows hadn't heard that one before. Untimely tragedy. He said, "Tell us about the security, Bob. Got any?"

"Are you kidding? Know what a nightmare is? A dead whale floating in a pool full of diluted arsenic, or a live one cruising around in a bubble bath. Can't strip-search your customers, Detective. Especially if they're from out of town. So we do the best we can with what we've got. Which is plenty. Round-the-clock security in the form of rotating four-man shifts of the very best personnel that money and a top-notch dental plan can buy."

Parker said, "What else, Bob?"

"There's a guard dog has the run of the outside premises as soon as the staff have gone home. Plus more than a dozen video cameras positioned throughout the complex. Plus we got fifteen heat-and-motion detecting devices strategically placed outside the perimeter."

"What breed's the dog?"

"German shepherd." Kelly smiled. He had very thin lips and his teeth were a shade too large for his mouth. He said, "I got a pal, a cop on the dog squad. He told me get a shepherd, you can usually depend on them to bite and hold. Dobermanns, on the other hand, they're a little scarier but they got a weakness for subduing people and then munching away just for the hell of it. Because it's fun. Like I said, shepherds got more self control. So, even though dobermanns are a lot scarier looking, we don't employ them, because of the risk of being sued."

Parker said, "Okay, your staff restrict themselves to the interior of the complex. The dog stays outside, patrols the grounds. Is that how it works?"

"Waldo is restricted to outside work, yes."

Parker said, "Waldo?"

Kelly bristled a little. "Yeah, Waldo."

Parker said, "There are also janitorial staff in the building at night?"

"Yes, of course."

68

"And I suppose there must be times when members of the staff work late?"

"Certainly."

"And groups of schoolchildren stay overnight as well, don't they?"

"Inside," said Kelly. "By the beluga pool. Kids just love those belugas."

"So there's quite a lot of traffic, then."

"Not really, no. The kids are restricted to the beluga's viewing area – it's kind of an open room down on the lower level. The cleaning staff are out of here by midnight. There's always a guy in the control room, watching the monitors. The other two guys are supposed to endlessly patrol the building. We don't have a checkpoint system but they're in constant radio contact with the control room."

Kelly smiled at Parker. "I schedule a surprise visit every two or three weeks. I catch one of my men taking a snooze, I fire him on the spot." He smiled again. "But, I have to admit, staying awake around here can be a real problem. Fish are a wonderful soporific. You got a problem with insomnia – buy yourself a nice fish."

Willows said, "Is there a camera on the whale pool?"

"Three of them. Like I said, it's considered a high-risk area. You got to watch out for pranksters, assassins, you name it. I already checked last night's tape. There's nothing unusual on it that I could see, except for the fact that I couldn't see anything at all."

Willows didn't let his irritation show. He said, "Why is that, Bob?"

"Well, the pool area's kept pretty dim at night, so Finna and Bjossa can sleep. Also, it seems three of the lights were burnt out. You could've dumped a whole truckload of bodies in there last night and it wouldn't have showed up on the tape."

Parker said, "Bob, are you sure the lights were burnt out – not tampered with?"

"Burnt out. Just like a couple of maintenance men I could mention, who've recently had a yard-wide strip tore off them."

Parker said, "Wait a minute. Something happened last night, whether it was taped or not. Where was the dog?"

Kelly nervously ran his fingers through his hair. Parker noticed

69

that his nails were bitten to the quick, and that a thin half-circle of blood followed the line of his thumbnail. He said, "Waldo is missing and has not yet been accounted for. It's remotely possible that he's running loose somewhere in the park. We just don't know. We've looked everywhere, can't spot him."

"Is he dangerous?" said Willows.

"I've already suggested to your colleagues that he be shot on sight."

Kelly noticed his thumb. He sucked a little blood from the wound. Parker didn't blame him – he looked as if he could use the nourishment.

Willows said, "Tell us about Dr Roth. Did you know him very well?"

"He was a little eccentric. Or you could say weird."

"Could you be a little more specific."

"He liked to swim in the nude." Kelly turned to Parker. "Have you seen the big tank, the one with the black-tailed sharks?"

"No, not yet."

"Dr Roth's 'old swimmin' hole'. He liked to take his lady friends there, goof around."

"With the sharks," said Willows, wanting to make sure he had it right.

"Yeah, in the nude, with the sharks."

"With his girlfriends?"

"Right, right."

"How often did this occur?"

"Sometimes he'd swim in the pool every night for a month. Or he might not get his feet wet for six months or more. It depended how things were going, know what I mean?"

"Not really," said Parker.

Kelly hesitated. "Dr Roth was married, but I understand he and his wife split up a long time ago. And he took advantage of the situation, believe me. Whenever he had a new girlfriend he conned her into going for a swim in the tank. Nude. It was like a rite of passage."

"Was he aware that you knew what was going on?" said Willows.

"Yeah, sure. If he had a heavy date lined up, he always warned me well in advance that he was conducting an important experiment and told me to keep my boys clear of the area. He'd tape a piece of paper over the lens of the security camera, too. Not that he didn't trust me."

70

Parker said, "If Roth took all those precautions, how did you originally find out what was going on?"

"I peeked." Kelly sucked a little more blood from his thumb. "You have to understand that my primary responsibility is to the aquarium's board of directors. Once I'd satisfied myself that Dr Roth wasn't up to anything dangerous, I left him completely alone."

Parker said, "You don't consider the shark tank dangerous?"

"They're bottom feeders. They won't bother you, unless you stop swimming and walk around on the bottom of the tank."

"Was Dr Roth in the shark tank last night?"

"Must've been, because the security camera in that area wasn't working from about nine-thirty to midnight, due to an obstruction in front of the lens."

"Who did he have with him?"

Kelly screwed up his face as he resumed nibbling at his thumb. "I'm afraid I can't say."

Willows said, "You don't have any choice, Bob."

"No, what I mean is, I don't know who he was with, or if he was with anyone at all. Maybe I forgot to mention it, but he often swam alone."

"Nude?"

"Yeah, nude. But come to think of it, if he was by himself he didn't care if we patrolled the area or if we had him on video. So he must've had company last night."

Willows said, "Dr Roth was an exhibitionist?"

"You betcha."

"What happened to the tapes?"

"Of him swimming alone with the sharks?"

Willows nodded.

"They were recycled. Listen, every member of my staff is a fully functioning heterosexual. I'm not saying they're saints. I examine the previous night's tapes each and every morning. If a tape was missing, heads would roll."

"What about copies?"

"Well, sure. I guess it could happen."

Parker said, "So it's possible someone had film of Roth in the pool, and tried to blackmail him?"

"It would've been a hard way to make a dollar. I mean, Dr Roth was plenty circumspect when it came to his girlfriends, but

71

when it came to flaunting his own slice of cheesecake he was a pretty uninhibited guy."

Parker said, "How did he get along with the rest of the staff?"

"Everybody more or less loathed him."

"You're sure about that?"

"Ask around."

"He was unpopular?"

"Believe me, it was a lot worse than that. I don't like to speak ill of the dead, but when it came to women, Gerard was a totally selfish creep. You saw what he was wearing when we fished him out of the pool. Swim fins and a mask. But no wedding ring, right?"

"But you said he was separated."

"But still married. To Iris, for something like a quarter of a century. Last year was their twenty-fifth anniversary. Sometime in the spring. There was a big bouquet of roses in his office, and a heart made out of little red flowers, and more flowers arranged into the number of years they'd been together. I assumed Roth had bought it to take home to Iris, but he laughed and told me it was the other way around. She'd sent it to his office. Pissed him off, too. He liked her to keep a low profile. Give himself room to move."

Kelly slid open the top drawer of his desk and withdrew a single sheet of paper. "We got a camera on the parking lot in front of the building. It's got a wide-angle lens, scans the area. This is a list of the plate numbers of cars that were in the lot last night, and these figures in the right-hand column tell you when the car arrived and departed, within a five-minute span."

He handed the list to Willows, who saw that a dozen cars had parked in the lot during the course of the evening, from nine at night through five in the morning. It was a surprisingly large number, given the weather.

Kelly said, "I can give you a copy of the tape, if you want."

Parker said, "I have to admit it, Bob. You've got a pretty impressive system. How much did it cost?"

Kelly frowned. "The aquarium's self-supporting. I don't know if you were aware of that. We pay our own way, the operation doesn't cost the taxpayer a dime."

And consequently the taxpayers didn't have an awful lot of say in how the operation was run, either. The aquarium was a bad joke, an anachronism. Parker had viewed killer whales in the open ocean. She'd seen the way they could move, given room. Bjossa's yard-long dorsal fin was bent over so that it lay almost flat across his body. The reason for this was unknown. One theory was that it was caused by the backwash of water from the pool pushed against the fin as the whale circled endlessly in a counter-clockwise direction. Well, maybe so. Or perhaps the bent fin indicated the state of Bjossa's mental health.

Either way, the whale had been disfigured by its claustrophobic environment.

Kelly was watching Parker, smiling. "You're no friend of the aquarium, are you, Detective?"

Parker said, "Did anyone here dislike Roth enough to kill him?"

Kelly pursed his lips, shook his head. "Not to my knowledge. The guy was a real dork, but I wouldn't say he deserved to die. I mean, he manipulated women but as far as I know he never forced anyone to do anything she didn't think she wanted to – even if she eventually realized she was wrong. If you follow me."

"Roth was badly battered," Willows said. "Is it possible the whales would attack him, if he entered the pool?"

"If you want an expert's opinion, you're talking to the wrong guy. Tony's the resident authority. But yeah, they'd rip him apart, if they were in the mood. Don't get me wrong. I'm not saying they'd go after him because they were pissed off. They might figure he was some kind of new beachball – a toy."

Willows turned to Parker. "We finished here?"

She nodded.

Kelly said, "Want me to give Tony a call?" He leaned forward, reached for his phone.

Parker said, "That's okay – he's expecting us."

The phone on Kelly's desk warbled. He hesitated, then turned and snatched up the receiver, identified himself. Parker saw his knuckles whiten as he clutched the receiver. He wiped a tear from his eye, visibly fought to bring himself under control. In a flat, calm voice that seemed to have been deliberately stripped of all emotion he said, "Okay, Travis. Thanks. Yeah, a hell of a way to die."

Kelly hung up in slow motion. He turned towards Parker. His plum-colored face contorted in a horrible twisted smile.

Parker said, "Maybe you better sit down, Bob."

Kelly collapsed into his swivel chair. He said, "Guess what – they found Waldo."

And burst into tears.

8

Chris slept fitfully. He dreamed in vivid color of the near-unbelievable events of the previous evening, his mind following the original script but hoping, as he tossed and turned, for a happier ending. A wind had sprung up, come at them from the west, passing over a stand of tall fir trees and the children's zoo and miniature railway, dropping down the grassy slope and hitting the zoo. Somewhere high above them a peacock blared its discomfort. Without warning, the cloud cover began to break up. In minutes, the snow stopped falling and the air cleared and grew even colder. Here and there a star made a brief appearance and abruptly vanished.

After about a quarter of an hour of this, it began to snow again.

Robyn and Chris stayed right where they were, held each other for warmth and companionship as they huddled on the mock-sandstone wall beneath the scant shelter of a dwarf cedar's low spreading branches. Chris couldn't stop talking about what they'd seen – or what he believed they'd seen.

Robyn knew what she believed. She believed there was something mixed up in the dope, some weird chemical, fertilizer or whatever, that had twisted their minds and made them hallucinate.

Chris said, "That doesn't make sense to me, Robyn. People don't hallucinate in tandem. Why would we both share the same nightmare? – it doesn't make sense."

Robyn had an answer for that one. "Because we're so close to each other. You're always telling me how close we are, and how we think so much alike. Remember last week when I asked if you wanted to go see a movie at the exact instant you asked me if *I* wanted to see a movie?"

Chris nodded. It'd been two weeks ago, or maybe it was three. But it had happened. Coincidence. Mainly he talked about stuff like that – how much alike they were – when they were in bed.

Robyn was more or less sitting in his lap. He kissed the back of her neck and she told him to cut it out. He kissed her again. She elbowed him in the ribs, hard enough to sting despite his bulky leather jacket.

She said, "You've got a pretty strange attitude, for somebody who thinks he saw some poor guy get pushed into a pool, and drown."

"Death makes people sexually aroused. Sudden death arouses them instantly."

"How would you know?"

Chris laughed, and gave her a hug. But he had to admit she was right about his mood. He wasn't exactly stricken with grief. So, why was that? He stared down at the smooth, slick black surface of the pool. He'd heard the thump of the dolly's hard rubber wheels and crackle of ice, and glanced up. Through the grey haze of marijuana smoke, the fog-like mist rising from the pool and the curtain of falling snow, he'd seen something slide off the dolly and on to the snow and then into the water.

And behind the dolly a naked figure, turning away.

He pictured the scene in his mind. Long blonde hair. Hips. Long pale legs with not much between them.

A woman. Definitely a woman.

She'd turned away from him and, in the space of two or three steps, vanished. His attention had been drawn back to the water. He'd kept waiting for the body to surface. Stared stupidly at the gleaming expanse of black water while his imagination ran amok, dipping him in a succession of macabre scenarios.

He saw a splayed hand rise out of the water. He saw a sudden panicky splashing followed by a shrill scream and super-quick vanishing act. He saw the excruciatingly slow rising of the corpse's upper body from the depths, saw the head loll face-down just beneath the surface. He saw the body roll over, black water stream from gaping eye sockets.

But none of that had happened. He'd waited for a long time, for nothing. Then, finally, a whale surfaced without a fuss on the far side of the pool. The whale cruised around for the space of a minute or less, then submerged.

Chris squinted across the pool. He thought he saw two faint parallel tracks in the snow where the dolly had been. But he wasn't sure. With each moment that passed, the falling snow obscured the evidence.

The whale surfaced again, vented. It was business as usual, as if the brittle crunch of ice and the naked body sliding into the pool were nothing more substantial than a snowflake.

Chris pictured himself making a statement to the cops. *I saw a naked woman push a dolly down the amphitheatre stairs to the pool. There was a naked man on the dolly. The body was tilted into the pool and vanished. What was I doing at the whale pool? And who was I with? Uh . . .*

Suddenly he wasn't at all sure *what* he'd seen, or even if he'd seen anything at all. He was just about to lean forward and whisper the good news into Robyn's ear when, less than twenty feet away, the surface of the pool exploded in a white froth and the massive black head of a killer whale rose up before him, a naked corpse clamped firmly in its jaws.

Robyn screamed.

Writhing and twisting, the mammoth creature threw itself high into the air and then crashed down upon them. Chris tried to jump clear.

He was tangled in the sheets, trapped. The back of his skull hit the edge of a cinderblock holding up the bookshelf next to the bed. Groaning, he rolled over and found himself staring into Robyn's wide, terrified eyes.

Very lightly, she touched his shoulder. "Are you okay?"

Tentatively, he probed his head with the tips of his fingers. A bump, but no blood. He'd live. He smiled at Robyn. "How're you doing?"

"Okay."

"Yeah? Then why were you screaming?"

She frowned, gave him a puzzled look. Finally said, "That wasn't me – it was you."

Chris punched the pillow into shape, lay back and thought about it for a minute, realized she was right. His stomach did a slow roll.

He said, "What time is it?"

Robyn took his hand, rotated his wrist. "Quarter past seven."

The alarm was set for half-past. Chris rolled out of bed. He went over to the bedroom window, cracked the blinds and looked out. It was barely snowing but there was snow everywhere except for twin black ruts down the middle of the street. Despite the window's double-glazing, he could hear the dull throb of traffic. The sky was an ugly shade of grey, like the skin of a sick old man.

77

So, in short, everything seemed normal. He rubbed his jaw and his beard made a sandpaper sound that only he could hear. When he released the blind it snapped as if trying to bite him. He turned and walked out of the room.

Robyn said, "Where you going?"

"The bathroom."

"Stay out of the shower, okay?"

"Got to have that shower, Robyn. A clean mind is a healthy mind."

Robyn sat up in bed. Chris, standing at the bedroom door, made his eyes open wide and leered at her breasts. She hadn't even had her first cup of coffee, but just look at her – so perky.

Robyn said, "Wipe your chin. You're drooling."

Chris smiled. Robyn was so casually immodest, so effortlessly carnal. It drove him crazy day and night, and he always enjoyed the ride.

She said, "Go on, get out of here. If you're going to take a shower, get it over with. I don't want to be late for work. Again." She smiled sweetly. "*Somebody* has to pay the rent."

Chris turned so his back was to her. He reached down and patted himself gently on the rump. Robyn sat there in the middle of the big, unruly bed, watching him. He said, "Next time you want something, kiss me right here before you start begging for it, okay?"

Robyn tossed a pillow at him. It hit the bedroom wall with a dull thud that reminded Chris of the sound the dolly's wheels had made. His smile faded.

Robyn said, "What?"

Chris shrugged. "Nothing, toots. Just another lewd thought, that's all."

He showered, dressed in a pair of faded black jeans and a pale blue denim shirt, battered black Nikes. He snatched his leather jacket from the back of a kitchen chair as he headed for the door. Robyn was still in the shower. Usually she sang a little, but not today.

Chris took the elevator down to ground level, walked to the 24-hour convenience store at the end of the block and bought the city's two dailies from a fat girl in a red and white checkerboard smock and complexion to match.

Back at the apartment, he helped himself to a fresh cup of

coffee, sat down at the table with the papers. The toilet flushed and then Robyn came out of the bathroom and sat down opposite him, smoothing her skirt so it wouldn't wrinkle. Chris stared at her. He had been gone less than ten minutes but in the interval Robyn had dressed and put on her makeup, turned herself into a stranger – a responsible young woman with a job, a downtowner.

He pushed away from the table and fetched her a cup of coffee. Black, no sugar. Robyn noticed the papers, reached for the *Sun*. Chris favored the splashy tabloid style of the *Province*. He browsed through the sports section, stood up and moseyed over to the kitchen counter, poured himself some more coffee. He peeked over Robyn's shoulder.

As usual, she was reading the comics.

He said, "I thought you were worried about being late?"

"Shows what you know. Not much. You read 'Calvin & Hobbes'?"

"Do I look like I've got X-ray vision?"

"Yeah. As a matter of fact you do."

Chris stared hard at the table. He said, "You are wearing black silk panties . . ."

Robyn giggled. She batted her eyes. The paper made a brittle sound a little bit like ice crunching underfoot as Robyn turned the pages around so Chris could gasp at the crazy shenanigans of her favorite cartoon characters. He began to read. Robyn peered at his watch. "Holy shit, I'm gonna be late!" She dropped the paper and grabbed her coat and mimed blowing him a kiss as she rushed out of the apartment.

Chris sat there, listening hard. After a moment he heard the drone of the elevator. He walked quickly over to the open door, stepped out into the hallway and leaned against the wall. Robyn was waiting at the turn in the hall, about thirty feet away. She turned and looked at him, started a slow smile as he unbuttoned his shirt all the way down to his belt. The elevator arrived and the doors slid open. It was crowded in there. Where was everybody going? Shopping, she supposed.

Not quite shouting, Chris said, "Thanks, honey. I had a wonderful time!"

Robyn stuck her tongue out at him. She vanished into the elevator.

Chris yelled, "I'm gonna recommend you to *all* my friends!"

Robyn's arm shot out, her hand balled into a tiny fist, middle finger extended. She was working on a Saturday because Chris wasn't bringing in any money, and they both knew it. That's why he was giving her a hard time. Guilt.

Chris went back into the apartment. He shut the door and – atypically – shot the deadbolt.

On working days, all Robyn ever had for breakfast was a cup of black coffee; a jolt of caffeine on an empty stomach to get her cranked. It was a weight thing – she hit the scales every morning and every night, and her weight never varied by more than half a pound.

Chris was only twenty-three. He wouldn't need to worry about his figure until his metabolism slowed down, and that unhappy event was at least ten years down the road. But he'd always made a point of not eating either, until Robyn had left the apartment. Chris kicked in what he had, but she was paying most of the freight and they both knew it. He owed her a lot, and paid his debts any way he could.

He and Robyn had been a love unit for close to a year. They'd met in early December, at an animated film festival. Bumped into each other in the lobby and found out right away they had mutual friends. Chris was well known in local showbiz circles, primarily for his work in a soap commercial that had received saturation coverage nationally. Robyn watched too much television. She'd seen him lovingly sud his butt maybe a thousand times. So she was familiar with his body, knew right away that he had a pretty decent build. Plus he had a great smile and a totally new-age voice, masculine but sensitive.

What she'd told him when she agreed to let him move in with her, about a month later, was that she couldn't do without the way he looked at her after they made love, with such tenderness and care.

And the amazing thing was that it was the way he genuinely felt about her. He did care about her, deeply. But there was a wildness about him that he believed she was strongly attracted to as well, even if she wouldn't admit it; a spontaneous craziness that she wasn't capable of but admired in others.

They were as different, if you stopped to think about it for a minute, as the tiger and the kid in "Calvin & Hobbes". And got along together just as well, too.

Chris poured himself a bowlful of Kellogg's Cinnamon Mini

Buns. He doused the cereal with milk, thumped down at the table, turned the *Province* towards him and began to eat. The paper was noted for its crime coverage. On the third page, Chris found a piece on a loosely knit gang of homeless people who roamed Stanley Park at night, plundering and cooking the wildlife and generally making merry as best they could. During the previous evening the gang had apparently been attacked by a vicious German shepherd. They'd managed to overpower the beast by force of sheer numbers, debated the merits of eating it versus hanging it by the neck until dead from the welcoming arms of a tarnished bronze statue of Robbie Burns located about a quarter mile from the zoo area.

Chris studied the small photograph of Lassie twisting in the wind. He wondered briefly if there could be a tie-in with the drowning in the whale pool.

His day lay before him. He had an audition at a downtown studio at ten o'clock, for a bit part in a pilot for a TV series about a day care worker. Great concept. He was supposed to play a single parent picking up his kid for a dentist's appointment. Now there was a role he could sink his teeth into. The audition would take about an hour, somewhere in there. Including about fifty-eight minutes of wait time. Afterwards, he'd take an aerobics class and then find a Starbucks, order a *latte* and slouch on to a stool by the window. Study the way the world moved, as it drifted past.

Chris went into the bathroom. He removed the water tank's heavy ceramic lid, balanced it on the toilet seat and unscrewed the hollow white plastic ball floating upon the surface of the water tank. The ball was attached by a brass rod to a gizmo that made the water shut off at a prearranged level, instead of overflowing on to the floor. Good idea. Also a great place to stash a half-ounce of finely chopped marijuana – all leaf, no stems or seeds.

He shook enough weed into the palm of his hand to make two fat joints, then put the toilet back together. In the kitchen, he rolled the joints and slipped them into a plastic sandwich bag, which he put in one of the many inside pockets of his black leather jacket.

Dope? Check. Wallet? Check. Keys? Check. Buck knife with fake bone grips and six-inch blade sharp as a razor? Chris yanked open the door where he kept the can-opener and potato-masher and cookie cutters and all that stuff, rooted around until he found the knife and slipped it into one of his pockets.

Dope, wallet, keys and knife? Check. He was armed and dangerous, ready to roll.

9

As Robert Kelly escorted Willows and Parker to Tony Sweeting's office, the bereaved head of the aquarium's complex and many-layered security system whined and moaned incessantly about the fate of his beloved German shepherd. If Travis, the *Province* reporter who'd phoned Kelly could be believed, Waldo had been strung up from the arm of the statue of that drunken Scottish poet across from the yacht club. Much worse, Waldo's body had been spray-painted in alternating bands of red and white.

"What's the point?" wailed the anguished chief of security. "I mean, I don't get it. Am I missing a barber's pole joke? It was a barbarous act, is that it? My God! Why would anyone paint Waldo in red and white stripes?"

"Beats me," said Willows, feigning interest in a potted plant, turning his head away so Kelly couldn't see him smiling. There was nothing funny about a hanged dog. Hanged dogs weren't funny. He'd have to hold on to that thought. Make it the thought of the day.

"Maybe red and white was all they had," said Parker.

Willows chuckled. Kelly shot him a hard look. They passed a reception area done in beige carpeting and off-white paint and pale oak veneer. Willows noticed that the woman behind the desk only had eyes for Bob.

They walked down a short hallway to another expanse of bleached veneer. Kelly put his knuckles to work, and then pushed open the door and stepped aside.

Anthony Sweeting had removed his suit jacket but hadn't gone so far as to loosen his fish-shaped tie. He was standing at a large picture window looking philosophically out at an access road blocked with chunks of fragmented concrete and a couple of tons of twisted iron reinforcing rod and rusty sheet steel.

Willows thanked Kelly for his help, told him he'd be talking to

83

him again and firmly shut the door in his inquisitive, grieving face.

The aquarium director's desk was made of a lustrous black synthetic material in the shape of a large fish, possibly a flounder. Sweeting welcomed them, shook hands with professional enthusiasm. He sighed heavily enough to weigh them all down, and then crossed to the fishdesk and dropped into an overstuffed black leather chair.

Sweeting leaned forward. Two huge albino spiders – reflections of the director's hands – floated up from the bowels of the desk. Sweeting clasped his hands together. The spiders jumped.

Sweeting had not worn the morning well. All the starch had gone out of his suit. His skin was the colour of jaundiced marshmallow. His ears seemed to droop and his whisky-coloured eyes were rimmed with red. He said, "You heard about the damn dog?"

Parker nodded.

"Waldo. What kind of name is that for a guard dog? I'm surprised it didn't commit suicide."

The office walls were covered with photographs of large sea creatures devouring smaller sea creatures. The colors were carnival bright. Willows looked into the placid eyes of a moray eel chomping thoughtfully on a small golden fish. He experienced a queasy sensation in the pit of his stomach, and looked away.

Parker said, "There were two parallel ruts in the snow, that ran down the middle of the amphitheatre stairs to the edge of the whale pool. Do you know what might have caused those ruts, Mr Sweeting?"

"I didn't notice them."

"They were about an inch wide and twenty inches apart."

Sweeting massaged his forehead with the tips of his fingers, so vigorously that it almost seemed he might be trying to rub himself out of existence.

Willows said, "Probably Dr Roth simply drowned. We won't know until we have the autopsy results. But in the meantime, there are a number of questions that have to be answered."

Sweeting stood up. His suit jacket was draped over the back of the leather chair. He put the jacket on and fastened the middle button, shot his cuffs and sat back down again.

He said, "Gerard wasn't simply a colleague; he was also a friend."

Parker said, "We weren't aware of that. This must be very difficult for you."

Sweeting nodded.

Parker said, "If it's any consolation, rest assured that we sympathize with your loss."

"He wasn't an easy man to get to know. If you make enquiries, you'll find he wasn't terribly popular. This may have been due to his academic accomplishments, which were remarkably impressive and which he liked to discuss at length. He had a rather large ego." Sweeting rubbed his chin. "When I say he was a friend, what I mean is that I was an admirer of Gerard's dedication, his drive. I sure as hell wouldn't want to play eighteen holes with him. Not that he'd waste his time on such a frivolous pursuit. He was an absolute genius, both in the lab and the field, and that's extremely rare. But Mother Nature has a way of balancing the scales, don't you agree?"

Willows nodded. His roving eye focused on a picture of a shark tearing a manhole-sized chunk out of another shark.

Sweeting said, "Makos. Bankers evolved one rung up the ladder. Nasty bastards."

"Would you mind explaining what you mean about nature balancing the scales?" said Parker.

"Professionally, Gerard was brilliant. But his interpersonal skills were virtually nonexistent. His personal life was an absolute shambles, a monument to incompetence."

"He was married, wasn't he?"

"To Iris. Lovely woman. He simply didn't know how to behave – what was correct. When he spoke to you he scrutinized you with the intensity and complete lack of inhibition of a small child. It was very unsettling. He'd stand too close to you, that sort of thing. If you had something he wanted, his strategy was invariably to tell you what it was and wait for you to hand it over."

"Are we speaking of a particular object or event?" Parker asked.

"Not really. I'm attempting to give you a general impression of the man, that's all."

Parker said, "We've been told Dr Roth was . . ." She hesitated. "Extremely fond of women."

"Who told you that?"

Parker smiled. "Was it true?"

"No, certainly not. Well, I'd better qualify that. He may have been emotionally involved with a member of the staff. But I have no reason to think it was anything but a platonic relationship. In fact I was under the impression it was more of a father-daughter situation."

"What's the young lady's name?" asked Parker.

"Just give me a moment to be absolutely clear about this – the rumours I've heard are, as far as I am aware, unsubstantiated."

Willows said, "What was her name again?"

"Susan Carter."

"Married?"

"I believe she is unattached."

Parker said, "Dr Roth's wife's name is Iris?"

"Yes, that's correct. I've only met her once or twice, and not recently. But my recollection is that she was a very attractive woman. Have you spoken to her?"

"Not yet, no."

"Someone should inform her of Gerard's death. Did you want me to do it?"

"That isn't necessary," said Parker. "Does Iris live in the city?"

"West Vancouver. Quite far out. Do you know Eagle Island?"

Parker shook her head, no.

Sweeting said, "Would you like to see Gerard's office?"

Parker glanced at Willows. He was looking at the picture of the sharks. She said, "Why don't we have a little chat with Miss Carter?"

Sweetings nodded reluctantly. "I'll show you the way."

It was immediately obvious that Susan Carter wasn't in her office. The door was wide open and the cluttered, tiny room offered no place to hide.

Sweeting, looking a little flustered, checked his watch. "It's a little early for lunch. I could check with Marian, the receptionist . . ."

Willows said, "We'll wait for her. She'll probably be back in a few minutes."

Sweeting nodded uncertainly, glanced around as if to itemize the office's valuables and then turned and strode quickly down the corridor.

Parker pointed at the untidy heap of used Kleenex in the wicker wastebasket next to the desk.

Willows said, "It looks as if there might have been some basis for the rumors."

Parker moved a little closer to the desk and took a long look at the colorful bar graph on the Mac's screen.

"What is it?"

"An analysis of the sexual performances of fifty of the aquarium's male staff." Parker smiled. "Now, what made me *say* that?"

Two small, framed photographs hung on the wall to the left of the desk. The first was of a young blonde girl of twelve or thirteen. Susan, no doubt. She was lying beneath a tree reading a book. A small black dog lay curled up in her lap. The second photograph had been taken at a beach. Two divers in shiny black wetsuits, flippers, tanks and face masks stood awkwardly at the water's edge. A tendril of blonde hair trailed from beneath the cap of the smaller diver's wetsuit.

Susan Carter and Gerard Roth?

A wraith moved across the window. Parker turned. A bewildered young blonde woman stood in the doorway, her hands in the pockets of an expensive chocolate-colored full-length suede coat.

"Susan Carter?"

The woman nodded. She slipped gracefully out of the coat. Beneath the coat she wore a cream silk blouse and a pleated skirt in grey wool with a windowpane pattern in burgundy. She stood about five foot two in her sensible black shoes. Parker doubted she weighed much more than a hundred pounds. Her skin was very pale. Her full red lips gave her small mouth a look of compression, almost disapproval. Her blue eyes were set a little too far apart.

Susan's most striking feature was her long blonde hair. Parker estimated she was in her early twenties. The skin around her eyes was dark and puffy, and there was a tinge of red to her nose. She wasn't wearing any makeup, but perhaps she'd cried it all away. She was pretty enough, but bland. Somehow, there wasn't much to Susan Carter. Parker tried to think of the word that best described her. Insubstantial.

Parker introduced herself, and Willows. She pulled the chair away from the desk and told Susan to go ahead and sit down, relax.

Susan said, "This is about Dr Roth, isn't it? He was such a sweet, sweet guy."

Parker had to repress a smile.

"We were told that you and Dr Roth were very close."

87

"Really?" She smiled at Willows. "If we're going to get into my personal life, would you mind shutting the door?"

Perhaps there was a little more to Susan than showed on the surface. Willows did as he'd been told.

Susan said, "Dr Sweeting suggested Dr Roth and I were involved in some way?"

Parker shook her head. "No, not at all. He did say he'd heard rumors about the two of you. But he insisted he didn't think they were credible."

Susan said, "I don't know what the hell it is about this place. All those little fish swimming around in all those tanks, maybe. Like *sperm*, turning everybody on."

Parker said, "So you're saying the atmosphere here results in a lot of tongue-wagging . . ."

Susan smiled. "Nope. What I'm saying is, Gerard was doing it to me every chance he got, and I loved every minute of it."

And then she burst into tears, and collapsed across her desk. An elbow hit the Mac's keyboard. The computer bleated like a deeply offended sheep.

Parker handed Susan a Kleenex from the family-size box on her desk.

Willows took a moment to study the larger of the two wet-suited figures in the photograph. Maybe it was Roth and maybe it wasn't.

Parker offered Susan some more Kleenex. The sobbing segued into intermittent snuffling.

Willows said, "Tell us about him. What kind of guy was he?"

Susan's head came up. She pushed back her hair and tossed a balled-up Kleenex at the wastebasket, missed by a foot.

"He was wonderful. So caring. Attentive and sexy. He knew all the best restaurants and how to order wines and how to wear clothes. He was smart and he was witty and he had a really nice apartment in False Creek. He loved to cook, too, and he was good at it. Italian food was his specialty. He'd spent a couple of years in Italy when he was younger, and spoke the language fluently."

Willows said, "That's you in the picture, on the left?"

Susan nodded. She dabbed at her bright blue eyes, loudly blew her cute little nose.

The beach dropped steeply down to the water, and it looked as if the guy standing beside Susan was a little higher up the slope, which would give him an artificial height advantage. If

Susan was five foot two, the guy standing beside her had to be well under six feet.

Roth was six-two, easy, even without his flippers.

Willows tapped the picture with the tip of his pen, loudly enough to get everybody's attention. "Who's the diver standing next to you?"

Susan blew her nose again, missed the wastebasket again. "That was taken up in the Queen Charlottes, the summer before last. God, but the water's cold up there! I think his name was Walt. He was a local, and he was a really good diver."

"Was Dr Roth present on that trip?"

She nodded. "But at the time, we didn't know each other. Hadn't met. His wife might've been with him, I'm not sure."

"You knew he was married?"

"Yes, of course. We talked about it all the time." Susan misinterpreted the look on Parker's face. "I don't know if you're aware of this, but they'd been separated for more than a year."

"Yes, Mr Kelly mentioned that."

"Gerard spent so much time in the field that eventually he and Iris lost touch with one another."

Parker said, "I can see how that might happen."

"He was never home. Even when he was in town, he worked incredibly long hours. Iris was very lonely. She resented Gerard's work habits but never said anything. Then she found out somehow that he was having an affair. When she confronted him he admitted he'd had a whole lot of affairs, and that was that. She kicked him out and hired a lawyer. About six months later he invited me out. To the opera. He has season tickets. We've been inseparable ever since."

Or at least until recently, thought Parker. It was odd, the way Susan kept referring to Roth in the present tense, and didn't think to correct herself.

Willows said, "Did Dr Roth ever talk about the women he'd had affairs with before he met you?"

"I questioned him about his past in detail, after we'd started sleeping together. I wanted to know what kind of woman he was attracted to, and I was looking for a pattern, trying to see how I fit into the scheme of things. And also, I admit it, I was desperately curious to find out what turned his crank. Well, Gerard loved to talk about himself. And I was careful not to appear judgmental. He'd gone out with just about anything in a skirt, before he started

89

up with me. Married or single or anywhere in between – it didn't make the slightest bit of difference."

"But you felt he changed, when you started going out together?"

"Definitely. We were very serious about each other, right from the start. Gerard was remarkably intelligent and he was brutally honest with himself. Believe me, he was quick to see the error of his ways."

Parker waited a moment and then said, "Do you have any idea what Dr Roth was up to, last night?"

"You mean the fact that he was naked?"

Parker nodded.

"He liked to swim inside, in the big tank with the black-tailed sharks."

"Did he ever swim with the whales?"

"No, never. It was too dangerous."

"If he did, would you know about it?"

"There were no secrets between us. That's part of the reason the relationship worked so well."

Parker said, "Do you have any idea why else he might go outside on such a chilly night?"

"No, I'm afraid I don't. I've thought about it and thought about it, but I just don't know."

"Did any of his research involve killer whales?"

"No, absolutely not."

"How did he feel about the aquarium's policy of capturing and displaying whales?"

"The aquarium doesn't capture whales. Bjossa and Finna aren't local – they're Icelandic."

Willows saw the logic of the aquarium's policy – if the whales weren't local it made it that much harder for animal rights groups to fight their capture. But that wasn't the point, and he said so. "Regardless of where the whales originated, how did Dr Roth feel about their capture and display?"

"He strongly disapproved. I mean, he didn't make a fuss about it – the aquarium was instrumental in funding a great deal of his research. But everyone, even Tony, knew how he felt."

"Did you ever go for a midnight swim with Dr Roth?"

"Almost every week, usually on Thursday nights. We swam with the belugas, too, a couple of times. But it's kind of boring, so we gave it up."

Parker said, "Why is it boring?"

"Because you can't have sex in the pool. They take too much of an interest. They want to get involved, if you know what I mean."

"Were you at the aquarium last night?"

"No, I left at five o'clock and went straight home."

"Then what?"

"I showered, made dinner. Watched television and went to bed."

"You weren't expecting a visit from Dr Roth?"

"No, I wasn't."

"What did you have for dinner?"

"Leftover tuna salad and a glass of dry white wine. Okay, I confess. Two glasses of wine."

"What was on television?"

"A movie. A really old one called *The Birds.*" She smiled at Parker. "Have you seen it?"

"Years ago."

"It starred . . ." Susan frowned, bit her lower lip in frustration, then turned and stared at Willows. "Am I a *suspect*, Detective?"

"No, of course not." He smiled. "How could you be? As far as we're aware, no crime has been committed."

Parker asked Susan Carter a few more questions about the killer whales, and then Willows interrupted to say he was pretty sure it was Ray Milland who'd had the male lead in the Hitchcock film. Parker said no, it'd been Darren McGavin. They stared down at Susan sitting there at her desk in her tiny office, waiting patiently for her to tell them who was right and who was wrong.

God, she'd damn near memorized every line of the film; but all those birds swirling around in her brain had her completely confused.

Which was not a good thing, because the detectives seemed so suspicious.

She told herself to calm down. They were trained to be inquisitive. It was bred into them. They simply couldn't help themselves.

Willows said, "We may want to talk with you again, Miss Carter."

"Anytime."

Parker said, "You do have our sympathies. We want you to know that."

"Thank you."

Willows said, "If you think of anything . . ."

91

She nodded, turned to the computer and worked the keyboard for a few moments, then turned the machine off. By now the detectives would be almost to the reception area. She called out.

A moment later, Willows appeared in the open door.

She smiled at him, putting a little extra into it, and said, "I just thought of something."

He cocked an eyebrow.

She said, "You're right – it was Ray Milland."

10

The single parent with the dentist's appointment was, according to the script director's scribbled notes, an automobile mechanic. Speaking with his agent on the phone, Chris said, "Oh yeah? Cool. What kind of cars does he work on?"

Actors. Sherry bit down hard on the plastic tip of her cigarillo, inhaled deeply. "What kind of cars would you prefer to work on, Chris? I mean, if you really were a mechanic, instead of a chronically unemployed actor."

"Jaguars?"

"That sounds just fine."

"Or maybe, on second thought, that's too elitist. BMWs? How about a BMW – everybody's got one of them suckers."

"BMWs would be perfect."

Chris said, "What's the director's name again?"

"Rusty Arnold."

"Yeah, right. I could pop the hood of the Subaru, poke around in there. Get a little grease under my nails . . ."

Ten per cent was ten per cent. Sherry told herself to hold on to that thought. She forced a laugh. "Whatever works, Chris."

Chris said, "How old's my little boy?"

"Young. Very young."

"He's my only son?"

"Daughter."

"Uh, okay. I can live with that, I guess. What's her name – or has she got one?"

"Read the script, Chris."

"If I get the part, can I keep her?"

"Only if you can afford her."

Chris said, "Maybe I should work for Mercedes Benz. I can do a great German accent . . ."

Very calmly, Sherry said, "Oops!"

Predictably, Chris kept on about the accent. Sherry had to cut in. She said, "I lit a cigarillo a minute ago, tossed the match in the wastebasket and now I got a three-alarm fire, the office is full of smoke. Catch you later, okay?"

Click. Buzz.

Chris was downtown, the Subaru double-parked. He waited thirty seconds and dropped a quarter, called back. Sherry's secretary, Bobbi, picked up on the first ring. Chris asked her if the fire was under control.

"What fire?"

Chris said he had a message for Sherry. Tell her not to worry, he said, he'd decided on the Jaguar after all. Bobbi said, "Wait a minute, what fire?"

Chris hung up, got in the car and started driving. He'd never in his life made it to an audition on time. He was always early. Always.

Or didn't bother to show up at all.

The auditions were being held in a drab three-storey brick structure on Hastings, a couple of blocks from Gastown. Inside, an area roughly the size and shape of a boxing ring had been separated from twenty thousand square feet of unused space by the simple expedient of laying down strips of white tape. A couple of overworked space heaters glowed red in a futile attempt to dispel the chill.

Rusty Arnold was sitting in a director's chair that had the word "Rusty" printed on the back in clumsy block letters. Arnold was wearing a six hundred dollar brown leather bomber jacket with a sheepskin lining, silvery-grey widewale cords and a pair of scuffed workboots, a cheap straw cowboy hat.

He looked at Chris, did a stylized double-take and then put a finger to his lips, cleverly miming silence.

Or maybe he was about to throw up.

A gopher in black jeans and a tight black sweater eased up on Chris from his left flank. She put an arm around him and got up on her tip-toes, let him take the weight of her breasts as she leaned into him, whispered could she get him a cup of coffee? Chris was about to tell her she could get him any way she liked, remembered the silence edict and nodded his head, miming "yes".

An actress was reading from a script laced through with blue and pink rewrite pages. Chris watched her drop to her knees. He listened as she patiently told an invisible little girl Mr Dentist

94

was waiting for her and he was so looking forward to her visit. And besides, if she didn't do what she was told all her teeth would drop out the minute she fell asleep tonight.

Rusty said, "Can you just run through those last few lines one more time for me, honey?"

The actress nodded, smiled.

Rusty said, "Be really threatening, okay? Think of a recent situation when you've felt intimidated, and then turn it around and use it. Can you think of a situation recently when you've felt intimidated, honey?"

The actress nodded enthusiastically.

"Good girl. Now grab the surly little bitch – I'm talking about your daughter here – and shake her so hard her teeth damn near fall out. Remember, this is *comedy*! Broad strokes, sweetheart."

Chris mulled the situation over, tried to drum up the motivation a typical Jaguar mechanic would need to grab his tiny little darling girl and shake the living bejeezus out of her while screaming threats into her face in front of several horrified day care workers who would surely call the cops the minute he walked out the door.

He sighed wearily, glanced around. The cheesecake who'd offered him coffee was off in a corner necking with a guy he vaguely knew, Stan, a failed actor who was now a lighting technician and probably could afford a Jaguar, if he wanted one.

Chris stood there in the shadows, memorizing his terminally stupid lines as his blood congealed and the actress screamed at her daughter until her voice failed her.

Chris got set. Rusty ignored him. Another would-be child abuser came out of nowhere and did her level best to emotionally scar her child for life.

Finally, about quarter past eleven, the director shot out of his chair and turned and pointed at him in shocked disbelief, "Are you *Chris*?"

Chris reluctantly admitted it.

Rusty asked him who his agent was. Chris mentioned Sherry's name. Rusty told him he was terribly sorry for wasting his time, even though it sure as hell wasn't his damn fault.

Chris said, "Excuse me?"

Rusty explained he was a hundred per cent sure he'd told Sherry he was looking for a woman. He made a crack about Chris's name being kind of ambidextrous. Then asked Chris how old he was, and how in hell he thought for one moment he could play the father of a five-year-old child.

On his way out, Chris fingered his buck knife and enjoyed a full-color fantasy about cutting Mr Director into even thinner slices of baloney.

He walked three blocks to his car, paid the parking lot attendant three dollars and asked for a receipt. Either the guy smoked a lot, or he'd neglected his teeth ever since they arrived. Chris thought about grabbing him by the throat and delivering his lines, but reasoned that any parking lot guy who valued his life probably kept a sawed-off baseball bat clamped between his knees.

So he just drove anticlimactically away.

Earlier, he'd toyed with the idea of downing a *latte* at Starbucks. But the disastrous audition had left him in no mood for world-watching. What a much better idea it was to head over to the zoo for a little stroll, some fresh air.

He could ogle the otters. Bait the bears. Menace the monkeys. Maybe go inside the aquarium, admire the anchovies.

He drove straight out of Hastings, past the boarded-up picture windows of what used to be the downtown branch of the Woodward's department store chain. When he was a kid his mother used to take him downtown on the bus during the Christmas holidays to admire the animated display in the store's big plate-glass windows. Every year it was the same. The whole gang turned out. Elves and gnomes, reindeer. Santa and Mrs Claus.

When Chris'd finally had enough of the spun-floss snow and the elves' inhumanely repetitious chores, his mom would take his hand and lead him inside, along a maze of aisles and then downstairs to the basement cafeteria. He and his mom would get up on stools at the horseshoe-shaped counter. She'd order a coffee for herself and a grilled cheese sandwich – hold the pickles – and a coke for him.

After lunch, they'd walk a couple of blocks down Hastings to the Army & Navy. His mother never bought anything except bathroom and kitchen supplies, but she'd let him wander around the sports department, check out the guns and the fishing tackle. Huge salmon, fish as big as he was, had been stuffed and mounted and hung on the walls . . .

What a ritual it had been. It just about knocked him out, remembering the child he'd left behind.

Well, those happy carefree times were dead and gone. It'd been years since he'd counted on his mother to take him by the hand.

But now, instead of his mother, he had Robyn.

He continued along Hastings to Georgia, and then followed the same route he and Robyn had taken the previous night, past Lost Lagoon and into the park. He'd read somewhere that it had once been a tidal pool. Hence the name. Whatever, the lagoon was frozen solid except for a smallish patch of open water near the causeway. Hundreds of assorted ducks and inbred Canada geese were milling around in the water, their feathery little faces pinched and worried. Or was he projecting?

Bright yellow "No skating" signs had been placed on the ice. If it was thick enough for a city employee to walk out on so he could put up the signs, why wasn't it safe to skate on?

Chris drove past the Robbie Burns statue. A large stuffed toy dog hung by the neck from one of the famous dead poet's benevolently extended arms. A crowd of people stood on the snowy slope, looking up. Was that a television camera?

Behind him, a horn blared loud and long. He frowned into his rearview mirror, saw the twinkling bar of red and white and blue that straddled the patrol car's roof. He moved over, into the curb lane. The police car sped past. Chris saw that it was headed towards the aquarium. He followed, turning left up a slight gradient, the parking lot suddenly coming into view. There was another patrol car already in the lot, plus a couple more cars Chris suspected were unmarked units.

He noticed the ghoul patrol's drab brown station wagon with its curtained windows and whip antennae, was wondering what it was when he was distracted by a burst of dopey music on the radio. It was time for the noon news.

Chris pulled into a parking slot near the aquarium complex. He put the transmission in "Park" and turned the radio's volume up a little. The lead item on the local news concerned an apparent death by drowning at the city aquarium. Chris leaned back and closed his eyes.

An employee, Dr Gerard Roth, had been discovered in the whale pool early that morning by a senior member of the staff. An ambulance had been called, and Dr Roth was pronounced dead at the scene. A homicide detective named Jack Willows had declined comment.

Next came an item about three bodies discovered in a parked

97

car on the city's east side. All three deaths had resulted from an overdose of heroin . . .

Chris didn't hear a word. All he could think of was that he'd been right – *he had seen what he had seen.*

He switched off the ignition and got out of the car, dropped the keys in his pocket. He walked about fifty yards to a ticket dispenser, fed two quarters and in exchange received a ticket valid for one hour's parking. He went back to the car and laid the ticket in plain view on the dashboard and locked the door.

The cold seeped into his bones. He thrust his hands deep into the pockets of his Levis, walked down a pathway that led past the low-slung building that held the zoo's collection of exotic, if somewhat bedraggled and morose, birds.

The central zoo area was deserted except for a few elderly men and several determined-looking mothers towing small, unhappy children.

Chris walked towards the aquarium. He had reached the foot of the steps when he saw that the complex was closed.

A uniformed cop stood by the door, watching him. He jogged up the steps and asked the cop if the aquarium was closed because of the guy who'd drowned.

The cop stared at him for just a heartbeat too long, then nodded tersely.

Chris asked when the aquarium would reopen. Was it worth waiting around?

The cop removed his hat. He ran his fingers through his hair. He put the hat back on. Finally, he shrugged.

Not far from the monkey house there was an antique fire-engine: a red wagon with big wood-spoked wheels, that had been converted into a popcorn stand. Chris bought a brown paper bag of fresh popcorn. He asked for extra salt and an extra squirt of butter and then took three napkins, because the bag was so greasy. The popcorn guy apparently considered three napkins a bit excessive. He gave Chris a mildly disapproving look.

Chris wandered off eating popcorn and licking his fingers. He'd have liked a cup of coffee or maybe a hot chocolate, but the concession stand was closed for the winter. He sat down on a wooden bench and stared at the granite and green-glass wall of the aquarium.

What did the cops think – that it was an accident? He knew better. He remembered the snow falling silently down out of the

98

black sky and the sound of the dolly as the wheels thumped on the concrete steps. He remembered the body – Dr Gerard Roth's body – sliding silently into the pool. He wondered if he'd be able to identify the killer, if he saw her again.

Chris sat there on the bench and imagined tracking the killer down. Think of the publicity! He fantasized selling film rights, starring in the lead role . . .

Susan Carter pushed the glass door open. The cop hitched up his belt and gave her a hopeful but hopeless smile.

The popcorn guy stomped his feet against the cold, rubbed his hands up close to the hissing propane lantern that warmed his fare. He admired Susan's long blonde hair, the movement of her hips beneath the heavy winter coat. Full of juice, she was. You could see it just looking at her.

Meanwhile, Chris sat there on his bench with his bag of double-buttered popcorn in his lap, dreaming of wealth and dreaming of fame.

Oblivious to Susan, as she walked briskly past.

11

They went back down to the pool again. The whales were still there, but the body had been removed and the techs had come and gone. Crouching, Willows used a borrowed tape to measure the span of the parallel ruts in the snow and ice, that led all the way from the main building down past the outdoor viewing area to the pool.

Parker said, "You're starting to think Roth's swim was involuntary, aren't you?"

Willows nodded. Twenty inches, approximately. The tape was old and rusty. He had to gently encourage it back into its dispenser.

Parker said, "I'll give Kirkpatrick a call, see if I can get him to put a rush on the autopsy."

"Tell him you're particularly interested in comparing the water in Roth's lungs to the water samples we took from the pool."

"He was dead when he was dumped in the whale pool, is that your theory?"

"He might've been unconscious, but alive. I hope he wasn't, though, because if he was alive the fluids would match." A knee creaked as Willows stood up. "Let's go find that dolly."

The aquarium's public viewing area was all fresh paint and gleaming terrazzo floors, polished acrylic and glass panels, bright information signs in primary colors.

Below decks it was a completely different situation.

A warren of narrow corridors led to various offices and storage areas and unexpected dead ends. Each of the larger display tanks had a dedicated filtration system, and the sound of the complex state-of-the-art machinery was muted but pervasive. Willows tried an unmarked door and found that it was locked. He and Parker made their way down a narrow corridor past a churning pool of water. They turned a corner and came upon a stack of 25-kilogram bags of fine white powder.

Parker said, "If they've got 'Product of Colombia' stamped on them we're going to be famous."

Willows indicated a hopper attached to one of the filtration units. "It must be part of the purification system."

They continued their search. In ten minutes they'd found three dollies, all of them identical, with wheel spans measuring twenty inches.

Willows said, "That's three out of how many? We could wander around down here for the rest of the week and still not see everything."

Parker nodded in agreement. They'd explored less than a third of the basement level, and had already come across a dozen locked doors. She said, "We need a master key, and somebody who knows the terrain."

"A guide dog. But even if we had one, we'd have to wait for a positive autopsy report before Homer'd let us spend any more time on this."

"We could hand the search over to a uniform. Get him some help from Sweeting, tell him to round up every dolly he can find, hogtie them with crime scene tape. Explain that we might want to dust the damn things for prints."

Willows nodded his agreement. Except for the small matter of the unexplained wheel marks left by the dolly in the snow, they had no reason to suspect that Roth's death was anything but accidental. There wasn't an awful lot more they could do at the aquarium. The staff was so large that questioning them all simply wasn't practical.

Parker said, "I skipped breakfast. Want to take a break, grab something to eat?"

"We could drive over the bridge into West Van, have lunch and then drop in on Roth's wife."

"Widow, Jack."

"Want to give Homer a call?"

"And tell him what, that we'd like to have lunch in West Van, at a nice restaurant by the sea?"

"Tell him about the wheel marks. Tell him we think Roth might've been dumped in the pool. That's plenty of reason to talk to his wife."

Willows' conversation with the aquarium's director took considerably longer than Parker's call to Inspector Bradley. By the time he eased into the passenger seat of their unmarked Ford the interior of the car was cozy and warm. He said, "Homer give us a green light to cross the border?"

Parker nodded. "A Victim Services Unit has already paid Mrs Roth a visit, so we're clear to talk to her, see what she has to say. Tony going to co-operate?"

"Yeah, he said he'd get somebody to show the uniform around, and arrange a locked room to store the dollies." Willows shrugged out of his overcoat and tossed it in the backseat. He turned the heater down a notch.

Parker backed the car out of the parking slot. They drove down a curving, gently sloping hill towards the one-way road that followed the sea-wall around the park. The swimming pool that Willows had frolicked in as a child had long ago been filled with sand and topped off with asphalt. It was called a waterpark now. The Parks Board claimed maintenance costs were considerably lower.

Willows believed it.

Their car picked up speed as they drove past Lumberman's Arch – a massive cedar log spanning a pathway through the park. The inner harbor was on their right; a steep green wall of vegetation on the left. After a mile or so the road curved away from the water and then forked. Parker turned left. A couple of hundred yards further on a narrow branch road connected with the three-lane causeway that bisected the park on its way northwards over the Lion's Gate Bridge and into the suburbs of North and West Vancouver. A system of lights controlled the traffic flow; the causeway's middle lane was dedicated to north or southbound traffic according to need. Parker checked and saw that the light above the center lane was red. She waited impatiently for a break in the single lane of northbound traffic.

Willows checked his watch again.

Parker said, "What're you going to do, time me and then race me back?"

A yellow van shot past. She hit the gas, cut in between the van and an accelerating grey Mercedes.

The Mercedes' driver flashed his lights, leaned on the horn.

Parker glanced in her rearview mirror. "If he was any closer, he'd be in the trunk."

Willows rolled down his window.

She said, "What are you going to do?"

"Shoot him right between the eyes." Willows unclamped the

portable magnetic gumball, stuck it out the window and hit the on/off switch. Red light splashed across the Mercedes' windshield. The shiny grey car fell back.

Willows rolled up his window, switched off the light.

They hit the apex of the bridge, and the white-clad mountain peaks suddenly seemed to jump out at them. A freighter passing beneath the bridge on its way to the inner harbor pushed through the quiet water. Beyond the freighter the sea gradually darkened from grey to black.

Sometimes, due to a trick of the light, Vancouver Island rose up out of the horizon so it seemed only a few miles away, rather than twenty-five. But not today – the clouds were too thick, too low.

Parker said, "Think it's going to snow?"

Willows managed a shrug.

Parker almost asked him what he was thinking about, but caught herself in time. The kids – what else? They were approaching the roundabout at the end of the bridge. Below them and to the right, mobile homes on concrete pads occupied a narrow strip of land between the bridge and the Capilano river. You could buy cheap cigarettes down there. No taxes – it was reservation land. Parker braked slightly. The road widened to two lanes and the Mercedes took full advantage, passing them on the inside at a pace the Ford couldn't possibly match.

Parker said, "What a jerk."

"Yeah, but a rich jerk."

"It's probably a lease."

"He wasn't worried about getting a ticket. How'd he figure out we weren't West Van cops?"

"Your clothes, probably."

They rolled over the old metal-girdered bridge that spanned the river, then past a hotel and a gas station and a monstrous, sprawling shopping center. A small park appeared on their right, and then the police station, at the head of a retail strip several blocks long.

Willows pointed out a McDonald's.

Parker kept driving.

Willows watched the McDonald's go by. He said, "Do you know something I don't know?"

"Just worked that out, did you?"

A few minutes later Parker turned off Marine Drive. The Ford

103

bumped across a set of railway tracks and then they pulled up beside a long, low red-painted woodframe building.

"Alonzo's?"

"Relax, Jack. The food and the view are both great. Best of all, they've got a liquor licence."

In front of the restaurant a wooden pier thrust a hundred feet or more into the harbor. In the shelter of a small gazebo at the very end of the pier an elderly man with a shock of white hair and a close-cropped white beard sat with his back to the wind, smoking a pipe and reading a paperback. The man wore a bulky, bright red jacket and a green scarf and matching mittens. He was wearing wire-rim glasses, and his nose and cheeks were red with cold.

Willows said, "Getting close to Christmas, isn't it?"

Parker smiled.

The restaurant was built on two levels with most of the window tables at the front, on the lower level. The bar was upstairs, at the rear. About half the tables on each level were occupied.

A waitress hurried towards them, menus in hand.

Parker said, "Where would you like to sit, Jack?"

Willows asked if it was possible to have a table by the window, and the waitress smiled and said she thought it was extremely possible, and led them to a corner table for two.

Parker knew exactly what she wanted; bouillabaisse, with a spinach salad to start, and a Perrier to wash it all down. Willows ordered halibut and chips and a bottle of Granville Island Lager.

Out on the pier a gust of wind tore at the old man's beard, ruffled the pages of his book, made his red jacket billow like a spinnaker. He sat up a little straighter, looked out to sea as if to gauge the weather. Smoke and a flurry of sparks billowed from his pipe. He bent his head and went back to his book.

The waitress arrived with their drinks, Parker's salad and a wicker basket of bread.

Willows said, "The two clocks over the bar – one of them's running a little slow, isn't it?"

The waitress laughed. "That's the time in Bagheria. Do you know where that is?"

Willows shook his head as he poured a little beer into his glass.

"Have you ever been to Sicily?"

"Only in the movies."

Smiling, the waitress moved away.

Parker said, "She thinks you're cute."

"She's right."

"Cute, but old."

"*Very* old," said Willows, "but *very* cute." He drank some beer. It tasted fine. It was Laphroaig weather but since he was on duty he'd settle for a beer. But beer was alright. No, it was more than that, it was very good. Wonderfully good. He tried the bread and found it moist and a bit yeasty, with a fine crust. He sipped the beer and looked out the window at the old man fighting the weather on the end of the pier. He could have been Hemingway. Yes, it was possible. Why not? Elvis was alive. Why not Ernest?

He watched Parker devour her salad. Such a ladylike attack, ruthless yet delicate. She wiped her mouth and it seemed as if her napkin was bleeding. Lust hit him a bodyblow so fierce he almost dropped his glass in his lap. Maybe that wouldn't have been such a bad thing.

Parker smiled across the table at him. She said, "What did you think of Susan Carter?"

"Cute. Very cute. Not as cute as me, though."

Parker's bouillabaisse arrived, and Willows' fish and chips. He reached across the table and speared a scallop from Parker's bowl. There was a small west coast fishery but for reasons he didn't understand, restaurant scallops always came from the east coast, three thousand-odd miles away. You could buy west coast scallops at fish stores. Why not restaurants?

He asked Parker. She said, "Fish stores sell them fresh. Restaurants prefer a frozen product. There's a lot less waste, and they're probably cheaper to begin with."

Willows helped himself to a chunk of red snapper and then another scallop. Parker stabbed him lightly in the wrist with her fork. "Be a good boy. Stay on your own side of the table."

The waitress drifted past. Willows ordered another beer, by way of compensation. He tore into his halibut.

Parker said, "It's nice to see you making the best of a bad situation." She speared a scallop, gave her fork a little shake to stop the sauce from dripping, and leaned across the table. "Open wide."

Willows said, "You sound just like my dentist." But not until he'd chewed and swallowed.

They ordered coffee to go. Parker insisted on paying for the meal, but let Willows take care of the tip. Outside, the wind had freshened and the harbor was flecked with white. Sometime during their meal, the old man had abandoned the pier. Willows had an urge to walk out there, lean into the wind and feel the pilings quiver underfoot.

Parker said, "You want to drive?"

"Not particularly."

"You're okay?"

"After two beers and three scallops? Yeah, I think I can manage."

Parker said, "Don't be such a hard-ass, Jack." She went around to the Ford's passenger-side door, unlocked it and tossed him the keys. He unlocked, climbed behind the wheel. Shut the door and started the engine. Their fingers touched between the seats as they buckled up. As always, timing was crucial.

Willows smiled.

Parker said, "What?"

"Nothing," said Willows, but he kept on smiling as he reversed out of the parking slot and headed back up the road and over the railway tracks.

When Parker had tossed him the keys her weight had been perfect, the throw so accurate he'd hardly needed to move his hand. He found her so beguiling partly because she could do so many small things so very well, with such effortless grace.

Plus she was the kind of woman who willingly shared her scallops. And he might have got a chunk of crab out of her too, if he'd thought to ask.

Next time.

They continued along Marine Drive, the narrow road rising and falling and curving endlessly through thickly treed terrain sprinkled with a few small cottages dating from the thirties and many newer, studiously lavish homes situated on huge, immaculately landscaped lots.

Money money money.

Eagle Island was a long way from the city. They drove past West Bay and the neighborhoods of Altamont, Sandy Bay and Lighthouse Park. The winding streets had names like Sunset, The Dale, Water Lane and Bear Lane, The Byway and The Halt, Daffodil Road. Willows knew a cop who'd lived way out here, in an area called Lower Caulfield. The cop and his girlfriend had lived in a rented log cabin with a close-in water view. It had seemed like a great place to live, but the cop and his girl were

106

city people and after a year of it they'd had about as much of the idyllic life as they could stand.

Pilot House Road, that's where they'd lived, right next door to a stone and cedar church. It had bothered the girlfriend, living in sin in such close proximity to a place of worship.

Willows told Parker about the log cabin on Pilot House Road – but not about the girlfriend. They talked for a while about the street names – were they charming or merely pretentious? Then a discreet varnished pine signpost warned them that the West Vancouver Yacht Club was coming up on their left.

Willows cursed softly.

Parker said, "Something wrong?"

He nodded. They'd overshot the mark. The road movie had gone off the reel – they were lost.

12

Chris finished his popcorn and turned the bag upside-down and gave it a shake. A couple of scruffy-looking pigeons turned towards him, pecked at the ground near his feet in a desultory fashion and then ambled away, cooing softly in disappointment. Chris crumpled the bag into a compact brown ball and lobbed it overhand into a green-painted metal wastebasket fitted with a wire mesh cap to keep the crows from making a mess.

He stood up, stamped to get his blood circulating. A grotesquely fat woman pushing a stroller overflowing with two screaming toddlers glared at him as though she could read his intention to snatch her beloved infants as clearly as if the words were tattooed across his forehead.

But she was the sadist, thought Chris, taking her kids to the zoo in weather this bad.

Chris waited until she'd put a reasonable amount of distance between them. Unfortunately, she had chosen the same route through the park that he intended to follow – past the monkey cages and down along the west side of the aquarium, towards the cenotaph.

The way he saw it, he had a maximum of two choices: he could dawdle in the area of the monkey house, spin his wheels until she was out of sight, far ahead of him. Or he could accelerate past her, let *her* catch up with him, if she chose to take the risk. Chris sighed woefully. The simple truth was that no matter what it cost him in terms of hypothermia, he wasn't going to risk exposing himself to another icy stare, that high-octane mother's mix of venom and suspicion that was so unnerving.

He remembered reading somewhere that even the most harmless snakes were potentially lethal for a short time after birth. Maybe nature had blessed new mothers in a similar fashion.

Loitering in the passive madness of the monkey house, he thought about a recent television program on cryogenics that he'd watched but hadn't paid sufficient attention to. By the time a quarter of an hour had crawled past he felt he could allow his body temperature to plummet no further. Abandoning the monkey house's dark and gloomy charms, he marched briskly along the path that led in the general direction of the aquarium.

He'd had some dope on him then – he had some dope on him now. He glanced around. He was alone except for a couple of hard-eyed, hunchbacked crows perched on the iron rail of the fence the Parks Board had built to keep people out of the moat that surrounded this side of the aquarium. The crows had the casually ruthless posture of professional gangsters. But the pair of them together weighed less than a pound, and they were smart enough to know it. Chris veered abruptly towards them and they spread their black wings and flew blackly away, fouling the air with their tongues.

He took another quick look around, fished in his leather jacket for a joint, moistened the paper with his tongue to slow the burning, lit up.

He pulled the smoke deep into his lungs, squeezed tight.

A picture came into his mind of Robyn at work. She was busy but he couldn't quite see what she was up to. He took another hit. She had not encouraged him to visit her when she was on the job. If they had lunch, she met him at a restaurant. So was it his fault if things were a tad out of focus when he tried to picture her at work? Was it his fault if he had very little idea what Robyn actually did for a living?

Chris walked quickly along the path parallel to the moat. A fat, mottled brown duck kept pace with him for a while, quacking softly as it swam effortlessly through the muddy water. Eventually it became discouraged by its inability to make eye contact, lost momentum and dropped away.

Chris walked through a green-painted iron gate, made his way down two levels of wide concrete stairs. Now he was at the point where he and Robyn had jumped up on the wall. He took another powerful hit on the joint, flicked away the burning end and ate the roach.

He scrambled up on the wall. Now he had a much clearer view of the aquarium complex, and anyone looking in his direction would have a much clearer view of him. But the aquarium was deserted. He was alone. He spread his arms for balance and walked rapidly along the top of the wall until he reached the scrim

109

of evergreens and shrubbery growing on the berm behind the pool.

Fallen leaves lay hidden beneath the crust of snow; the ground was slippery and treacherous. Chris stepped carefully – if he lost his footing, he'd end up in the moat or in the whale pool. He shivered, remembering how careless he and Robyn had been the previous night. He imagined what might have happened if she'd fallen into the pool. He'd have tried to save her. Gone in after her, right? Yeah, sure. Of course. Naturally.

They'd have drowned, both of them.

Chris wiped the thought from his head. Crouching low, he made his way through a patch of bushes thick with hard, shiny green leaves. Without the aquarium lights to guide him, it was impossible to tell exactly where he and Robyn had been the previous night. He moved closer to the lip of the sand-colored rock overhanging the killer whale pool.

He saw the small cedar tree and remembered holding Robyn tightly, enjoying the warmth of her body as they sheltered beneath the tree's branches.

Crouched under the tree in almost exactly the same position he'd occupied the previous night, he stared across the dark, calm surface of the water. Over there where the wide concrete steps came down to the edge of the pool, that's where he'd seen the pale figure moving through the snow. He shut his eyes and tried to conjure up the memory of something it was possible he had never seen in the first place.

He saw, or imagined he saw, a body slip into the water, silently vanish. He saw a naked figure turn and start up the steps. The figure paused. It looked right at him.

Chris squinted into the swirling snow, harsh glare of the lights.

Directly in front of him, no more than fifteen feet away, one of the whales breached. He held his breath as the huge black and white creature rose high into the air and then fell back into the pool with an enormous splash.

The water slowly settled. Chris waited a moment and then crawled on his hands and knees to the edge of mock-sandstone, peered straight down into the water.

It was impossible to see past the surface glare; it was like looking into a mirror. He cupped his hands funnel-like around his eyes. There was *something* down there, that vanished and then

110

reappeared as the water glittered and heaved and the light came and went.

He leaned out a little further. The thing was lying on the bottom of the pool, wavering and insubstantial. No, wait. It was a small metal dolly – the kind you'd use to move a stove or refrigerator. Or maybe a corpse.

A hoarse shout carried across the water, hit him like a slap in the face. He looked up. A guy in a suit was yelling at him, waving his arms.

Chris jumped to his feet. Crows shrieked at him. He turned and ran.

13

Willows braked hard and swerved into the left turn lane. The road was clear. He turned into the yacht club's grounds past the pair of slightly neglected totem poles that flanked the entrance.

Off to the right, a smaller pole with widespread wings and a made-in-Taiwan look about it towered over several neatly ordered rows of trailered boats of various size, all of them protected from the weather by bright orange and blue tarpaulins.

There was parking for two or three hundred cars, but there were only a couple of dozen vehicles in the lot and they were all huddled together down by the water, next to what had to be the clubhouse – a sharp-angled, steep-roofed building faced with reddish-brown rock.

It was drinking rather than sailing weather, Willows supposed.

Parker said, "Somebody in there ought to be able to give us directions."

Willows nodded. He rummaged in his jacket pocket for a breath mint.

As he drove across the empty parking lot towards the building he saw that only part of it was used by the yacht club. There was also a chandlery, its big plate-glass windows bright with the gaudy foam and plastic products that seemed so much a part of modern boating. He braked, put the transmission in "park", got out of the car and walked up the wide, heavily salted steps and pushed open the door. The shop was even larger than it had looked from out-side, and was well-stocked with a mix of basic necessities and problematical luxuries. To Willows it looked like the kind of place where the staff knew everyone by name, and the customers kept a running account or paid with gold cards.

A woman wearing faded jeans and a striped blue and white polo shirt appeared from behind a circular rack of mournful black rubber wetsuits that made Willows think of a scarecrow's funeral. He asked her if she could give him directions to Eagle Island.

112

Her smile was more amused than sympathetic. "You've gone right past it. Go back towards the city and make a right at the second intersection. There's a sign – if you look for it. Got a boat?"

"No."

"Care to buy one?"

"Thanks anyway." Salt crunched underfoot as he navigated his way down the icy steps to the car.

Parker gave him an enquiring look. He said, "We have to go back. We missed the turnoff. Apparently there's a sign – if you look for it."

Parker said, "I had a feeling we should've looked for a sign."

"Rules to live by," said Willows. "Always look for a sign." He started the engine and they drove down the length of the parking lot, past the gaily shrouded boats and snow-drifted totem poles and back on to Marine Drive.

At the second intersection on their left a white-painted wooden signpost with black letters about an inch high directed them towards Eagle Island. Willows drove down a narrow, winding asphalt road past a mix of older cottages and huge, architecturally aggressive houses that seemed determined at all costs not to blend in with the rainforest landscape.

A minute or two later an expanse of flat, greyish-green water came into view. As they drew closer, Willows saw that there was a small beach at the end of the road, and a parking lot to the right. He started to turn in and then spotted a sign warning that the lot was the property of Eagle Island Yacht Club members and that all other vehicles would be towed away at the owners' expense. He continued to drive slowly down the narrow road. There was parking on both sides, but every space was reserved for a named resident of Eagle Island. In the slot marked "Sinclair" was an old split windshield Studebaker that had been kept in showroom condition. He slowed to admire the car.

Parker said, "Organized, aren't they?"

Willows nodded, backed the Ford into a driveway paved with interlocking blocks of pink cement, and then drove down the road and parked illegally.

Parker said, "It's a long walk home, Jack."

"We'll steal a yacht." He pulled down the sun visor so the Ford's POLICE VEHICLE placard showed clearly, and then grabbed the gumball and wedged it on the dashboard. "That ought to do it."

113

The two detectives got out of the Ford and walked back down the road. Iris Roth's slot was fifth from the end on the right, and was occupied by a shiny white BMW cabriolet.

The road climbed gently through evergreens and thick undergrowth. The surface hadn't been salted or ploughed, so Willows and Parker went slowly. In a few minutes the island, located at the head of a smallish harbor crammed with moored sail boats, came gradually into view. Then the road abruptly disintegrated into an unpaved footpath. Willows and Parker followed it down to a narrow pier jutting out into the water. Thick planks echoed hollowly underfoot as they walked the length of the pier and then down a steeply pitched ramp to a floating dock.

The island was no more than a hundred and fifty feet away, but the water, a lovely clear green, was too cold to swim and too deep to wade.

A dozen small boats were moored at the dock, held in place by chains draped casually over galvanized iron posts. There were several variations on the basic design but the boats were all about twelve feet in length, with a six-foot beam, sheetmetal aluminum decks and waist-high pipe rails. Willows noticed that they were all powered by 9.9 horsepower outboard motors, the majority electric start models equipped with remote controls.

An equal number of similar vessels were moored at a small dock on the island.

Willows stepped cautiously on to one of the boats. It wobbled slightly under his weight. He grabbed the rail and made his way to the controls.

Parker said, "What are you doing, Jack?"

"The key's in the ignition."

"Are you familiar with the word *piracy*?"

"How about I take us over and then you come back and wait for me here?"

Parker waved her arm at the island, taking in the homes lined up along the shore and high up on the hill above the water. "Look at all those windows. You think we aren't being watched? Somebody's watching us. What if they call the cops? And please don't tell me we're the cops, because we won't be much longer, with your attitude."

Willows said, "If we don't take a boat, we'll have to call Mrs Roth and ask for a ride."

Parker nodded. "That's right, Jack."

114

Willows stepped back on to the dock. The miniature ferry, relieved of his weight, moved restlessly in the water. The chains binding it to the dock chimed softly. He said, "There's a phone booth back at the parking lot."

"You want me to walk back there and call her, is that what you're saying?"

"Or we can take a boat."

Parker gave Willows a look perfectly suited to the cold weather. She started up the ramp, then paused and turned back to him. "Gimme a quarter."

Willows thrust his hand into his overcoat pocket, came up with some loose change. He segregated a quarter and walked up the ramp and laid it gently in Parker's open palm.

"Got her number?"

Parker smiled sweetly. "I've got everybody's number, Jack. Even yours."

The ramp trembled slightly as Parker continued back towards the pier. But Willows had to admit it, she was extremely light on her feet. He turned and rested his elbows on the frosty wooden railing and studied the island. It was very small, about ten acres or so. At the near end, the moss-covered roof of a small white house looked as if it was about to cave in. Directly across from him there was a large, obviously expensive home with a detached guest cottage and private dock with about forty feet of sail boat moored to it. A nice lifestyle, very attractive. But there wasn't much open ground on the island, and very little flat area that he could see. Except for a few of the waterfront lots, the houses all seemed to have been built on about a thirty-degree slope. It was no place for small children; one misplaced step and you were in the saltchuck.

A woman in a shiny red jacket and bright yellow boots suddenly appeared between a stand of evergreens. He wondered where she'd come from and then saw the narrow path that ran between the trees and down to the dock. He wondered if the woman was Iris Roth and then decided it was unlikely because she was making her way down the path with a quick, fluid agility far beyond a woman Mrs Roth's age. He felt a vibration in the pier, and turned to look behind him. Parker had made her call. She didn't look very happy.

Willows said, "What's the problem?"

"Either she isn't home or she's refusing to answer the phone."

115

A badly scuffed fibreglass dinghy lay keel-up at the far end of the dock. The butt-ends of a pair of oars protruded from beneath the stern. Parker knew Willows would have noticed the boat. And she knew damn well he wasn't going back to the city without talking to Roth's widow, no matter what he had to do to see her.

Willows said, "Well . . ."

"Well what, Jack?"

"Well, gimme back my quarter," said Willows, and then turned away, deflected by the shrill whine of an outboard motor. Across the water, the woman in the red jacket stood at the wheel of one of the little ferries. Behind her a puff of blue smoke hung in the air. The woman cast off. The sound of the motor steadied and deepened as she put it in gear.

Willows said, "Tell me, Claire, are you familiar with the word *hijacking*?"

"Keep it up, Jack. Before you know it you'll be the funniest ex-cop in maximum security."

They stood there on the dock as the woman expertly steered her small craft across the span of water that lay between them. As she drew nearer, Willows saw he'd been right about her age; she was in her early thirties, slim and fit-looking, with sensibly cut auburn hair.

When the blunt prow of her boat touched the dock he moved forward and helped her tie up, then gave her a good long look at his badge. Before confusion could turn to apprehension he introduced himself and Parker, explained that they needed to get across to the island.

"Who is it that you want to see?"

Her voice was surprisingly firm. Willows wasn't in the mood for a debate. He made sure she got a good look at his clamshell holster and the butt of his .38 Special as he put his badge case back in his jacket pocket. Her eyes widened satisfactorily. He said, "We need to speak with Iris Roth."

The woman nodded. She looked a little surprised, but not much. She'd have made a good poker player – or maybe she already was.

Parker said, "Do you know Mrs Roth?"

"Yes, of course. On the island, everybody knows everybody. It's unavoidable, I suppose."

Parker said, "Do you know why we need to speak with her?"

"Should I?"

Spiky. Willows was careful not to let her see how much he approved.

Parker said, "Mrs Roth's husband has been seriously injured."

"Gerard? I'm sorry to hear that."

Parker thought it was just as well that the woman had said so, because otherwise she wouldn't have had any idea how she felt. She said, "Did you know him very well?"

"No, I didn't. As a matter of fact I tried to stay away from him." The woman glanced behind her, as if she expected Roth's ghost suddenly to appear on the island.

Parker said, "You avoided him? Would you please tell us why?"

"My husband and I held an open house shortly after we moved to the island. We invited everyone. Dr Roth had been drinking when he arrived. He asked me to dance, and . . ."

"Made advances?" said Parker.

"He tried to put his hand up my skirt. When I asked him to leave he acted as if he thought I was joking. The next morning, shortly after my husband left for work, Dr Roth showed up with a bottle of champagne. He apologized for his behavior and sug-gested we have a drink. I told him I wasn't interested. His reaction was to reach out and fondle – grab, really – my breast." Unexpec-tedly, the woman laughed. "My God, it was eight o'clock in the morning!"

Parker didn't see how that was relevant, but held her tongue.

"I slammed the door in his face. When my husband came home I told him what had happened and he walked over and had a talk with Dr Roth. He didn't bother me after that. But I doubt if there's a woman on the island he hasn't had his hands on. Except his wife, of course."

"They didn't get along?"

"You'll have to ask her. But I very much doubt it. She seems like a really nice person to me." She pushed back the sleeve of her raincoat and looked at her watch. "Look, I'm late. I can give you a ride to the island, but you'll have to make your own way back."

Parker said, "That's just fine, thank you." She and Willows stepped aboard. The engine made the little boat vibrate beneath their feet. They reversed away from the dock and turned towards the island.

A few moments later Parker found herself struggling to keep pace with Willows' longer stride as he hurried up the narrow

117

footpath that serviced the island's homes. The only vehicles she saw were the wheelbarrows residents used to transport groceries and other heavy items from the dock to their homes. Except for the crunch of snow and ice underfoot, it was eerily quiet. The air smelled fresh and green. Parker took a deep breath. She exhaled noisily, and said, "Nice neighborhood."

"Depends what you're looking for. There isn't as much traffic – or trafficking, as you'd find at Main and Hastings."

"I wonder what it costs to live here."

"Lots," said Willows.

They crested the low hill and started down the other side. Almost all the houses on the island seemed to have grown out of the landscape. The island's populace appeared content to coexist with nature rather than dominate it. Willows hardly knew Roth, but he didn't seem like the kind of man who'd thrive in such a pastoral environment. Maybe that had been a contributing factor in the breakup of his marriage.

Parker pointed through the trees at a long, low house with a wood-shingled roof and walls. She said, "That must be the one, Jack."

They walked down a limestone path through mature fir and cedar trees, and then across a span of open, grassy ground towards the rear of the house. There was only one window and it was at the far end.

They followed the path around to the side. Parker stepped up on the porch and knocked on the door. At the front there was another small patch of lawn, and then what appeared to be a sheer drop to the sea.

Willows glanced at his watch. It was mid-afternoon, but it seemed to him that the sky was already darkening. Despite his heavy coat, he could feel the cold seeping into his bones.

Parker knocked again, more vigorously.

Inside the house a dog yapped shrilly and then there was the clatter of claws scrabbling on linoleum.

The door swung open. A large woman with a small, snarling dog tucked under each arm and a lowball glass in her hand glared coldly at them and then said, "No, I do not wish to sell my house, you bloody vultures. Now get the hell off my property, or I'll tell Mr Jigs and Hot Stuff to piss all over you. And they'll do it, believe me."

Willows said, "They're Boston bulls, aren't they?"

"None of your damn business."

Parker said, "We're police officers. We'd like to ask you a few questions about your husband." She flashed her tin.

Iris Roth eyed the shield. Her gaze shifted to the color photo ID. She held out a large, calloused hand. Parker handed over her badge case. Squinting, Iris held the photograph up to the light streaming in from the open door. Mr Jigs and Hot Stuff were mostly black and partly white, like tiny cows, but with wildly bulging eyes and sharply pointed ears, stubby legs and no visible tails. Ruthlessly manipulated genetics had given them faces that were mashed flat and accordioned, as if they spent their spare time wilfully running full tilt into a brick wall. One of the dogs licked Parker's badge. Iris said, "When was this picture taken?"

"A little less than a year ago. Last January."

Iris nodded thoughtfully. She handed the badge case back to Parker, turned to Willows. "You're a policeman, as well?"

Willows nodded. He introduced himself.

Iris turned back to Parker. "How did you get across from the mainland?"

Willows held his peace, but he thought *mainland* was a little weighty. A few years ago he'd have damn near been able to take a running jump across to the island.

Parker said, "We were able to hitch a ride."

"Old man Sinclair came out for you?" Before Parker could deny it, Iris said, "Well, why shouldn't he, if he feels like it?" She pushed open the door and stepped aside. "Come on in out of the weather, and I'll tell you more about Gerard than he'd ever have wanted you to know. Would you like a drink?"

"No, thank you," said Parker very quickly.

Willows, following his partner into the house, gave her back a sour look.

Iris made a beeline for the kitchen counter. "Well, I think I'll freshen this up just a little, if you don't mind." She shifted a dog to her shoulder, unscrewed the metal cap from a bottle of rye whisky and topped up her glass. She smiled at Willows. "Sure you won't join me, Officer?"

"We aren't supposed to drink while we're on duty," said Parker. The dogs eyed her suspiciously, as if she was lying in her teeth, and they knew it.

"Well then, let me know when quitting time rolls around." Iris led them out of the kitchen and into the living room. A third dog

119

virtually identical to the pair tucked under her arms lay curled up on the hearth in front of a cheerful fire. As they entered the room the animal reared its head and silently bared its teeth.

Iris said, "Relax, Fireball, they're friends." She affectionately nudged the dog with the toe of her foot. Reassured, it licked its chops, yawned hugely and went back to sleep.

The wall facing the ocean was all glass. Orange firelight danced on the low, open-beamed ceiling. A pale grey light from the sea moved restlessly on the walls. Iris sat heavily on an overstuffed chair by the fire and waved Parker and Willows towards a matching sofa on the far side of a coffee table made out of a varnished slab of polished driftwood.

Parker said, "Mrs Roth . . ."

"Call me Iris. I got a call about an hour ago, from Tony Sweeting. He said Gerard's death was an accident. The woman who came around – from Victim Services – said she didn't know what happened. But she wasn't with the police. So what can you tell me?"

Parker said, "It was an accident, as far as we know . . ."

"But you think that could change?"

"Tell me," said Willows. "Why do you ask?"

"That's a very good question, young man. And I'm happy to be able to give you a very good answer."

In the kitchen, the phone rang stridently.

Iris said, "I sensed when I spoke with Tony that he was a little uncertain as to what had happened to Gerard. As a matter of fact I asked him straight out if he was sure Gerard's death was accidental."

"What did he say?"

"That he only knew what the police had told him. But I could tell he was being less than candid. Do you mind if I answer the telephone?"

"No, of course not."

Glass in hand, Iris pushed herself out of the chair and made her way back into the kitchen.

Parker and Willows exchanged a look. Parker removed her overcoat. In the kitchen, Iris picked up. There was a pause and then she told whoever she was talking to that he was a damn vampire and deserved to roast in hell, and slammed down the phone.

She came back into the living room with the bottle of rye tucked under her arm. Meeting Parker's eye, she said, "Suddenly I'm getting a million phone calls from real estate agents. Somehow they've already found out about Gerard's death. Disgusting creatures. Has there been something in the newspapers already?"

"Not that I know of," said Parker. "It may have been mentioned on the radio. We have no control over that, although we do ask that the news be withheld until the victim's relatives have been notified."

"Well, I was notified, wasn't I, so I suppose that means I have no reason to complain. But from now on I've got to remember to get the bastard's names, so I can complain to the fools who employ them."

Parker waited a moment, letting the dust settle, and then said, "Is it fair to say that when you first heard about your husband's death, it occurred to you that it might not be an accident?"

Iris drained a quarter-inch of whisky. "Oh yes, I'd say that was more than fair."

"It occurred to you that someone might have killed him?"

"Absolutely." One of the dogs tried to wriggle free of her grip. She said, "My goodness, Mr Jigs, I forgot all about you, didn't I! Poor thing!" She released both animals and they scurried down from the sofa and raced into the kitchen, claws clicking like tiny castanets on the linoleum. Fireball growled in his sleep, and curled into a marginally tighter ball.

Iris said, "Gerard trained all three of the dogs to urinate on people's legs. It took him months and months, but he never lost patience. He bought a mannequin and dressed it up and put it out in the yard. He'd say 'heel' and then urinate on the damn thing, and give them a piece of biscuit. Eventually the dogs caught on. 'Heel', he'd say, and they'd trot over to the nearest shoe and piss all over it. It was the only trick he ever taught them. If he was out for a walk and he saw somebody he didn't like the look of . . ."

She spoke Fireball's name. The animal raised its blunt, over-sized head, sleepily wagged its stump of a tail.

"They're such wonderful dogs, so affectionate and brave. Gerard perverted them. But that's the kind of bastard he was – somebody who thought it was hilarious when his dog filled your shoe with hot piss."

Willows said, "I understand you've been separated for the past year or so."

121

Iris picked up the lowball glass and brought it to her lips, drank deeply. "Who told you that?"

"An employee of the aquarium."

"A junior employee, I imagine. Some sweet young thing with loose morals and a tight skirt."

"Is it true – *were* you separated?"

"No, absolutely not. Gerard kept a small apartment in the city, but it was primarily because he often worked late into the night. Worked until he was exhausted; too tired to drive home. He was a workaholic, as I'm sure you've been told."

Parker murmured noncommittally.

"And Gerard absolutely hated crossing the bridge, especially when the weather was bad. He thought it was dangerous, and he was right."

"So he stayed over fairly often."

"Quite often." Iris reached down and lovingly scratched Fireball behind the ear. The dog licked her hand. Iris waved her empty glass at Willows. "Sure you don't want a drink?"

"Thanks anyway."

"Have to drink alone, then, won't I?" She unscrewed the cap from the whisky bottle a little too forcefully, and it spun out of her fingers and bounced off the hearth into the fireplace. Fireball twitched nervously. Iris poured herself a generous refill, drank half of it down.

Willows said, "Maybe I'll have one after all, if you don't mind."

"Good idea!"

Willows stood up, took the bottle and went into the kitchen and returned a moment later with a quarter-inch of whisky in a water glass. Parker noted approvingly that he'd left the bottle behind. He caught her look and smiled and raised his glass. Tricky bastard.

Slurring her words a little, Iris said, "Well, he had girlfriends from time to time. I knew that much. It wasn't always work or rotten weather that kept him over there." She glanced at Parker and then looked away, at the fire and then out at the darkening ocean. "We'd been married a long time. I suppose you could say he went his way and I went mine. Isn't this a lovely house?"

Parker hesitated, and then said, "Lovely."

"Gerard always took very good care of me. It wasn't one of those horrible situations you read about in the newspapers, where the poor woman has to account for every last penny. If I wanted a new dress, or anything at all, really, all I had to do was say so, and it was mine."

"He'd buy it for you?"

"Almost always. And if he wasn't around all that much, so what? The dogs were a lot more affectionate and a lot less demanding." Iris dipped her finger in her drink. She tilted her head back and held the finger over her open mouth. A fat drop of amber whisky trembled and fell. She smiled at Willows and said, "Yummy."

Parker said, "At the time of his death, was Gerard seeing anyone, Mrs Roth?"

"You mean, who was the other woman – 'scuse me, who was the other *lucky* woman?" She shrugged massively. "I have no idea. Spot her at the funeral, maybe."

The whisky had suddenly taken effect. Iris Roth was slurring her words badly now. Her chin bumped her chest. Her eyes popped open. She focused on her glass, drank deeply and sighed wearily.

Willows shot his cuff and glanced at his watch.

Iris said, "Time to go?"

Willows nodded, and stood up. He and Parker put on their coats. Willows went over to the fireplace, pulled the screen to keep the sparks at bay.

Iris said, "Thank you."

Willows smiled down at her.

She said, "Want a ride back to the mainland?"

Parker said, "We'll be okay."

Iris nodded. She thumped her glass purposefully down on the driftwood table, fell back against the sofa and closed her eyes.

As they walked along the pathway to the dock, Parker said, "Now what're we going to do – any bright ideas?"

"Old man Sinclair'll give us a ride, I bet."

"You're on," said Parker.

And lost.

14

Because of the continuing cold snap and treacherous streets, a lot of people had left their cars at home in favor of the city's already inadequate public transport system. Consequently the queue at the bus stop stretched well beyond the confines of the plexiglass shelter.

Robyn fell in at the end of the line and waited for her bus. When it finally arrived it was ten minutes late and the seats and aisle were jammed with forlorn-looking office workers just like her. For reasons unknown to her and possibly to himself as well, the driver pulled up and opened his door. No one got off and there was no room for anyone to get on. The bus sat there for about thirty seconds, its diesel engine staining the air, and then a passenger standing by the open door complained loudly about the cold.

The door hissed shut and the bus lurched ponderously away.

Robyn made sure her collar was all the way up and that her scarf was secure, snuggled a little deeper into her coat. Her legs below her hemline were numb. Her nose felt as if it was frozen stiff and would snap like an icicle if anyone happened to bump up against it.

She might as well have volunteered to stay late at the office. She'd have scored a few brownie points with Jerry and probably arrived home at about the same time anyway.

Another bus pulled up in front of her. It was empty but going in the wrong direction. The doors hissed open. A man in an ankle-length black leather coat broke free of the queue and stepped on board. He dropped his fare in the glass box and walked halfway down the bus and thumped down in a window seat. Robyn and everyone else in the queue watched him settle in, unbutton his coat and make himself comfortable.

The man looked out the window, surveying the frigid street. Robyn stared at him. He looked right at her, stared right through her. He seemed totally unaware that he was snug and secure on

124

a nice warm bus, and she was freezing her ass off on a sidewalk cold and hard as a slab of ice. There was certainly no hint of compassion in the look he gave her. In fact, there was nothing at all in his eyes that she could see.

Robyn was beginning to think her parents had been right. It *was* a cold, uncaring world.

Three-quarters of an hour later she was standing in the corridor fumbling numb-fingered for her keys when the apartment door swung wide and Chris put his arms around her and, his eyes full of laughter, told her he thought he'd heard the rattle of chains. Then he kissed her cold mouth and shivered and kissed her again and told her how much he'd missed her, as he pulled her into the apartment and locked the door.

He'd showered recently. His hair was damp, and his body still carried the lingering scent of soap. He kept on kissing her as he led her towards the bedroom, helped her with the clothes. The smell of spaghetti sauce, thick with meat and spices, wafted in from the kitchen. She could hear the pot bubbling softly on the stove. There was a vase of flowers on the table by the bed. Winter roses . . .

It was past eight by the time they finished dinner. Chris had bought a bottle of Australian red, and after they'd stacked the dishes in the sink he emptied the rest of the wine into their glasses, blew out the candles and then they went into the living room to watch "Cheers" on television.

During a commercial break, Chris snuggled closer and told Robyn about all the fun he'd had at his audition.

"He let you stand there for almost an hour, and then told you he thought you were a woman?"

"Yeah, right."

She squeezed his thigh. "Somebody ought to point him in the direction of an optometrist."

Chris chuckled. He was leading up to his trip to the aquarium and was feeling a little tense, but did it show? No way.

Robyn, playing straight man, said, "How was the rest of your day?"

Chris casually mentioned that he'd been back to the aquarium. He neglected to tell her how he'd crept around in the shrubbery while fantasizing that he was a hot-shot detective. Even so, Robyn was pretty upset.

She said, "His name was Gerard Roth. He drowned, and then the whales attacked him. They kept talking about it at work. Making sick jokes."

Chris told her he believed he could identify the killer.

Robyn said, "What killer?"

Chris gave her a look. Incredulous.

Robyn said, "You don't get it, do you? The man's death was an accident. They said so on the radio. He was in the pool doing some kind of research and drowned. And that's all there is to it."

"I don't think so," said Chris firmly. He used the remote to flip through half a dozen channels and then turned the TV off. The light in the room changed. The walls suddenly turned into an animated quilt, abstract grey shadows creepy-crawling and slippy-sliding down rectangles of white. Spooky. A shiver of fear ran the length of his spine. Turning, he peered apprehensively behind him.

It was snowing.

Robyn, watching him and somehow knowing what was going on in his mind, said, "It's the dope."

"Huh?"

"We smoke too much."

"You mean *I* smoke too much."

"Is that what I said?"

"Yeah, that's exactly what you said. You work your butt off all week while I lie around watching TV and smoking dope. You come home wet and cold, tired. *I* don't give a shit. All *I* care about is me. That's what you're saying, isn't it. I'm cute, but useless."

Robyn didn't actually move away from him, but Chris felt her tighten up, withdraw into herself. It amounted to more or less the same thing. Rejection. He felt a quick surge of anger. He said, "What I saw – a woman shove Roth into the pool – was a hallucination, and I should forget about it. Is that what you're saying?"

She nodded.

Chris was silent for a little while, looking over Robyn's shoulder at the snow. He liked the fact that he'd noticed the amoeba-like shadows crawling down the walls and Robyn hadn't. That he knew it was snowing and she didn't. He played with her hair, twisted it in his fingers and made it curl in on her neck. A few

126

minutes slipped past. Very quietly, he said, "I don't want an argument . . ."

"Good."

"But I know what I saw."

Robyn gave him a withering look. The yellowish glare of the streetlight didn't do a lot for her skin tone. She looked kind of *microwaved*.

He said, "I saw a woman with a dolly, remember? The body slid into the pool and I saw a blonde woman with a dolly turn and disappear into the snow."

"How many times do I have to tell you – I don't want to talk about it!"

"When I went back this afternoon, I looked down into the water and saw it lying on the bottom of the pool."

Robyn's eyes bugged out. Her jaw dropped. She'd have been laughed off the stage for overacting, but Chris believed her.

He said, "Not the woman – the dolly."

Recovering fast, Robyn said, "Bullshit."

"No, it's true."

"You said before that this person you saw with the dolly dragged it *away* from the pool."

"She must've come back later, after we'd left."

Robyn took a deep breath, held it for a moment. She said, "Okay, let's say Dr Roth was murdered and you play detective and actually identify the killer. Then what?"

Chris had been thinking about it. He had his answer down pat. "A certain unemployed but extremely talented actor becomes internationally famous overnight. His ruggedly handsome face is seen on every television screen on the continent. He's offered more work than he could handle in a lifetime." Chris hesitated and then added, "And he and his sweetheart live happily ever after."

"What about the police?"

"They're envious, but mature. Professionals. I'm sure they'll get over their embarrassment."

"No, Chris. What the police are going to do is ask us questions. Lots of really *difficult* questions. For starters, I'm sure they'll be curious about why I was trespassing at the aquarium after hours with my deadbeat boyfriend, the so-called actor with a criminal record for assault and battery."

"That was a long time ago."

"It was last summer, Chris. And have you given even a moment's thought to the more than three hundred dollars you owe for unpaid speeding and parking tickets?"

Chris said, "Jeez, Robyn. You make me seem like such a jerk."

Robyn moved in on him, gave him a perfunctory kiss on the cheek. "I'm trying to show you their point of view, that's all. And another thing, Chris. Jerry's going to ask me exactly the same questions as the police, and he won't like the answers any more than they do."

"We don't have to tell the cops we were smoking dope."

"Yes, we do. If Roth was murdered we have to tell the police everything. Everything, Chris."

"Why?"

"Because they'll find out anyway, believe me. And then Jerry'd find out, and he'd fire me."

"For smoking a couple of joints?"

"Listen, there's nothing more tight-assed than an accountant. When Jerry farts, he squeals like a goddamn smoke alarm."

Chris stared at her. Sometimes Robyn came home feeling a little low. But he'd never before heard her speak negatively about her job, the people she worked with.

Robyn said, "Yeah, he'd fire me. The bastard would fire me like a match. Then where would we be?"

"Still with each other, I hope."

She smiled for the first time since he'd turned off the television. "You're a sweet guy, Chris."

He said, "But kind of dumb?"

"Naive, maybe."

Chris thought, Unlike you. But all he said was, "It's snowing again."

Surprised, Robyn turned and looked out the window. Chris showed her the snowflake shadows drifting down the walls. He asked her if she'd like to catch a breath of fresh air, take a stroll.

Robyn thought that was a wonderful idea.

They bundled up in their warmest clothes, took the elevator down to street level, hurried through the tiny mirrored lobby and then the wide glass doors into clean-smelling air and a blizzard of white.

Chris said, "You'd think God was shaking the spots off every dalmatian in the world."

128

Robyn laughed. "Dalmatians are white with black spots, not the other way around."

He scooped up a double handful of snow, packed it into a ball, went into a major league wind-up and threw it at a nearby stop sign and missed by a mile.

Robyn said, "Watch and learn." She made a snowball the size of a grapefruit, turned her body at right angles to the stop sign, went into a complicated wind-up and side-armed a sly shot that exploded against Chris's head.

Then, with her out-of-work, assault-and-battery boyfriend in hot pursuit, she ran laughing and screaming down the pure white, sparkling city street.

By the time they arrived back at the apartment they were cold and shivering. There was a brief but spirited argument over first use of the shower, that was settled when Robyn suggested they wash together. Afterwards, she crawled straight into bed and waited impatiently as Chris opened a bottle of Chilean red. They made love with the curtains pulled and the snow drifting silently down the white-painted walls. When they were finished, Chris lay on his back with Robyn nestled in the crook of his arm. The snow had continued to fall. He stared out the window and dreamed lazily of fame.

Robyn said, "Chris?"

"Yeah?"

She rolled on top of him. "You awake?"

"Getting there."

"Do you really think you could identify the person you saw last night?"

Chris nodded. He put his arms around her and slid his hands down the sweet curve of her back and over the sweeter curves that followed.

Robyn said, "Instead of telling the police what we know, why don't we tell the killer?"

He buried his head between her breasts.

"Chris?"

He moved his hands lightly over her body, lingering here and there, pleasuring in the slow tingle of renewed desire.

Robyn said, "Blackmail – doesn't that sound like a good idea to you? We could give the money to an animal rights group, then turn the killer over to the police."

Chris pulled his head back. He said, "That sounds risky as hell to me. A lot riskier than just turning her over to the cops." His fingers grazed on her as if all the sustenance he needed was to be found right there on the smooth pale surface of her flesh.

"You're certain it was a woman?"

"Yeah. The more I think about it, the surer I am."

"Well then, it wouldn't be as dangerous, would it?"

Chris cupped her breast in his hand. He kissed her gently and then took her nipple into his mouth.

Robyn arched her back. Her cry of pleasure was soft and fragile as the sound of a snowflake falling to earth.

Chris was a very good lover. He knew when to be gentle, and when to be cruel.

His only problem was, sometimes he didn't know when to stop.

15

Willows dropped Parker off at her apartment. As he drove away, leaving her standing at the curb, he tried not to think about the many things she could have said but didn't, and the utterly direct way she'd looked at him as he'd grimly told her there was nothing he'd love more than to come in for a drink, but it was impossible because he had to drive straight out to the airport to pick up his kids.

"Wife and kids," said Parker, and gave him another piercing look. For a long moment he thought she was going to say a great deal more, none of it very pleasant. But all she'd done was get out of the Ford and shut the door with exaggerated care, stand there looking down at him through the glass with her shoulders set a little too square.

Willows drove down to Southwest Marine Drive and made a left, followed miles of road past the towering cedar hedges and granite walls that separated the real world from the south side's huge lots and multi-million dollar residences. What kind of people lived in those gigantic mock-Spanish and Tudor houses? Willows had no idea. No one had ever been murdered in any of them, yet.

Dual railway tracks marked an abrupt deterioration in the quality of the neighborhood. Willows turned right past a cluster of California-style condominiums in pink stucco, then made another slow left, cruised through an area of light industry, and then on to the Arthur Laing Bridge and over the wide sweep of the Fraser River to the flatlands of Sea Island, the straight run to the airport.

There was a radar trap on Grant McConachie Way. Willows had been speeding since he'd dropped Parker off – he was late – but was saved from a ticket by the vagaries of the traffic flow.

He parked on the arrivals level, shuffled through his pockets and discovered he didn't have change for the meter. He lowered the sun visor. Old man Sinclair had been quick to agree to ferry them back to the "mainland", but slow to actually do it. He had a captive audience, and a disarming, oddly charming assumption that they'd be fascinated by a detailed verbal history of Eagle Island, cleverly and tantalizingly intertwined with every fat and juicy scrap of gossip he knew about Gerard and Iris Roth. The chance of a titbit of useful information kept Willows from cutting the old man short. As a result, he arrived at the airport almost twenty minutes late.

Fortunately, due to unexpected headwinds, Air Canada flight 857 was a full half-hour behind schedule.

Willows bought himself a foam container of airport coffee. He found the flight listing on a monitor and wandered over to the baggage carousel.

Now all he had to do was wait.

He'd just finished his coffee when the flight began blinking rapidly on the monitor, indicating that it had arrived. He began distractedly pinching small chunks of foam out of the cup and depositing the pieces inside it. Before long he had so thoroughly demolished it that there wasn't enough of it left to hold the pieces. He tossed the whole mess in a waste container. He could feel the tension in the back of his neck, his shoulders.

He checked the monitor. No mistake. The flight had arrived safely. By now his family must have deplaned.

A trickle of rumpled-looking, slightly disoriented travellers began to enter the carousel area through the arrivals gate. The trickle became a flood. It looked as if Sheila's plane, a 737, had been fully booked.

The first pieces of luggage slid down a metal chute on to the black rubber carousel.

Willows looked in vain for Sheila. He suddenly had a truly horrifying thought – what if he didn't recognize her?

A burgundy-colored leather suitcase that might've been Sheila's drifted past. Willows snatched at it, and missed, watched it disappear from view.

Annie came through the gate. She craned her neck, seemed to peer right at him. Willows waved violently but she didn't see him. A moment later she was swallowed by the crowd.

Sheila was close on her daughter's heels. Sean, always the straggler, brought up the rear. Willows' son had suddenly shot up – he'd grown taller than his mother.

Willows cursed under his breath as Sheila's suitcase went by.

Had the carousel accelerated or had he suddenly slowed down? His family had vanished. Where was Annie? The air stank of jet fuel. He was sweating buckets. His heart pounded. He should've taken off his coat . . .

He caught a flicker of movement and turned just as Annie shouted, "*Daddy!*" and threw herself into his arms. He hugged her tightly. She was wearing a new coat, and a beret. Her hair was longer, down past her shoulders. She looked up at him, eyes sparkling. "I just *knew* you'd be here!" she said.

A fat man in a raccoon coat pounced on a suitcase that looked like an oversized turtle, grunted in triumph and lunged away. Willows tried to make eye contact with Sheila. Sean loitered at a distance.

Willows moved towards his wife. He was smiling but terrified. The turbulent mix of apprehension and rage that had bubbled just beneath the surface for years was in danger of suddenly erupting. He felt overwhelmingly fragile. Suddenly, Sheila thrust a hand towards him as if to ward him away. He stared at her, shocked. Then, divining her intention, took her hand and solemnly shook it. Sean continued to hang back. Willows had to skirt a baggage cart to get to him. He put his arms around his son and hugged him, without response.

Willows said, "It's good to see you, son."

Sean grunted noncommittally. All domestic flights were non-smoking, but even so, his breath smelt of stale tobacco. Willows relinquished his grip and patted him awkwardly on the shoulder.

After greeting Willows, Sheila had gone directly to the carousel, where she had already retrieved several pieces of matching luggage in a coarse black fabric with a multitude of zippers. Willows asked her about the burgundy leather and she smiled for the first time, and told him, with obvious satisfaction, that it wasn't hers. She snatched another bulky suitcase from the passing parade and told him that was it.

Willows tried to take the largest bag from her but she was having none of it. She and Sean and Annie could handle their own baggage.

Willows felt as if he'd been punched in the heart. Well, what had he expected? He realized he hadn't given the reunion much thought, other than to hope everything would go smoothly. But what else could he have done? There were times when it was

133

necessary to give in to a sort of mindless optimism simply because it was the logical thing to do.

Willows led his entourage out to the unmarked Ford. The snow had stopped but as they crossed the parking lot it began again, fat white flakes that fell straight down out of the sky. No one except him seemed to notice. Having spent a couple of winters in Toronto, he supposed they'd become inured to inclement weather. He unlocked the trunk. While the luggage was being packed he unlocked all four doors and then climbed into the car and started the engine. He'd already learned to let them stow their own luggage, so he was making progress, wasn't he? He switched on the heater and windshield wipers.

The Ford rocked on its springs as Sheila slammed shut the trunk.

Willows had thought all three of them might scramble to squeeze into the back seat, but to his intense relief, Sheila chose to sit up front.

He waited until everyone had buckled up, then drove slowly through the parking lot, braked for a stop sign and merged with the flow of traffic heading back towards the city.

Sheila said, "I have to tell you, Jack, that I didn't expect you to be here to meet us."

Was he being complimented or lectured? He glanced at her but she was staring out the windshield and he couldn't read her face. He concentrated on the traffic.

"I want to make it clear to you that I very much resent the way you assumed it was perfectly all right to show up without warning, just . . . take over."

She'd started out all right, but now she was using that bitchy, pedantic, lecturing tone of voice that so quickly wore him down.

Willows said, "If you didn't want a ride in, Sheila, why did you leave your flight number on the answering machine?"

"So you'd know when to expect us."

Willows said, "Oh, I see. My mistake."

"No, Jack. It wasn't a mistake, it was a deliberate attempt to undermine my authority, to compromise my sense of independence."

In the back of the car, a match flared. Willows peered into the mirror. Sean slouched low in the seat, a cigarette dangling from the corner of his mouth.

134

Annie stared rigidly out the window. Everything in her face said she was determined not to get involved.

Wary of making a serious misstep, Willows glanced at Sheila. No help there. He was beginning to understand why she'd come back to Vancouver.

He pulled the Ford over to the side of the road and turned off the engine. Sean's leather jacket creaked as he sat up a little straighter. Willows said, "This is a non-smoking vehicle, Sean."

"So?"

"So, if you're going to smoke, you'll have to step outside."

"You're going to *leave* me here?"

"No, of course not. We'll wait."

Annie giggled softly.

Sean said, "Hey, shut it!"

Quietly but firmly, Willows said, "Don't talk to your sister like that. Or me. Or your mother. Now get rid of the cigarette or get out of the car."

Sean muttered a few words no one was intended to hear, pushed the door open and flung himself out of the car, slammed the door shut. A passing truck caught him in its headlights. The Ford's side window was streaked with melting snow; through the pebbled glass Sean looked like a weirdly distorted apparition as he paced back and forth in the slush, his cigarette glowing red.

Annie said, "Nice one, Daddy."

Willows turned and smiled. It was a comfort to know he had an ally.

The car door jerked open. Sean glared at him. He flicked the cigarette away, climbed inside, slammed the door and exhaled fiercely.

There was a lengthy pause and then the seatbelt clicked sharply. It was the last sound anyone made until Willows pulled up in front of his house.

He waited until everyone was out and then grabbed Annie and Sean's suitcases and strode briskly up the walk towards the house.

Behind him, the trunk slammed shut.

He unlocked the front door, stepped inside the house and deactivated the burglar alarm, switched on the hall light, turned up the thermostat. He'd left the door open and was acutely aware of Sheila struggling up the front steps. He made his way along the hall to the rear of the house and put Annie's and then Sean's suitcases in their rooms.

Sean said, "I need an ashtray."

Willows said, "When this was my parents' house, my dad had to smoke out on the porch. The same rule applies to you, son."

Annie disappeared into her room and softly shut the door.

Sean slammed his.

Willows would have to talk to him about that, put a stop to it before it became a habit. But not now, not now.

He found Sheila standing in the middle of the living room. She had the slightly off-balance air of someone who'd been dropped off at a station long after the last train had departed.

She said, "You've been busy."

Willows nodded. At one point after they'd split up he'd intended to sell the house, and had gone through it ruthlessly, piled a small mountain of unwanted valuables in the lane and paid a kid with a pickup truck to haul it all away to the recycling depot and dump. He'd done a lot of painting, as well. But that had been more to give himself something to do than anything else. Sheila had paid a kid with a ponytail serious money to paint the dining room walls flamingo pink. He'd used a big sponge, instead of a brush. Willows had bought a can of latex paint and spent a pleasant Sunday afternoon listening to a ball game while restoring the room to its original eggshell white.

He said, "Nothing major's been done. The kitchen is still in the kitchen. The dishes are still in the sink."

Sheila studied the couch. It and a matching chair had been recovered in her absence, but with identical material, in the original pattern. Something had changed but she wasn't at all sure what it was. Willows couldn't blame her. He glanced covertly around, trying to see the house through her eyes. It was amazing how many fiddly things he'd done, especially during the first year she was gone, simply to keep himself moving. He said, "I put the spare bed in the sewing room. I hope that'll be alright."

Sheila nodded. The "sewing room" hadn't seen needle or thread since Willows' mother had died. "That'll be just fine, Jack."

There were three bedrooms upstairs; the master and two smaller rooms. One of the rooms had been turned into a den. Willows did his reading there, and it was where he kept his trophies and citations. He kept his firearms there, as well, in a wall-mounted safe hidden behind a framed 25-meter pistol target with the bullseye shot out. The other room, which was the smallest of all, was used from time to time as a guest bedroom. Sheila

136

could have stayed there if she had wanted to, but he'd correctly guessed she'd prefer to sleep as far away from him as possible.

Sheila yawned hugely. She apologized automatically, and glanced at the fireplace mantel, did a double-take that was almost humorous.

She said, "Where's the clock?"

"In the basement."

"Why – is it broken?"

Willows said, "The ticking never stopped. It drove me crazy." He didn't see any point in adding that what drove him even crazier was the fact that the ticking was often the only sound in the house.

"Why didn't you just let it wind down?"

"I'll put it back, if you want."

"No, leave it in the basement."

Willows said, "I'm going to have a drink. Would you like a Scotch or a glass of wine?"

"I don't think that's a good idea, Jack. What time is it?"

Willows checked his watch. "Quarter to ten."

"Almost one o'clock, in Toronto. I'm tired, I'm going to bed."

Willows couldn't leave well enough alone. He said, "We've got to talk, Sheila. I don't have any idea what the hell's going on, and that isn't right."

"Not tonight, Jack."

He'd heard that line before, though in a completely different context. He grinned. Sheila gave him a look made up of equal parts pity and disdain, snatched up her suitcase and hurried lop-sidedly out of the room.

Willows went into the kitchen and poured two fingers of Cutty into a lowball glass. The freezer was working just fine but the ice-cube tray was empty. He sipped at the Scotch, decided he'd survive. He left the kitchen, strolled down the hall and knocked on Annie's door, and was given permission to enter.

His daughter had changed to a sloppy sweatshirt and faded jeans. She was sitting cross-legged on the bed with a magazine in her lap.

Willows said, "Got a minute?"

"Sure." Annie's eyes were red and puffy. Two years ago, Willows would have known what to do. Now, he wasn't so sure.

He said, "What're you reading?"

She shrugged. "A trashy magazine aimed at the heart of the easily exploited pre-pubescent female market."

"Trashy but popular, I bet. So tell me, what's Elvis been up to lately?"

Annie smiled. She snatched a tissue from her sleeve and blew her nose.

Willows said, "He out of the army yet?"

She nodded, blew her nose again and tossed the used tissue into the wastebasket next to her desk. "Did you clean my room?"

"Yeah."

"Thanks for the daffodils."

Willows smiled.

Sheila said, "You cleaned the whole house, didn't you, Daddy?"

"It needed it."

"Did you put flowers in Mummy's room?"

"Hers are on the dining room table."

"How is she supposed to know that?"

"She's a pretty smart cookie – she'll figure it out if she wants to."

"Daddy?"

"What is it, sweetheart?"

"Do you love her?"

Willows sat down on the edge of the bed, leaned over and kissed his daughter lightly on the tip of the nose, just as he'd always done. He said, "Yes I do," and gave her nose a tweak.

She said, "I knew you did. I just knew it."

Willows checked his watch. He said, "It's past one o'clock, Toronto time."

"But I'm not in Toronto any more."

Willows laughed. "True, but you've had a long day. Unless you don't mind sleeping in until noon tomorrow, I think it's probably a good idea to get some sleep."

"You're such a diplomat! I'm going to have a bath before I go to bed, okay?"

"Whatever you like, Annie." Willows had washed or sent to the dry cleaner all the clothing she'd left behind, including her flannel Bugs Bunny pyjamas, but she'd outgrown everything and would probably want to chuck it out or give it away.

She said, "Are you going to be here in the morning?"

He nodded. "You bet, but not for long. I'll be on my way downtown by eight-thirty at the latest."

"Gonna catch some bad guys?"

"Let's hope so."

138

"Catch any lately?"

"Sure, lots of them. But they were too small, so I threw them back. Night, honey. Sleep tight, don't let the bugs bite."

Annie smiled, remembering the old catechism. "See you in the funny papers."

Willows softly shut her door, and walked down the carpeted hall to Sean's room. He knocked lightly. There was no answer. He hesitated, knocked again, and called his son's name as he opened the door. The room stank of cigarette smoke. Sean lay on his back on the single bed that suddenly looked much too small for him. He was still wearing his black leather jacket. His skin was pallid. A lock of oily hair fell carelessly across his forehead. He didn't seem to be breathing. Willows' eyes darted wildly about as he looked for a hypodermic or empty pill bottle. He stepped into the room, turned on the bedside lamp.

Sean blinked. He sat up and then fell back, stared blankly up at the ceiling as he told his father to please go away and leave him alone.

Willows went back into the kitchen. His glass was empty. He poured himself another and drank most of it down and helped himself to a refill. He carried the glass upstairs, took a long hot shower and went to bed, sipped his drink as he read a book called *Five Summers*, about a family growing up on the seashore.

In the small hours of the night an unfamiliar sound yanked him from a shallow, restless sleep. He switched on the bedside light. His stainless Smith & Wesson lay snugly in the rich burnished leather of the clamshell holster he'd owned for fifteen years. Somewhere in the house, someone was crying softly.

A spring creaked as he eased out of bed and reached for his terrycloth robe.

He stood quietly in the bedroom doorway, listening. The crying had stopped.

Willows went back to bed, shrugged out of his robe and slipped under the blankets. There hadn't been time to locate the source of the crying. It could have come from anywhere in the house, and it might've been Annie or Sean or even Sheila who'd been weeping.

The way he felt, lying there all alone in the middle of the night, it could even have been him.

16

In the morning there was two inches of fresh white snow on the windowsill. Looking a little farther afield, Chris saw a quintet of fluffed-out rock pigeons loitering on one of the powerlines that ran down the lane past the apartment block. His feathered friends had a shifty-eyed look about them – or was he a victim of his own larcenous mindset? Chris turned and looked fondly down at Robyn. She was sleeping quietly. Her hair was rumpled and her lips were slightly parted. He knelt beside the bed and kissed her just below the ear. In her sleep, she swatted at him as if he was a small, essentially harmless insect, then rolled away from him, taking the bedclothes with her.

Chris stood up, stretched. He lingered for a moment, admiring the curve of her hip, and then made his way into the bathroom. He shut the door, urinated and flushed and ran the shower.

One of the things he liked best about weekends was that most of the apartment block's tenants slept late, so there was plenty of hot water, for a change.

He tried to think of a clever remark about his penchant for getting into hot water, but couldn't come up with anything smooth enough. He wondered what Robyn'd think of her blackmail scam when she woke up.

He was in the kitchen spooning coffee into the machine when she breezed past the open doorway on her way to the bathroom, and he was just getting to the bottom of his first cup when she sat down opposite him with her hair wrapped in a florescent orange towel.

Chris said, "Morning, sex kitten."

"That was then – this is now."

"What's that supposed to mean, I get to watch you dance with the vacuum cleaner, maybe wax the kitchen floor?"

"I'll wax your ass."

140

Chris got up and poured her a cup of coffee, sliced a poppyseed bagel in half and dropped it in the toaster. He got butter from the fridge and a plastic container of cream cheese from the cupboard, put everything down on the table in front of her.

The morning paper, folded in half lengthwise, lay on Chris's side of the table. Robyn frowned as she tried to make sense of the lead headline.

The toaster decided enough was enough, and forcibly ejected the bagel.

Chris retrieved the bagel, put it and a dollop of cream cheese on a plate, put the plate down on the table in front of Robyn. She stared grimly at the food until Chris snapped his fingers in exasperation and fetched her a knife.

As she spread cheese on the bagel, Robyn indicated the newspaper with her chin. "Any good news?"

"Some really good news," said Chris. He picked up the paper, pinched his nose and waved it above his head. "Extra! Extra! Read all about it . . ."

"You keep reading your lines like that, you'll be an extra all your life."

"Funny . . ."

Robyn drank some coffee. "So what's the good news – that I only dreamt we made love last night?"

Chris said, "Even better – I dreamed it. You weren't even there."

Robyn rolled her eyes, took a huge bite out of her bagel.

He said, "So am I an ace cook, or what?"

Robyn swallowed, drank some coffee. "Totally ace." She pointed at the newspaper. "You were saying . . ."

"Gerard Roth was murdered."

Robyn almost said who, but caught herself in time.

Chris said, "Front page stuff, Robyn. He drowned, but probably not in the whale pool. The new thinking is that somebody dumped him in there with the killers."

"So, you did see something?"

"Bet your bagel, sweetcheeks."

"Please don't talk to me like that. It's demeaning, and I love it, and it makes me feel so utterly helpless I want to puke."

Chris went over to the kitchen counter, stole the pot right out of Mr Coffee's arms and poured Robyn and then himself a refill.

She said, "What else is in the paper?"

141

Dramatically lowering his voice, Chris said, "The investigation continues."

"That's it?"

"Yeah, that's it. The news probably broke at the last second. The way the article's written, it's pretty vague. But the bottom line is, somebody bumped the guy off."

Robyn nodded, distractedly chomped the last of the bagel to paste. Chris thought it was typical of her not to want to read the newspaper article herself. A lot of stuff, what she considered boring, she was happy to leave up to him. He read the newspaper for awhile, the "Help Wanted" section first, to verify the situation was still hopeless, and then the comics.

Robyn wet the tip of her index finger and chased down and captured the last few crumbs of her breakfast. She said, "You're telling me the news is good because now we know for sure there's somebody out there that we can blackmail. Is that right, is that what you meant?"

"Yeah." He looked up the weather in the index and rattled the pages until he found what he was looking for.

High of minus three. Low of minus nine.

Robyn said, "You think I'm going to chicken out, don't you?"

"*Chicken out*? That's pretty darn sophisticated terminology, young lady. Exactly what do you mean? Act responsibly? Exercise a little common sense? Yeah, I kind of expected something along those lines."

"I still want to go through with it."

"No way."

"We can do it, Chris."

"Do what – risk our lives to save a few trees, or a hoot owl or whatever? No way. Forget it."

Robyn stood up, moved her hips as she walked around to his side of the table. Looking down at him, she told him in a low sexy voice to give her a little room. He pushed his chair back. She sat lightly on his lap and started nibbling his ear.

He said, "I'm impervious to that kind of behavior – you ought to know that by now."

Robyn kept nibbling.

Chris said, "Tell you what. If you promise to do the dishes for a week, you've got a deal."

Robyn kept right on nibbling.

Chris said, "Want to take a little after-breakfast nap? Settle the digestion, maybe get laid?"

Robyn said, "No way. I want to blackmail a murderer and make lots of money. You do all sorts of exciting things like drive too fast and go to auditions and mingle with the stars, and all I ever do is sit at a cheap desk, entering meaningless information into a stupid computer."

"Maybe we could compromise."

"How?"

"Engage in both activities. A little blackmail, a little sex . . ."

"Not necessarily in that order, I bet."

"Necessarily *not* in that order," said Chris. "Race you to the boudoir."

She put her arms around him. "Carry me."

Laughing, he said, "Don't I always?"

Despite the murder, it was business as usual at the aquarium. And despite the weather, business was good. The roads had been plowed, and the park was a study in white, the branches of the evergreens bent under the weight of snow.

Chris parked the Subaru, bought a ticket from the dispenser and tossed it on the dashboard, locked up. He and Robyn strolled hand in hand into the zoo area. There was a lineup at the popcorn stand. He and Robyn loitered by the sea otter pool, watching a fat, bright-eyed toddler in an electric pink snowsuit wriggle towards certain death while his dull-eyed mother rooted around in her purse for her matches.

Was the kid going to make the jump into the otter's gaping maws?

Nope. Mom lit up. Casually hauled junior back into her arms.

They strolled past the Bill Reid sculpture and up the steps and into the aquarium. Chris borrowed twelve dollars from Robyn and bought two tickets. "What'd you like to see first?"

"A fireplace and a waiter with a couple of hot rum punches."

"The only way you're going to get something to drink around here is in the washroom, slurping from the sink."

"How delightful."

"Let's check out the Amazon exhibit. It's so steamy in there, you'll feel right at home."

They followed the signs past a small tank filled with pint-sized alligators, through a wide, open doorway into a miniature rainforest. Robyn unzipped her jacket. The humidity was sauna-like and the temperature verged on uncomfortable. An artfully laid-out plank path tunnelled through the dense undergrowth. A bird so flamboyantly feathered it might've been a client of Liberace's tailor flitted giddily past, swerved and vanished in a shiny green mass of shrubbery.

Chris reached out and pinched a leaf big enough to roll into a canoe.

Robin said, "Plastic?"

Chris shook his head. "Nope. It's the real thing. Genuine vegetation. Makes you wonder – what'll they come up with next?"

They continued to wander through the rain forest. If you had a weakness for trees and vines and creepers, it was definitely the place to be. But for a hardcore downtowner like Chris it was just another part of the world were it was hard to snag a cab.

Possibly Robyn was thinking along similar lines, because she suddenly clutched Chris's arm and uttered a fetching shriek in the very best Fay Wray tradition. Expecting nothing less than a giant ape, he followed the line of Robyn's trembling finger to a huge cockroach that had decided to free-climb the north slope of his pants leg.

He knelt and flicked at it with his fingers, made solid contact.

The cockroach spread its eight legs slightly, as if intending to give him a hug.

Chris said, "Look at the size of the thing. If it ever got out on the highway, they'd have to put license plates on it." He shook his leg. The roach continued to laboriously gain altitude. He swiped at it with the edge of his hand. The insect dropped, skittered across the plank pathway and dove headlong into a bathtub-size body of brackish water. A large mouth with a small fish attached to it swam out of the coffee-colored depths and swallowed the cockroach all of a piece.

Chris said was, "Bon appetite, pal." The roach had gotten in over its depth, and paid a heavy price. But if there was a lesson to be learned, Chris apparently hadn't paid attention.

Thunder rolled overhead. The exhibit darkened and the air filled with a fine grey mist.

It was raining, kind of.

Chris said, "C'mon, let's get out of here before we start to rust."

What he was really worried about was getting out of there before something happened. He'd known Robyn a long time, close

144

to a year now, and was confident she'd soon lose interest in the bounty-hunting game and move on to something else. She was a frustrated joiner who hadn't joined anything lately. It was as simple as that. If she wasn't bored, they'd be safe at home in bed.

"Want to check out the whales?"

Robyn shook her head, no. "The heart and soul of this operation's got to be the gift shop." Already, she was moving away from him. Hurrying to catch up, Chris caught an unexpected glimpse of himself in an expanse of polished acrylic. He stopped and stared. A school of angelfish drifted through his skull. He looked harried, off-balance. Like someone who was forever trying to catch up.

In the gift shop, Robyn was talking animatedly to the two elderly women guarding the cash register. Both women were expensively dressed and sported plastic tags that said they were volunteers. There names were Judith and Katherine. Chris arrived just as Robyn said, "A hundred people work here? You're kidding me!"

But no, these women were not kidders.

Robyn said, "We were here last week, talking to a woman about . . . octopuses." Chris waggled his fingers in a mock-groping motion. Robyn ignored him. "She was so helpful. I wanted to send her a card of thanks. But I didn't get her name . . ."

The women leaned forward expectantly. Katherine, who was the taller of the pair, was wearing silver killer whale earrings and a matching necklace.

Robyn smiled up at Chris. What, what? Finally, he realized he'd been cued.

He said, "I'm not very good at describing people, but she was about medium height . . ."

"Blonde," said Robyn. "Wasn't she a blonde?"

Chris said, "Yeah, that's right."

Judith and Katherine mulled it over, thinking hard. After a moment Judith said, "Are we speaking of natural blondes?"

"Not necessarily," said Robyn.

"Well, then. I can think of three."

"Two," corrected Katherine promptly. "Yvonne's been on maternity leave for nearly two months, so it couldn't have been her."

"That's right, she is! I wonder how she's doing, I haven't heard a thing since she left."

145

"She had a girl. What did she call her . . . It was an old-fashioned name, quite lovely. *Charlotte McKenzie*. Doesn't that have a lovely, lilting ring to it? She sent a picture. It's on the notice board in the lunch room."

Robyn said, "Charlotte's a wonderful name. Tell me, was she named after the actress?"

The women looked at her, then burst into laughter. Katherine said, "We went off on a wee bit of a tangent, didn't we, dear? Let's see now . . . Who is it that works in the lab . . . Moira?"

"Mary," said Judith.

"She has beautiful hair. She wears it in a pageboy cut." She smiled warmly at Robyn. "Is it Mary you're thinking of?"

Robyn said, "Chris . . . ?"

Chris wrapped his octopus arms around Robyn and squeezed her tight. "I don't know. Could be. I spend so much time looking at you I hardly notice what anyone else looks like."

Robyn laughed and returned his hug, but one of her lively green eyes shouted *You* and the other screamed *Asshole*.

Chris said, "You said that there are two blondes working here?"

Katherine and Judith exchanged an uncertain look. Judith said, "I suppose it could have been Dr Carter."

"Carter?" said Robyn.

"Susan Carter."

"She's a research assistant," said Katherine, "and she does know an awful lot about octopuses and just about everything else you can think of."

"But," said Judith.

Katherine nodded in agreement.

Chris said, "But what?"

"She isn't overly friendly," said Judith. "Don't you dare tell her I said so, but it's true."

Katherine said, "It's not that she's rude, just that she doesn't seem to have much time for anyone. Always in a rush. If you say hello, she'll say hello right back to you. Like an echo. But that's it. Nothing extra."

"Such a busy young lady."

"Yes, she certainly is."

Judith nodded. "Busy, busy, busy."

Robyn said, "You've both been very helpful. Thank you *so* much."

"It was a pleasure talking to you, dear."

146

Chris said, "Does Dr Carter have an office in the building?"

"Yes, but you can't get to it from here. You'll have to go outside, towards the parking lot, and then walk down the sidewalk to the far end of the building."

"Towards the harbor," said Katherine.

"Door number five. The receptionist will help you."

"But if all you want to do is take a peek at her, just look in the last window before you get to the door."

"That's her office."

"If she's in, she'll be sitting at her desk in front of her computer."

"I wouldn't disturb her, though."

"Not if she's working."

"And she will be, you can be sure of that."

Chris smiled. "We'll find her. Thanks for your help."

"That's what we're here for," said Judith. "It's what volunteering is all about."

Chris thanked them again, and then he and Robyn wandered back to the viewing area. Chris looked out the window, down at the killer whale pool. He thought about the dolly. Would twenty-four hours under water destroy any fingerprints that might be on it? Had the cops found it yet? He said, "Now what?"

"What do you think, Mr Octopus?"

"I think we should go home and take a nap."

Robyn playfully whacked him with a mitten. "Dream on, loverboy."

"Okay, go home and have lunch and take a nap."

"Oh, I see. If you can't lure me away with sex, maybe a can of tomato soup will do it."

Chris said, "What do you want to do?"

"Locate Susan Carter. See if you recognize her."

"Naked would be best," said Chris.

Robyn gave him a look. She said, "Tell me about it. Isn't it always the way?"

147

17

Willows was at his desk by quarter to nine. No one else was in the office, although he had the cork bulletin board's display of several hundred mug shots to keep him company.

At home, he'd tiptoed around the kitchen in his stockinged feet as he made his morning coffee. The pot had burbled so vociferously that he was sure he'd wake the household. But if he had disturbed anyone they hadn't complained. Willows was solitary by nature. He'd lived by himself for more than two years. Suddenly the house seemed crowded. It was going to take a bit of time, getting used to the mob.

He glanced across the aisle to the clutter on Eddy Orwell's desk. All those photographs of his wife and kid; Eddy had only been married a few years but his relationship was already falling apart. Well, that's the way things were, for cops. The job took so much out of you that you had nothing left for your family. For the uniformed constables, it was the shift work that did them in. Detectives had another problem – the lengthy and unpredictable hours they worked played havoc with their family lives. Either way, in uniform or civvies, all you saw was the rotten side of the log. A lot of good cops looked down the road, didn't like what they saw, and took early retirement or quit. Some made a conscious decision to switch off their emotions, deal with the world as if it was nothing but a tangled heap of machinery. Others hit the booze.

Orwell had started messing with fast women with slow minds. It wasn't an original solution but it was a popular one.

Willows slid open his desk drawer and took out his personal phone directory. He slid the plastic indicator arrow down to the YZ section and pressed the metal bar. The directory flipped open. Annie and Sean smiled up at him from their two-inch-square school photographs. He leaned back in his chair. Parker had lent him a pair of scissors so he could cut the margins off the pictures to make them fit on the index card.

That had been more than three years ago. The adhesive tape holding the pictures in place had yellowed with age, curled around the edges.

Sean and Annie had been children when the pictures were taken. They were something else now; neither adults nor children, but somewhere in between. Especially Sean. The boy's narrow, bony face seemed permanently twisted by rage. Willows hoped his son was angry at something in particular. He'd seen what could happen when a kid made up his mind that life wasn't worth living.

Down at the far end of the squadroom there was the scratch of a key in the lock. The door opened and Homer Bradley limped in. He hadn't complained, but it was clear that the cold, damp weather was playing havoc with his rheumatism. He pocketed his keys, saw Willows and nodded in a friendly way.

Willows stole a last quick look at his children, snapped shut his telephone index and put it away in his desk.

Bradley, approaching, said "Morning, Jack."

"Morning, Inspector."

"Anything new –" Bradley dropped his voice to a growl and did a fair imitation of Marlon Brando in *The Godfather*" – on duh nude dude got took for a swim wit' duh fishes?"

"Not yet, Inspector."

"But you're working on it, right?" Bradley gave Willows a fatherly pat on the shoulder and headed towards his office.

Willows' phone rang shrilly. He picked up. Parker told him she was calling from the RCMP forensic laboratory on Alberni Street. The water in Gerard Roth's lungs had come from the big saltwater tank inside the aquarium, the tank with the black-tailed sharks.

Willows remembered it.

Parker said, "Roth was dead when he went into the whale pool, Jack."

Willows gripped the telephone a little tighter as he felt that familiar adrenalin rush. He'd known Roth was murdered.

Farley Spears entered the squadroom. He shrugged out of his overcoat and tossed it on his chair, walked up to Orwell's desk and used a heavy black felt pen to draw Groucho Marx moustaches on each and every picture of Orwell's wife and son. He saw the look on Willows' face and said, "It's on the glass. It'll wipe off."

Parker said, "Somebody dumped him in the whale pool, Jack.

149

It wasn't the tide that put him there." There was some background noise at her end, and then she said, "Now the bad news."

"What's that?"

"Read the *Province* yet?"

"Haven't gotten around to it."

"Roth made the front page. Big headline, gigantic color photograph. The article's only about fifty words. There's nothing concrete, but it hints strongly that he was murdered."

"Who got the byline?"

"Nobody, Jack. The piece's uncredited."

Willows chair creaked. He sighed heavily. Popeye had a fatal weakness – once he'd had a few free drinks poured down his throat he was prone to idle conjecture. Willows said, "Want me to pick you up?"

"I've got a car."

"I'll meet you at the aquarium. Twenty minutes?"

"See you there."

Willows said, "But not in the building. Outside, by the popcorn stand."

"Forget it – it's too cold."

"In your car, then. What're you driving?"

"A dirty brown Pontiac equipped with all the usual optional accessories. Blackwall tires. Mini hubcaps. Twin antennae. Manually operated windows. Don't worry, Jack. You'll know it when you see it."

"Twenty minutes," said Willows. He heard somebody with a very deep voice ask Parker if she'd like another cup of coffee, or maybe a drink somewhere.

Parker said, "Gotta run, Jack."

Willows flinched away from a sudden earful of hearty masculine laughter.

Parker hung up.

Willows walked the length of the squadroom to Bradley's office, knocked and walked inside, and filled his inspector in on recent events.

Bradley said, "I'm assigning Orwell and Spears to the case. Viney and Wilkinson are in court for the next couple of days, but the minute they're done I'm going to put them on it too." Willows' eyes darkened. Bradley said, "Don't fight it, Jack. You've got a hundred alibis to verify, and that's just the full-time staff. If I can find a couple more bodies, you'll get them too."

150

Fifteen minutes later, Willows found Parker's dirty brown Pontiac pointed nose out in the parking lot next to the aquarium. He pulled in next to her, turned off the engine and climbed out of the Ford.

Parker's door was locked. He knuckled the glass and she leaned across the seat to let him in.

Willows hurriedly got into the Pontiac, shut the door, rubbed his hands and held them out to the blast of hot air coming from the dashboard vent.

"Cold out there, huh?"

He nodded.

Parker said, "The preliminary autopsy report's being dictated even as we speak. There's no doubt in the coroner's mind that Roth was murdered. Somebody drowned Roth in the aquarium and then dragged him outside and dumped him in the whale pool."

"Was Roth beaten before he died?"

"It's impossible to say. Having a leg ripped off was the least of Gerard's problems. The killers really scrambled him. He suffered internal damage the coroner described as cataclysmic. Given a choice, he said he'd rather try to put Humpty Dumpty back together again."

Willows said, "We've got to have another chat with Iris. She's plenty big enough to slamdunk Roth. And she's already told us she knew he was cheating on her. She must have resented his sexual antics and the tight financial control he kept over her. Roth had a master key to the aquarium complex. He probably kept a spare at home. Even if he didn't, Iris must've had ample opportunity to make a copy of the original."

Parker said, "Okay, she's a suspect."

"You don't think so?"

"Yeah, I do. But let's not be so quick to rule out the rest of the world. What about Sweeting?"

"Drowning sounds perfect for him. He wouldn't have to get his hands dirty."

"Or maybe he and Iris did it together. It's a long haul from where Roth was murdered to where he was found. Getting him all the way from the shark tank to the whale pool would be a tough job for someone working alone – man or woman."

Willows said, "True, but that's where the missing dolly comes in."

151

Parker nodded, acknowledging Willows' point. Five identical dollies had been rounded up by Constable Lambert. All five were liberally sprinkled with fingerprints but devoid of any traces of flesh or blood or other evidence indicating that the dolly might have been used to transport a naked corpse. Naturally not all the aquarium's staff had agreed to be voluntarily fingerprinted.

There was general agreement among the staff that a sixth dolly was missing. A hunt was underway.

Willows told Parker about Homer Bradley's decision to assign two more teams of detectives to the case.

Parker said, "Good, that'll give us the time we need to concentrate on the two people who knew Roth best – his wife and Anthony Sweeting."

"And Susan Carter," said Willows. "Who performed the autopsy?"

"Christy Kirkpatrick."

"Yeah?" Willows didn't try to hide his scepticism. Christy Kirkpatrick was notorious for the rigidity of his scheduling. Nobody butted in for free.

Parker said, "I had to get on the phone – he was standing there listening in – and use my credit card to buy him a pair of tickets to the Canucks–Kings game. It cost me almost sixty dollars, Jack."

Willows smiled. "Bill me."

"Count on it." Parker was no hockey fan, but in order to get Kirkpatrick to fit Roth's autopsy into his crowded schedule she'd also had to promise to accompany the old goat to the game. Willows owed her more than he knew, but she'd make sure he found out about it, sooner or later. She turned off the ignition, opened her door and got out of the Pontiac.

Sweeting was expecting them, and they were already late.

As they walked down the sidewalk that skirted the east wall of the aquarium complex, Parker said, "How do you want to handle this?"

"Got any ideas?"

"Not really. I think we better go easy on him – he seems like the kind, you push him too hard, he's going to roll up into a tight little ball and hibernate."

Willows averted his head, grinned at a snow-clad azalea bush. Parker was always telling him to behave himself, keep a smile on his face and his hands in his pockets. But the reason the partnership worked so well was because the two of them instinctively

152

attacked from radically different angles. Whether Claire knew it or not, she was the sugar coating on his poison pill.

Parker pushed open the glass door numbered five. She held the door for Willows, smiled at the receptionist lurking behind the curving wall of blonde oak veneer. The receptionist reached for her phone. She said, "You're here to see Dr Sweeting?"

Willows said, "Save your nickel – he's expecting us."

He and Parker walked briskly down the sombre, beige-carpeted hallway to Tony Sweeting's office. The door was open. Sweeting was standing by the window, watching a fat man in coveralls balance precariously on a stepladder as he strung Christmas lights on a small spruce tree overhanging the concrete retaining wall.

Parker knocked lightly on the doorframe.

Sweeting turned, saw them and smiled. He said, "I thought you'd forgotten me."

"Never," said Parker, returning his smile.

Sweeting indicated the man on the ladder. "I should send somebody out there to give him a hand, shouldn't I, before he breaks his stupid neck."

Willows said, "Go ahead. We'll wait."

Sweeting started towards the telephone on his fish-shaped desk and then made an abrupt gesture of dismissal. "Ah, to hell with it. *Qué sera, sera.* You're absolutely sure Gerard was murdered?"

Parker said, "We're sure."

Sweeting's shoulders slumped. He went over to his desk and collapsed in the leather chair. He said, "I saw his picture in the *Province*. It was a real shock, let me tell you. Brought it all home, know what I mean?"

Parker nodded.

"Who'd want to kill him?" said Willows.

"I have no idea."

Willows said, "Why not? I thought you and Gerard were friends."

"We got along. As I said earlier, Dr Roth did good work and I respected him for it. However, I thought I'd made it clear that we were far from the best of buddies. I mean, he wasn't exactly what you'd call a warm person. He certainly didn't confide in me."

"Did he have any close friends that you know of, anyone at all?"

"I'm afraid not."

153

"There was no one here at the aquarium that he was close to?"

"Not a soul." Sweeting hesitated. "You've talked to Susan, I suppose?"

Parker said, "Dr Carter?"

"Yeah, Susie."

"We spent some time with her."

"Couldn't she help you?"

Parker hesitated.

Willows said, "Do your recall where you were Friday night?"

"You mean – when Gerard died?"

"Was killed," said Willows, correcting him.

"I spent the entire night at home."

"With your wife."

"I'm not married."

"Boon companion? Significant other?"

"I was alone."

Willows said, "No kidding, I didn't know people still did that."

"Just me and my shadow." Sweeting yanked open the top drawer of his desk. He twisted the foil wrap from a roll of breath mints, popped several into his mouth and chewed furiously. "Am I a prime suspect?"

"Certainly not," said Parker.

"Unless," added Willows, "there's a motive floating around that we don't know about."

"I had no reason to kill Gerard." Sweeting balled up the foil and placed it carefully in the breast pocket of his suit jacket. He said, "Let me amend that. What I should say is that I had no more reason to kill Gerard than anyone else who knew him."

Willows said, "Well, to tell the truth, I'm not too surprised." He smiled. "You don't seem like the kind of guy who'd bump someone off just for the fun of it."

"That's very gratifying. Would you like a breath mint?"

"Not while I'm working, thanks."

Sweeting smiled at Parker. "You two must have a lot of fun together."

"An awful lot of fun," said Parker, smiling back.

Willows said, "You saw Dr Roth virtually every day, isn't that true?"

"Unless he was in the field."

"Did he do much field work?"

"Not really. He'd be gone, at most, two or three months out of the year."

"Had he been on a field trip recently?"

"Not since late August."

"Three months ago."

Sweeting counted it out on his fingers. He nodded.

Willows said, "Had you noticed a change in Dr Roth's behavior during the past few months?"

"How do you mean?"

"Well, for example – did he seem unduly depressed?"

"Not from my perspective. Unduly cheerful, maybe."

"He was a happy fella?"

"He was so happy, he could've been in love."

Willows went over to the window and looked out. The lights had been plugged in and the man in the coveralls was leaning far into the tree, making minor adjustments. There were only four colors – red and green and yellow and blue.

Parker said, "Dr Roth didn't seem tense, or agitated in any way?"

"Well, at times, sure. It's the twentieth century, right? But most of the time he was pretty much a smile in his eyes, song on his lips kind of guy."

"Would you be aware of it, if Dr Roth wasn't getting along with another member of your staff?"

"I think so. In fact, sure, why not?" Sweeting devoured another breath mint. "Gerard would have given me an earful if something was bothering him. As I've said, he was an aggressive personality." Sweeting ate another mint. "I'd even go so far as to say he was most content when he was upset about something."

Parker said, "You're telling me he liked to sail when the wind was up."

"Yes, exactly."

"But nothing was bothering him – that you know of – when he died."

"That's true, I guess. Although if you're referring to the actual moment of death, I bet all sorts of stuff was nagging at him."

Willows turned away from the window. He said, "We'd appreciate it if you kept this discussion confidential, Dr Sweeting."

"Can't say I blame you." Sweeting gobbled the last of the mints.

Parker said, "Are you sure you were alone the night before last?"

155

"Fairly sure."

Parker softened her voice. "Dr Roth's death has been a terrible shock to you, hasn't it?"

"Yeah, kind of."

"Pretty stressful?"

"I'll say."

"Would you mind telling me what medication you're taking?"

Sweeting fumbled in his jacket pocket, came up with an orange plastic vial. "Valium." He kept digging. "And these cute little blue and white babies. Which I do not hesitate to highly recommend, especially when washed down with a shot of single malt."

Outside, the fat man shouted an oath and disappeared into the spruce tree.

"Oops!" Anthony Sweeting gave Parker a slack-jawed, foolish grin. He slumped in his chair. His eyes sagged shut. He began to snore.

Parker said, "Now what – Susan?"

"Yeah, let's talk to Susan. If she's coherent." Willows popped an imaginary mint in his mouth, chewed with great relish.

"May I have one of those?"

"Unfortunately, that was the last one."

Susan Carter's office door was locked. Willows hit it with his fist but got no response.

Parker said, "Step aside, Jack. Let me show you how it's done."

"Want me to hold your purse?"

"No, but I'd appreciate it if you held your tongue."

Parker slapped the door hard with her open hand, as if it were a recalcitrant witness. There was no response. Frustrated, she rattled the knob.

Willows said, "Still locked, huh?"

At the receptionist's desk they learned that Susan Carter was ill and not expected to return to work for several days.

Willows said, "Whatever she's got, I wonder if it's contagious."

"Nowadays," said Parker, "isn't everything?"

18

There was a payphone next to the dreary, crumbling ruins of the old monkey house, now occupied by a band of wallabies. Chris couldn't understand why the Parks Board had bothered to acquire the animals. To his mind they were nothing but pint-sized kangaroos, lethargic, lacking in charm, morose and pathologically introspective.

He thought for a humiliating moment that he'd have to bum a quarter from Robyn, but luckily found some loose change in his jeans pocket.

In Vancouver, the telephone company has the heart and soul of a dehydrated walnut, and a policy of refusing to provide outdoor pay telephones with phone books. The official rationale is that vandals torch the books, using them to fry the phone booths. But the truth is, that like any large bureaucracy, they take great satisfaction from inconveniencing their customers.

Chris fed three nickels and a dime into the phone's maw, dialled up an operator and asked for Susan Carter's number.

The operator asked him for an address. Improvising, Chris said he'd lost it, chuckled grimly into her ear.

He was told an address was required.

Chris told her to hang on a minute, gave her the address of the warehouse in Gastown where he'd gone to audition.

No Susan Carter there.

He tendered the address of the Subaru dealership where he and Robyn had bought her car. No Susan there, either.

Chris gave the operator the address of a public health clinic on Fourth Avenue.

Still no luck.

He started to give her his dentist's address. Robyn reached past him and disconnected. His nickels and dime jingled merrily into the coin return slot.

Collecting his change, Chris said, "What's up?"

"My blood pressure. Is this how you like to spend your time, wasting everybody else's?"

Chris said, "Hey, relax. I was just trying to get my money's worth – I didn't know they gave refunds!"

Robyn laughed despite herself.

Chris said, "Joy joy. Happy happy. Smile and the world smiles with you. Frown and you frown alone. Know what we need?"

"Tell me, big boy."

"A phone book. And I'm pretty sure I know where we can find one."

"You do, huh?"

Chris nodded. He assembled his face into a sneaky, underhanded look, got it right the first time.

Playing it straight, Robyn said, "Maybe you better show me what you've got in mind."

"Can do, babe."

In a hurry to get out of the park, Chris took the shortcut that skirted the miniature train and rose gardens, then eased into the turgid flow past Lost Lagoon. In the grey light of day, the Christmas tree on the fountain had a sad and bedraggled look about it.

Robyn said, "They should use brighter lights, lots of tinsel."

"And put an angel on top."

"If they can find one."

As soon as the Subaru's cabin warmed up, Chris pulled off his black leather gloves with the rabbit fur lining.

He rested his hand lightly on Robyn's thigh.

She slapped him lightly. "Cut it out."

"You want me to put the leather back on, that what you're saying?"

"No, I'm saying I want you to pay attention to the road."

In an off-key voice, Chris sang, "I'm a trucker and I don't mean maybe, rather ride the road than fondle my baaaby . . ."

Robyn guided his hand back to her jean-clad leg. "Just stop singing, okay?"

"For now," said Chris. "Until I can free up this other hand."

Back at the apartment, Chris made lunch while Robyn perused the phone book. There were no listings under the name Susan Carter, but there were eighteen S. Carters, six of whom lived in the city.

Robyn dialled the first number. The phone rang three times and then a young-sounding woman picked up, said hello. Robyn

158

said, "Is this the Susan Carter who works at the aquarium?"

Yes, it was.

Robyn hesitated. Now what? She hadn't given it much thought, actually.

Susan Carter wanted to know who she was talking to.

Robyn tried to think of a name – any name but her own. All she could think of was Smith. Mumbling like a fool, she said she was a reporter.

Susan Carter hung up.

From the kitchen, Chris shouted that lunch was on the table.

Susan lived in the West End, on Davie Street. Robyn circled the address with a black makeup pencil. A tinny, computer-generated voice emanating from the phone advised her to hang up and please try to call again. She disconnected.

Chris had made toasted-cheese sandwiches and tomato soup. Robyn sat down at the table. She watched him crush a handful of Stone Wheat Thins, drop the crackers into his soup and poke them under with his finger.

He bent over his bowl, began to eat.

Robyn picked up her spoon. She balanced it on the rim of her bowl.

Chris said, "Something wrong with the soup?"

"No, it sounds delicious."

"Add milk, stir well and heat carefully. What could go wrong?"

Robyn shrugged.

Chris lowered his head over his bowl. He said, "So eat up, before it gets cold."

Robyn pushed away from the table. She went over to the sink, pulled open a drawer and chose the sharpest knife that she could find. Chris continued to burrow into his soup. She sat down at the table and quartered her sandwich.

"Sorry about that." Chris grinned. The soup had stained his teeth red. A scarlet rivulet dribbled down his chin.

Robyn kept chopping up the sandwich, cutting it into smaller and smaller pieces.

Chris said, "Now what?"

"I talked to her. I mean, she spoke to me."

"Yeah? What'd she say?"

Robyn tried her soup. It was surprisingly good.

Chris said, "You mutilated my sandwich because the murderous bitch said something rotten to you, am I right?"

159

Robyn glanced down at the mess on her plate. She looked shocked. Or maybe just bemused. "I did that?"

"You and your butcher knife."

"Well . . ."

"So . . . what'd she say?"

"She said, 'Hello'."

Chris shook his head, miming amazement. "You phoned her and she said hello? Wow! No wonder you're feeling a little shaky."

"Don't be a smartass." Robyn picked up the smallest piece of her sandwich, ate it and moved on to the next.

Chris thought about it for a while, finally said, "It was a shock, wasn't it? You heard her voice. She spoke to you. All of a sudden she turned into a real person."

Robyn nodded, kept eating.

"And now you want to back off. Leave her alone. Forget the whole thing."

Like a very attractive toreador lining up a doomed bull, Robyn pointed with her index fingers at the remains of her sandwich. Then she pointed at her mouth. Sign lingo.

While he waited for her to finish chewing, Chris noticed he'd left a burner on. He went over to the stove and turned it off, then made his way down to the other end of the counter and stood a bottle of red wine on end. Robyn watched him but kept silent. He rummaged around in a kitchen drawer until he found the corkscrew.

"Are you planning to open that?"

"It's the weekend. The sun's past the yard-arm. I'm thirsty."

"Answer the question, please."

Chris popped the cork. "Care to join me?"

"Not particularly."

"Maybe I should rephrase the question. Would you like a glass of wine?"

Grilled cheese was good, but greasy. Robyn licked her fingers clean. She said, "Yes, please."

Chris poured two glasses of wine. He put a glass down in front of Robyn and set the bottle down between them, raised his glass in a toast.

"To us."

Robyn smiled. "To you, and to me." They touched glasses and drank. She smiled.

"What's so funny?"

160

"Nothing."

"I could tickle it out of you!"

"Better not try."

Chris made as if to crawl across the table towards her.

Robyn said, "Remember Linda?"

"Should I? Is it safe?"

"She and that guy she was going out with, the bicycle courier . . ."

"Donny."

"They rented that place up on Tenth Avenue . . ."

"The duplex."

"Right, and they had a housewarming party, forty or fifty people, and somebody proposed a toast and then we all threw our glasses in the barbecue . . ."

"That was the outside crowd," said Chris. "The inside mob demolished the microwave."

"You're kidding – really?"

"Yeah, really."

Robyn said, "What happened to them? Are they still together?"

Chris's face suddenly sobered up. He said, "Donny jumped a red and got wiped by a punk in a pickup truck. I thought you knew."

"Run over by a truck – was he badly hurt?"

Chris poured them both a little more wine. "Yeah, he was almost killed. See, he got tangled up in his bike chain and dragged across the intersection by his . . ."

"His what?"

Chris glanced circumspectly down at his lap.

Robyn said, "Oh my God."

"The surgeons did what they could, but there were parts of Donny that were never found." Chris emptied and refilled his glass. "*Important* parts."

Robyn said, "Poor Linda. How awful for her."

Chris nodded in agreement. He said, "That's life, I guess." He leaned over the table and turned Robyn's hand palm up and softly kissed her. He kissed her again and seductively whispered, "No one knows what the future holds. Life's best lived to the fullest, my love."

Robyn nodded sorrowfully and then glanced up and caught the glint of lust in Chris's eye. She slammed her glass down on the table. "You really are a grade-A asshole, aren't you!"

161

Chris admitted it, happily confessed he'd say or do whatever it took to get her into the sack.

"Even the dishes?"

"But not the pots."

In bed, Robyn suddenly turned serious. She told him about the eighteen possibles, how she'd narrowed it down to six and struck paydirt on the first number she tried.

"What'd she sound like?"

"Stuffed up. Congested. Like she had a cold or had been crying."

"Remorse," said Chris.

Robyn said, "That's right, that's what it must have been. Remorse. She sounded guilty as hell, now that I think about it."

Chris raised himself up on an elbow so he could see her face more clearly. She didn't seem to be kidding. He said, "You're serious, aren't you?"

She nodded. He stroked her golden skin, ran his thumb along the smoothly curving white line that marked the southernmost boundary of her bathing suit. Summer was long gone. Her tan was fading fast. He kissed her throat. Summer was a memory but Robyn still tasted of the ocean: salty and warm.

She turned into him. "What're you thinking about?"

"August – the sexiest month of them all."

"And what page of the calendar are we on now?"

"November."

Robyn laughed. "I should have known."

Chris turned his back on her. He said, "Now I know how Donny felt when he came out of the anaesthetic and the surgeons told him he was going to have to learn how to ride side-saddle."

Robyn giggled and said, "She probably doesn't have much money anyway."

"Susan Carter? Probably not."

"We should forget about blackmailing her. Just drop it. Tell the police what we know and let them take over. It was a pretty stupid idea, if you stop to think about it."

"My sentiments exactly," said Chris.

"But at the same time, I don't *want* to quit. The truth is, I don't care if she has any money or not. I just want to . . . keep on going."

Chris said, "I've been thinking. Now we know where she lives, maybe I should break into her apartment. That seems like the best way to find out what kind of person she is."

"Please don't tell me that all your life, if you wanted to get to know some woman a little better, the first thing you did was ransack her apartment."

Chris moved cautiously across to Robyn's side of the bed. "That's exactly right. Want to know what I did next?"

"Actually, I don't think I do."

"Kissed her breasts."

"What a cheap obvious trick."

"But it worked."

Robyn pushed his head away. "Those must've been the good old days, eh sport?"

Chris moved effortlessly into the feeble, antiquated voice he'd used in a lucrative voice-over for a product that cleaned and disinfected your teeth when you weren't using them. He said, "I suspect they were the good old days. Hard to recall 'em, lately. Everything's kind of all mixed up and hazy-like. Know what I mean?"

Robyn laughed and reached out to him, took him in her golden arms and pulled him close.

Squinting down at her, Chris said, "You sure are a pretty young thing, ain'tcha?"

They made love again, slowly and carefully, getting it just right, and then Robyn snuggled into his arms and drifted off. Chris stared up at the ceiling for a while, then doubled up his pillow and read a couple of chapters of a paperback. Then he must've dozed off for an hour or two, because somehow the book ended up on the floor and dusk was settling over the city. He happened to glance out the window. Four of the five rock pigeons had gone. The remaining bird, tiny feet still clamped to the power line, hung head down with its wings spread wide.

A gust of wind raced down the alley, blew swirling clouds of snow off the roofs. The frozen corpse swayed slightly, and was still.

19

Parking was always tough in the city's overpopulated West End district, but Willows managed to find a spot in a loading zone in an alley. He let Parker out of the unmarked Ford and then pulled up against the graffiti'd flank of a building, turned off the engine and got out of the car and locked up.

An orange tabby with a pronounced limp and most of its left ear missing slunk out from behind a dumpster. The animal eyed the two detectives with the air of a jaded beggar sizing up a prospective customer. Meowing plaintively, it picked its way across the landscape of ice and snow, rubbed against Willows' leg. Willows knelt to stroke the cat's wide, blunt head. It pressed against him, purring furiously. He scratched vigorously behind a bristly nub of scar tissue – all that remained of its ear. The cat's ringed tail whipped at the snow. It jumped suddenly into Willows' lap.

The creature had bright green eyes, good teeth, a great personality. But it wasn't wearing a flea collar and the fleas knew it. Willows ran his hand along the length of the cat's body, felt the bones lurking beneath the fur. The tabby was big, but it wasn't fat.

He slipped his hand under its belly and put it down on the snow. The cat gave him a shocked look.

Parker said, "Look at him. He's been jilted, and knows it."

Willows stood up.

The tabby followed them as far as the mouth of the alley and then, still mewing, fell back.

Susan Carter lived on the fourteenth floor of a drab concrete highrise on the corner of Davie and Bidwell. The wide brass-trimmed glass doors leading to the block's cramped lobby were kept locked to deter lazy door-to-door salesmen, thieves and vagrants, maybe even cops. Willows ran his finger down the list of tenants until he found Susan's name, dialled her apartment number on the intercom. The machine emitted a raucous buzzing sound, like a crow with laryngitis.

Willows dialled her apartment again. Nothing.

Parker said, "Maybe she's sleeping."

"Or watching TV or filing her nails." Willows tried a third time, then buzzed the manager.

Following another pause a disembodied androgynous voice said, "Yeah, who is it?"

Willows identified himself, explained the situation.

"She don't answer her buzzer?"

"Don't answer it one little bit," said Willows, affecting the patois.

Parker gave him a look.

The voice said, "Probably she ain't home."

"Yeah, probably. But we'd like to check it out."

"Got a warrant?"

Willows said he hoped it wasn't necessary.

There was a pause and then the unseen woman told him she couldn't open up the apartment unless he had a search warrant. The law was the law. If he really was a cop, he ought to know better.

Parker said, "A colleague of Miss Carter's recently died. She called in sick at work. We're concerned about the general state of her health. We just want to make sure she's okay."

"What's that?"

"This is Detective Claire Parker speaking."

"No, what the hell's a *colleague*?"

Willows said, "Tell you what, let us into the lobby and we'll take it from there."

Raucous laughter, fading into silence.

Parker said, "She hung up on you, Jack."

Willows had to agree. He wondered what was wrong with him, that he didn't recognize the symptoms after all this time. The nearest payphone was a block away. He asked Parker if she wanted to wait in the car.

"I better not. I might be tempted to shoot that poor starving cat, put it out of its misery."

They trudged down Davie, wary of the patches of ice and trampled snow that made the sidewalk treacherous.

Parker said, "Isn't there a city bylaw requiring landlords and shop owners to clear the sidewalk in front of their premises?"

"I think that might be the exact wording," Willows said, grinning. "It sure has the right tone."

He unbuttoned his overcoat so he could get at his sports jacket, found a quarter. He wiped the pay phone's mouthpiece on his sleeve, dropped the coin and dialled.

An operator new to the job picked up on the first ring. Willows gave him Susan Carter's address, was told to wait. The computer kicked in. An eerily human voice gave him Susan's number. By then Parker had notebook and pen in hand. Willows repeated the number aloud and she wrote it down. He hung up. The quarter rattled in the coin return. He dug it out and used it to dial Susan's number.

The phone rang twice and then Susan Carter picked up and said hello.

Willows identified himself. He told her he and Parker were only a block away, and would like to talk to her about Gerard Roth's death.

Susan said, "You're a block away?" She sounded a little confused, as if she had trouble believing him.

Willows said, "I buzzed, but you didn't answer. The super wouldn't let me in. I'm calling from a payphone at Denman and Davie."

There was a pause. He thought he could hear her breathing, but wasn't sure because the light had changed and there was a noisy rush of traffic.

"Miss Carter?"

"I'm not at my apartment. I have call forwarding. I'm . . ."

Willows felt himself losing control, the situation slipping away from him. Cutting in, he said, "Where are you now?"

"Gerard's. I'm at Gerard's."

"The house on Eagle Island?"

"No, of course not. His apartment – the condo."

Willows said, "You'd better give me the address." He gestured to Parker, and she passed him her notebook and pen. He wrote down Roth's address, thanked Susan Carter, told her they'd be arriving in twenty minutes or less and hung up.

They walked in silence back to the Ford. Willows unlocked his door, got behind the wheel and started the car. He pulled into the middle of the alley and reached across to open Parker's door. As she got in he said, "Straight up Davie and then left on Homer and right on Nelson and over the bridge. What'd you think?"

166

Parker fastened her seatbelt. She said, "Sounds good to me, Jack," and slammed shut her door.

The Ford fishtailed as Willows gunned it towards the mouth of the alley.

Gerard Roth's condominium was located in the eight-hundred block West 7th, on the trendy north-facing slope above False Creek. Fifteen years ago the area had been a mix of light industry, warehouses and falling-down drunk clapboard houses. Now it was a mass of three-storey apartments; wall-to-wall stucco in a thousand shades of pink and green. Prices started at about a hundred and ten thousand and went up to twice that amount. The area was convenient to the downtown core. If you had a view, the scenery was terrific. But Willows had always thought the area somehow looked like a gestating slum.

As they turned up Davie, he said as much to Parker.

"The whole world's a gestating slum. Or you could say it's nothing but an over-tended graveyard. Depends on your attitude, doesn't it?"

Ice crunched under the tires as Willows pulled over to the curb, braked. Parker had a bit of an attitude herself, and he thought he knew why. He said, "Look, there's something I think I better explain. On the way in from the airport, Sheila and I hardly said a word to each other. She spent the night in the guest bedroom. She was still sleeping when I left the house this morning. Claire, I don't have any idea what's going on. I don't know any more than you do what's on her mind."

"She's your wife."

"No she isn't."

"Yes she bloody well is."

"*Legally*," said Willows. He thumped the wheel as if he'd made a crucially important point.

"Did you sleep with her?"

"Hell no."

"Did she ask you to sleep with her?"

"No, Claire, she didn't. In fact she hardly said a word to me."

"She will, if she wants to stay."

Willows nodded sagely. He was confused. Was Parker predicting an onslaught of meaningless sex, or meaningful dialogue?

She said, "Does she want to stay?"

"I have no idea."

167

Parker said, "I want you to invite me to dinner this evening. After the kids go to bed maybe we can work out what everybody else is up to."

Willows said, "The three of us?"

"You think I'm going to put up with a situation like this – not knowing what the hell's going on?"

"You're serious, aren't you?"

Parker leaned across the seat and kissed him on the mouth. In his peripheral vision Willows saw one of the new patrol cars cruise past, the uniformed constable behind the wheel eyeing him with a mix of suspicion and envy. The department was saving three hundred dollars a unit by sticking with an essentially off-the-rack factory paint job. White, with a blue racing stripe. What was the world coming to? Willows remembered a time, not so long ago, when police cars were black.

He hadn't recognized the cop and was pretty sure the cop hadn't recognized him. The Ford's tires spun on ice and hard-packed snow as he pulled away from the curb.

As advertised, he drove down Davie to Homer, made a left and continued down Homer to Nelson, hung a right and merged with the southbound flow across the Cambie Street Bridge.

He turned off Cambie at Seventh Avenue, drove three blocks west and parked in a "Residents Only" zone. He dropped the visor.

Roth's building was virtually identical to all the buildings that surrounded it – three storeys of miniature balconies and blank aluminum-framed windows, the whole package wrapped in pastel stucco. The California look.

This time, Parker hit the intercom button.

Susan Carter answered immediately, as if she'd been waiting for them and didn't care if they knew it. She gave Parker directions and buzzed the door, unlocking it.

The lobby was small. Smoked mirrors lined the walls from waist level to the white-painted ceiling. There was only one elevator. Willows punched the UP button. The elevator – as Eddy Orwell liked to put it – immediately "spread 'em".

Parker stepped inside and held the door for Willows. There was just room enough for the two of them and a chaperon.

Parker hit the third floor button. They ascended so lethargically that Willows wouldn't have been surprised to learn that down in the basement somebody was sweating over a cheap bicycle. He

168

said, "If this thing went any slower, somebody'd have to offer us a cold meal."

"The world's first elevator with an in-flight movie. Good concept."

The third floor button lit up. The elevator crawled to a stop.

Willows said, "Spread 'em!"

The doors split apart, opening on a minimum-width hallway studded with heavy metal fire doors that had been painted a leprous shade of green. The two detectives walked down the hall until they came to apartment 304.

Willows knocked.

The door swung open. Susan Carter said, "I should have warned you about the elevator, but I forgot. They keep saying they're going to fix it . . ."

She was wearing a sleeveless black cocktail dress, diamond earrings and high-heeled shoes, in red. Her legs were bare. Her blonde hair was brushed straight back. She'd been crying but had recently made herself up. When she smiled, her teeth were very white against her full red lips. The way she looked, her general appearance, she should've been riding in a pink Cadillac convertible, next to a guy named Ken.

The cocktail dress was backless, Willows observed as he and Parker followed Susan down a short entrance hall and into the living room.

The apartment faced north; through the plate glass there was a spectacular view of False Creek, the city and mountains.

Parker said, "Beautiful view."

"It really is, isn't it? Would you like me to show you the rest of the apartment?"

"If you don't mind."

Parker waggled her fingers at Willows, who suddenly found himself standing alone in the middle of an expanse of pale blue carpet that he'd have bet a month's child support payments had been specially chosen to compliment Susan Carter's gorgeous eyes.

The only furniture in the room was a big, pillowy-looking black leather sofa, matching loveseat and heart-shaped mirrored-glass coffee table with stainless steel legs. There was a lowball glass on the table. Willows picked it up, sniffed. Gin. He put the glass down. The living room was L-shaped with the dining room at one end, cleverly sited to take advantage of the view. The oval mahogany table was set for two. Cutlery and crystal caught the light. A slim crystal vase held two long-stemmed roses; one red and one white.

White for purity, red for passion.

The kitchen was a relentless blinding white except for the stainless steel double sink and matching fridge and stove. It looked more like a morgue than a place to prepare food. Willows trusted that was more by accident than design.

The counter was bare except for a four-slice toaster and small microwave, an empty ice-cube tray and a bottle of tonic water.

Willows opened the fridge. There was a variety of cheeses in an enclosed tray in the door. Three champagne bottles lay neck-out on the bottom shelf. Willows knelt and read a label. Lanson Père Black Label Brut. Good stuff. The fridge also held two six-packs of Paulie Girl and a litre of Mexican tequila, a pewter bowl of limes, a solitary apple long past its prime, and an unopened pound bag of Murchie's coffee.

Willows tried the freezer. It was crowded with a lifetime supply of ice-cubes, a pack of individual-size pepperoni pizzas and three blue plastic trays of frozen herring marked "Not For Human Consumption".

He checked the cupboards, found a few tins of crab meat and a bottle of Perrier, three bottles of Beefeater gin and a bag of wild rice harvested, if the artwork was credible, by authentic naked Indians toiling in birchbark canoes. Roth apparently ate out a lot, but did at least some of his drinking at home.

Willows heard Parker's rising voice. He eased shut a cupboard door and strolled back into the living room. The wall opposite the dining room was covered with dozens of photographs of various sizes in identical shiny black anodized aluminum frames. Willows was staring at a picture of Susan and Gerard and a couple of black-tailed sharks when Parker strolled into the living room with Susan close behind. The sharks were stark naked, but the humans, both of whom faced the camera, were decked out in oversized swim fins and masks equipped with snorkels.

Susan said, "I suppose I should take that down, shouldn't I?"

Willows glanced at her, and saw that she was looking at a *different* photograph. He shifted his gaze. There were actually quite a few pictures she might think about removing, if modesty was a consideration. And there was that small black dog again, at a barbecue, sharing a hotdog with his mistress, now fifteen or sixteen. He became aware that the grown-up version was standing behind him, very close to him. He asked her about the dog, if it was the same as the one in the picture in her office.

"That's Elvis." She saw the look on his face and said, "We called him Elvis 'cause he was a hound dog." She smiled. "I love animals. All of them, great and small. If you treat them right, they never let you down." She smiled again, wistfully, a little girl smile that only an older woman could pull off. She said, "I wanted to be a veterinarian, believe it or not."

Willows could smell her perfume, the gin.

As if reading his mind, she said, "Would anyone care for a drink?"

Parker asked for a glass of water. Willows said he wouldn't mind a beer, if she happened to have a cold one.

Susan said, "Coming right up." Was she slurring her words a little? Willows wasn't sure.

He took one last look at the underwater picture of the two lovebirds in the shark tank. Gerard had been in pretty good shape for a guy old enough to be Susan's father . . . He heard the chime of ice from the kitchen and a moment later Susan appeared carrying a silver tray. She'd poured herself another mostly gin and partly tonic, dusted off the Perrier and sliced into a lime, cracked open a Paulie Girl.

Parker and Susan sat at opposite ends of the black leather sofa; Willows took the loveseat. He poured an exact measure of beer into a cold, freshly rinsed glass and drank swiftly but deeply.

Parker sipped at her Perrier. Turning to Willows, she said, "Susan tells me this is where Dr Roth lived after he separated from his wife."

"The fact is," said Susan, "that he spent most of his time here even before he officially left her." She caught Willows eyeing her and shyly looked away.

Willows said, "Well, we weren't aware of that."

Susan wore a slim gold watch with a gold band and diamond bezel. She studied the watch for a moment, then glanced up and again caught Willows watching her.

Parker said, "Are we interrupting something – were you expecting someone?"

"Gerard gave me this watch. I was looking at it because I was thinking about him, that's all."

Parker indicated the table. "I thought you might be having someone over . . ."

"Who would that be? I don't have any friends left. God, that sounds awfully dramatic, doesn't it? What I mean is Gerard and I didn't have any mutual friends. It was the nature of our relationship. And of course the fact that he was so much older made it difficult." She glanced at Willows, a quick look that took him in all at once. "Gerard and I went out to dinner with another couple not long after we first met. My girlfriend's date kept treating Gerard as if he was infirm. Opening doors for him, that sort of thing. Can you imagine?"

Parker made small sounds of sympathy. She grinned wickedly at Willows as Susan delicately knocked back an inch of gin and tonic.

Susan said, "The horrible part is that he was trying to be nice." She shrugged. "Well, that was the end of our experiment in mingling."

"From then on, you kept to yourselves," encouraged Parker.

Susan nodded. "He was all I needed, and he felt the same way about me. Don't misunderstand me – we continued to go out a lot, but always by ourselves."

Willows said, "Who took the pictures?"

"Of the two of us together in the pool?"

Willows nodded. Yeah, that one.

"Gerard had all sorts of photography equipment. One of his cameras had an automatic timer. He'd set it and then jump in the tank with me."

"Did you swim there often?"

"No more than five or six times altogether. It was fun, but kind of risky."

"The sharks?"

Susan laughed. "No, the security guards. At night, you never knew where they were. Skulking around. Have you been up on the roof?"

Willows nodded.

"Gerard had a key – a master key – that opened all the doors. He'd buy a bottle of wine and something from a deli and we'd take the food and a blanket or sleeping bag up on the roof. He'd unlock the door and we'd slip inside and have a picnic, get a little bit drunk and take a swim in the tank and then come out and make love under the lights and that big blue

172

tarp that hung from the ceiling and looked like the sky sagging down."

Susan tucked her legs beneath her. She gave Willows a very direct look, gently bit her lower lip. "Gerard was a wonderful lover. He never seemed to get enough of me. I really liked that. And it wasn't just . . . carnal. He was a true romantic, always buying me perfume and sexy clothes, flowers . . ."

Parker said, "Have you met his . . . ex-wife?"

"Iris."

"Yes, Iris."

Susan nodded. "Once, by accident, at the aquarium. She wasn't very nice. I remember thinking that she still hadn't gotten over Gerard."

"How do you mean?"

"Well, she acted as if she hoped they might get back together, or even as if he'd never left her. But I guess that's the point, isn't it? I mean, *he* left *her*. So for him it was an easy adjustment but for her it must've been just the opposite. Have you talked to her?"

Parker nodded.

"How strange it must be, to live all alone on that tiny little island. So isolated." Susan straightened her legs. She tugged at the dress, stood up. Her center of gravity seemed to have shifted slightly. She started towards the kitchen. "Anybody ready for another drink?"

Parker said, "We're fine, really. Are you sure . . ." Her voice trailed off. She gave Willows a *why don't you do something?* look.

A bottle thumped down on the counter. Ice rattled in the sink. The refrigerator door slammed shut. Susan, as she made her way back into the living room, followed a route too circuitous for any self-respecting crow to fly. A small mouthful of gin spilled across her fingers and vanished into the rug as she leaned over to put another bottle of Paulie Girl on the table in front of Willows. He lowered his gaze and found himself staring into the mirrored surface of the table and a reverse image of his grieving host's impeccable cleavage.

Susan straightened up, almost overbalanced and caught herself just as he reached out for her. Willows hastily withdrew his extended hand. She looked past him, at the pictures on the wall, and then gave him a goofy, lopsided smile. By the time Willows figured out that he had no idea how to respond, the chance had passed. Susan tossed back a couple of inches of gin and tonic, ran

173

her fingers through her hair. She tottered back to her spot on the couch and collapsed in a seductive heap.

Parker said, "Susan, there was a stray cat in the alley behind your apartment on Bute. Are pets allowed in the building?"

"No way. I wish they were. People are terrible, aren't they, the way they just abandon animals, leave them to fend for themselves . . ."

Willows sneaked a look at his watch. In less than twenty minutes Susan Carter had progressed from slightly tiddly to borderline falling-down drunk. He sighed, saw he'd finished his first Paulie Girl and poured half the second bottle into his glass. Waste not, want not, after all.

Parker was radiating animosity.

Willows asked Susan for directions to the bathroom. She offered to show him the way, but Parker cut in, told Willows to go through the kitchen and down the hallway, take the first door on his right.

Curled up in a corner of the black leather sofa, Susan adroitly managed the tricky business of attacking her drink while simultaneously pouting up a storm.

The bathroom was much larger than Willows expected. There were side-by-side sinks, a mirrored wall and jetted bathtub big enough for two. Or even three, if you were in the mood. He swung open the cabinet doors above the sinks. Susan had a supply of prescription drugs varied enough to satisfy the most venal of pharmacists, but he could see nothing unusual or illegal.

He checked the drawers beneath the counter on both sides of the sinks and found the usual line of brand-name products and a wide variety of designer contraceptives.

He flushed the toilet and went back into the living room.

Parker said, "Ready to go, Jack?"

"All set."

Susan Carter had slumped a little lower in the sofa. Her skirt had ridden up on her thighs. Her head rested on the cushion and her silky blonde hair was a golden fan against the curve of black leather. She was sleeping deeply. Her scarlet lips were slightly parted.

Willows smiled down at her. He thanked her for the beer and said not to get up, that she looked perfect just as she was. He and Parker would find their own way out, no problem.

Parker said, "Perfect just as she is?"

"Well, a little immodest, maybe. If that's what you're getting at."

"The snoring doesn't bother you?"

"I kind of like it," admitted Willows with a mock-sheepish grin.

"Turns your crank?"

"Just a little."

Shaking her head in mock-pity, Parker said, "Just a little, but still too much. Right?"

They took the fire stairs down to ground level. The Ford had been ticketed. Willows unlocked Parker's door. He waited for a Volvo station wagon to pass, then stepped into the street, unlocked his door and got in.

Parker smiled at him, then laughed out loud.

Willows said, "Okay, I admit it. She's young enough to be my daughter. But she isn't my daughter, is she? And all I did was look. You'd be worried if I didn't."

Parker's smile widened. "What are you talking about, Jack?"

"Nothing. Forget it."

Parker said, "Take a look behind you. It looks like we've got a stowaway on board."

Willows turned around. A big-boned marmalade cat lay curled up in the middle of the seat. It opened a huge green eye and stared at him.

Willows leaned back, scratched at the nub of an ear. The eye squeezed shut. There was a sound like a distant airplane revving its engines.

Parker said, "Looks like you've got yourself another dependent. What're you going to call him?"

"I've always wanted a cat named Barney."

"Well, that's a Barney if ever there was one."

"Lucky for him." Willows started the Ford's engine. He switched on the windshield wipers. The parking ticket skittered back and forth across the glass and then fell away. He turned the wipers off. "What was the bedroom like?" He smiled. "Tell me all about the bedroom."

"You'd have liked it."

"Yeah?"

"More plate glass, the same great view of the city and mountains."

Willows made a left on Laurel.

Parker said, "Wall-to-wall pink carpet. A king-size bed with a mirrored headboard. The ceiling was mirrored, too, Jack. And so were the doors of the walk-in closet. The bedside lamps had pink shades. There was a VCR and a television, and a library of the kind of films that are short on plot but long on something else."

"You're referring to the complete works of Jacques Cousteau?"

Parker shook her head, no.

"Ah," said Willows, "I see." A clot of pedestrians shuffled lethargically past. He improvised a little two-fingered music on the steering wheel. The intersection cleared. He turned right on to Broadway. "So tell me, was Miss Carter broken-hearted, or what?"

"You're asking me for a woman's point of view?"

"Exactly."

"I'd say she was genuinely upset by Roth's death."

"She loved him?"

"Apparently."

"Okay," said Willows. "Now tell me this – why?"

"You mean, what was the attraction?"

"No, more than that. Why did she love him?"

Parker stared at him, seeing him in profile as he concentrated on the traffic. After a moment she said, "Beats me, Jack."

20

She filled the sink with hot, soapy water and then used the electric opener on a can of Dr Ballard. Claws rattled and scrabbled on linoleum as Fireball and Hot Stuff and Mr Jigs raced wide-eyed and panting into the kitchen. It wasn't din-dins time yet, but unscheduled treats were always welcome.

The dogs rubbed up against her ankles, panting and whining in a display of ravenous affection.

She stacked their bowls, then picked them up and put them down on the kitchen counter by the open can of dog food. Hot Stuff sat on his hind legs and barked twice. Untalented Mr Jigs snapped at him and then head-butted him and bowled him over.

Iris snatched up Fireball and stuffed as much of him as as she could into the hot water. His hind legs pushed against her breasts. He wriggled and squirmed and the soapy water bulged and frothed. Her eyes stung. Fireball shuddered and then all the starch went out of him at once.

Suddenly he felt – there was no other word for it – *lifeless*.

Iris shoved his sodden body along the counter until it bumped into the toaster. She dumped a few spoonfuls of Dr Ballard into Mr Jigs' bowl and put the bowl down on the floor by her feet.

Mr Jigs gobbled the food into his mouth. He was still licking his chops when she pushed him under. His body heaved and twisted. A cupful of water sloshed over the lip of the sink. Mr Jigs was much stronger than he looked.

But not quite strong enough.

When Hot Stuff realized what Iris was up to he ran about as far away from her as he could, all the way to the tiny guest bedroom at the other end of the house.

Iris had to get down on her belly and crawl under the bed to get at him. Dustballs made her sneeze. She yanked his nub of a tail and he snarled and snapped, bit her in the soft web of flesh between finger and thumb.

She retreated to the bathroom and rinsed her wound under the cold water tap.

Blood ran into the sink, swirled down the drain. She bloodied a towel drying herself off.

Hot Stuff had put a tooth right through her – in one side and out the next. She needed a cork more than a bandage.

When she'd tended to her wound she went into the kitchen, poured an inch of rye into a water glass and drank it down.

Hot Stuff was still wedged into the corner under the bed. She attacked him with a spray bottle of window cleaner and then a pressure can of oven cleaner. He bristled and moaned, but refused to budge.

She tried to sweep him out. He bit the straw, and laughed in her face.

She got the poker from the fireplace and hit him hard. Howling, he scurried for his life.

My, but he was agile. She chased him through the living room, in and out of the kitchen. She thought she had him when he ran down the hall, because she'd shut the door to the guest bedroom. But he made a U-turn and scooted between her legs and got away again.

Disappeared.

Iris checked the doors and windows. He had to be somewhere in the house – there was no way out. She took a break, had another drink.

There was soapy water all over the kitchen counter and the floor.

She cleaned up, had another drink.

When she finally found Hot Stuff, it was entirely by accident. He'd wedged himself in behind the toilet, curled up in a ball and gone to sleep.

She shut the door, raised the poker. Hot Stuff whined and snarled. She struck at him and missed, and struck again.

He bolted. Panic-stricken, he bounced off the door and ran straight at it again.

The poker clanged against the bathtub. Chips of pink enamel rattled against the tiles. Terrified, Hot Stuff pissed on his own shoes.

The poker caught him square on the head. He sank to the floor, eyes bulging and legs splayed out. He'd been killed between one breath and the next.

178

Iris wasn't taking any chances.

By the time she'd finished with him, he had all the stuffing knocked out of him, was flat as a bathmat.

Hot Stuff, indeed.

21

Bradley said, "Remember a couple of years ago, I'd come to work in the morning and find somebody'd been at my Coronas?"

Willows nodded politely.

Parker said, "You thought it was a janitor."

"Yeah, the guy with the curly black hair, all those gold chains. But I couldn't prove it. Then the rotten bastard's parents were killed in a train accident and he skipped back home to grab the estate. An olive orchard, something like that."

Willows looked out the window. The tar and gravel roof of the adjoining building was covered in what he couldn't stop himself from thinking of as a mantle of white.

Bradley said, "Anyhow, I haven't lost a cigar since he left. Then, this morning, guess what happens?"

Parker said, "Somebody stole *all* your cigars, box and all."

"How did you know?"

"The box is always on your desk – but now it isn't."

Bradley said, "Jack?"

Willows turned his gaze from the mantle of white to the inspector's eyes, which, God help him, he suddenly realized were a piercing blue.

He said, "Yes, Inspector?"

"When I got here this morning, my office door was, contrary to regulations and the way I like things done around here, wide open."

Willows said, "Yeah, I noticed."

"You were first person in, right?"

"As far as I know."

"The door was open when you arrived?"

"Wide open."

Bradley leaned back in his chair. "At this point, I suspect I've been victimized by a joker. Maybe I should say I'm hopeful that's

180

the case." He turned to Parker. "Have you heard any rumors to that effect?"

Parker shook her head, no.

"Jack, I'm wondering if Eddy's wife recently gave birth . . ."

"Not to my knowledge, Inspector."

Bradley didn't try to hide his disappointment. The missing cigar box had been carved from a solid block of red cedar by a well-known Haida artist and was worth at least two hundred dollars. It had been a farewell gift from his ex-wife; the last thing she'd given him – except for several years' worth of heartburn. As he grew older, Bradley's personal history vanished with quickening speed into a kind of roiling mist that swallowed good memories and bad. The cigar box was an important signpost in his life – it served to reinforce his fading belief that he'd actually had a past.

He valued the box tremendously.

He wanted it back.

He said, "Listen, I wouldn't want this to get out of the squad-room, but I'm posting a reward."

Willows said, "How much?"

Bradley gave him a pained look.

Willows said, "Face it, Inspector. It's the first question everybody's going to ask."

"Fifty bucks?"

Willows looked out the window.

Bradley said, "Okay, a hundred. And another buck per cigar."

"How much for the perp?"

"Nothing, not a cent. I want my cigar box. That's what I'm paying for, nothing else."

Bradley shifted a stack of files from one side of his desk to the other, and back again. "Okay, so much for the vitally important stuff. You get Roth's killer yet?"

"Not yet," said Parker.

"But soon?"

Willows said, "No promises, Inspector. Roth wasn't a tremendously popular guy. Everybody who knew him is a potential suspect."

"Somebody must have loved him. Somebody loves damn near everybody."

"He was going out with a woman named Susan Carter."

"Works at the aquarium, right?"

Willows nodded.

181

Bradley said, "That's what I'd focus on. His love interest." He smiled with teeth that were old and yellow but still had plenty of bite. "Passion's *always* been my favorite motive."

Parker said, "We just talked to Susan. Or tried to."

Bradley lifted an inquisitive eyebrow.

"She was in mourning," explained Willows.

"Drunk," said Parker.

Bradley shrugged. "She'll sober up eventually. What's next on the agenda?"

"Another talk with Roth's widow."

"Iris."

Willows said, "We've been phoning on and off all day. If she's home, she isn't in the mood for company."

Bradley said, "There's two of you, and you're both young and strong – why don't you go over there and beat her door down?" He shut his eyes, massaged his temples. "Just kidding, folks."

Willows said, "Tony Sweeting gave us his files on the animal rights groups that have harassed or threatened the aquarium or its personnel during the past few years."

"Yeah?"

"A guy named Archie Brock seems our most likely suspect. In the past five years he's written quite a few vaguely threatening letters addressed to various staff members, including Roth."

"How many letters is 'quite a few'?" asked Bradley.

"In excess of five thousand."

"My goodness. What a busy fellow."

Willows smiled.

Bradley said, "How many members does he have in his organization?"

"Just the one."

"He must be a hell of a typist. What else do we know about him?"

Parker said, "Archie's done some time at Riverview, mostly awaiting psychiatric evaluation. I had a brief off-the-record with the psychiatrist who evaluated him most recently – that'd be about a year ago. In his learned opinion Archie writes a mean letter but that's about as mean as Archie gets. The shrink said Archie thinks too highly of the whales to feed them something as morally deficient a human being."

"Why bother with him, then?"

"People do change."

"True."

"Usually for the worst."

"Equally true."

"Another thing," said Willows, "There was a copy of Roth's will in his desk. He was insured for five hundred thousand dollars. His wife gets most of it, but fifty grand goes to Archie Brock."

Bradley didn't say a word, but his chair squeaked as he sat up a little straighter.

Parker said, "Archie isn't our only suspect, or even the best. Anthony Sweeting was alone the night Dr Roth was killed. No alibi. So we can't rule him out. And we definitely need another session with Iris before we can cross her off our wish list."

Willows said, "By the time Eddy and his gang finish with the rest of the aquarium's employees, we'll have so many pissed-off citizens on our hands that we won't know where to put them all. In the meantime, it seems wise to tread where Eddy hasn't stomped. Besides, if Archie didn't kill Roth, he might have an idea who did."

Bradley nodded. "Where's Archie like to roost, when he isn't hanging out at the asylum?"

"That's the serendipity part. He lives in Horseshoe Bay, just a few miles past Eagle Island."

"And he's home, and in the mood to entertain?"

"So his mother tells us."

Archie Brock was doing fairly well, judging by his address, which was screwed to the wall of a Tudor-style gatehouse in custom-made foot-high polished brass numbers that must easily have cost a thousand dollars the set.

Willows drove down a narrow road that meandered artfully through a tangle of undergrowth studded with mature evergreens. The driveway made a sudden turn, then dipped sharply. A small animal darted in front of the car and vanished beneath a boxwood hedge pruned in the shape of a whale. The road twisted again. The house suddenly reared up in front of them.

Archie Brock's sprawling, cedar-shingled home sat hunched on a granite foundation. A deep wraparound porch gave the building a warm, welcoming aura. Willows parked the car next to a Range-Rover. A red Jaguar convertible and a white Buick station wagon were parked in a triple garage. He and Parker got out of the Ford. Barney raised his head. He yawned hugely and then went back

183

to sleep. It was as if he instinctively knew that he was still a long way from home. The house was situated on a rocky bluff a hundred feet or so above the ocean, in at least an acre of grounds.

High overhead, metal squeaked on metal. Willows glanced up. Above the steeply pitched roof's ridgeline a large weathervane in the shape of a killer whale turned slowly in the wind.

As he and Parker walked towards the house, Willows said, "I'm starting to think I'm in the wrong profession – the animal rights biz obviously pays top dollar."

Parker smiled. "If he can afford the postage for five thousand letters, it stands to reason he's going to be reasonably well off."

"Anybody who lives in a place like this would have to be unreasonably well off."

"You sound like the government, Jack."

Willows laughed. He said, "I don't want to tax him out from under his roof, I just want to know where he got the money to pay for it."

They climbed the granite front steps. Despite the inclement weather, a trio of glossy white wicker chairs were grouped around a wicker table at the far end of the porch, where there was a sweeping view of the water. The polished brass door knocker was, naturally, in the shape of a killer whale.

Willows used his fist. Through the bevelled and leaded glass he saw a distorted movement deep inside the house. A moment later a shadow darkened the glass, and then the door swung open.

An elderly woman who looked like everybody's idea of a grand-mother gave Parker and then Willows a rosy-cheeked smile.

"You must be the detectives from across the water!"

Willows smiled and nodded. He introduced Parker and then himself.

"Well, I'm Archie's mother. Always have been and I suppose I always will be." She waved vaguely towards the driveway. "Is there a Jaguar in the garage?"

"Yes, there is," said Parker.

"Red as a whore's first blush?"

Parker nodded.

"Good. That's Archie's flavor of the month. Whore's blush red. If the car's there, he's here." She pushed the door open a little wider. "Don't just stand there – come on in."

Willows followed Parker into the house. As Willows shut the door Mrs Brock said, "Be careful you don't slam it. And please

184

speak quietly at all times. We who live here treasure this house as an oasis of peace and quiet in what has become an increasingly strident and uselessly noisy world. Am I making any sense to you?"

Willows said yes.

"Well, good. Archie said it first. *Strident and uselessly noisy world.* That child's got a way of talking that is extremely seductive. When he's at his best he can read the instructions off a container of anti-freeze and make it sound like ten rules to live by."

She smiled at Parker. "Tell me, Claire, do you know anybody like that?"

Parker jerked her thumb towards Willows.

"No! Really? Isn't that interesting?" Peering over her gingham shoulder at Willows, Mrs Brock led them down a wide hallway with a dully gleaming plank oak floor and white-painted walls covered with hundreds of pictures of killer whales. She paused to open a door and Willows found himself being stared down by a pair of bloodhounds stretched out on an oval carpet in front of a blackened fieldstone fireplace.

Then that door was shut, and another opened on what must have been the music room. A girl, no more than ten or eleven years old, lay on her stomach on an ebony grand piano, carefully picking out a tune with her toes. She wore an orange top hat and leopardskin leotards, and seemed to be enjoying herself immensely. She looked up and smiled prettily.

Mrs Brock said, "That's Lillian She lives not far away. Her father and mother are actors. She wants me to adopt her. What do you think of that?"

Parker said, "How old is she?"

"Nine. But she's very mature for her age. When she's in the mood, she can tickle those ivories fit to break your heart."

A third room held a large painter's easel standing on a polar bear rug. Blank canvases, many tubes of white paint and a jar of white-tipped brushes of various size stood on a small white table. Mrs Brock said, "This was the sewing room until my eyes started to go. Don't ask me about the artwork. Ricardo knows what's going on but he isn't the sharing type."

Parker said, "Ricardo?"

"He must be a friend of Archie's, because he's far too young for me. You know the type. Tall, muscular. Reddish-blonde hair. He's a therapist but wants to be a painter. At the moment, he's

185

feeling extremely involved and passionate about purity, which he currently defines as a complete absence of impurity. So, everything he paints is white. Which is, of course, the antithesis of darkness. He's painted a dozen pictures in the last few months and I can't tell one of them from the next, even with the aid of a magnifying glass."

She smiled at Parker. "He asked me to pose for him, and I did, for hours and hours. By the time he was done with me I had a terrible neckache. And do you know what I ended up looking like?"

"No," said Parker. "What?"

"A freshly ironed bedsheet. A white bedsheet, I hasten to add."

Mrs Brock led them further down the hall and into the living room – a huge room with a beamed ceiling that spanned the width of the house and was dominated by a massive fireplace and long wall of leaded-glass windows overlooking a wind-blown expanse of rock studded with patches of snow and tufts of grass, that descended so steeply it seemed as if it was falling into the sea.

Pointing, Archie's mother proudly said, "There he is, there's my darling boy."

Willows made his way around a sofa, stepped over a rusty child's tricycle. A small gazebo had been built in the shelter of a precariously sited clump of three or four red cedars. A man wearing a dark green windbreaker and a floppy off-white hat sat in the gazebo with his back to them, looking out at the view.

Mrs Brock said, "He's always liked being outside. I can ring the bell if you like."

Parker said, "No, it's alright. We'll go down to him." On the wall above the fireplace was a very large photograph of a naked man juggling five black and white kittens. He was grinning maniacally, his eyes alight with pleasure. There was blood on his hands, streaks of blood on his chest, a thin, curving red line just below his right eye.

Willows opened a door, stepped on to the wide porch that ran all the way around the house.

Mrs Brock gently took Parker's arm. Indicating the picture, she said, "That's Archie's father. He juggled poisonous snakes, too, for a while. Archie hates that picture and what it stands for, but I won't take it down because it's the only one of Bob enjoying himself that I've got left."

Parker said, "There were others?"

"Lots and lots. I burned most of them and tossed the rest into the ocean. You bring your arm across your body as if you were throwing a Frisbee. Frame up. If you do it just right, you can throw a medium-size canvas a long, long way."

Nodding, unable to think of anything to say, Parker slipped out the door. Willows was waiting halfway down the steps. A slate path traversed the yard diagonally, and he and Parker followed it down to the gazebo. As they drew near, Archie Brock turned and stared at them, his eyes flicking from Parker to Willows and back again.

The gazebo was an octagon made of unpainted cedar, with a steeply pitched roof and waist-high walls topped with a wide railing. Inside, a plain wooden bench ran all around the inside wall.

Willows sat down opposite Archie, taking care that he didn't block the view. Parker sat midway between the two men. She smiled. Archie thrust his hands into his pockets and looked away.

The ocean heaved against the rocky shore. A gust of wind made the grass lie flat. Something moved under Archie's jacket. Parker stiffened. A white rabbit with pink eyes stared unblinkingly at her for a fraction of a second, and then was gone.

Archie said, "That's Louie-Louie."

Parker nodded. She said, "Shy, isn't he?"

"You'd be shy too, if you were a rabbit."

"I bet I would," said Parker, laughing.

Archie's jacket bulged crazily as the rabbit turned round and round. Archie said, "I'm a murder suspect, am I? Is that a good thing? Somehow I doubt it. Please explain. For example, will I lose my driver's licence? Also, do I need a lawyer?"

Willows said, "Not unless you're guilty."

Archie nodded, mulling it over. "Nine hundred thousand gallons of water, that's how much the whale pool holds. Sounds like a lot, doesn't it?" He looked out at the water. His nose was thin and straight, his mouth a little too wide. His pale skin was smooth and unlined, even though he was thirty-six years old. His eyebrows and eyelashes were so light in color that they were hardly there at all.

Finally, he said, "A mature killer cruises at thirty miles an hour. Pods often travel more than one hundred miles a day. Know how many times you'd have to lap that pool to do a hundred miles?"

Not expecting an answer, Archie ducked his head, buried his nose in his jacket.

187

He spoke quietly to Louie-Louie and then raised his head and stared directly at Parker. "Killer whales require more than one hundred pounds of protein a day. Three-quarters of their time is normally spent foraging for food. Have you ever thought what it must be liked to be snatched out of the ocean and dropped in an oversized bathtub?"

"Not too happy, I guess."

Archie turned and looked back up the slope at the house. "What did you think of my mother?"

"She seemed nice enough."

"But a little eccentric, maybe?"

Parker smiled.

Archie said, "She works *so* hard at it." He returned Parker's smile. "This is the first time in my life I've been a murder suspect. It's kind of neat – makes me feel dangerous." Louie-Louie poked its head out again. Its nose twitched as it tested the breeze. Archie scratched it behind the ears. The bunny perked up a little. Its close-set pink eyes scrutinized Parker.

Willows said, "Can you tell us where you were Friday night?"

"Right here at the old homestead. I had dinner with mother and a wonderfully talented painter who specializes in snowstorms."

"Ricardo."

"Yeah, Rick."

"How much of the evening did you spend with them?"

"Well, it seemed like forever. But I probably left the table about eight or eight-thirty."

"Then what?"

"I came down here to the gazebo."

"Alone?"

"No, I was with Louie-Louie. He's a wonderful pal. Never interrupts, never complains."

"How long did you stay down here, Archie?"

"Until about seven in the morning. That's when mother rang the breakfast bell."

Parker said, "What did you do here, during all that time?"

"Listened to the snow. Rain can be so violent, but the sound of snow falling is the most gentle sound in the world." He shifted on the wooden bench so he was facing Willows. "Don't you agree?"

Willows said, "Can your mother or Ricardo confirm that you spent the night here at the gazebo?"

188

"Mother always watches me. She's very considerate, turns out all the lights in the house so I won't be able to see her standing at the window. But all the same, I know she's there. I can *feel* her eyes on me." Archie glanced at Parker, quickly looked away. "Can you tell when someone's watching you, Miss Parker?"

"Almost always."

Willows stood up. "Thanks for your time, Archie."

"I hope you learned something."

"Well, you never know." Willows paused. "One more question. Were you aware that Gerard Roth mentioned you in his will?"

"He said he would. Phoned me a couple of years ago and told me I'd be fifty thousand dollars richer, the day he died. But that I had to spend every last dime on the whales. Educating people. Helping them see the light."

"He cared about the whales?"

"I doubt it. The killers are a big draw. There's no way the aquarium could survive without all the cash they bring in. They paid Roth's salary. He was guilty of exploiting them, and he knew it. His posthumous donation to the cause was a last-ditch shot at balancing the books, that's all. In case God noticed that he'd died."

Archie gave Parker a sly look. He said, "Lots of people hedge their bets. There's a woman who works at the aquarium, sends me a check every month . . ."

"Susan Carter?"

"How'd you know that? She told you?"

"No, Archie, just a lucky guess."

Willows drove the Ford back through West Vancouver, over the falling-down bridge and through the salt-grey causeway and into the city. It was late, approaching end of shift. He asked Parker if she wanted a ride home and she told him she wanted to be dropped off at 312 Main. She wanted to ask Bradley about getting a court order to obtain BC Tel records of outgoing calls from Gerard Roth's and Susan Carter's apartments, Iris Roth's house and Anthony Sweeting's home.

Willows said, "You want to know if any of them were in contact with each other?"

"Something like that."

"It's a good idea. Bradley should go along with it, if you ask him nicely."

Parker said, "Dinner still on?"

189

Willows nodded, checked his watch. "Seven-thirty okay?"

"Fine," said Parker, a little too vigorously. "I'll bring some wine – what are we eating?"

"Guess," said Willows, showing his front teeth and wriggling his nose.

22

He'd been calling her all morning, letting the automatic redial do the work for him as he held the phone loosely in his hand, hearing a sharp click as the connection was made and then the steady ringing that went on and on and on, until he finally hung up. Since it was Monday, maybe she was at work . . .

People had all kinds of phones now – you could rent or buy hundreds of different models and they all sounded a little different. But no matter what kind of phone the person you were calling owned, the sound of the ringing was always the same.

Chris didn't think that was right. He believed that if the person you were calling had spent a few extra dollars on a phone that warbled, then you should be able to enjoy the sound of warbling as you waited for her to pick up. And it'd be even better if instead of a ringing in the ear you got a real sexy voice that whispered "call me again and again and again".

Unfortunately that kind of phone didn't exist, or if it did, wasn't available to the public. And if Susan had an answering machine it wasn't plugged in. Chris hit the redial number again.

He was beginning to think she'd left town for the weekend and hadn't come back yet. Maybe driven across the border to Seattle, or up the deathtrap Sea-to-Sky highway to Whistler for a little skiing. Or maybe she went home so she could lay her head in her mommy's lap, be a small helpless child once again.

Still no answer.

Chris tossed the phone on the floor. He climbed out of bed, dressed in faded jeans, a baggy, blindingly white cotton shirt, thick white sports socks and his black Nike Hi-Tops, the black leather jacket with the heavy brass zippers.

Outside, it wasn't snowing but somehow smelled like snow. Chris unlocked the Subaru, got in. He started the engine and turned the heater on full, then climbed out to scrape the frost off the windows. He slowly worked his way around the car, held his

191

breath as he scraped clean the rear window, exhaust fumes pluming around him.

When he'd done the windows he climbed back behind the wheel and hit the gas. The engine revved smoothly. He fastened his seatbelt and slipped a Neil Young tape into the cassette deck.

There was a payphone on Davie, less than two blocks from Susan Carter's apartment. Chris had written Susan's number down on a scrap of paper. That was the problem with automatic redialers, wasn't it? Your brain could take a holiday but it had to go back to work sooner or later. He dropped a nickel and two dimes and dialled Susan's number. Her phone rang slavishly until he disconnected.

He scooped his money out of the coin return slot, got back into the idling Subaru and continued up Davie. There was a parking spot on Bidwell, right across the street from her highrise. He pulled in, checked his watch. Five minutes had passed since he'd last called her. What could happen in five minutes? He got out of the car and locked it, pocketed his keys and zipped up as he trotted across the street.

He buzzed Susan's apartment.

No answer.

He hit another button, at random. Again, there was no response. He punched several more buttons, running straight down the row. A voice – he thought it was a woman's but wasn't sure – said hello. He said he lived down the hall, gave the voice a name plucked from his subconscious and laughingly explained that he must've left his keys in his apartment door. Did she remember him? Would she please let him in, because his mother was coming over and he had to get the roast into the oven?

The woman buzzed him in. He took the elevator up to Susan Carter's fourteenth-floor apartment.

There was no response to his lighthearted knock. He pushed his eye up to the peephole, but it was designed to work the other way around and all he could see was a tiny disc of fuzzy grey light.

He stepped back, got set, and hit the doorknob hard with the heel of his running shoe. Ouch. Next time he'd wear his boots.

He kicked the door again. It didn't move so much as a fraction of an inch. He kicked again, putting all his weight into it, holding nothing back. His foot slid off the rounded knob. Pain zapped his ankle, knee.

He was sitting on his ass grumpily ministering to his wound when a fat guy in striped coveralls and a green corduroy Mohawk gas-station cap decorated with gold braid pushed through the fire door at the end of the corridor. The guy held the fire door open with his left foot while he dragged a wooden stepladder and a cardboard box full of light bulbs into the hallway. He noticed Chris, did an unintentionally comic double-take and asked him who he was.

Chris told the guy he'd hurt his ankle. He said he realized he'd left his keys in his other jacket just as the door was closing behind him, had stupidly tried to stop it with his foot.

The guy asked him what he was doing with keys to the apartment, since he wasn't a registered occupant.

Chris explained that Susan was his sister. He said he was in town for a day or two because her boyfriend had been killed and she was pretty upset about it. The guy nodded sympathetically, his gold braid glinting. He was aware that Susan worked at the aquarium and knew all the gory details of Dr Roth's murder. Imagine being drowned and then used for a beanbag. Brother, what a way to go. He asked Chris what his name was and Chris, caught off guard, told the truth and nothing but. Oh well. The guy shoved his cap back on his sloping forehead, dug around in his coverall pockets, came up with a brass key on a Mohawk keyring. He unlocked the door, pushed it wide open but stood in the way as he mentioned he hadn't seen Susan around lately. Where was she?

Chris said she was right there in the apartment, taking a bath. He winked and asked the guy if he wanted to come in for a minute, say hello. The guy hesitated, thinking it over. Finally he shook his head and said he better not, his wife'd break a frying pan on his skull if she got another complaint.

Chris thanked him for his help, held on to his smile while the door slowly swung shut.

He looked in the bathroom first, just in case he'd inadvertently made a lucky guess.

The bathtub was empty. No water. No Susan. He moved quickly through the apartment. It was a compact unit. There wasn't a whole lot of exploring to be done. He checked the bedroom first. From the hall he could see that there was no one in the kitchen nook or combination living and dining room.

Wherever Susan was, it had to be somewhere else.

Chris went back into the bedroom and switched on the light. The walk-in closet was stuffed with expensive clothes. A dozen pairs of shoes were laid out neatly on the floor. The dresser had five drawers, three of them stuffed with the kind of kinky silk lingerie Chris was always trying to get Robyn to buy, and she was always telling him they couldn't afford.

In the bottom drawer of the dresser Chris found a ripped-open package wrapped in plain brown paper covered with cancelled American postage stamps. The package had Susan's name and address printed on it in heavy block letters. Under the brown paper was a sturdy cardboard box stuffed with hundreds of contraceptives. It was a sample pack; a selection of guaranteed-to-please rubbers from all over the world.

Was the girl weird? Or merely economical?

The bed was a king-size model. Chris bounced up and down on it a couple of times, testing the mattress, which he judged to be the extra-firm model, fairly new because it still had plenty of life in it.

There was a purse-size black leather telephone book on the night table. He found Gerard Roth's name in the book under "a" for "amazing", "h" for "hunk", "l" for "lover" and "s" for "stud" and "sex machine" and "satyr". It went on and on. There he was, every two or three pages, in large red letters. Sometimes there was a small but elaborate, oddly erotic illustration.

Chris turned to the last few pages. Roth was listed under "w" for "wanton".

It occurred to him that since Susan wasn't here, but must be somewhere, maybe she was there. At loverboy's love nest.

Acting on impulse, he dialled the number. The phone started ringing . . .

In the drawer of the night table he found more contraceptives and two hand-held mirrors. He held the mirrors up on either side of his face. He smiled.

The damn telephone had been ringing almost all day long. Was it the handsome detective having second thoughts? Or maybe Iris? Or some woman from Gerard's past that she didn't know about . . . Susan's head throbbed. Too much alcohol. She picked up and said hello, trying to sound sexy but grief-stricken, a little angry.

Chris said, "I know what you did, Suze. But I'll keep my mouth shut, for twenty-five thousand dollars."

Susan slammed down the phone.

Chris thought, Well, at least she hadn't said no.

He finished searching the bedroom and walked down the hall to the bathroom. It was clear that Susan spent an awful lot of her disposable income on makeup. The medicine cabinet was crammed with elegant little jars and tubes and squeeze-packs, expensive brands Robyn raved about but rarely bought.

A gold lipstick tube stood upright on the counter. Chris opened it. The lipstick was a rich, creamy-looking red. It looked brand new, unused. He put the cap back on and dropped the tube in his pocket.

The sink, bathtub and toilet were all the same putrid green. Chris lifted the toilet seat, urinated, zipped up. Deliberately neglected to flush.

He checked himself out in the mirror over the sink, squared his shoulders and tilted his head in an exact imitation of James Dean. The dead and buried poster boy. Some actors were like artists – unpopular until they'd died. It was a chilling thought. Chris wandered into the kitchen. There was nothing of interest except the pyramid of champagne bottles in the refrigerator. He crouched and examined a label. Lanson Père Black Label Brut. French. He laid a hand on the top bottle. It was icy cold. Why was he surprised?

He found a half-full bottle of Absolut vodka under the sink, behind a pressurized tin of disinfectant. He unscrewed the cap and sniffed, poured a drop on the tip of his index finger and gingerly licked it, then put the bottle to his mouth and helped himself to a stiff shot.

As he lowered the bottle, he happened to notice his watch.

He'd been in the apartment for over half an hour, almost forty minutes. She could have walked in at any moment, could walk in right now. Or what if she happened to bump into the halfwit Mohawk dude?

Chris screwed the cap back on the vodka bottle and tried to remember where he'd found it, if the label was facing out, what possible difference it could make if he got it right . . .

He made a last quick circuit of Susan's apartment, emptied the dresser of a handful of exotic rubbers and several pairs of frothy silk panties with the price tag still attached. He carried his loot back into the kitchen, put it in a brown paper bag taken from a stack of neatly folded bags wedged between the fridge and the

195

kitchen counter. What else did she have that he wanted? Champagne.

He was standing there in the kitchen with the paper bag in his arms when it finally sunk in that he'd made a connection. Demanded the cash. Now all he had to do was wait a day or two and then give her another call. She'd get the money somewhere – what choice did she have?

He helped himself to a bottle of bubbly, tore off the foil and wire cage and popped the cork. A little wine spilled on to the linoleum floor. He drank deeply. The champagne was so cold it made his throat ache. But it tasted wonderful.

He was confident Susan Carter would never miss any of the things he'd taken. If she noticed the urine in the toilet she'd blame herself. Who wouldn't?

But still, it was a creepy thing to do, piss in a woman's toilet and then leave it there.

Chris carried the open bottle of champagne and his brown paper bag back down the hall towards the bathroom.

The phone rang. He hesitated, standing there in the gloom of the unlit apartment. Susan didn't want any more threatening phonecalls so she'd cancelled her call forwarding – but Chris had no way of knowing that.

There was a knock on the door. More of a pounding, actually.

The phone rang again and then the answering machine in the bedroom picked up. Susan's pre-recorded voice said she wasn't home and please leave a message after the beep.

Chris waited for the beep. It didn't come.

The door shook.

In the bedroom, a woman's voice rambled on. Robyn? No, of course not. Impossible.

A key scratched in the lock.

He stepped into the bathroom. It was a very small bathroom. If there was somewhere to hide, he couldn't find it.

The hall lit up as the door swung open. The Mohawk guy said, "Anybody home?"

The woman who'd called was in a chatty mood. She wouldn't stop talking, no matter how much Chris willed her to.

The Mohawk, easing into the apartment, said, "Miss Carter?" The door swung shut, leaving him in darkness. He said, "Oh, shit."

A light snapped on.

196

Chris stepped into the bathtub. He slid shut the frosted glass shower door and lay down, tried to make himself very, very small.

The Mohawk guy had fallen silent. Chris studied a place on the tiled wall where the grout was starting to fall away.

The Mohawk guy cleared his throat. He said, "Miss Carter? It's Tony. You there? Everything okay? I hope I'm not disturbing you?"

Suddenly the bathroom was ablaze with light, the fan rumbling, heavy footsteps on the tiles. Champagne gurgled out of the bottle he held tightly in both hands. He lay perfectly still.

Tony said, "What the hell!" Then he said something else, that Chris missed because of the sound the toilet made, and the sudden cataclysmic drumming of his heart.

Tony's hand was on the pebbled glass of the shower door, and the door was moving.

23

On his way home Willows made a slight detour to the neighbour-hood supermarket. He'd been cooking for himself for a long time. There wasn't much food in the house and the spices were all stale-dated. If the cupboard wasn't bare, it certainly was scantily dressed.

He paid a quarter to free up an ice-cold shopping cart from a long line of carts in front of the store, then pushed inside and idled up one brightly lit aisle and down the next, taking his time, making sure he had everything he needed. Tinned and fresh tomatoes. A large onion. A paper bag of brown mushrooms. Shallots. A crisp Romaine lettuce, bunches of carrots, radishes and green onions, a huge, lumpy field tomato and a horribly expensive English cucumber imported from California.

At the meat counter he tossed two shrink-wrapped six-packs of chicken breasts into the cart. Further down the aisle he helped himself to a plastic container of fresh pasta.

The section devoted to pet foods was enormous, and there was a wide range of prices. Willows decided to buy only the best – Barney was obviously in need of a few solid meals. He dumped a dozen small round tins and as many flavors of cat food into the cart, added a kilo box of Purina Cat Chow. What else did a cat need? A matched pair of bowls; one each for food and water. Flea powder and soap, a flea collar, name tag and soft wire brush. He added a five-kilogram bag of scented kitty litter and a plastic basin to put it in. So far, he'd spent almost twice as much on the cat as he'd spent on the family dinner.

He rounded a corner and nearly drove his cart into a small table covered in a display of pre-cooked meats. Thin slices of blood-red sausage simmered in an electric frying pan. A woman in a white smock smiled at him and offered him an obsessively neat arrangement of toothpick-skewered slices of meat on a paper plate. His stomach churned. He hadn't realized how tense he was. He went over to the dairy counter and leaned into the cold air, took a few deep breaths and then pushed his cart along to the section devoted to cheese.

He eyed the shelves, searching for a block of fresh mozzarella. Finally he chose a quarter kilogram priced at nearly three dollars. The cost of food being what it was, no wonder people ate most of their meals out.

At the bakery he plucked a loaf of French bread from a wicker basket and then, with an unfamiliar twinge of guilt, passed over the English muffins Sheila had always been so fond of.

At the last moment, as he approached the lineup at the checkout counter, he remembered the garlic.

Twenty minutes later the belt was pulling his groceries steadily and remorselessly towards a red laser beam and a girl whose name tag said "Lucinda" was ringing up his purchases and bagging them at a pace Willows found exhausting just to watch.

Foot-long lengths of black rubber heavy enough to make a decent sap were used to separate groceries at the checkout. Willows had dropped one down to keep his purchases separate from those of the customer in front of him. The man behind him hadn't bothered – was waiting for Willows to do it for him. Willows covertly looked over the man's purchases. The first items were three tins of sliced pineapple and a *Province* newspaper. The pineapple was on sale; he'd almost bought a couple of cans as he'd wandered the aisles. He let the checkout girl ring up and bag all three tins, but not the paper. He'd paid her and was waiting for his change when the guy behind him finally realized what had happened.

Pointing, he said, "That's my pineapple!"

Willows ignored him.

Lucinda said, "Excuse me?"

"He took my pineapple."

Willows accepted his change.

The guy said, "Hey now, wait a minute . . ."

Willows had read Lucinda correctly. She had plenty of front-line experience and wasn't combat shy. Sounding cheerful and spiky, she said, "What am I supposed to do? He paid for it. If it was yours, you should've kept it separate . . ."

Except for the outside security lights, the house was always dark when Willows got home at the end of the day. Old expectations die hard; it was a shock to drive up and find the house ablaze with light. Willows turned off the Ford's engine. He reached behind him for the cat. Barney hissed and dug his claws into Willows' coat, but allowed himself to be picked up. He held on tight as Willows carried him up the walk to the house, unlocked the front door. He called out, but there was no answer. He shut Barney away in the bathroom and went back outside for the groceries.

For the first time, he noticed that someone had shovelled the snow from the porch stairs and from the walk in front of the house. He unlocked the car and retrieved the groceries, carried them inside and down the central hallway into the kitchen, dropped them on the counter. The tap was dripping. He turned it off. Somewhere in the house, someone was playing a radio. Willows tracked the sound to Sean's bedroom. He knocked and waited and then opened the door. The bed was in ruins and the room stank of stale cigarette smoke. Willows turned off the lights and radio. He left, shutting the door behind him.

The door to Annie's room was open. Willows glanced in, just to make sure she wasn't there. A vase of fresh-cut flowers stood on her desk by the window. She'd hung the burgundy cashmere sweater he'd given her the previous Christmas over the back of her chair. He doubted if the sweater still fit, and was touched by the gesture.

He walked back down the length of the hall and stood at the bottom of the stairs for a moment, then went up, a tread creaking underfoot.

The television in the den was on, but the sound had been turned off. There was no one in that room or in any other upstairs room.

In his bedroom, Willows pushed the night table away from the wall. His Beretta hung inelegantly from a nail. He ejected the pistol's clip and racked the slide, clearing a round from the breach. Like a lot of cops, Willows firmly believed there was nothing more dangerous than an unloaded gun. But Sean was clearly not stable. Willows wasn't going to risk coming home and finding his son in the basement with a bullet through his heart.

He stood up, dropped the clip in his pants pocket, hung the pistol on the nail and pushed the night table against the wall.

Back in the kitchen, he opened a can of crabmeat-flavored cat food and spooned it into a bowl, poured fresh water into another bowl. He dumped half the kitty litter into the plastic container and took it into the bathroom. Barney was under the tub, meowing pitifully. Willows put the cat box on the floor next to the toilet. The cat shifted around, showing Willows his stern.

Willows went into the living room, slipped a Lyle Lovett CD in the player and went back into the kitchen and cracked open a Kokanee. He sipped at the beer, then crouched and pulled a big, black iron pot from the bottom shelf of the cupboard . . .

An hour later the kitchen smelled very tasty indeed, and Willows was still busy. He dumped mushrooms in a colander, washed them thoroughly, cut off the stems and quartered them and tossed them into the pot. He dipped a wooden spoon in the pot, sipped and frowned, added a teaspoon of oregano. By now he was deep into his second beer, wailing happily along with Lyle's Large Band. How had he managed to forget what fun toiling over a hot stove could be?

Soon the sauce was simmering away nicely, steam rising into the heat, bubbles heaving up to the surface and bursting with a fat lethargy that was almost insolent.

Willows went to work on a salad. By the time he'd finished, Lyle had long since packed it in.

Willows set the table for five. He made a trip to the bathroom and checked on Barney. Man's second best friend was still wedged under the tub.

He went back into the kitchen, opened his third beer of the evening, wandered into the living room and slipped a Rita Mac-Neil CD into the player.

Time was slipping by. It was getting late. Where in hell was everybody?

Half an hour later, Parker knocked twice and walked in the door. Willows tried not to look startled. She slipped out of her coat and tossed it on the banister. He turned down the stereo. She gave him a warm smile. "Forget you invited me?"

He started to deny it, caught himself.

Laughing, Parker put her arms around him. He kissed her lightly on the mouth and asked her if she'd like a glass of wine.

Parker said, "Something smells delicius. Could it be you?"

She'd brought a bottle of cold Chardonnay. In the kitchen, Willows fought the cork as she dipped a spoon into the pot, sipped.

"Too much garlic?"

She shook her head. "No, it's perfect."

He poured the wine. As Parker accepted her glass she said, "Where is everybody?"

Willows shrugged. "The house was empty when I got home." He told her about the blazing lights, the dripping tap and the radio.

"Have you noticed any spaceships hovering over the house lately, Jack? Tractor beams, that sort of thing?"

Willows said, "Let's eat."

They'd finished the meal but were still sitting at the table, drinking coffee, when Sean arrived. The boy slammed the door behind him and slung his black leather jacket across the sofa. He started towards the kitchen and then saw Parker and stopped short.

Willows said, "Sean, you remember Claire Parker . . ."

"Yeah?" Sean fished a cigarette out of his shirt pocket, leaned over a candle and lit up, turned his back on them and strolled into the kitchen.

Parker lifted her wine glass and then put it down on the table without drinking.

Willows said, "I'll be right back." He followed his son into the kitchen. Sean was leaning against the fridge, his skin pallid in the harsh light, cigarette dangling from his tight disapproving mouth.

"I told you not to smoke in the house."

"Maybe you should've asked me."

"Put it out or take it out, Sean."

"Or what – you'll shoot me?"

Willows took him by the arm and led him down the hall to the front door.

"Kicking me out, *Daddy*?"

"Not you – just the cigarette."

Sean stood there on the threshold, looking sullen. Something pressed against Willows' ankle. An orange blur scooted across the porch and down the steps, vanished in the darkness.

Willows called Barney's name, swore.

"Temper, temper."

Willows fetched Sean's black leather jacket off the sofa. He went back outside, handed the jacket to his son and gently shut the door. Sean shrugged into the jacket, zipped up. He leaned against the porch railing with his hands in his pockets. The cigarette glowed red. Under the porch light his thin, angry face was a jigsaw puzzle of black and white.

202

As Willows made his way back to the table Parker smiled and said, "Rebel without a pause."

He nodded grimly.

"So what's bothering the kid, aside from holes in the ozone, the rainforest stuff, puberty, and the fact that he's being bounced around like a pinball?"

Willows said, "I don't know how I forgot, but he doesn't like chicken."

"Well, that explains almost everything." Parker turned and looked behind her, out the window. "He's a nice-looking kid, isn't he."

"Think so?"

"Got his daddy's looks, I'd say. He just flipped his cigarette on to your neighbor's lawn. Why don't you invite him back in?"

"He doesn't need an invitation – he lives here."

"Maybe he isn't too sure about that."

Willows sighed heavily. He pushed back his chair, stood up and walked towards the door.

Sean waited until Willows stepped outside and then, timing it perfectly, lit a fresh cigarette.

Willows went back into the house.

Parker was on her knees in front of the fireplace. Willows had prepared a fire and she was trying to light it with a candle.

Willows said, "I'll do that."

"No, you won't. And next time, use more kindling. I don't think this is going to catch."

"It'll catch." Willows knelt and pushed the iron lever that opened the flue. Parker gave him a look. He said, "Like a Scotch?"

"I better not, Jack. I'd hate to have to badge my way out of a roadblock." She put her hands out to the rapidly growing fire. "Have one yourself, though, if you like."

Sean had his back to them. Willows kissed Parker's hand. Her dark eyes were lustrous and unfathomable, her hair backlit by the fire. He kissed her on the mouth and she made a small, hungry sound.

The front door swung open. He looked up expecting to meet his son's contrite and apologetic eyes. But it was Sheila and Annie who stood in the doorway, not Sean.

Parker stood up. She and Sheila exchanged smiles, shook hands. Annie smiled at her father and then at Parker. Willows asked her

203

if she remembered Claire, and she nodded and smiled again. Willows offered Sheila a drink. Annie warmed her hands by the fire. He asked her if she'd like a hot chocolate.

Sheila said, "Annie's tired. She's still adjusting to the time-zone change."

"I'm not *that* tired."

Willows said, "It'll only take a minute. She can take it to bed with her, how's that?" Before Sheila could respond he added, "Let me get your wine," and beat a dignified retreat to the kitchen with Annie skipping alongside. As he mixed sugar and cocoa into a mug, he asked her where she'd been.

"Downtown, for dinner."

Willows added milk, set the microwave at two minutes on high. "Better get ready for bed, Annie."

"Okay."

In the living room, Claire and Sheila were talking about the weather. Where was Sean? And when was Sheila going to ask what had happened to him? The microwave beeped. Willows gave Sheila her wine. He was in the kitchen stirring the cocoa when Annie reappeared wearing the flannel Mounted Police pyjamas he'd given her – along with a moderate sum of cash – for her last birthday.

"I'm washed and brushed and flossed and I kissed Mummy goodnight. Where's my cocoa?"

"Right here, Miss Wonderful."

"Tuck me in?"

Willows nodded happily. Annie ran down the hallway ahead of him. He heard her jump into bed. The lamp came on. When he caught up with her she was lying on her side by the light with a paperback in her hands. *The Old Man and the Sea*.

Willows put the cocoa down on the night table. "What happened to science fiction?"

"I read it all."

He sat down on the edge of the bed, straightened the duvet. Annie said, "Where's my crazy brother?"

"He'd must've gone for a walk."

"At this time of night?"

"I had to enforce the local no-smoking bylaw."

Annie said, "Don't worry about it. He'll be back, probably."

"Probably?"

"He had an argument with Mum a couple of months ago, ran

204

away and broke into an empty house. He stayed there three days, until a neighbor called the cops."

"Police," said Willows.

"Cops!"

Willows bent and kissed Annie on the cheek. "Drink your cocoa and read your book. One chapter, okay?"

"Mum said we could stay with you as long as we want. Is that true?"

Willows hesitated.

Annie said, "She was talking about us – me and Sean. Not her."

Willows said, "Your mother's right. I love you both and you can stay with me as long as you like." He kissed her again. "Lights out in ten minutes."

"Good night, Daddy."

"Night, Sweets."

Annie said, "I love you too . . ."

Under the circumstances, Willows thought it best to get straight to the point. Entering the living room, he said, "I understand you're going back to Toronto."

"Annie told you?"

"Inadvertently."

Sheila drank some wine. "I've had them for three years, Jack. It's your turn. If that sounds a little harsh . . ."

Parker stared at Sheila, her eyes flat, offering nothing and expecting very little in return.

Willows said, "You've talked to Sean?"

"He knows what's going on. They both do. We talked it over, all three of us, before we left Toronto."

"Too old, are they? Not quite as cuddly as they used to be?"

"Don't be sarcastic, Jack. It demeans both of us."

Willows heard the heavy thump of boots on the front porch steps. The door opened and Sean came in. He shut the door behind him. Barney's head poked out of the top of his jacket. The cat's ear lay flat on his head and his green eyes looked very angry.

Sean grinned at Willows. "I found him in the garage. He'd stuffed himself in between a couple of logs in the woodpile. Strange cat. Where'd he come from?"

"An alley in the west end. He sneaked into the car this afternoon."

"Climbed into a *cop* car?"

Willows nodded.

205

"Weird." Sean went over to the fire, sat down on the tiled hearth. He took a can of cat food out of his pocket, hooked his finger in a metal ring and pulled off the lid. Barney's ear came up. His eyes widened. Sean unzipped his jacket. He used his fingers to pinch a bit of meat from the tin, offered it to the cat.

Barney began to purr, and to eat. Willows had never seen a cat purr and eat at the same time. Sean continued to feed him as he fished his cigarettes from his shirt pocket, lit up. He turned and winked at Willows, leaned forward and exhaled carefully into the fireplace.

Sheila said, "I'm booked on a return flight leaving tomorrow afternoon. Maybe it would be better if I spent the night in a hotel."

"The kids know you're leaving?"

She nodded.

"Want me to call a cab?"

"I'll do it." Sheila stood up, gave him an icy look and went into the hall to use the phone.

Sean used his index finger to scrape the last of the cat food from the tin. He said, "What's his name?"

"Barney," said Claire.

Five minutes later, Sheila told Willows she could manage her own luggage and that she'd be in touch, said goodbye to Parker and walked out the door.

Ten minutes after that, Parker said it was getting late. She thought Willows and Sean probably had a lot of catching up to do . . .

Willows walked her out to her car. He kissed her goodnight and stood there at the side of the road until she turned a corner and disappeared from view. He went back into the house. Sean was stretched out on the sofa with Barney on his lap and a pair of Walkman headphones in his ears. Fire danced in the cat's eyes as he watched Willows walk towards him. Willows tapped Sean lightly on the shoulder. Sean opened an eye, pointed at his ears and put a finger to his lips.

Willows said, "You want to talk?"

"Maybe tomorrow."

"Good night, Sean."

Sean blew him a kiss.

Willows looked in on Annie. She'd fallen asleep with the Hemingway in her hand and the light still on. He marked the page, turned off the light and left the room. As was his custom, he checked the locks on the back and front doors, made sure the security lights were on.

It had been a long and eventful day, and he wasn't quite ready to put it to bed. There was a bar fridge and a bottle of Cutty Sark in the den. He slowly made his way up the stairs, the tinny wailing of Sean's Walkman following him all the way. He'd take a long, hot shower and then have a drink and watch the news – even though it was bound to be anticlimactic.

24

Scattered lights glimmered along the Eagle Island shoreline and across the water at the yacht club moorage. Even so, it was very dark beneath the drab, windswept sky. Late afternoon was slipping into early evening and depth perception in the rapidly fading winter light was difficult. Susan had good reason to go slowly as she made her way down the pier towards the water. A skin of crusted snow lay on the narrow railing. The wooden planks beneath her feet were slick with frost. Not for the first time, she wished she'd brought a flashlight.

She reached the end of the pier and began to make her way down the treacherous, steeply sloping gangway. An unseen bird screamed shrilly as she stepped upon the tiny dock that serviced Eagle Island, and a moment later she heard the dry rattle of wings overhead. The air shivered, and was still.

The small floating dock moved slightly under her weight. A chain rattled softly. Light gleamed on black, rippling water.

A hooded light hung from a tall pole at the end of the pier, but the bulb had burnt out, or been shattered by vandals. Susan tried to read the dial of her watch, but the light was too dim. Cold seeped through the thin soles of her shoes. She had left Gerard's apartment in a rush, and hadn't thought to wear her boots. She rubbed her hands briskly together. A gust of wind tore through her heavy coat and chilled her flesh. The black surface of the ocean was flecked with white. Where was Iris?

The temperature was dropping rapidly. She began to pace back and forth to keep warm. A fragment of glass crunched underfoot. The dock shifted beneath her weight, and the disturbed water splashed faintly. Alarmed, she moved well away from the edge. The dock had no railing. How long could she survive if she lost her footing and slipped into the water? Not very long. The weight of her sodden clothes would pull her down. Hypothermia would quickly steal away her strength. In a few minutes she would lose consciousness, and drown.

She walked back up the ramp to the end of the pier, where she felt she was most visible, and safest.

There was a payphone at the bottom of the road, near the yacht club's parking lot, but she had been told not to call. She bent her head and peered at her watch again. She was sure she'd arrived on time but it might have taken her longer than she'd expected to walk down the road from the parking lot . . .

Susan stamped her feet but that only made it worse; the frozen planks were hard as concrete and jolts of pain stabbed up through her legs.

She heard the creak of wood on metal, and looked out across the water, towards the island. As she strained to penetrate the gathering darkness, a pale shape materialized out of the gloom, gradually assumed the shape of a small dinghy.

Iris Roth glanced over her shoulder, towards the dock. Susan was making her way down the gangway. The boat lost way as Iris released her grip on the starboard oar and waved hello. Cursing like a sailor, she bent to the oars. The dinghy's stern dipped and the little boat once again moved smartly through the water. A few moments later Iris skilfully worked the oars to make the boat swerve sharply, altering course so it was drifting parallel to the dock. A moment later the port gunwale bumped gently against the dock. Iris reached out to hold the boat steady. It was of a lapstrake design, constructed of fiberglass with built-in flotation tanks. Even so, Susan was very careful not to let the boat slip out from under her as she eased on to the stern seat. It was unsinkable, but because of the certainty of hypothermia the end result, were they to swamp, would be no different than if the boat sank like a stone.

Susan crouched low, on the damp, narrow seat. The dinghy had only a few inches of freeboard, and there was very little room. She was so close to Iris that despite the dim light she could see that the older woman's face was set and grim.

The stern dipped as Iris pulled strongly away from the dock and turned the bow into the wind.

Susan said, "Why didn't you use the ferry?"

"There's something wrong with the engine. Gerard kept promising to fix it, and I kept believing him. So typical! Anyway, I can use the exercise."

209

Susan had expected Iris to row straight across the narrow strip of water towards the Eagle Island dock, but to her alarm she saw that they were heading for the open water of the harbor.

"Why don't we go straight across?"

"Because I've no way of locking up the dinghy and it cost eight hundred dollars and I don't want it stolen." Susan flinched as the bow crashed into a wave and a spray of icy water flew high into the air and was swept away by the wind.

Already, the water was noticeably choppier. Iris adjusted her stroke.

Susan said, "Shouldn't we be closer to the island?"

"No, because the bottom swells up rapidly, and that causes rougher water. We'll much safer staying this far out, believe me."

Susan gripped the plastic gunwales on either side of the boat. She decided to start screaming immediately they began to take on water.

As if reading her mind, Iris gave her a reassuring smile and told her not to worry; that she had been out in heavier weather than this and they were perfectly safe.

A few minutes later the lights of Iris's house came into view. The dinghy turned in, towards the island. Now they had a following sea, and Iris was forced to row hard to avoid taking water over the stern. A curving strip of pebbly beach gleamed in the faint light from the house. Iris began to stroke more powerfully, and they picked up speed.

They were a boat's length from shore when Iris shipped her oars, turned completely around on the seat and moved with surprising grace towards the bow. The sudden shift in weight made the dinghy's stern rise higher out of the water. The boat began to drift sideways to the surf, and then the keel grated harshly on the beach. Iris stepped out of the boat. She hauled on the painter in concert with the impetus of a timely wave and the dinghy rode well up the beach. Smiling at Susan, she said, "You can abandon ship now, if you like."

Susan was impressed with the effortless way in which the potentially dangerous landfall had been accomplished, and said so, as she stepped out of the boat. As the two women hurried across the snowy lawn towards the warmth and safety of the house, Iris took Susan's hand and held it tight.

"You're still frightened, aren't you?"

Susan laughed nervously. "A little."

"Of course you are. Who wouldn't be? But there's no need. Everything's going to be just fine – just you wait and see."

"Someone broke the light on the dock. I stepped on a piece of glass."

"It's the local kids. Little buggers. I saw them at it this afternoon, throwing snowballs and laughing their stupid little heads off."

Susan followed Iris up the porch steps and into the kitchen. The brightly lit house felt wonderfully cozy after the chill air and very real threat of a dunking. She glanced around the kitchen. Three empty bowls stood in a row on the freshly polished linoleum floor. Susan wondered where the dogs were. In this weather, it was inconceivable that the animals were outside.

Smiling, Iris said, "Let me take your coat, Susan, and then we'll go into the living room. I've had a fire burning all day long. I'll say one thing about Gerard; he always kept a good supply of firewood. I don't know if he ever told you, but he absolutely loved to use his chainsaw – if he spotted a decent-sized log drifting by he'd be on it like a shot."

On the driftwood table in the living room there was a bottle of red wine and a plate with a variety of cheeses and biscuits. A colorful throw rug of Navajo design covered the sofa. Its soft earth colors and the warmth and flickering orange light from the fire combined to give the room a casual yet intimate cheerfulness.

Iris sat down on the sofa, so close to Susan that she could feel the heat of the older woman's body. Iris poured them both a large glass of wine. She handed a glass to Susan and then tipped her own glass so the rims touched with a clear, ringing chime. She smiled. "Here's to . . . What *shall* we drink to, Susan?"

Susan's mind was a blank. All she could think of was her glass, which was so brimful of red liquid that she had to hold it steady with both hands.

"Here's to the triumph of justice over adversity," said Iris. "If that sounds a little pompous, well, what the hell! Cheers!"

She touched glasses again, and drank deeply.

Susan sipped delicately.

Iris said, "Try the Stilton – it's delicious. Is something wrong with the wine, dear?"

"No, it's fine. Perfect." Susan forced herself to swallow a mouthful. She obediently took a little cheese. The food caught in her throat. She drank a little more wine. She could feel the warmth

211

of the fire on her legs, and the erratic hiss and pop of the burning wood provided a lovely counterpoint to the soft murmur of the sea.

Iris said, "The tide's still coming in, but it'll turn in another half-hour." She leaned forward to poke at the fire with a blackened iron rod. "You have to pay attention to that sort of thing if you live on an island – even a little one like this."

"It must be a wonderful life."

Iris patted Susan on the knee. "Are you ready to tell me about the phone call?"

Susan nodded. She drank some more wine.

"You said the man was young?" Iris prompted.

"Yes."

"And you haven't changed your mind – you're still quite sure you didn't recognize his voice?"

Susan shook her head, no.

"It couldn't have been someone from the aquarium?"

"No, I don't think so."

"But you aren't sure? This is vitally important, Susan, as you must be aware."

"No one from work or anywhere else knew where I was. And besides, if it had been someone I knew, I'd have recognized his voice."

"But who else could it be? Gerard had an unlisted number. He didn't hand it out to just anyone, especially men. You must have told someone where you were."

"No, I didn't. No one knew!" The wine danced in Susan's glass. She drank deeply.

Iris waited until Susan had calmed down a little and then said, "What about the police? How did they find you?"

"They went to my apartment, but couldn't get in. Then they phoned, and I talked to them and had to explain about the call forwarding, and where I was." Susan's face looked as if it was being pinched from within. She said, "Well what was I supposed to do?"

"There, there, dear. Don't be upset." Iris stroked Susan's back, moved the flat of her hand in small circles up and down her spine. She picked up the wine bottle and replenished Susan's glass. "The homicide detective, could it have been him?"

"No, the voice was younger. Much younger."

"And what did our anonymous caller say, exactly?"

"I already told you!"

"Tell me again," said Iris patiently.

"That he knew what I'd done. And if I didn't pay him twenty-five thousand dollars, he'd tell the police!"

"That's it?"

"He was going to say something else, but I hung up on him."

Iris's hand hovered above the cheese plate. After a moment she chose a small triangular cracker. She brought the cracker to her mouth, turned it slowly in her hand as she nibbled industriously. The cracker rapidly dwindled in size, but continued to retain its original shape.

Against her fading better judgement, Susan drank a bit more wine.

Iris said, "We agreed that you'd stay away from Gerard's little love nest, didn't we, dear?"

Susan nodded.

"Well then, would you please tell me what you were doing there?"

"Picking up some things that belonged to me."

"Oh, I see. What sort of things?"

"Personal things," said Susan. The look she shot the older woman was defiant, triumphant, nakedly sexual.

Iris snatched up another cracker. This one went down quickly, in a frustrated snap of teeth and crunch of jaws.

Susan raised her glass and saw that it was empty. Iris sighed wearily. She filled Susan's glass and topped up her own.

"The homicide detectives," said Iris.

Susan brushed a strand of naturally blonde hair from a naturally blue eye.

Iris said, "Did they mention my name?" Her face was all eyes and teeth.

Susan shook her head. She looked away.

"Did you mention my name, dear?"

"No, of course not!"

Iris sighed. She said, "I wish you'd tell me what you were doing at his apartment, I really do."

Susan hesitated and then said, "I was upset about some things that happened between us."

"What sort of things?" Iris smiled warmly, as she raged inside.

"Photographs. He took some photographs. I'd been drinking,

213

and I was upset." She shrugged. "It was a lucky thing, really. The police thought I was grieving for Gerard."

Iris nodded, smiled encouragingly. "This threatening young man – whoever he is – how could he have known where to call you?"

Susan said, "I don't know."

"But you must have talked to someone . . ."

Susan said, "Whoever it was, couldn't he have been a friend of Gerard's?"

"I doubt that, dear. Gerard liked young women, not men. As we both know all too well."

Susan said, "When I found out he was . . . That I wasn't the only . . . God, but I hated him."

"Of course you did. We both did. We hated him. But it made things so much easier, don't you agree?"

Susan wondered what had happened to Fireball and the other two Boston bulls. Gerard had been so proud of his dogs, the way he'd trained them. She turned to ask Iris where they were.

Iris said, "He was addictive, wouldn't you say? So good in bed, and he had a special knack for making you think everything you did together was unique; the first time for both of you."

Susan felt herself blushing. She turned her face towards the heat of the fire.

Iris said, "If you think you hated him, imagine how I must have felt."

Susan felt Iris's hand on the nape of her neck, the older woman's thick blunt fingers twist in her hair.

Iris said, "Look at me, Susan."

Susan stared down at the cheese plate.

Iris tightened her grip on Susan's hair. "I want you to know that I don't blame you one little bit for what happened. You didn't have a chance, once Gerard had made up his mind to go after you. He was so experienced. And I know how you must have suffered; the emotional turmoil. You may not believe it, but I was about your age when I first met him."

Iris smiled. Her eyes and teeth seemed to rise up out of her face. "Stay right where you are, dear. I'll just be a minute."

Susan lay back against the sofa. The wine had made her sleepy. Or perhaps it was the lullaby of the ocean, which was a little louder now. She remembered that Iris had told her the tide was coming in . . . The Navajo rug smelled faintly of woodsmoke. She ran her fingers across the material. A few moments later she became aware of a faint gurgling sound. Iris stood over her, filling her glass with wine from another bottle. She handed her the glass and sat down next to her on the sofa. "Tell me about the photographs, dear. Did Gerard use them to threaten you in some way?"

"No, I just . . . I was embarrassed. I was afraid that someone would find them. I wanted them back."

Iris refilled Susan's glass. She stroked her head as if she were a cat. "Such lovely hair . . . Did you find them, dear?"

Susan bit her lip.

Iris said, "What did you do with them?"

Susan told Iris how she'd tried to tear Gerard's collection of Polaroids to bits with her hands, explained that they were made of a special kind of paper and were very tough. She'd used a pair of scissors to cut the pictures into tiny little pieces. She'd cut them and cut them and cut them until they were so small she couldn't cut them any smaller. Then she'd scooped them up and carried them into the bathroom.

She had stood there in the bathroom for the longest time, flushing the toilet over and over again . . .

Iris said, "About a month before we killed him, he called and said he wouldn't be coming home that night. He didn't bother to say why, to make up an excuse. But what really hurt was that he was so *cheerful*. He didn't care about me enough to bother with a lie. I felt so terribly humiliated. I cried for hours, Susan, and then I suddenly realized I'd had enough of him, and started to work out how to kill him. And then, when you came to me and told me how he'd betrayed you, I knew you'd do what you could to help. And I was right, wasn't I?"

The fire crackled and a spark shot into the air and bounced off the metal screen. Susan made a small sound of fear, but Iris ignored her.

"The night we killed him, I cooked a ten dollar steak and cut it into chunks and slipped a codeine tablet into each one. I put the pieces of steak in a plastic bag and drove through the snow all the way to the park. Gerard had told me about the security cameras, so I left the car down by the water. I wasn't sure if the guard dog would accept the meat, or if he'd been trained not to." She smiled. "You should have seen him gobble it down! In ten minutes he was sound asleep. I picked him up in a fireman's lift and dumped him over the wall, into the moat. The cold water must've revived him. Then I took the stairs up to the roof and used Gerard's spare key to let myself into the room above the shark pool, and hid behind a potted plant. A potted plant! Gerard arrived about an hour later. I waited until he'd stripped and dived into the pool and then went in after him. The poor man kept trying to turn around, but I wouldn't let him. I'm sure he thought I was you, Susan, and who can blame him? As a jilted lover, you certainly had a wonderful motive. But then, didn't we both."

Iris stroked Susan's silky hair. Susan had told her about her date with that unwitting bastard Gerard, the romantic late-night swim. Iris had instructed her to show up half an hour late, but neglected to explain why. She'd drowned Gerard in Susan's absence and then, when she finally showed up, forcefully recruited her to help with the really hard part – shifting all that lard to the whale pool. Susan had been really useful, but Susan was weak. Her rage towards Gerard had died with him. Love was seeping back into her heart. Like Gerard, she had become a liability that must be disposed of.

Iris said, "Did it ever occur to you that we look very much alike, dear?" She smiled a sad, sweet smile. "If you'd only known me when I was your age . . ." A single teardrop, burning like liquid gold in the firelight, trickled down the older woman's wrinkled cheek.

The second bottle was half-empty. Where had all the wine gone? Susan looked at her glass. There it was, some of it. She raised the glass to her lips. A little wine trickled down her chin. Iris offered her a napkin, and she took it and held it tightly.

Iris said, "He died thinking it was you, dear."

Susan shuddered. She'd already consumed at least two full glasses of wine. Iris was watching her. She knew she would have to be very careful. She tried to put her glass down. The driftwood table was a bit unsteady. Or perhaps the glass slipped from her hand. *Something* went wrong.

A mouthful of wine spilled across the shiny yellow wood.

Iris said, "So you killed him, in a way. Didn't you? Not that it makes the slightest bit of difference. We couldn't have done it without each other. In the end, that's what counts, don't you think?"

Susan began to cry; tears flooded her cheeks and great racking sobs shook her body.

216

Iris picked up Susan's wine glass and tossed it into the fire. She was quite sure the silly girl hadn't touched anything else. But in the morning she'd clean the house from end to end and top to bottom, just to be sure.

Susan had curled up into a tight ball of grief. The tears continued to flow. Her body heaved and shuddered. But who was she grieving for – Gerard, or herself?

Iris went into the bedroom. She stripped down to her bra and panties and then wriggled into her wetsuit, dressed again in her baggy jeans and black sweater. She stuffed her mask, gloves and swim fins into an Eaton's shopping bag, carried the bag into the kitchen and hung it on a hook by the door.

When she returned to the living room she found that Susan had cried herself into a state of exhaustion. She told her it was time to go home, pulled her to her feet and helped her with her coat.

Susan said that she was frightened. Laughing, Iris told her not to be ridiculous.

Outside, darkness had fallen and the tide was on the ebb. It was so cold that the rhododendron's leaves had curled into hundreds of tiny green fingers. A gust of wind made the shrub's branches scratch against the side of the house. Bits of debris blew down upon them from the surrounding trees. Iris roughly propelled Susan across the snow-swept lawn towards the beach. The wind howled around them. A wave crashed upon the shore in a burst of white froth.

As they drew near the dinghy, Iris released her grip on Susan's arm. She tossed the plastic bag into the boat and ordered Susan to help her carry the small craft down to the water.

On the far side of the harbor, the city glittered as if many thousands of stars had fallen from the sky, and lay stricken and dying upon the land.

25

The way they worked it, Parker and Willows split the foot-high stack of witness reports right down the middle. Willows read carefully. As he finished each report he added it to the growing pile on Parker's desk.

Parker followed the same procedure with her stack of reports. When every report had been read, each detective skimmed rapidly through his partner's stack, searching for a previously overlooked, telling detail. The teams of detectives Bradley assigned to the case had conducted preliminary interviews with one hundred and six aquarium employees. Almost all of those interviewed had firm but uncomplimentary opinions about the deceased. But no one – so far – had any hard information that might lead Willows and Parker to Roth's killer. The investigation was going nowhere, and it was getting there in a hurry.

Willows glanced at his watch. It was quarter past eleven. He'd been at it almost three hours; no wonder his vision was starting to go.

Parker tossed him another witness report.

Eddy Orwell's chair creaked as he leaned towards Willows.

"That Ellen Murata's statement?"

Willows nodded. Orwell's initials, a block letter "E" inside a flamboyant "O" had been scrawled at the bottom of the page.

Orwell said, "I spent a little extra time with her."

"Yeah?"

Orwell nodded sagely.

"Why?" said Parker.

"Because she was real cute," said Orwell. "Why else?"

"Good question, Eddy."

Willows half-rose from his chair, leaned across his desk and tossed a report on Parker's desk.

"Great body," said Orwell. "And real friendly, know what I mean? Made me long for the bad old days."

218

"When dinosaurs roamed the earth," said Dan Oikawa, "and a bottle of Coke cost a dime."

Orwell ignored him. "There's lot of times," he said, "when I really envy you, Jack."

Willows slid open a desk drawer, slammed it shut.

"Must be nice, being single again. Ready and able to pick and choose . . ."

Oikawa and Farley Spears exchanged a quick glance. Oikawa put his pen down on his desk.

Orwell said, "Man, I bet there's times you can hardly believe your luck . . ."

Willows pushed back his chair. He stood up.

Parker said, "Jack . . ."

Orwell caught her tone. In a gesture of surprised innocence he brought his hands, knuckly fingers spread wide, up against his burly chest. "Did I say something to offend?" He winked at Oikawa. "Could it be that Jack don't want Claire thinking he's fooling around on her?"

Willows moved away from his desk.

Parker said, "Hey, wait a minute . . ."

Willows pointed across the squadroom. Homer Bradley was lounging in the open doorway to his office, an unlit cigar dangling from his mouth.

Parker turned the witness reports face down on her desk and followed Willows towards the door.

Bradley took the cigar out of his mouth, studied it for a moment and then put it back where it belonged. He stepped aside, waved Parker and Willows into his office and shut the door behind them.

Orwell waited until Bradley's shadow moved away from the pebbled glass of his office door, and then said, "So what was Jack upset about? He looked as if he was gonna slug me."

"No way," said Oikawa, a little too promptly.

"He was pissed off about something," Orwell insisted.

Spears said, "You better tell him, Dan."

Oikawa frowned. He stared up at the ceiling for a moment and then said, "You're better qualified. You do it."

"It's about the babe," said Spears. "The witness, the one who came on to you."

"Ellen Murata?"

Oikawa said, "Yeah, Ellen."

"What about her?"

"She dropped by earlier this morning, looking for you."

"She did?"

"Jack took one look at her, fell in love."

"You're kidding."

"He asked her out, Eddy."

"He did?" Orwell looked surprised, even a little upset. "He's a little old for her, wouldn't you say?"

"Lots of girls like older men," said Spears. "Older men tend to have more money. Also, most women consider them superior sackmates."

"Absolutely," said Oikawa, deadpan.

Orwell said, "Well, I'm *getting* old."

Spears smiled. He said, "The truth is, she turned him down cold."

Recovering fast, Orwell said, "I knew she would. Jack's at least thirty-five, right? Must be a bitch, knowing the high ground's all behind you."

Oikawa was in his late forties. Spears was getting close to mandatory retirement. Neither man said a word.

Whistling jauntily, Orwell consulted his spiralbound notebook. He picked up his phone, made the call, slammed the receiver back in the cradle.

"Busy?" said Spears.

Orwell nodded.

"Probably she's trying to get through to you."

"Right, right." Orwell dialled the number again. He made a face, disconnected.

"Got the automatic redialer there, Eddy."

"Yeah, right. Thanks."

Bradley poured tea from a rose pattern Royal Albert pot into a matching cup. He added three spoonfuls of sugar, squeezed a slice of lemon. He picked up the cup, sipped. "How's the Roth thing coming along?"

"Slowly," said Willows.

"You talked to the animal rights screwball?"

Parker said, "Archie isn't exactly a screwball, Inspector. In fact he was kind of nice, in a way."

"Nice," said Bradley, "but innocent." He spooned more sugar into his cup. "That's it – no other leads?"

220

Parker said, "Aquarium security sweeps the parking lot every couple of hours throughout the night. They get a lot of kids smoking dope, turning the family car into a motel on wheels. Any car in the lot after hours, they run a flashlight over it, record the tag. We asked the head of security, Bob Kelly, to provide us with a list of licence numbers recorded the night of the murder. There was a Saab registered in Roth's name, a motorhome from California. It took a while to track that one down . . ."

Bradley sipped his tea and thought about how much pleasure his cigar would give him, when his working day finally came to an end.

Parker said, "There was a black Porsche belonged to a low-level coke dealer named Maury Grescoe AKA Two-Coat Tony. Kearns says he's called Two-Coat because he's got emphysema, circulation problems. So he's always cold . . . Anyway, we cleared all the cars except one – a late-model four-wheel drive Subaru owned by a woman named Robyn Davis, DOB 11 October 1971. MVB had an address on Pendrell but she's moved, no forwarding address."

"How long's she been gone?"

"Too long, Inspector. The building manager gave her notice six months ago. Apparently she had a rambunctious boyfriend; he liked to stay up all night, listen to loud music. The manager warned Robyn twice, and then gave her the boot."

"She got a sheet?"

"No, she's clean."

"What about the boyfriend?"

"All we've got is a first name – Chris." Before Bradley could vent his displeasure Parker hastily added, "The Subaru's at the top of the hotsheet lists. It'll show up sooner or later."

"If we're lucky. How you doing with the witness reports?"

"We're making progress, Inspector."

"Stick with it. But in the meantime, do whatever you can to track down Robyn Davis. Understood?"

Willows nodded, but Bradley had already moved on to the next problem on his list, was reaching for the phone. Willows waited until Parker was clear of the door and then shut it behind them. He checked his watch. High noon. Orwell and Oikawa and Spears had already left for lunch. He said, "Can I have another look at the MVB report on the Subaru?"

Parker unlocked the top drawer of her desk, handed Willows a buff-colored folder. He glanced briefly at it. "What's today's date?"

"The twenty-eighth. Why?" She gave Willows a look. "Her insurance is due to expire, isn't it?"

"Midnight of the thirtieth."

In British Columbia, automobile insurance is mandatory. If Robyn Davis wanted to keep her Subaru on the road, she'd have to fill out an insurance form – and update her address – within the next two days.

There was a Chinese restaurant on Keefer, just off Main, that served terrific Won Ton, as well as a decent plate of bacon and eggs. Parker waited for the food to arrive, and then asked Willows if he'd thought about what he was going to do when Sheila came back. The question caught him by surprise, and it showed. He said, "She just left, Claire. The door's still closing behind her."

"She's dumped your kids – *her* kids – for some guy so unimportant to her she didn't even think to mention his name. Some guy who didn't even *care* that she dumped her kids. What kind of jerk would let a woman do something like that? How long do you think it's going to take her to realize she made a mistake? She'll be back, and it'll be sooner rather than later."

Willows stabbed viciously at a chunk of pan-fried potato, missed. The fork's tines screeched across the plate. He struck again, and this time his aim was true. He stirred the potato into a puddle of egg yolk, chewed and swallowed, gave Parker an infuriatingly bovine smile.

The remainder of the day was spent on the witness reports, fruitless calls to the Traffic Detail, Motor Vehicle Branch and ICBC – the Insurance Corporation of British Columbia. Robyn Davis's driving record was clean. She hadn't yet reported her change of address. If she'd been involved in a motor vehicle accident, she'd failed to report it.

Willows phoned Medicare. Robyn had fallen behind in her monthly payments – her health insurance had been cancelled six months earlier.

During the afternoon Willows repeatedly phoned Susan Carter and Iris Roth. Neither woman answered. Factor in Robyn Davis, and he was zero for three. Nobody answered at his own home, either. At five o'clock he tried Susan Carter one last time, let the phone ring while he cleared his desk.

Parker said, "Packing it in, Jack?"

Willows nodded.

"Got time for a drink?"

"Yeah, sure."

"Freddy's?"

"Sounds good."

"I've got a few odds and ends to tidy up. Meet you there in half an hour?"

Willows nodded. He cradled the phone, locked his desk and walked out of the office.

Freddy's bar was a lot like Freddy – low profile and well-worn. Unpretentious. Before he got into the bartending racket Freddy had been a fairly decent piano player and wonderfully indecent ladies' man. Both pursuits had come to a bloody, grinding halt when a jealous boyfriend with a tin ear stuck his hand in a blender set on purée.

A few years later Freddy settled down, became a happily married man. Because the three middle fingers of his left hand had been chopped off at the knuckles, he wore his wedding ring on his thumb.

Freddy turned from the television over the bar as Willows walked in. He snatched an open bottle of Cutty Sark off the shelf and slammed it down on the wide oak bar. Reaching for a glass, he said, "All by yourself, Jack?"

Willows said, "Yeah, but I've got a friend I could call if I was lonely."

Grinning, Freddy thumped a lowball glass down on the counter, dumped in some ice and poured a generous double. The jealous boyfriend and a couple of pals had taken Freddy to a five dollar room in a skidrow hotel, chained him to the radiator and plugged in the blender.

The night clerk heard Freddy's screams and, against all odds, dialled 911. Willows and his longtime partner, Norm Burroughs, had kicked in and saved most of Freddy from being turned into a strawberry milkshake.

About six months later Norm Burroughs succumbed to stomach cancer. No one had thought to notify Freddy of the funeral but he showed up anyway, paid his respects and dropped a thousand

223

dollars in the widow's kitty. A year or so later he invited Willows to the grand opening of his new bar. He'd been pouring Jack doubles ever since.

Freddy gave the drink a push. The glass slid along the bar and came to a stop directly in front of Willows. He picked it up, sipped.

On the television over the bar, a commercial for an environmentally friendly four-wheel-drive vehicle was replaced by a shot of a boxing ring, a square of bright blue canvas, a pair of overweight fighters slumped on wooden stools. A bell rang shrilly. The fighters came lethargically to their feet and shuffled towards the center of the ring.

"Pugs," said Freddy. "It's the third round, neither of em's been hit yet. Care to make a small wager?"

Willows said, "The fight's on tape. It happened last night, in Atlantic City. The black guy knocks out the white guy in the middle of the sixth."

"Yeah?"

"It was in this morning's paper, Freddy."

Freddy was clearly amazed. He said, "I gotta get myself a subscription. No wonder I been losing so much dough!"

Willows helped himself to a bowl of shelled peanuts. He started towards the back of the bar.

Freddy said, "Hey, wait a minute. Whaddya say we make it a *small* bet?"

Willows slid into a booth near the emergency exit. He unbuttoned his jacket and sat there with his back to the wall, watching Freddy polish glasses. A couple of guys in ski jackets came in and sat down at the bar where they could watch the TV. Both men ordered Beck's out of the bottle at five dollars a pop. Freddy started talking about the fight, pointing at the TV and shaking his head. One of the jackets said something. His buddy laughed a little too loudly, punched him hard on the shoulder.

Freddy popped the cash register, slapped a twenty down on the bar. The jacket covered the twenty with one of his own. Freddy gave Willows a conspiratorial wink.

The door swung open and Parker walked in. Willows knocked back the last of his Scotch. Freddy pointed at Willows, and Parker said something that made him smile. She started towards the rear of the bar. The sports fans swivelled on their stools as she walked by, then turned their attention back to the fight.

Parker slid into the booth, shrugged out of her coat. "Sorry I'm late. The roads are a mess. How do all those idiots ever get a driver's license?"

Willows smiled. "Talk to a traffic cop – he'll tell you that a lot of them don't."

Freddy arrived with Parker's ginger ale, a fresh bowl of peanuts and another Cutty for Willows. He said, "I got the ski bunnies down for twenty. We're into the fourth round. The white guy gets hit hard enough to wake him up. He's looking so good they want to double their bet. What am I gonna say? People want to throw money at me, I'll catch it."

Willows hadn't appreciated the wink, Freddy trying to involve him in his dumb-ass scam. He said, "If your liquor licence is only worth forty dollars to you, go ahead and sell it."

"Excuse me?"

"The guy near the door works for the liquor control board. His name's . . ." Willows frowned. He snapped his fingers, trying to remember.

Freddy laughed nervously. "You're pulling my leg, am I right?"

"Why don't you go take a hike, and see if you walk with a limp."

Freddy gave Willows an irritated look. He snatched the empty peanut bowl off the table and hustled back to the bar.

Parker said, "What was all that about?"

Willows told her. Then, without preamble, he said, "Sheila isn't coming back, Claire. Even if she did, it wouldn't make the slightest bit of difference. She and I are finished. We're through."

Parker nodded carefully. She sipped at her ginger ale.

Willows sank half his Cutty. "I'd have invited you over for dinner, but I'm a little worried about Sean – I don't know what kind of mess is waiting for me at home." He hesitated, and then said, "But I was thinking, maybe we could do something a little later on . . ."

"What kind of something?" said Parker.

"*Everything*," said Willows, and leaned across the table and kissed her on the mouth.

26

After he left Susan's apartment Chris made a beeline for a liquor store, bought a bottle of Johnny Walker Red. By the time Robyn arrived home from work he had a pretty good idea what the Scotch tasted like, and had managed to convince himself he'd brained the Mohawk guy strictly in self-defense.

Robyn sat there at the table, her generous portion of tuna casserole losing its gloss as Chris told her most but not quite all of the weird stuff that had happened in Susan's apartment. He watched Robyn very closely as he selectively described the surprising turn of events that had occurred. By the time he'd come to the end of his tale of rainbow contraceptives and spilled champagne, he believed he had convinced her the Mohawk guy's fate was inevitable.

Which was almost as good as desirable, hopefully.

Robyn turned her attention to the casserole. She chewed voraciously. Her eyes widened.

Chris said, "Something wrong?"

Robyn spat the food back on to her plate, snatched up her glass of Chilean white and put her mouth through the rinse cycle as she pushed away from the table and marched over to the sink. She spat again, vigorously, and patted herself down with a paper napkin.

Chris said, "Something is wrong, isn't it?"

She gave him a thoroughly disgusted look, putting her whole face into it. "What's wrong with you?" She stabbed a finger at the casserole. "Tuna?"

"It's politically correct tuna. Read the label! They catch it with special nets, that aren't dangerous to dolphins."

"You expect me to swallow that?"

"It says so right on the can!"

"Show me!" Robyn tore a chunk off the end of a loaf of French bread, chewed angrily.

As far as Chris was concerned France's nuclear policy was, at the very least, debatable. Just look at the way they'd pushed those Greenpeacers around! But Robyn hadn't stopped drinking French wines or eating French bread, had she?

Sighing theatrically, Chris dropped to his knees in front of the sink. He yanked open the cupboard door and started rooting through the garbage. He was supposed to have removed the can's paper label, then washed the can and crushed it and put it in the city-provided "blue box" to be recycled into a motorcycle. But what was the point? The collection process was a sham and everybody from the mayor on down knew it. Ninety per cent of the city's recyclable garbage ended up in the municipal dump.

He found the damned tin, wiped it clean of coffee grounds and placed it on the table. While Robyn perused the label, Chris picked up her plate and put it in the microwave, punched in ninety seconds on high.

Robyn said, "You're supposed to recycle, Chris. Be good to the planet, and the planet will be good to you."

"I recycled the Mohawk guy – isn't that enough for one day?"

Robyn lowered her wine glass. She gave him a very serious look. "You said you knocked him out. Now you're telling me you killed him?"

Chris went over to the kitchen counter and poured himself another shot of Johnny Walker. "He'll be okay. I never whacked a guy with a champagne bottle before. It's kind of hard to judge the weight. But like I said, he'll survive."

"And you talked to the woman – Susan?"

"Yeah, Susan. Susie. Sue, for short." He knocked back the Scotch, looked darkly up at the ceiling through the bottom of the glass.

"And . . . what? You told her you wanted twenty-five thousand dollars to keep your mouth shut."

"Well, that's not exactly how I put it. I believe 'Exercise discretion' was the phrase I used."

"And she hung up."

"Yeah, right."

"You should've phoned her right back. Kept up the pressure." Chris shrugged.

Robyn nibbled at the bread, sipped at her glass of politically correct Chilean vino.

Chris said, "It's hard work, burgling. Prowling around in a

227

strange apartment. Knowing you don't belong there. Never knowing what you're going to find around the next corner. You'd be surprised how tiring it is. By the time Susie slammed the phone in my face I was so worn out that my only ambition was to take a nice long nap."

"You had enough energy to bash the maintenance man, though, didn't you?."

"He was replacing burnt-out lightbulbs in the hall," said Chris, "and then I put out his lights." He tried a light-hearted chuckle, to let Robyn know he was just kidding, and made a sound like a length of barbed wire being dragged through a rusty pipe.

Robyn gave him a motherly look. Jeez. He turned his back on her, and was pouring another drink when his fickle and wilful imagination suddenly transported him back into the bathroom in Susan's apartment. The shower door thundered back on its rollers and there was the Mohawk guy, staring down at him as he lay curled up in the bathtub like a cowardly fish out of water. The ceiling fan grinding away overheaded, spot lights blinding him. The Mohawk guy rubbed his chin and then dipped a grimy hand into the back pocket of his coveralls, came up with a foot-long screwdriver.

Chris scrambled sideways. The screwdriver's blade chipped enamel from the tub. He swung from the hip and the champagne bottle caught Mr Mohawk flush on the ear. The screwdriver clattered in the tub. Chris lashed out again. The champagne bottle ricocheted off Mr Mohawk's skull and hit the shower door, which exploded in a burst of frosted glass. Blood splashed red as ketchup across the tiled wall as Mr Mohawk collapsed in a heap. Where had the screwdriver gone? Blood poured from Mr Mohawk's battered ear, and there was lots more blood leaking from a hole in Mr Mohawk that Chris couldn't see. Mr Mohawk made gurgling noises. Blood trickled merrily down the drain.

Mr Mohawk had a look in his eye that plainly said he'd never make that mistake again . . .

Chris turned on the shower, adjusted the taps until the temperature was just right. At the time, he had no idea why he'd done it. But later it had all made sense, kind of . . .

The microwave beeped. Chris yanked open the door, scorched his thumb and index finger on the plate. The tuna steamed delicately.

Cursing, he pulled on a bright yellow oven mitt decorated with tiny red steaks, picked up the plate and put it down in front of Robyn.

She scooped up a forkful of casserole. She said, "You're sure he's going to be okay?"

"Pretty sure." Chris turned on the cold water tap, held his wounded fingers under the stream.

"I hope you didn't hit him too hard, Chris."

"Yeah, me too. But don't worry about it. He'll be fine."

But, just in case Mr Mohawk had cashed in his chips, Chris had used a pink and blue striped bath towel to wipe down the apartment. The way he saw it, if the cops ever did find a body, there was a good chance they'd assume Mr Mohawk had surreptitiously gained entry to the apartment with his master key, helped himself to a little too much bubbly and, inebriated, accosted Susan in the shower.

She'd slapped him down, naturally. Who wouldn't? He'd gone after her with the screwdriver . . .

It sure sounded good to Chris. But what if Susan went back to her apartment? What if she called the cops? Would she risk drawing their attention to one murder and perhaps becoming implicated in another? Chris told himself the answer was no.

But who could tell, really. And if he *had* killed Mr Mohawk, well, what did he have to lose by knocking Susan off? Now, wasn't that a horrible thought.

Robyn said, "Did you make a salad?"

Chris shook his head, no. He couldn't help noticing that she seemed to be having a little trouble keeping him in focus.

He had drifted away on a sea of murderous thoughts, and he saw that while he had been gone Robyn had hardly touched her tuna casserole but had managed to drain the wine bottle.

He went over to the closet and grabbed his leather jacket.

"You leaving me again?" said Robyn. No doubt about it, she was a little on the tipsy side. Or, a somewhat less charitable way to put it, drunk.

Chris said he was going out to make a call.

"Why don't you use the phone in the bedroom?"

"I don't think that would be wise, Robyn."

"How come?"

"Because, depending on how things turn out, we might not want the cops to be able to trace the call."

"I'm going with you."

Chris said, "Maybe you better not." But she was already moving towards him, smiling.

She pressed up against him as she reached for her coat. "Gimme a kiss, big fella."

Chris put his arms around her. She played with his jacket, rubbed up against him as she worked the zippers. He kissed her all the way down the hall, continued to kiss her while they waited for the elevator. He kept on kissing her as they descended to ground level and made their way through the lobby and outside, into the cold, cold world.

There was a payphone a couple of blocks away, near a Shopper's Drug Mart. Robyn wanted to hang on to his ear but Chris told her she'd make him nervous so she went into the store to browse around, maybe read a magazine. He dropped a quarter, dialled. Susan picked up on the first ring, which Chris thought was promising.

He said, "Susan?"

"Yes?"

Chris said, "Is that you?"

"Who else would it be?"

A black kid in an oversized Chicago Bulls jacket and impossibly baggy jeans sauntered by. Chris said, "You know who this is, don't you?"

The kid's head snapped around. His baseball cap was on backwards, as were his pants, so it was a mildly weird effect.

Susan said, "Yes, of course." She sounded very calm.

Chris said, "So . . ."

"Well, I don't have a great deal of choice, do I?"

"That's the way I see it. How long's it going to take?"

"To get the money?"

Chris, tired of dicking around, said, "Yeah, that's right. How long's it gonna take you to get the money?"

"I already have it."

Chris said, "Huh?" Recovering, he added, "All of it?"

"Every last penny."

Her voice sounded a little different. Not much, but a little. Deeper, somehow. Chris mentioned it.

Susan said, "I've been crying."

The kid in the Bulls jacket cruised past again, like a deconstructed shark moving in for the kill. He flipped a quarter high

230

into the crisp neon-zapped air, caught it behind his back and gave Chris a triumphant look.

Distracted, Chris asked Susan if she had a pen and a piece of paper, then told her what he wanted her to do – put the cash in a brown paper bag and get on the SkyTrain at the Royal Center station, and then . . .

Susan broke in, told him if he wanted his filthy money he was going to have to meet her at the east end of Trout Lake.

Chris said, "Hey, wait a minute . . ."

The kid in the jacket had moved in unannounced, was standing almost within reach, rocking from side to side on a pair of monster Nikes that must've added at least two inches to his height. But even without them, he was pushing six foot six.

The coin whirled high into the air, vanished in a huge black fist.

Susan, talking fast in that tear-stained voice of hers, told Chris she wouldn't do it any other way – that she was going to be all alone, and was afraid he might overpower her, take the money and kill her. All the odds were in his favor, but this way she'd feel she at least had a chance. Was he afraid of her?

Chris said no.

The kid had put on a pair of oil-on-water wraparound sunglasses.

Susan told him to look for a litter bin down by the shore; a big green metal drum chained to a wooden post. She'd meet him there at one a.m. Sharp.

Chris said okay.

She asked him how she'd know who he was. Chris told her he looked a lot like Tom Cruise, except he had whiter teeth, a nicer smile.

It sounded to him then as if she burst into tears.

Chris hung up, moved away from the phone. The black kid swooped, sprayed the receiver with disinfectant from a pressurized can.

Robyn was at the cosmetics counter, sampling a new shade of frosted pink lipstick. She asked Chris what he thought.

"Nice."

"Nice?" She made a face. "It's supposed to be sexy. Or you could say decadent, or hot. Anything but nice. God, what an utterly *limp* word." She paused. "You talked to her?"

"Everything's all set."

"It is?"

231

"It'll all be over by a few minutes past one."

Robyn said, "Mr Quick."

Chris smiled. "That's what they call me and that's who I am." He'd already decided not to tell Robyn that he'd caved in under pressure, agreed to meet Susan at the lake of her choice.

But come to think of it, he wasn't at all sure he'd be able to find Trout Lake. Maybe it'd be a good idea not to search too hard. Maybe he should take a pass on the one o'oclock meeting, take some time to think things over.

But then, what about Mr Mohawk?

If Mr Mohawk was dead, he was looking at arrest, a trial – the whole law-and-order shtick, and who could say what the consequences might be. He couldn't see himself doing time. He'd been a little worried about the kid in the Bulls jacket. Imagine what it'd be like bunking down with a maximum-security prison full of genuine convicts.

On the other hand, the twenty-five grand would last a long time, in Mexico. Even if it turned out that Mr Mohawk was a little bruised but otherwise okay, wouldn't it still be a good idea to blow town?

Naturally Robyn wanted to be there when he picked up the money.

Chris said no, he had to go alone. Why? Because they couldn't risk spooking Susan.

She tried another shade of pink. "Like this one?"

"Hot," said Chris.

"It should be. It's called Frosty Pink Hot Melt, by Luscious Lips. You really like it?"

"Cross my heart."

"Want to go home and try it out?"

Chris had scheduled a very serious meeting. He knew he should arrive early, check out the terrain. But Robyn was standing there, hip-cocked, giving him a mischievous grin, challenging him.

He said, "Tell you what. Why don't we go back to the apartment and find out just how quick Mr Quick can be . . ."

He left the apartment at eleven-thirty, studied a map of the city as the Subaru's engine warmed. Trout Lake was about four miles east and maybe twenty minutes or half an hour's drive away. Chris scrubbed at the frosty windshield with a gloved hand, trying to clear the thin layer of iced-up condensation. He'd been meaning

232

to buy a plastic scraper all week, but somehow hadn't gotten around to it.

That was another thing about Mexico – the weather was better.

He turned on the radio, fiddled his way across the dial, stumbled across a Garth Brooks tune and cranked up the volume until he could hear the music over the blast of the heater.

At twenty-five minutes to twelve he put the Subaru in gear and set out upon his crosstown voyage.

Thirty minutes later he pulled into the tiny public parking lot at the far end of Trout Lake. The trash can was no more than two hundred yards away; a dark green rectangle silhouetted against the snow.

The lake was so perfectly oval that it looked as if it had been man-made. It was fairly large; about a quarter of a mile across and half a mile wide. Except for a black, kidney-shaped area of open water at the near end, the lake's surface was frozen solid and covered in snow.

The park itself was a perfect rectangle about four blocks long and two blocks wide. There were a few small trees down at the far end, but otherwise the whole area was open as a desert. Chris turned off the car lights but let the engine idle. Either Susie was tucked away in the trash can, or she hadn't showed up yet.

Chris figured he better find out which was which. He turned off the engine. The door squeaked as he pushed it open. Snow creaked under his boots as he made his way down a gentle slope to the trash can.

The can was big – waist high and almost a yard across. Big enough to hold a woman.

He walked right up to it, peered inside. There was nothing much in there except a few non-returnable bottles at the bottom and a Domino's Pizza jacket with the right arm ripped off.

No Susan, though.

Chris walked across slippery, hard-packed snow to the shore of the lake. The small body of open water was shiny black and very still, reflecting pinpoints of light from the street. A few small dark birds floated in the middle of the water. A yellow sign said "Thin Ice – No Skating".

Chris walked along the shore until he came to where the ice started. He walked a few more feet and gingerly put one foot on the ice to test its strength. It held. He edged out inch by inch until he was about a foot from shore. The ice felt solid as concrete.

He moved out a little further and then walked along parallel to the shoreline. There were marks on the ice, that he was sure had been made by skates. He broke into a kind of shambling trot and then braced himself and slid almost twenty feet, came to a gentle stop.

Somewhere in the darkness behind him a duck quacked plaintively.

Chris skated clumsily along the shoreline until all the fun had gone out of it, then went back to the Subaru and started the engine. It was important to keep the car warm. When he made his getaway he wanted it to start with the first turn of the key.

He switched on the radio. The country music station had changed to a talkshow format. A woman wanted to know why her trucker boyfriend refused to make love except in his eighteen-wheeler, at highway speed . . .

At quarter to one Chris left the warmth of the car and walked back down to the trash can. Behind him, there was a sudden burst of alarmed quacking. The open water was chopped to a white froth as the flock of ducks lifted off, wheeled past him and rose up into the city lights and vanished in darkness. He peered towards the lake, crouched down low so anyone creeping towards him across the frozen surface would be silhouetted against the lights on the far shore.

He saw no one. He began to relax; could feel the tension easing out of him as palpably as if someone had pulled a plug. He told himself the ducks had smelled a cat or raccoon, or some other predator.

Directly in front of him, about fifty feet away, the surface of the lake bulged. A pinpoint of light swelled and burst, reformed, trembled and was still.

Chris, squinting down at the dial of his watch, saw nothing of this. All he knew was that it almost one. Christ, where could she be?

Somewhere high overhead the birds were circling, the wind in their pinfeathers making an eerie, high-pitched whistling sound.

Distracted, Chris looked up.

On the lake, the surface of the water fractured in thin streamers of light. A shiny black form rose out of the inky blackness. It was as if the lake was giving birth. A gleaming oval disc of light seemed to levitate above the surface of the water, glide slowly and silently towards the shore. A bright spark of moving light marked a lightning-rod of steel. Small waves pulsed against the muddy shore with a sound like muted laughter.

Chris turned. He slipped on the snow.

He thought, *There she is.*

The spark of light dipped towards him. There was a snapping sound, as if someone had released the tension on a gigantic rubber band. The air vibrated.

Chris felt something *slither* into him. He looked down. A thin black shaft – the last few inches of a three-foot-long teflon-coated anodized aluminum spear – protruded from his chest. The barbed stainless steel point had struck him just below the breastbone, pierced him through and chopped his spine in half.

He collapsed in a heap on the hard-packed snow.

The slap of Iris Roth's fins sounded like scattered applause as she made her way up the slope. She knelt, gripped the bloody shaft with both hands, grunted loudly as she pulled it free.

Chris saw his faint, ghostly image reflected in the glass of her face mask. He looked very pale. The woman who had hurt him slung her speargun across her back. He felt nothing as she dragged him towards the water.

There was the sound of an engine. A car swung into the parking lot, stopped with the headlights focused on the green-painted metal trash can. Chris heard laughter, car doors slamming. The woman who held him in her arms crouched low but kept moving. He saw that her mask had begun to fog. Was that why his image was so indistinct, faded and blurred? She reached the shoreline and backed slowly into the water.

The engine and headlights died. Chris heard more laughter and the squeaky crunch of footsteps on the snow. Black water closed around him, burying him.

He heard screams. Flashlight beams skittered across the snow.

Iris backpedalled until she bumped gently against the edge of the two-inch thick shelf of ice that covered the lake.

She let the kid drift while she struggled with the thirty-pound weight belt, slipped it around his narrow waist and cinched it tight.

Chris was still alive. Water sloshed in his gaping mouth. A skullcap of ice had already formed on his head.

But he was alive. He was still alive.

A widening beam of light swept across the surface of the lake.

Someone cried out. Someone else laughed and laughed and laughed.

Iris rolled Chris over and pushed him down and away as hard as she could, with all her strength.

She felt the pressure of the water swirling round her as his drowning body glided silently beneath the ice.

27

Willows arrived home at six-thirty. He'd planned to throw together a salad while a couple of steaks thawed in the microwave, cook a few Idaho potatoes in the microwave while he pan-fried the steaks. It wasn't exactly *cuisine gourmet*, but it wouldn't take more than fifteen minutes to prepare.

He unlocked and swung open the door and the mouth-watering smell of good food that had been simmering for a long time hit him flush on the nose. He went down the hall and into the kitchen. A huge pot of spaghetti sauce burbled quietly on a back burner. Water boiled in a two-quart pot on another burner. Willows called out and Annie cheerfully responded. She was in the dining room. The table had been set for four. Candles had been lit and she'd used the good napkins, his mother's linen. She gave him a bright smile, got up on her toes and kissed him on the cheek.

Willows eyes strayed to the four place settings.

Annie said, "I thought you might invite Claire over for dinner."

Willows nodded. He said, "I see."

"You thought Mummy had come back, didn't you?"

"The possibility crossed my mind."

"Pretty scary, huh?"

Willows smiled. "Sean around?"

"He's in his room. He told me he got kicked out of the 7-Eleven for trying to steal a pack of cigarettes."

Willows saw the tears welling up. He put his arms around his child's thin shoulders.

Snuffling into his shoulder, Annie said, "I don't care if she never comes back. From now on, I'm staying with you."

Willows said, "That would make me very happy, Annie." It seemed such an inadequate response. He held his daughter close, trying to convey his love for her with all his heart and soul.

Annie pulled away from him. She fished a thick wad of tissues from her sweater pocket and blew her nose. "That creep's going

237

to dump her sooner or later, and she knows it. But she wanted so badly to get away."

Willows kissed her on the forehead. She wrinkled her nose. "You've been boozing it up."

"In moderation."

"At Freddy's?"

"Yeah, at Freddy's."

Annie wiped dry her eyes. "Well, that's not *quite* so bad, since he's famous for watering his drinks. Hungry?"

"Starving," said Willows.

The meal was as good as it had smelled, and Willows refused to let it bother him when Sean decided to eat in his room, and then left the house without explanation. Annie had baked an apple pie for dessert. She insisted that Willows phone Parker and invite her over.

Parker arrived a little before nine, with a liter of expensive designer icecream. The three of them lingered over fresh pie *à la mode*. Annie chatted animatedly with Parker about the new school she'd start attending in the morning. A few minutes past ten, all the energy seemed to drain out of her at once. She yawned hugely, apologized to Parker, kissed Willows goodnight and went off to bed.

"Sweet child," said Parker.

Willows had to agree.

Parker said, "She's going to be a real knockout in a few more years, Jack. You'll be beating the boys off with a stick."

"A large, sharp stick," said Willows. He suggested they go upstairs and watch a little television.

Parker said, "Is that a euphemism?"

"Come and see." Willows offered her his hand, and she took it.

The phone rang twice and then the alarm went off. Willows rolled over. He turned off the alarm and picked up, realizing in a moment of clarity that Parker had left him so long ago that her side of the bed was cold.

Homer Bradley was an early riser. He expected the same from his squad.

"I wake you, Jack?"

"Not yet."

An alert city sanitation employee had noticed a smear of blood

238

leading from a garbage can to the shore of Trout Lake. He'd taken a look in the can and found a Domino's Pizza deliveryman's jacket with an arm ripped off. The man had called his supervisor, who'd promptly passed the call on to *his* supervisor, who'd called the cops. A car had responded, parked right next to Robyn Davis's hotsheet Subaru.

Willows said, "I'll call Parker."

"Claire's already on it, Jack. I talked to her a few minutes ago. She expects you to pick her up on the way to the lake."

Willows showered and shaved, dressed in jeans and a flannel shirt.

He heard a noise downstairs in the kitchen, found Annie pouring freshly made coffee into his stainless steel thermos.

She said, "I heard the phone . . ."

Willows said, "You're a sweetheart, but I don't want you to do this again, understand?"

Annie nodded, added cream to the coffee and screwed the lid down tight.

Willows shrugged into a brown leather bomber jacket with a sheepskin collar.

Annie hurried to the front door, held it open for him. "Got your keys and gloves? Gun?"

He gave her a sourpuss look, and then a quick hug.

She said, "Don't forget your smile . . ."

Willows told his daughter to shut the door before she caught her death of cold.

Alfred Cortez was a small, dark man in his early fifties. Tight black curls streaked with grey sneaked out from beneath his wool hat. His black plastic framed glasses rode high up on his snub nose. Beneath his down-filled jacket he wore a crisp white shirt and tartan tie. When he pulled off a heavy leather workglove to shake hands, Willows noticed that his skin was soft and white, the nails clean and recently trimmed.

Alfred had been employed by the city close to twenty years. He enjoyed his job and worked very hard to ensure that he was the sort of employee in which the city could take great pride. The first words he spoke to Willows echoed his opening statement to the uniformed cop who'd answered his original call.

"I didn't touch nothing. Soon as I saw the blood I backed off."

239

Willows said, "That's good, Alfred."

"I got a schedule, but I ain't gonna worry about it. It's my duty as a citizen to co-operate with the police, and I take that duty real serious. So what if I miss a coffee break. Did *you* ever miss a coffee break?"

Willows nodded.

"Well then, there you go."

The problem was, Alfred hadn't seen anything and he didn't know anything.

Willows offered him a card. Alfred put the card in a battered, seam-split eelskin wallet stuffed with cards. He gave Parker a lingering smile. She gave him one of her cards. Alfred maintained eye contact with Parker as he said, "If I think of anything, I'll give you a call."

"But *only* if you think of something," said Willows.

"Whatever." Alfred adjusted the knot of his tie, which in his opinion was practically brand-new, since he'd scavenged it out of a garbage can hardly more than week ago. He tossed Parker another fetching smile, waved as she and her partner made their way towards the cop brass parked down by the water.

Homer Bradley, Mel Dutton and Bailey "Popeye" Rowland stood facing each other in a tight, black-coated circle down by the frozen lake. A strong wind ripped dark tendrils of cloud from the churning mass overhead. The sky was so dark that there were no shadows. All three men wore dark blue or black wide-brim hats that obscured their features. To protect themselves against the chill they had pulled up the collars of their drab winter coats, stuffed their hands deep in their pockets. Their heads were bowed, shoulders hunched against the cold. Bundled into themselves, they were motionless and silent. Their posture suggested an introspective, moody and amoral attitude. They resembled crows. A stranger coming suddenly upon them would have been alarmed. They looked as if they were plotting murder.

Bradley and the others turned inquisitively as they heard the crunch of snow underfoot. They saw Willows and Parker moving down the slope towards them. There was an exchange of greetings.

The smear of blood in the snow was twenty feet long and a handspan in width, framed on either side by shallow grooves in the snow. Heel marks.

A small flock of ducks paddled lethargically in the shrinking body of open water. Behind them, the surface of the lake was flat and white, featureless, bland. On the far shore stood a copse of elms, branches shivering in the wind.

Mel Dutton said, "Pretty, huh?" He tapped the Nikon slung around his neck. "I shot half a roll. Next year's Christmas cards."

Popeye gave Dutton a disgusted look. The ME's Monocle reflected a disc of light. A large brown paper bag stood open on the snow beside him. Willows took a peek inside. Popeye had collected a generous sample of red-stained snow. He caught Willows looking and bent to pick up the bag. Turning to Bradley he said, "Since you don't have a body for me to examine, Homer, there isn't much I can do here. How about I head back downtown, drop this off at the lab, let Goldstein have a look at it."

Bradley said, "I'd appreciate that, Popeye."

The ME nodded. He smiled at Parker. "You're a single woman, aren't you?"

Parker nodded.

Popeye smiled approvingly. "Good girl. Minimizes the risk of domestic violence." He settled the paper bag in his arms and started up the slope towards the parking lot.

Parker caught Dutton's eyes. She said, "The trouble with Popeye is, I can never tell when he's serious."

Dutton said, "He's never serious. I know because I asked him once, and that's what he told me."

Bradley said, "You finish taking pictures, Mel?"

"Yeah, I'm finished."

"Well then, I guess the sooner you get back to your darkroom, the sooner we'll see what you've got."

Dutton trudged up the slope. If he'd had a tail, it would've been tucked between his legs.

Willows said, "Find anything in the Subaru?"

"It's locked. I'm having it towed to the impound lot for examination." He crooked a finger. "Take a look at this."

Willows and Parker followed Bradley up the slope to the source of the bloodstain.

Bradley crouched, pointed down at the thin streaks of frozen blood radiating outwards in the snow. "What's that look like to you?"

"A splash pattern," said Parker. "I'd say somebody shot him with a small-caliber weapon, a twenty-two, maybe. Any casings?"

"Nope."

Willows said, "Anybody hear a shot?"

"It's a very quiet neighborhood, Jack. Nobody ever hears anything."

Behind Bradley a yellow tow-truck, lights flashing, drove down Semlin towards the park.

Willows turned and looked at the lake. Dutton was right, it was a picture-postcard scene. He thought about the body that was surely out there, drifting under the ice. Somebody's daughter, or somebody's son.

Willows and Parker tailed the Subaru to the impound lot beneath the east end of the Georgia Viaduct. The car was driven over a sheet of heavy-gauge plastic. The tow-truck disengaged.

A mechanic unlocked the Subaru with a master key. Ident swarmed over the vehicle's interior, dusting down every square inch of surface area that could possibly hold a fingerprint.

Willows popped open the glove compartment, found a stamped, pre-addressed BC Telephone Company envelope. He ripped it open. Inside was a BC Tel statement of account. The customer, Christopher Rand Spacy, was in arrears. He owed the company thirty-seven dollars and forty-nine cents. Twenty-two dollars and fifty-six cents of that amount was overdue. The envelope also contained a personalized cheque made out in the full amount owing. Spacy had signed the cheque.

The billed address was 808-East 8th Avenue.

Robyn had been up all night, worrying. She'd called all of Chris's crazy actor friends, and then half a dozen emergency wards. Maybe he'd spent the night in the drunk tank – wouldn't that be nice?

She was angry when she answered the door, ready to give him hell for losing his keys and whatever other stupid things he'd done. But it wasn't Chris who stood there in the hall, it was a clean-cut but somehow kind of hard-edged couple that looked as if they'd been standing there forever. The last thing she needed was a high-powered doom and gloom religious pitch. She tried to shut the door, and the guy in the bomber jacket stuck out his foot. Robyn looked down. The guy was wearing oxblood brogues, size ten and a half or eleven. Same as Chris.

Robyn looked up.

The woman had a badge. Correction. They both had badges.

Cops.

Robyn suddenly knew that Chris had lost a lot more than just his keys. She stepped back, leaned against the wall. The woman reached for her but missed. She slumped to the carpet. The cops knelt beside her. The woman had a weakness for expensive perfume; her partner was chewing on a mint.

Robyn took a deep breath. She said, "What happened to Chris?"

"He's missing," said Willows. "That's all we know."

"Bullshit."

Parker said, "No, really." She introduced herself, and Willows.

Robyn tried to stand up. Her knees were a little wobbly. Parker steadied her.

Willows said, "Do you own a white ninety-two Subaru Justy?"

Robyn nodded. She bit her lip, hard.

"We're looking for Chris."

"He isn't here, obviously."

Willows smiled. "Mind if I take a look?"

"Help yourself."

Willows wandered through the apartment, letting his eyes do the work, find what they may. There was a framed picture in the hall of Robyn and someone he assumed was Christopher Rand Spacy, basking in sunlight on a white sand beach.

The kitchen was a mess.

The bedroom was worse. Clothing, male and female, was strewn everywhere.

A tap dripped in the bathroom. The tub was half-full of cold, soapy water. A washcloth floated like a blank white face.

In the living room, Willows loitered quietly while Parker told Robyn what little they knew: that her Subaru had been found abandoned by the lake and that it appeared someone who was bleeding heavily had been dragged down to the water.

Robyn told Parker she didn't see what that had to do with her.

Parker asked Robyn if Chris had driven the Subaru the previous night. She asked Robyn when she had last seen Chris. She wondered what Chris was doing at Trout Lake. She asked Robyn if Chris owned a gun.

Robyn wasn't sure, couldn't remember, had no idea, doubted it.

Parker kept asking questions. She was infinitely patient.

Robyn went into the kitchen and wiped clean the counter. She

243

asked Parker if she wanted coffee and then neglected to make it. She came back into the living room, straightened a cushion on the sofa. Chris had left a wine glass on the windowsill. She picked up the glass and held it as he had held it, covering his hand with her own.

The male cop was staring out the window. What was he looking at? She followed his gaze. The dead pigeon still clung to the power line in the alley. Its body and widespread wings were glazed in snow and droplets of ice. The bird glittered and sparkled as it swung stiffly in the erratic, gusting wind. It was so lovely that it might have been an angel come to grief.

Like Chris.

Robyn sat down. Parker held her hand. Willows took notes as Robyn confessed to a disjointed, weepy tale of base opportunism, sudden greed, foolhardy naïvety.

When Robyn had finished talking and dried her eyes, Parker said, "You're sure it was Susan Carter that Chris tried to blackmail?"

"He had proof she was having an affair with the man we saw pushed into the whale pool."

"Gerard Roth."

Robyn nodded.

Willows said, "What kind of proof?"

Robyn shrugged.

"You didn't ask?"

Had Chris collected the twenty-five thousand and then abandoned her? Robyn wanted to believe it. He was impetuous and sometimes he was weak. It was possible . . . She felt hollowed out, empty. Desolate. Awash in grief. The cop in the brogues had knelt down in front of her. What was he saying? He looked so sincere, but the tears had begun to flow again, and she couldn't understand a word he said.

Willows used the phone in the bedroom to dial Susan Carter's home number. He counted a dozen rings, hung up and dialled again. No answer. He tried the aquarium. Susan was apparently still sick. She hadn't called in.

He hung up, went back into the living room. Robyn had managed to bring herself under control. He waited while Parker explained the functions of the Victim and Witnesses Service Unit, asked Robyn if she would like someone to give her a call.

Robyn said she'd think about it.

Parker asked her if she had any relatives in the city. Robyn shrugged and said no.

"Friends?" said Willows.

"No one I want to talk to."

Parker and Willows exchanged a glance. Parker went over to the phone and dialled the VWSU. She was told to expect a counsellor in half an hour or less.

Willows went into the kitchen to make a pot of tea.

An hour later, Willows parked in the alley behind Susan Carter's apartment block. There was no answer when he buzzed her. He rang the super. A woman who would only identify herself as Esmerelda told him she had no idea where her drunken lout of a husband was, that he'd been missing since mid-afternoon of the previous day.

Willows told her that was quite a coincidence, since Susan Carter had been missing for roughly the same period of time. He and Parker stamped their feet against the cold while they waited for Esmerelda to let them in. The super's wife was in her mid-fifties, wore a charcoal-grey cardigan and brown slacks, bifocals in hot-pink plastic frames. Esmerelda wasn't wearing lipstick or any other makeup, but Parker was certain her hair had recently been tinted and permed. Her eyes behind the glasses were red and swollen. In silence, the two detectives and their escort rode the elevator to the fourteenth floor.

Willows used Esmerelda's master key to unlock the apartment door. He draped a handkerchief over the knob, delicately turned it until he could push open the door. It was a straight run down the entrance hall to the living room. The apartment was dark. He could see from the open doorway that the living room curtains had been pulled.

He used the handkerchief again as he snapped on an overhead light.

Parker told Esmerelda to wait in the hall, and she and Willows entered the apartment. The smell of blood hit them and Parker immediately turned and shut the door in Esmerelda's bleached, tear-stained face.

They found Mr Mohawk exactly as Chris had left him. Willows turned off the shower, knelt and searched for a pulse. Mr Mohawk's eyes flicked open. He showed his teeth. Parker hurried off in search of a phone. Willows told Mr Mohawk to take it easy,

245

assured him he was going to be all right. Mr Mohawk swung wildly, and sank a number eight Phillips screwdriver deep into Willows' forearm.

Willows fell back. Mr Mohawk fainted dead away. The screwdriver clattered in the tub.

Parker appeared in the bathroom doorway. She said, "An ambulance is on its way."

"Great." Willows stood up. A stream of blood ran down his wrist, splattered on the bloody floor. Parker's face was white. He managed a shaky grin.

Parker said, "Christ, Jack."

"I'm okay – it's nothing."

"What happened?"

"He woke up on the wrong side of the bed." Parker helped Willows ease out of his jacket, gingerly rolled up his bloody shirt sleeve. The neat round hole in his arm was about a quarter-inch in diameter. She remembered the small-caliber splash pattern in the snow at the lake.

As Parker rinsed his wound under the cold water tap, Willows tried unsuccessfully to recall when he'd had his last tetanus shot. Long, long ago. He asked Parker if she had any aspirin.

Of course she did.

The paramedics stabilized Mr Mohawk, then dealt with Willows' relatively minor injury. Parker wanted to drive him to emergency, but he'd been on the hunt too long to give it up.

By the time Parker pulled up in front of Gerard Roth's expensive False Creek apartment Willows' arm was so badly swollen and painful that he had to ask her to loosen the pressure bandage hurriedly applied by the paramedics.

His mood improved slightly when he saw that Roth's door was off the latch. Parker knocked and loudly called out Susan's name. There was no response. Willows drew his revolver. Parker called out again, and then she and Willows entered the apartment.

The leather couch and loveseat had been slashed to ribbons. A chair had shattered the heart-shaped mirrored-glass coffee table. Dozens of framed photographs had been torn from the wall and stomped to pieces. Willows made his way down the hall, checked first the bedroom and then the bathroom. Gerard Roth's expensive

False Creek apartment had been violently but methodically ripped to shreds.

Parker dialled Iris Roth's number.

Busy. She dialled "O", gave the operator her badge number and asked for an intercept. Iris's phone was off the hook. With a mounting sense of urgency, Parker made a call to the West Vancouver police. The duty sergeant told her he had a major backlog but assured her he'd send a unit to check on Iris Roth as soon as possible. Parker insisted on knowing roughly how much time that was likely to take. Pressed, he told her the switchboard had logged two 911 calls from a residence on Blink Bonnie Road, out on Batchelor Point. An unidentified, extremely distraught female had reported a break and enter in progress and the presence of three bodies on the beach in front of the residence. Every available unit was en route, and likely to be tied up for quite some time.

Parker said, "How far is Batchelor Point from Eagle Island?"

"Half a mile, maybe a little more."

"And there were three bodies on the beach?"

"Yeah, three of 'em."

Parker thanked him and hung up.

Willows said, "I'll drive."

28

Feeling housebound, old man Sinclair had decided to spend an hour or two on the beach, spin-casting for whatever was dumb enough to climb aboard his hook. He had no real hope of catching anything, given the tide and his general lack of enthusiasm. But he'd learned early on in his retirement that carrying a fishing rod gave him license to poke around on the beach for as long as he wanted, no questions asked.

He'd barely wet his line when he saw Fireball and Mr Jigs. The two dogs lay on the beach by the high tide line, entangled in a lacy shroud of green nylon fishnet. He rested his rod against a log and hurried towards them. He noticed right away that neither dog was wearing his studded collar. As he drew closer he saw that their fur was matted and their weirdly bulging eyes had a dull, glazed look.

A stranger coming upon the two bodies might have thought they were cheap stuffed toys, but Sinclair recognized the dogs immediately. The feisty little buggers had escaped from the Roth household whenever they could, ever since they were pups. Many was the time he'd looked out the window and seen them scampering through the trees towards him, looking for a little affection, table scraps.

He poked Mr Jigs and then Fireball with a stick. The dogs were at least as dead as they looked, which was about as dead as it was possible to get.

Now that he'd had time to get over the initial shock he was able to see the dogs more clearly. It was obvious they'd been on the beach for a day or so; Mr Jigs had dried sand in his eyes and Fireball's open mouth was choked with hoar frost. Both bodies were badly mutilated; chopped up as if by a propeller. He remembered seeing that sad asshole Gerard trying to train them to piss on a scarecrow he'd set up in the backyard. What a dope.

If there was a doggie heaven, the Saint Bernards at the front door sure as hell wouldn't let Gerard inside.

Knees creaking, the old man crouched behind a log to escape the wind that swept in off the harbor. He stuffed and lit his pipe. The rotten weather had kept just about everyone indoors. Except for the dogs, he was alone.

He glanced behind him, at the dark, empty windows of the multi-million-dollar oceanfront homes that lined the beach. He couldn't walk away and leave Fireball and Mr Jigs lying there, but knew he lacked the strength to carry or even drag them to his car. What he needed was a little bit of help. He showed the wind his strong yellow teeth. He couldn't see himself asking some millionaire's wife to give him a hand with a couple of deader-than-hell dogs.

It was a goddamned quandary, wasn't it?

He could call the pound though, couldn't he? Let professionals deal with the problem. He tried to think where the nearest payphone was, puffed strongly on his pipe and was a little astonished to find it had gone out. His Zippo was in his pants pocket. He had to stand up to get at it. He was thumbing the lighter's wheel when he saw the third corpse. His first thought was that it was a seal, but then he saw it was a human being, probably a woman.

A wave struck the body in a welter of foam. Well, he knew what to do now, didn't he? He turned his back on the body and walked stiffly up the beach, towards the nearest million-dollar home.

The house's mahogany front door had a miniature porthole sunk into it. Cute. He peered through the glass, then pressed the doorbell. Behind him, a seagull flared its wings as it passed over the body, wheeled gracefully and settled lightly on the sand. Prepared to eat it or beat it, the bird approached the corpse with a peculiar sideways gait.

The old man pressed the doorbell again. He tried the door. It was unlocked. The entrance hall was lit by a massive, glittering chandelier. The floor was pink marble and the walls panelled in bleached oak. A garish Mickey Mouse telephone stood on an inlaid table. He was pleased to find that he much preferred his own modest dwelling to this one. He called out, then walked inside and shut the door behind him, went over to the table and picked up the phone.

The line was already occupied. A woman's voice said, "Bob, is that you?"

Old man Sinclair identified himself. He explained that he was a neighbor, almost.

The woman screamed.

A man with an Italian accent excitedly advised the woman to hang up and lock the bedroom door. He told her to be quick, shouted that he would call the police.

Old man Sinclair said that was a very good idea. He tried to explain about the bodies. The Italian swore vociferously. Upstairs, a door slammed shut.

He went back outside, took a deep breath of cold, salty air. The gull had vanished, but the woman's body still lay on the beach at the tide line. A wave rolled over it, roughly pushed and pulled it across the gravel. It was wrong to leave her there, but he'd done what he could. He'd seen more than enough corpses for one day. It made no sense to stick around and be arrested for trespass, or much worse. He retrieved his fishing rod and started towards the path that meandered through the fringe of woods skirting the golf course. It would take him to Marine Drive where he'd parked his Studebaker.

Half an hour later, as he sat at his kitchen window mulling over the wisdom of dropping by the Roth house to see if Hot Stuff was okay, he happened to spot the young couple on the pier.

Willows and Parker stepped on board the nearest of the little ferries. The boat rocked gently as Willows made his way to the stern. He checked to ensure that the motor was in neutral, adjusted the choke and pulled the starter cord. The motor sputtered. His wounded arm throbbed. He pulled again. The motor caught, faltered, and then held steady. He eased in the choke. Parker cast off the lightweight galvanized chains securing them to the dock. Willows put the engine in reverse, backed slowly out of the slip. His arm had started bleeding again; red drops splattered on the aluminum deck. He pointed the bow towards the island, shifted into forward and goosed it.

Old man Sinclair watched Iris Roth's boat speed across the narrow channel of slate-grey water separating the island from the mainland. The young fella at the tiller was going much too fast. Sinclair knew for a fact that most people who didn't know boats treated them as if they were nothing but floating automobiles. This was not a good idea. Boats were like horses – if you didn't tie them up, nine times out of ten they'd wander off first chance they got. He watched as Willows eased the ferry up to the small floating dock that serviced the island.

Parker fastened her detective's shield to the lapel of her overcoat. There was a lot that Willows wanted to say to her, but since he'd said most of it many times before, he didn't see much point in saying it again. As for the rest of it, well, that could wait. He reached out and gave her badge a yank, satisfied himself that the spring clip held it firmly in place. Claire smiled up at him. She checked the load in her revolver.

They walked in single file along the dark, narrow path that led through the woods to the Roth house. The porch light was on but there was no other sign of life.

Willows climbed the steps. Knocked. He tried the door and found it unlocked. He pushed it open a crack, called out Iris's name.

Parker said, "I'm going around to the front, to take a look through the french doors."

Willows nodded. He almost told her to be careful, but caught himself in time. He waited, giving her time to get into position, then pushed the door hard enough to make it bang against the kitchen wall. He loudly identified himself, entered, and shut the door behind him.

The cottage was overheated, the air hot and stuffy. Willows used his left hand to unbutton his jacket. He was all eyes, but saw nothing but the linoleum floor, which gleamed painfully bright beneath a bank of florescent ceiling lights. He was all ears, but heard nothing but the hum of the refrigerator. He smelled ceiling wax, woodsmoke. The overhead lights flickered as the furnace kicked in. A gush of hot air assaulted him from a vent in the floor. As he moved towards the doorway that led to the cottage's living room, his eye was caught by a small movement on the kitchen counter. He turned and saw his reflected image, distorted and shrunken, stare back at him from the polished chrome flank of an old-fashioned toaster.

The kitchen was spotlessly clean, except for the sink, which was full of dirty water. Impulsively, he walked over and dipped a finger. The water was cold and greasy, black with filth. He felt

251

a chill run up his spine. To Willows, an unnaturally clean room was a red flag; it indicated a sanitized crime scene. He shrugged out of his overcoat, pulled up the sleeve of his jacket and plunged his hand into the sink. His groping fingers touched something that might have been a sponge. In the same instant, his mind registered the sprinkling of dark brown freckles on the underside of the spigot-style tap. He lifted the object out of the sink. It was a dog's paw, and he had no doubt it had been chopped off one of Iris Roth's Boston bulls. He put the paw down on the sink, shook water from his hand and scraped one of the freckles away from the tap with his thumbnail.

The refrigerator throbbed and was still. Willows rubbed the freckle with a damp finger, watched it turn from brown to red.

Parker stayed close to the cottage's shingled wall as she made her way around to the front of the building. Wide steps led to a low sundeck and quartet of french doors that opened directly to the living room. Through a gap in the curtains she could see a fire burning in the hearth. She climbed the steps and moved across the deck.

She peered through the gap. Dark shadows and orange light flickered on the walls. In the corner of her eye she caught a quick, furtive movement. A pale oval seemed to float up to the glass, then drift away. She walked up to door. A perfectly round, fist-sized hole appeared in the glass at eye level. Her right eye filled with blood. She staggered, dropped to one knee.

In the kitchen, Willows heard a *thrumming* sound, as if someone had snapped a giant rubber band. Glass shattered. He ran towards the living room, slipped on the freshly waxed floor and cracked his head against a corner of the big cast-iron stove.

Parker fired two quick rounds into the deadbolt. She yanked open the door.

Willows was on his knees in the kitchen doorway, his gun in a two-handed grip, held steady on Iris Roth.

Iris stood by the fireplace, sweating in the heat of the flames. She had the bewildered, off-balance look of a small animal caught in the lights of an onrushing car. She wore a heavy wool sweater, jeans and a pair of bright yellow knee-high rubber boots. In her arms she cradled a diver's spear-gun loaded with a matt-black, yard-long metal shaft tipped with a barbed point.

Parker's stomach rolled over.

Willows scrambled to his feet, crossed the room in two swift strides, scooped up the spear-gun and shaft.

Iris said, "My God, I almost killed you!"

Parker nodded. The spear had missed by inches; a sliver of glass had struck her just above her right eye.

Iris said, "I'm so *sorry.*" She turned to Willows. "I . . . I thought she was Susan."

"Susan Carter?"

Iris said, "Let me take a look at that . . ." She moved towards Parker.

Willows said, "Stay right there, Iris."

Iris hesitated.

Parker said, "I've got to get this cleaned up. Where's the bathroom?"

"I'll show you . . ."

Willows smiled. He said, "Just point."

Meekly, Iris pointed. Parker headed towards the bathroom. Willows holstered his revolver. He removed the shaft from the spear-gun.

In the bathroom, Parker cursed softly.

Iris sat on the couch. She fixed her eyes on Willows, waiting patiently for whatever was coming next.

A tap squeaked. Willows heard water running into a sink. He balanced the shaft of the spear-gun on the ball of his thumb. Christ, he'd rather be shot.

The tap squeaked again. A moment later Parker appeared in the doorway. She'd taken off her coat. There was a smear of blood on her blouse. Her skin was pale. A butterfly bandage pinched the flesh above her eye.

Willows leaned the spear, point down, against a wall. "You okay?"

Parker nodded.

Willows had his notebook and pen in hand. He said, "When did you last see Susan, Iris?"

"Last night. She told me . . ." Iris faltered. Willows nodded encouragingly. Iris said, "She told me somebody phoned her at Gerard's apartment. He accused her of murdering Gerard. He

253

told her he wanted twenty-five thousand dollars, and that if she didn't pay him he'd go to the police."

If Parker hadn't known Willows so well she'd have sworn he was buying it all, every word.

Iris told Willows that Susan had told her the whole story – how she'd set up a meeting at Trout Lake, waited in the icy water and then shot the blackmailer with Gerard's spear-gun.

Parker said, "Why a spear-gun, Iris?"

Iris shrugged. "She didn't say. It was Gerard's. I recognized it immediately. She chose it simply because it was available, I suppose."

Willows said, "You're saying that this spear-gun is the murder weapon?"

"Yes, of course it is! She was going to use it on me. Make it look like a suicide. We fought, and I was lucky enough to get the gun away from her. She ran outside . . ."

"When did this happen?"

"Last night, late last night."

"Why didn't you call the police?"

"Because she smashed the hell out of the telephone, that's why."

Willows said, "I hate it when they do that."

Iris blinked.

Parker said, "Why didn't you get a neighbor to make the call?"

"I was afraid to leave the house. I was terrified that she'd be waiting for me. You don't understand, do you? *She wanted to kill me.*"

The funny thing was, she'd actually believed it was Susan at the door. She'd been expecting her, in a way. The moment Susan had hit the water the little bitch had started swimming like a goddamn fish.

Iris's face seemed to darken, as if a cloud had passed over her. Her skin twitched and fluttered. Watching her, Willows wondered what had really happened. He thought it most likely that Iris and Susan had murdered Roth together, that both women had planned to set the other up for the fall. Susan was beautiful, and very clever. Younger than Iris, and quicker. But not quite as smart. The cold front was expected to last three more days. By the time they found Chris Spacy's body it would be impossible to determine when he had died except within a very approximate time frame.

Willows said, "Claire, would you mind getting me a glass of water?" He had a sudden urge to make a bad joke about the paws that refreshes, but managed to hold back. Parker gave him an odd look, nodded and disappeared into the kitchen.

She was only gone a few moments, and as she re-entered the room she said, "Iris, I've been meaning to ask you, where are the dogs?"

Iris glanced at Willows.

Parker said, "What happened to the dogs, Iris?"

Iris said, "She killed them."

"Susan killed the dogs?

"Yes."

"All three of them? What did she do, blindfold them, line them up against a wall and shoot them with the spear-gun?"

Iris said, "I don't know what she did to them – they just disappeared. Vanished! Why are you treating me this way?"

Willows smiled at Parker, and she smiled back, both of them thinking about Barney, their conversation with Susan about stray animals in general. The photo on Susan's wall of Elvis.

Willows said, "You shouldn't have killed the dogs, Iris. It was a mistake,"

Iris was thinking so hard you could almost hear her. After a moment she said, "Susan killed the dogs, not me."

"Susan was an animal-lover. She wanted to be a veterinarian."

Sneering, Iris said, "That's what she told you, is it?"

Parker said, "No, Iris. That's what Elvis told us, from beyond the grave."

Parker called on Homer Bradley, to let him know he had a jurisdictional squabble on his hands. Bradley told her to hold her ground until a decision was reached as to who could have Iris first. A couple of uniformed West Vancouver cops arrived, and then, all in a rush, the bloodhounds from Ident, a bunch of plainclothes guys in two-for-one suits, West Van brass and a fat woman in a cocktail dress who turned out to be an ME.

Willows and Parker went outside to prowl around in the woods behind the cottage. Parker found Hot Stuff's skull beneath an overgrown boxwood hedge, and then, not far away, a shredded plastic garbage bag and several scattered bones nestled in the roots of a cedar tree. The bones had been stripped clean of flesh.

Parker said, "I bet she cooked him."

255

Willows stared at her. "And then what, *ate* him?"

"Or fed him to the other dogs," said Parker, "before she killed them."

Bradley phoned back. Parker took the call in the kitchen. He told her to give Iris up. The suburbanites could have her, for now.

Willows went into the living room. Somebody had thrown another log on the fire. The salt trapped in the wood gave the flames a greenish tinge. Willows knelt and pulled the screen. Sometimes, with fireplaces or love, it was best to keep the sparks at bay.

spices from the islands. Since most of her friends were from there, she had plenty of opportunity to sample the different foods. She looked forward to the times when they all got together and each—except for her— brought their favorite dish.

Jane was very familiar with the sad feeling that comes when you don't know where you belong. Yet she had always made the best of it, just happy to be alive. Now, however, it seemed that there was an urgency to find out who she really was. As she stepped into the hospital, Sue met her.

"Did you bring your letter?" she asked.

"Yes, I did. Here it is."

Jane handed her the letter with a smile. Sue was so excited. *But she gets excited about everything*, Jane thought.

As she turned and walked away, Jane thought of all the people waiting to be attended to. She didn't have time to dwell on her problems. She was so wrapped up in her work that she didn't pay much attention to the news. Then she heard the name *Davenport*. That was the name of the doctor from the island. Why was she having such a strange feeling at the sound of his name? She didn't have that feeling last night last when she addressed the letter to him.